Acclaim for *One of the Girls*

'Brimming with tension, with such perfectly drawn characters
I keep wondering what they're doing now. Lucy Clarke gets
better and better' CLARE MACKINTOSH

'With a fascinating cast of complicated female protagonists,
a raft of dark emotional back stories and a gloriously exotic
location, this story delivers in spades until the very last line'
ROSIE WALSH

'An addictive sun-soaked thriller with a killer twist. Un-
missable' *MARIE CLAIRE*

'I loved the beautifully realised setting, the evocative descrip-
tions of Greece, the food . . . This is going to blow everyone's
socks off' EMMA STONEX

'Lucy Clarke goes from strength to strength; this utterly addictive, trouble-in-paradise novel is her best yet' ERIN KELLY

'From the first page I was transported to the intoxicating Greek
island setting of *One of the Girls* and found myself held there,
breathless, until the last' CHARLOTTE PHILBY

'Expertly plotted and so compelling with twist after brilliant
twist, *One of the Girls* is the perfect addictive holiday read'
CLAIRE DOUGLAS

'Dark, delicious and glamorous. *One of the Girls* is the perfect
summer page-turner you'll want in your beach bag'
TASMINA PERRY

'Beautiful writing, suffused with menace, complicated female heroines, and an ending I couldn't predict'

GILLIAN MCALLISTER

'A taut, propulsive plot keeps the pages turning through twist after devilish twist. Lucy Clarke always delivers'

CHRIS WHITAKER

'With the sun-soaked setting and the emotionally-driven mystery, it's got all the hallmarks of a classic Lucy Clarke novel'

EMYLIA HALL

'Complicated friendships and old resentments surface on a hen weekend. Fabulous read'

JANE FALLON

'*One of The Girls* has it all: a propulsive plot full of hidden undercurrents, a brilliant cast of characters and a setting so vividly described you'll feel you're right there on holiday with them'

T M LOGAN

'Deliciously escapist and addictive, Lucy Clarke expertly juggles the secret desires and deceptions of six fascinating women. I really couldn't stop reading'

KATE RIORDAN

'Packed with secrets, drama and all the complexities of female friendship and the darkness that lurks within us, *One of the Girls* is the perfect beach read'

ALLIE REYNOLDS

'I devoured it in two heart-pounding sessions. Intriguing and compelling – I couldn't put it down'

IMOGEN CLARK

'Lucy Clarke has proved, once again, that she is a master of the thriller genre'

JULIE CLARK

ONE OF THE GIRLS

Sunday Times bestseller Lucy Clarke writes from a beach hut, using the inspiration from the wild south coast to craft her stories. Her debut novel, *The Sea Sisters*, was a Richard & Judy Book Club pick, and she has since published *A Single Breath*, *The Blue/No Escape*, *Last Seen*, *You Let Me In*, and *The Castaways*, which was a Waterstones Thriller of the Month selection. Lucy lives by the sea with her husband and two children.

Keep in touch with Lucy –

www.lucy-clarke.com
@lucyclarke_author
/lucyclarkeauthor

Also by Lucy Clarke

ONE OF THE GIRLS

LUCY CLARKE

HarperCollins*Publishers*

HarperCollins*Publishers* Ltd
1 London Bridge Street,
London SE1 9GF
www.harpercollins.co.uk

HarperCollins*Publishers*
Macken House, 39/40 Mayor Street Upper,
Dublin 1, D01 C9W8, Ireland

First published by HarperCollins*Publishers* 2022
This edition published by HarperCollins*Publishers* 2023
1

A catalogue record for this book is available from the British Library

ISBN: 978-0-00-859777-1

Set in Sabon LT Std by Palimpsest Book Production Limited,
Falkirk, Stirlingshire

Printed and bound in the UK using 100% Renewable Electricity by
CPI Group (UK) Ltd

For Mimi Hall

WEDNESDAY

~

Later, we would all remember the hen weekend for one reason: because of what happened on the night of the beach fire. Before that, there were good moments – even beautiful ones – like sharing dishes of tzatziki and glistening olives beneath the Greek sun, or laughing till our knees gave way about something that would never be funny if repeated, or dancing barefoot on the lip of the shore.

We mustn't forget those moments.

If we'd been more astute, if we'd listened more closely, if we'd not turned away from her – from ourselves – we could have stopped it. That's what makes this so much worse. We could have changed it.

Now it's too late. It's over. We can never unsee the trail of her red wrap as it fluttered in the morning breeze, caught in the zip of a body bag.

1

Lexi

Lexi unwound the taxi window. The warm wind was infused with pine and the arid scents of sun-baked earth. Tiers of whitewashed houses clustered close to the rising blue dome of a church.

The sky, Lexi thought. *My God, how wide and cloudless could a sky be?* It felt like a magician's trick, swapping the rain-slicked pavements of London for the shimmering heat of Greece. She couldn't quite believe that she was here.

'We're on a hen weekend,' Bella was telling the taxi driver, oversized sunglasses pulled down, lipstick freshly reapplied. 'Lexi's the bride,' she said, swivelling around in the passenger seat to point.

'Congratulations,' the driver said, warm, dark eyes flicking to hers in the rear-view mirror.

'Thank you,' Lexi smiled. *The bride.* She was the bride. She shook her head lightly, still a little stunned.

'I'm her maid of honour,' Bella announced proudly. 'You know: the best friend. The important one who organises the hen weekend?'

'Self-appointed,' Lexi added. 'I wasn't going to have a maid of honour.'

'Which I ignored since you weren't even going to have a hen weekend.'

'True.' Hen parties made Lexi think of twenty-something-year-olds dancing in cheap veils, shots slurped through phallic straws, blistered heels, and too-short skirts. In fact, had Lexi been twenty, she would have *loved* a hen party. She would have tossed back the tequila, danced on the podium in a wisp of a dress, and when her feet blistered, she would've kicked off her stilettos and danced barefoot. But she was thirty-one now – and done with waking in the morning with that queasy sense of regret and shame that had nothing to do with a hangover. She was finally – much to everyone's surprise, including her own – getting married to a man she loved.

I love you.

She'd actually said those words, aloud. Meant them. It happened over breakfast, the two of them sitting at his kitchen counter with sleep-ruffled hair, him laughing about his failed attempt at cooking lasagne the evening before. She'd begun saying the meal wasn't a total disaster – the wine was nice! – and then she'd added, *I love you.* Just like that. Three brand-new words. Settling between their pot of coffee and the stack of sourdough toast.

He had looked at her. Ed Tollock. Thirty-five. Thick, dark hair threaded with early silver. A low, deep voice. What was it about him? His calm confidence? The way he'd look at her for a long, intense moment, then shake his head, grin, as if he couldn't believe his luck?

He'd moved aside their mugs, reached for her hands. His fingers were tanned, with fine golden hairs on the backs of them, and he'd said, 'I love you, too. And one day, very soon, I'm going to ask you to marry me.' He'd smiled at her, so easily, so openly, that Lexi didn't snatch her hands away, grab her coat, and run. She'd met his gaze and said, 'Is that right?'

Three weeks later there was a ring box. No extravagant candlelit dinner nor down-on-one knee ceremony. Just a simple walk along the banks of the Thames, hands held as they watched the white wake from a shelduck taking flight. His question, then her answer: *Yes*.

She glanced at her engagement ring now, the emerald-cut diamond glittering wildly. She was intent on keeping the wedding small: a gathering of family and friends taking over an old mill licensed for ceremonies. Simple, intimate. She didn't want the big dress, the hairstylist, the photographer. She just wanted him.

'I hear you: *low-key*,' Bella had said when Lexi explained her wedding plans. 'But don't think for one minute that exempts you from a hen party. You are getting married once, which means we are going on a hen weekend, and that, Lexi Jane Lowe, is that.'

So here they were, the tiny Greek island of Aegos. They'd left behind the tourist hustle and a strip of noisy bars as they drove west from the airport. Now the road had emptied and narrowed, carrying them over a scrub-lined hillside where the music came from the tinkling of goat bells and a donkey braying in the lengthening shade of an olive tree.

She'd told Bella that she wanted to spend the weekend lazing in the sun, reading, swimming, and eating. Bella had nodded earnestly for about two seconds, before the corners

7

of her lips curled upwards and she wiggled her eyebrows, meaning she had other plans entirely.

Bella was saying something to the driver now, gesturing expansively while he quaked with laughter. Lexi smiled. God, she loved this woman. Bella was her *yes* person. The one who you could call day or night and pitch any outlandish idea, and Bella's voice would sparkle as she'd say, *Yes!*

Fen – Bella's girlfriend – was the calm to Bella's storm of energy. She was gazing from the taxi window, wind fingering her razor-short, bleached hair. The small tattoo of a swallow on the back of her neck looked so crisply drawn that it, too, might take flight. Her brow was furrowed and a ball of tension worked across her jaw. It was an expression so at odds with her usual relaxed, easy smile that Lexi touched her arm, asking, 'Fen? You okay?'

Fen startled. The tension slid away as she smiled. 'Fine. Sorry. Miles away.'

Lexi had sensed an atmosphere between Fen and Bella at the airport, something weighted in the pauses before they responded to one another. She'd ask Bella about it when they were alone.

'Thank you again for letting us stay in your aunt's villa,' Lexi said.

'It's a good excuse to return to Aegos.'

'Bella said your aunt designed the place.'

Fen nodded. 'Originally for a client. Halfway through the project his finances imploded. He couldn't fund the rest. She was so in love with the place by then that she bought the plot from him.'

'Has she lived here?'

'For a couple of years, but she found the winters hard. The villa is very isolated. There are no neighbours or even passing roads. She prefers to come in summer, bring a crowd. I think the remoteness unnerved her.'

Fen's gaze returned to the window as the road unwound ahead of them.

There would be six of them staying at the villa. The second taxi carrying the other hens had detoured into town to stock up on provisions. Lexi had offered to go with them, but Bella said she'd do no such thing. 'It's *your* hen party.'

Lexi had a feeling she'd be hearing those words more than once this weekend.

'Almost there,' the taxi driver said, changing into a lower gear as the tarmac gave way to a stony track.

Lexi gripped the door as they bounced over rutted ground, tyres kicking up clouds of dust. They swung wide around rock-strewn potholes, as the track drew them closer to the edge of the island.

When they crested a hilltop, for a moment Lexi could see nothing but the glittering blue kiss of sea. Then suddenly the villa appeared, stone-white with a Greek-flag-blue roof. It stood like a crown on the clifftop, reigning over a tiny, jewelled cove below.

Lexi could only stare.

Bella clapped her hands together. 'Oh! Wow!'

Dust billowed behind them as the taxi descended steeply, brakes complaining. Lexi leaned forward, peering through the windscreen as she caught the climbing tangle of bougain-villea framing the side of the villa in a riot of pink.

The taxi came to a halt, engine ticking.

In a low whisper, as if speaking to herself, Fen said, 'This is it.'

Lexi pulled down her sunglasses, then stepped from the taxi. Even this late in the day, the heat was something solid, weighted, pressing against her skin. She took in the white-washed villa with its fastened blue shutters. She could smell the first notes of the sea: salted and clean.

Stones crunched beneath sandals as the three of them fetched their cases from the boot of the taxi. Bella waved away Lexi's attempt to pay the driver, and she made a mental note to slip some money into the kitty in a quiet moment.

As the taxi pulled away, Lexi, a hand on a hip, turned on the spot, breathing in their surroundings.

Cliffs; ocean; mountainside.

Not another building in sight.

She caught the plaintive cry of a mountain goat somewhere in the distance.

Lexi felt a strange flutter of apprehension in her chest. She told herself it must be the anticipation of the weekend to come, a sense of pressure knowing that her friends had come all this way for her. Yet, as her heart rate began to gather speed, it felt like more than that, as if she were unnerved by the very villa, or its remoteness, or the occasion itself.

Bella appeared at her side, hooking an arm through Lexi's. She grinned, a strangely wolfish smile. 'This weekend is going to be perfect.'

2

Robyn

Robyn paused the trolley in the fridge section of the supermarket. She hooked a finger at the neckline of her T-shirt and waggled it. Cool air reached her skin. Bliss. She wanted to climb into the standing refrigerator and press herself against those large tubs of Greek yoghurt.

Her eyes stung. Flights always did that to her. It must have been some combination of air conditioning and exhaustion. Unless she was about to cry? That happened since she'd become a mother. It was like her tear ducts had been tampered with and could leak without the faintest notice: at a single thought, an advert, a warm look between a mother and son. Anything.

She waited a moment, and when no tears arrived she decided the eye-sting was exhaustion. She'd barely slept last night and couldn't even blame Jack, who'd only woken once. After she'd been through her nightly rendition of nursery rhymes and resettled his blanket twice, she'd returned to her

11

bed, too alert for sleep. She'd begun mentally running through the checklist of instructions for her parents. *Make sure you cut Jack's grapes in half. No more than twenty minutes of television, even if he yells. He must keep his hat on if it's sunny.*

She'd never left Jack before. She'd tried demonstrating how long four nights was by stacking coloured blocks into a tower, but he'd bashed them down with a chubby palm, chuckling delightedly at the game.

Still, she mustn't feel guilty about leaving: it was Lexi's hen party. She would've flown to the other side of the world for Lexi because she was the sort of friend who – no matter what – was there for you. Lexi's life had always been big and colourful and messy and beautiful, and Robyn felt privileged to be along for the ride.

Although, she wasn't feeling quite so privileged about doing the supermarket run. Typical of Bella to task her with it. 'You're always so wonderfully practical,' she'd said. 'I'd just come away with a trolley full of ouzo.'

She slung a large block of feta and a tub of herby olives into the trolley while imagining the others already in swimsuits, cooling off in a sparkling pool. *The B-list,* she was thinking. Isn't that what they were *all* thinking?

She always took things too personally. *That's your problem,* Bill, her ex-husband, had told her.

Funny how personal a series of affairs feels.

Anyway. She was looking forward to this weekend. She really was. She deserved it. It'd been a tough couple of years. No, *tough* was wrong. That's what she'd say in front of her parents' friends. Correction; the last two years had been absolute shit-kickers. She had been six months pregnant when she'd discovered Bill had been having an affair. In fact, not one affair: many. Oh, how many there were. And she, Robyn of the Lists, of the Great Plans, had had no idea. When he finally admitted it, red-faced and indignant, she'd looked down at the huge swelling where her waist used to be and thought: *How am I going to do this on my own?*

Bill stayed until Jack was born, but after three months, the sleepless nights and cold stares were too much for either of them. She and Jack had moved in with her parents – and they'd been there ever since.

Bill visited Jack every Saturday afternoon, bringing plush cuddly toys, and then returned home to his new girlfriend, who still had full breasts and a stomach that didn't showcase silvery rivers that ran to the source of a C-section scar. Robyn knew she was meant to embrace these bodily changes – *the map of her life* – but honestly, she preferred her old body, the tight one that could propel her up mountains, that didn't constantly give her backache, that came with a sharp mind unfogged by exhaustion.

She rolled the trolley forward, catching up with Eleanor in the confectionery aisle. Her pale forehead shone with sweat, and she looked uncomfortably hot in a blouse and pressed shorts. Eleanor was Ed's sister. She hadn't been at the engagement drinks, Lexi explaining that she'd recently lost her fiancé, so a gathering to celebrate someone else's wedding was probably the last thing she needed. In truth, with Robyn's divorce imminent, it hadn't been that high up her list of Fun Ways To Spend An Evening. Still. It was Lexi. She would always show up for Lexi.

'Even when it says Cadbury,' Eleanor said, brow wrinkled, 'you can't trust it, can you? Cadbury abroad doesn't taste like Cadbury at home. Have you noticed? I think it must be the milk.'

'Let's spread the risk and get a stash.'

'Excellent,' Eleanor said as she turned to reveal the basket slung over her arm, already stocked with a variety of chocolate bars and honeyed nuts.

They continued around the supermarket together, Eleanor gathering generous supplies of fruit, vegetables, herbs and fresh bread. Once they'd finished and paid, Robyn wheeled the trolley into the sweltering heat of the afternoon.

Ana was standing beneath the shade of the supermarket canopy, a flame-orange headscarf knotted over her braids, a mobile pressed to her ear. Now here was a woman who didn't have problems with leaky tear ducts, Robyn decided. They'd met for the first time on the flight, Robyn learning that she was a single mother to a fifteen-year-old and had put herself through night school to finish her degree. Now she worked as a freelance sign-language interpreter – inspired by her sister's deafness – juggling a busy work schedule to make herself available outside of school hours for her son.

When Robyn found herself apologising for currently living with her parents, Ana had fixed her with a firm, level stare: 'Don't you dare apologise. We do what we do to get by. The bravest thing any of us can do is ask for help.'

Having not noticed them approach, Ana was speaking in a low voice into her phone. 'It was a mistake to come here,' she said, eyes down, brow creased.

Robyn slowed her pace and, at her shoulder, Eleanor did the same. *A mistake? Why?*

Ana looked up. Seeing them both, her eyes widened fractionally. 'Talk later,' she said hurriedly into the phone.

'Everything all right?' Robyn asked, then wondered if it would've been better to pretend she hadn't overheard.

'Fine.' Ana slipped her phone away, smoothed down her dress, then came to the side of the trolley. Her expression lightened as she eyed the bottles of ouzo, gin, Metaxa, Prosecco and beer. 'The alcohol to food ratio is excellent.'

Eleanor smiled and, after a moment, Robyn did, too.

As they unloaded the goods into the taxi, Robyn couldn't quite believe that this was the start of Lexi's hen party. The news still felt so fresh, so surprising. Lexi had always claimed she'd never marry – and they'd believed her. She'd spent most of her twenties as a backing dancer for a host of pop stars. She'd partied on tour buses, in penthouse suites, and tripped through Soho knowing every club owner's name. And then, two years ago, she'd fractured her tibia and, just like that, the dancing, the partying, the lifestyle, was over. But life had a habit of slamming one door, only to open another. Well, it did where Lexi was concerned. Lexi retrained as a yoga teacher, met Ed, fell in love, and agreed to get married. Now here they were, in Greece, ready to celebrate. How was that for an about-turn?

Maybe that was the problem with Robyn's life. She'd never lived it hard enough. Never gone for broke. She'd always followed the straight path: law degree, homeowner, career, marriage, baby. Tick, tick, bloody tick.

Where had it left her? Thirty years old, living with her parents and an eighteen-month-old baby, with a career she'd been sidelined from and an ex-husband under her belt.

The B-list, she thought.

Always the bloody B-list.

~

We were a group – a party of hens – but we were never the same.

Not by a long shot.

Don't forget that.

Some of us started the day with a sun salutation, or a run, or by clutching a pillow to our chests in an empty bed. Some of us arrived on the hen weekend wanting to step out of our ordinary lives and dig into our wild, free selves, to remember that's where we roamed. Others wanted only to get through it, to chalk off the hours until we returned home.

We all had different reasons for being there. But one of us – well, she had a very specific reason for saying Yes to the hen weekend.

The problem was, none of us realised until it was too late.

3

Fen

Fen's body tensed as she turned the key in the lock, as if bracing for a blow.

She took a steady, low inhale, then pushed open the door.

Stepping into the cool expanse, the villa greeted her with its familiar chalky breath. She tried to recall arriving here seven years earlier, wide-eyed at the sheer beauty of the island, the fizz of possibility bubbling in her chest that a new world was unfurling before her. Back then, she'd only just cut ties with her parents and their strict, church-led demands, so Fen had been entranced by her aunt's bohemian lifestyle, filled with friends who visited with their paintbrushes and sketchbooks and wildly seductive ideas of how life *could* be lived.

That was the remembering she wanted.

But there were other memories locked here, too.

Dry-mouthed, Fen removed her sandals and moved lightly across the cool stone floor, eyes adjusting to the dim. She unlatched the shutters and flung them wide. Dazzling light flooded the villa, dust motes set dancing. She blinked into the sunshine.

She was wondering if she'd regret saying *Yes* to using the villa for the hen weekend. Her aunt had announced to Fen and Bella that she was selling the Greek villa over sashimi at her favourite Japanese restaurant – 'Another project has come up in Croatia and I need to release some funds to secure it' – adding that Fen absolutely must use the villa while it was standing empty.

Bella had flattened her palms to the table, leaning forward. 'Lexi's hen! Let's go to Greece for her hen!'

Fen's aunt adored the image of the villa teeming with women and music and celebration, and by the time a second bottle of saké was set on the low table, the plan had been cemented.

'My God!' Bella cried, rushing through the doorway, high heels clacking on the stone floor. 'Look at this place!'

The villa had been designed in the Cycladic tradition, with a minimal aesthetic, as if chiselled from the rock it perched upon. Thick stone walls were washed white, their corners smoothed. The furniture was wooden, low, and sparse, emphasising the feeling of space. It was complemented by domed whitewashed ceilings framed by beams of salt-bleached wood.

'Everything is so beautiful!' Bella marvelled, her fingers trailing across the tassels of a wheat-brown wall hanging, then moving to a wooden side table hollowed from a single tree trunk. 'Oh, look!' Bella exclaimed, picking up a framed photo. 'Is this you?' She tapped a neon fingernail against the glass. 'Girl, you're looking smoking with those curves!'

The photo had been taken on the terrace in front of the villa, Fen squinting into the evening light, face blooming with an easy smile. She was wearing a denim miniskirt, a scarf threaded through the belt loops, with a vintage *Let Love Rule* vest that she'd paid three pounds for in a second-hand stall. Red sunglasses were propped on her head. She remembered going for dinner later that night in the Old Town, abuzz with energy. The memory of what happened afterwards shouldered forward with such sudden force that it felt physical. The blood drained from her face, her skin turning to ice.

Fen snapped her gaze away, ducked past Bella, and hurried out onto the terrace.

She stood in the shade beneath the pergola and set her gaze on the blue oval eye of the pool. She focused on her breath, slowing and deepening each inhale and exhale.

'Babe?' Bella said, following her out onto the terrace. 'You okay?'

Fen told herself she was. 'Fine. Just a bit light-headed after the flight.'

Lexi joined them on the terrace, drawn to the edge by the glittering blue sea. She placed her palms on the low stone wall. 'This view,' she said, drinking in the empty stretch of the ocean. Then she startled backwards. 'Shit. That drop!'

Bella marched to Lexi's side, fingers pinning her sunglasses in place as she stared over the edge. 'Jesus! It's lethal.'

The drop was sheer, falling over two hundred feet onto the jagged slabs of rock below. 'It's why the villa has been slow to sell. People are put off by the cliff edge,' Fen explained.

Bella pointed east. 'Is that *ours*?' she said, looking towards the brochure-perfect cove nestled at the foot of the cliffs.

'Yep. Private beach.' A wooden rowing boat waited on the shoreline, the turquoise paint peeling. Fen concentrated on recalling the pleasure of dipping the oars in the early-morning sea, rowing out to the hidden cove around the corner where a tiny bay had been carved from the cliffs.

There were good things here, too.

'What about having a beach fire one evening? Could we do that?' Lexi asked, looking towards the empty cove.

'For sure,' Fen said. 'There'll be plenty of driftwood washed up.'

Bella's eyes glittered. 'A beach party! Yes! To end the hen weekend! I love it!'

Lexi moved across the terrace, crouching low to smell the herbs growing in terracotta pots.

Bella approached Fen, lifting onto her tiptoes to place a kiss on her cheek. 'We okay?' she whispered, resting a hand at her waist.

Fen could see herself reflected in Bella's sunglasses, her creased brow, the tightness in her jaw. She wanted to say, *Sure, we're fine*. She wanted to feel buzzed to be on holiday with Bella. But she didn't. Couldn't.

Hours earlier, standing in the departures terminal at Gatwick airport, she'd learned that Bella had been lying to her since the day they met. Bella, white-faced, a hand gripping a luggage handle, had begged Fen to understand – but how could she when it had always been Bella's unflinching honesty, her refusal to apologise for her choices, that had drawn Fen to her in the first place?

The conversation had been cut off when they spotted the other hens arriving. Bella had blotted her face, pasted on a smile, then bounded towards them with outstretched arms, while Fen had stood back, thinking: *How does she do that?*

Now Fen slipped free of Bella's embrace, saying, 'I'm going to open up the bedrooms.'

It was a relief to return to the cool of the villa. She picked up her case and carried it up to the bedroom. She opened the shutters, a dead fly tumbling stiff-legged onto the thick stone sill. Below on the terrace, she could hear the scrape of chair legs, the drift of Bella and Lexi's voices as they settled themselves beneath the pergola. Bella must have said something funny, as she heard the eruption of Lexi's laughter.

Fen wanted to join them, but her thoughts felt knotted, unsettled. Needing to clear her head, she changed into a pair of running shorts and a vest, then slipped on her trainers. Bending to tie the laces, she caught sight of herself in the bedroom mirror, the hard angles of her body reflected back at her. Her gaze roved to her muscular, thick thighs, exposed by her shorts, and she heard his voice: *You disgust me.*

The memory of those words was a slap, unexpected and swift.

She stood sharply. No, she would not listen to that voice. It had been seven years ago. It was done. Over. She picked up her water bottle and returned to the terrace.

Bella looked up, surprised. 'You're going running? We've just arrived.'

'A quick one before it gets dark.'

Bella shook her head. 'How did I end up with a runner?'

'You got incredibly lucky,' Lexi told her.

'Yes,' Bella agreed, her face suddenly serious, eyes on Fen. 'I did.'

Fen left the terrace, heading for the cliff path that would carry her into the foothills of the mountain, heels pushing into the dried earth. The scent of wild thyme lifted in the dusty heat. She set her sights on the zigzagging path, the villa soon becoming no more than a shadow at her back.

4

Bella

Bella had been looking forward to the hen party ever since Lexi had announced the engagement. If you're losing your best friend to marriage, you damn well better get a big party out of it.

Lexi Lowe, getting married. It still blew her mind. It wasn't as if there hadn't been plenty of offers over the years. Men only had to breathe the same air as Lexi to fall in love. The surprise was that Lexi had fallen in love with *Ed*. (Bella needed to stop saying – or even *thinking* – his name like that, like he was something vaguely distasteful, or as a question: *Ed?*) Ed was charming. He was generous. He was passionate about his work. (Whatever it was he actually did. Some type of lawyer. Robyn would know.) He was loyal. And most importantly, he adored Lexi.

But – and there was usually a *but* with Bella – he just wasn't what she'd been expecting. She knew Lexi was done with the party scene, but still. Couldn't she have fallen for some sexy French yoga guru who had his nipples pierced? Or some reformed band member who dropped CBD oil like they used to drop acid? Someone a bit more textured, a little less tailored.

'Which room shall I put my things in?' Lexi asked. Even after a day's travelling, Lexi still looked effortlessly fresh, caramel hair loose over slender shoulders.

'Master suite,' Bella said in a butler-crisp accent. 'Please, madam, do come this way.'

The wheels of Lexi's case clattered as they bounced up the stone stairway. Bella moved through the bedroom doorway and pushed open the stiff wooden shutters. Sheer white curtains billowed in the breeze, revealing glimpses of a sweeping balcony that looked out across the terrace and beyond to the sea.

'I can't take this room. You and Fen should have it!' Lexi said.

'It's yours. Guest of honour and all that.'

Lexi glanced towards the door, checking they were alone. 'By the way, is everything okay between you two?'

'Yes, great. We're great. Everything's great.' *How many times do I want to say* great?

'Seemed like there was a bit of an atmosphere at the airport.'

'Not at all! We were just busy making sure everyone got on the right flight!' Bella caught the shrill note in her voice as she lied.

Lexi's instincts were right, though. It wasn't that she couldn't talk to Lexi about her problems. It was that she couldn't talk about *this* one.

She replayed the deep, perplexed frown that had settled

25

between Fen's brows as they'd waited for the others in the departure hall. 'You know what I've always admired about you?' Fen had said.

Bella had waited, tears streaking her cheeks, her mouth empty of answers.

'Your honesty. Your forthrightness. That you never apologise for being you.' Fen had paused, head shaking, eyes large. 'But now . . . now I'm not sure I even know who *you* are.'

Bella swallowed hard, pushing down the memory. 'Right,' she said brightly, grabbing Lexi's suitcase and heaving it on the bed. 'Get your bikini on. We're going for a swim!'

A set of sun-bleached wooden loungers lazed around the swimming pool. Bella, abuzz with holiday excitement and a sharper beat of adrenalin, wanted to do everything all at once – sunbathe, swim, drink, eat, explore.

She picked a sun-lounger in the last slice of sun, laid her towel across it, then settled herself on top. She wore a brand-new leopard-print bikini with construction-grade underwiring that held her breasts high and proud, and mid-waisted bikini bottoms that sculpted her backside into peachy curves.

Where is Robyn with the shopping? She could have murdered an ice-cold beer.

From her beach bag, she took out a compact mirror and reapplied her lipstick. It gave her something to do while she waited for Lexi. She'd never been good at being still.

She glanced over her shoulder towards the mountains, wondering if she could catch sight of Fen. The landscape looked arid, mostly low-lying scrub and a few patches of trees further inland. She pushed her sunglasses onto her head, squinting into the light. No sign of her. *A quick jog* for Fen meant an hour of running at an unfathomable pace. She'd probably already crested the mountain.

She needed to carve out some time alone with Fen this weekend. Make things right.

'Ready to swim?' Lexi said, crossing the terrace in a simple black bikini.

Bella cleared her throat, pulled down her sunglasses, and pasted on a bright smile. 'Sure am.'

'The sea?'

Bella turned, gazing down to the empty cove below. A tiny pebble beach reached out into impossibly clear water, the turquoise sea gradually shifting to deeper shades of navy. The sleeping shadow of the neighbouring island rested on the horizon; clusters of white buildings clung like calcified barnacles to a whale.

Bella was more of a pool person. She didn't like waves. Or those drapey, reaching fingers of seaweed. Or fish. No, she hated fish with their slick, muscular bodies and flashing scales. The pool was her place. You could see the bottom. You knew what was in it. Chlorine was her friend.

But it was Lexi's hen party. 'The sea, then.'

Stone steps wound steeply down the face of the cliff, the white paint flaring in the sun. They went barefoot, the stone achingly hot. The scent of sun lotion lifted in the heat.

'How many bloody steps are there?' Bella muttered, skirting a gecko eyeing her from a step. She turned, squinting up towards the empty villa. It was so high, as if it had been designed that way to keep guard.

By the time they'd reached the beach, beads of sweat had gathered at her hairline. They hot-footed it across the heat-drenched pebbles, then dunked their singed soles in the mercifully cool shallows. The water was startlingly clear, sharpening the contours of the seabed.

Lexi, as in life, waded straight in, diving forward and disappearing beneath the sun-rippled surface. She rose moments later, face washed fresh.

'Don't splash me!' Bella warned as she edged deeper, stomach sucked in, checking for sea urchins. *No urchins in a pool.*

As she glanced back towards the villa, she saw a cloud of dust rising as the second taxi arrived. She watched Robyn, Ana and Eleanor as they climbed out, hauling bags of shopping towards the villa.

She didn't feel bad for tasking Robyn with the food shopping: she was the second bridesmaid and, so far, all Robyn had done was ask her typically boring questions about Wi-Fi access and travel insurance. For God's sake.

If Lexi noticed the others arriving, she'd insist on returning to the villa and helping them unpack the shopping. Bella was desperate for a slice of time alone with Lexi. She pushed off in breaststroke, keeping her chin stiffly above the waterline. When she reached Lexi, she pointed towards an outcrop of sun-baked rocks. 'Let's swim out there.'

As their arms parted the clear water, the lowering sun against their faces, Bella felt a settling deep in her body, like something that had been out of alignment had shifted back into place. *Just you and me.*

5

Robyn

Robyn shoved the salad items to the back of the fridge, making space for the white wine.

There. That was the last of the unpacking.

She closed the fridge, then flexed and arched her back, the familiar ache clawing into her pelvis.

She checked her watch. Bathtime at home. She pictured Jack's little body, slick and glossy in the scented bubbles. Some evenings she'd marvel at him: the perfect pale skin, his delighted expression as he slapped his palms against the warm water, or that sweet moment of wrapping him in a parcel of soft towel, clean and fresh and ready for bed. Other evenings she just wanted to rush through the bedtime routine so she could go downstairs and – what? Watch Netflix with her parents? Fire up the laptop and catch up on work?

She slipped her mobile from the pocket of her shorts. *Damn, no reception.* Didn't surprise her with these thick stone walls. Through the open doorway, she looked west towards the cliff line. She'd try for signal up there.

She called to Ana and Eleanor, who were unpacking their things in the twin room, then walked out into the warm evening. She followed the goat track that hugged the cliff line, the ground hard underfoot. Her knees flashed pale as she marched up the narrow path, her breath shortening with the exertion.

It felt good to move after a whole day of travelling. It was such a long way to come for four nights. Weren't trips like this part of the crisis the environment was facing – people like them zigzagging across the continent because a hen party seemed like a birthright? Once, a hen party had been about sharing food with your girlfriends the night before your wedding. How had it become so commodified, with hen party packs, drinking games, and pathetic quizzes? Did anyone even enjoy them?

Robyn hadn't enjoyed her own, that was for certain. She'd foolishly agreed that her mother could come. She'd never been able to say no to her mother, who was always so kind, so appeasing, and who loved Robyn *so* much. But on her hen do, she'd constantly felt as if she needed to tone herself down.

There were at least three Robyns inhabiting her body. There was the Robyn she was for her parents: sensible, kind, level, strong. There was the one for work: determined, highly organised, with a streak of fierceness. Then there was the Robyn for her oldest friends, who showed up after a few drinks: spontaneous, brave, and a little sweary. Having all those selves in the same venue for her hen party was hard work, like she couldn't quite remember which Robyn she was meant to be, and she was so busy switching roles that she exhausted herself and just wanted the hen party to be over.

A bit like her marriage, actually.

The problem was, she didn't know which was the real Robyn. Not anymore.

Cicadas sang unseen in the low scrub as she pushed on, calf muscles burning, a thin film of sweat gathering under her arms. Somewhere behind her, she heard a scuff, like a shoe kicking the dirt. She glanced over her shoulder, spooked.

No one there, of course. An animal perhaps, or a loosened rock shifting. In the softening light, the surrounding landscape had lost its definition. The villa looked lonely, crouched on the cliff edge and she had an uneasy sensation, wondering if she should turn back.

She glanced at her phone. Still no signal. If she wanted to catch Jack, she'd have to climb higher.

Her arms pumped at her sides as she ascended the cliff path, her breathing shallow. God, she used to be so fit. At school she had been on all the sports teams. Scabby knees, bruised shins, and strapped fingers were the look of her teen years. She and her brother, Drew, had spent their weekends climbing trees, building dens, and playing Manhunt in the woods. She missed those easy days.

Missed him.

She reached the top of the hill, out of breath, but with one bar of signal flickering in the corner of her phone. She pressed *call*, picturing Jack in his dinosaur pyjamas, the nape of his neck still damp, hair smelling of baby shampoo.

'Robyn!' her mother answered warmly. 'You've arrived?'

'Yes, we've just got to the villa. How's Jack?'

'Wonderful! We've had the loveliest day. We took the train to Brockenhurst for the afternoon. You should've seen his face when we saw the New Forest ponies!'

'Could I speak to him?'

'Oh, I'm sorry, darling. You've just missed him. He's already asleep.'

Robyn remained on the clifftop a moment, trying to swallow her disappointment.

Somewhere behind her, a goat cried. She turned, searching for it. As she did, she saw someone running along the cliff track, nimble, sure-footed. She watched for a moment, the broad shoulders, the short bleached-blonde hair. Bella's girl-friend. They'd been introduced briefly in the boarding lounge but hadn't exchanged more than a few words. She tried to recall her name – and finally landed on it.

Fen.

She ran effortlessly, like she was gliding, legs muscular yet lean. The lowering sun gilded her in a stream of golden light. Her shoulders were tanned and she wore an expression of easy, full focus. Robyn had recently listened to a podcast about being in a flow state, which was when you were fully present in the moment, pushing your edge, ceasing to be aware of the environment around you. Top athletes, artists and writers could access it – so could everyone – but it was fleeting. Something to be learned. *Fen of the flow state.*

She watched Fen with a rising sense of nostalgia, remembering the Robyn who was once athletic and strong. When she'd fallen pregnant, her muscular, lithe body had bloomed into an entirely new shape, and she'd felt like a spectator, watching it happen. When she went into labour, she was ready. She had every confidence in her strength, her physicality. She'd read a birthing book about wild women letting themselves roar, moving with the pain, not fearing it. But her body had had other ideas. After labouring for twelve hours, she began to vomit blood. An infection meant she had to be hooked up to a monitor on a hospital bed. She could no longer writhe on the floor – but she could still yell.

'Honey, not so loud.' That from Bill.

Not so loud?

She was bringing another human being into the world. 'I will fucking roar!' she'd told him, and honestly, it was the coolest thing she'd ever said.

And she had roared. She'd roared and roared – but still her body, with all its animalistic strength, hadn't done what it was meant to. Thirty-six hours and a hoarse voice later, she agreed to an emergency caesarean.

It shouldn't have mattered – Jack arrived safe and healthy, with a shock of dark hair and a pink face that she couldn't stop kissing – but afterwards it mattered, when she realised the surgery involved sawing through five layers of muscle and tissue. An infection extended her stay in hospital, and her once muscular body turned soft, weak. She had no core strength, so her back took the strain – and didn't like it.

Where she'd once had a six-pack, now there was a gap between her abdominal muscles where the inside of her stomach domed if she tried to engage them. She was doing physio, pathetic little exercises of tilting her pelvis. She'd told the woman, 'But I used to be able to do chin-ups. From any branch, I could jump up – cling on.' The physio had nodded patiently. 'Small steps. You've had a baby.'

Yes, but there were other women who had babies – who pushed out three or four of them – and were still strong. Her body had let her down. She didn't trust it anymore.

But watching Fen, she remembered herself like that. Powerful, fit, capable. She was in awe of Fen's body, the ripple of muscle.

Suddenly Fen glanced up, noticing Robyn. She smiled.

Robyn felt heat rise in her cheeks. She'd always been a terrible flusher.

Fen slowed her pace, jogging lightly towards her. Tiny puffs of dust rising with each step, her calves muscular and smooth. She came to a stop, hands on hips. She was wearing an old band T-shirt, the sleeves cut off, and was barely out of breath.

'How's the trail?' Robyn asked.

Fen briefly closed her eyes. 'Beautiful. Everywhere smells of wild rosemary. There's no one. Not a soul in sight. God, it's glorious.'

Robyn found herself smiling, too. On the flight, Fen had been hemmed in by Bella and, in truth, Robyn had thought, *If she's Bella's girlfriend, she won't be my kind of person.* What a ludicrous, judgemental thought. Too long living with her parents, she decided.

She took in Fen fully now. Her nose was pierced, a simple silver stud in her right nostril. Her bleached hair held an undercut on one side. Robyn wouldn't even know how to ask for it at the hairdresser. The sort of haircut that her parents would call 'alternative'. Everything was alternative to them. Tattoos. Body piercings. Dyed hair. Same-sex relationships.

She looked at this woman – drinking in the view, so full of life and vitality and confidence and wonder – and thought, *That's how I want to be.*

'Is there a phone signal?' Fen asked, looking at the mobile Robyn was gripping.

'Just about. I was trying to call my little boy. He'd just gone to bed.' She could feel her voice threatening to crack. What the hell was going on with her today?

'I'm sorry,' Fen said. 'You must be missing him.'

She nodded. 'First time I've left him. He's only eighteen months.'

'Brave of you to come. It's lovely that you're here for Lexi.' Robyn smiled. 'Wouldn't miss it.'

'You've known each other since school, is that right?'

'Yes. Met when we were eleven.' Lexi had been beautiful, even then, before they really understood what beauty was and the power it held, yet she always looked tired, shadows under her eyes. Robyn's mother often commented, *That girl needs to go to bed earlier.*

Robyn quickly understood that Lexi's parents were for talking about in hushed voices. Her mother was an ex-professional ballerina who drank every night, and her father raced cars. That was his actual job: racing car driver. It was like two children had been asked, *What do you want to be when you grow up?* and they'd drawn a blonde ballerina and a dark-haired racing car driver holding a trophy – and that was Lexi's family. Robyn had been fascinated by them – the rule-less bedtimes, the lack of questions over where Lexi was going and with whom, the bottles of champagne routinely drunk without celebration.

'Bella started at our school a couple of years later,' she told Fen.

'When she moved down from London?'

'That's right. Bella spent the first term telling anyone who'd listen that she'd be going back to the city the moment she could.'

'Always a people-pleaser.' Fen grinned.

Robyn remembered teenage Bella with her clumpy mascara and high, dark ponytail, two sections of dyed-blonde hair pulled loose around her face. 'Bella knew every Italian swear word. In her first week she taught our Geography teacher how to say "What a gorgeous sunset!" when it actually meant, *Eat shit and die!*'

Fen laughed.

In that same term, Bella had announced she was a lesbian. 'I prefer women,' she'd said with such ease and confidence that no one even blinked, no one questioned it, or laughed. 'I've got three older brothers, and there's only one bathroom in our house. If you'd seen the stuff I have, you'd be put off for life, too. Women, we smell nicer. We look nicer. Our skin is soft. We have curves. We're just – better.' She'd shrugged as if she'd decided it there and then. *Yep, women. Better.*

Lexi and Robyn were intoxicated. They wanted to keep her. They wanted Bella to fall in love with Bournemouth, so that she'd never leave and take her spark and sass back to the city. So their duo became a trio – and it worked. They each had their role. Lexi was the face of the group, wild, untameable and untethered by her parents. Bella was the voice, loud and deliciously outspoken, often honking with infectious laughter. Robyn was their collective conscience, loyal and thoughtful, ready to steer them right.

'Is that them?' Fen asked, gazing down towards the water.

Robyn saw the two of them wading towards the shore in bikinis and felt a pang of disappointment that they hadn't waited for her to swim. 'Yes,' she answered, watching as Bella doubled over with laughter. She'd always laughed hard and easily, her whole body weakening as if she couldn't carry the weight of the hilarity and she'd simply collapse onto whoever was nearest. They wrapped towels around their waists, then began climbing the stone steps to the villa, where Bella would start pouring the drinks and the night would begin.

She turned back to Fen. 'Did you run in the mountains?'

'I stayed near the cliff line, but there is a trail that takes

you right up into the mountains. I'm going to hike it tomorrow.'

'Really?'

'Not much of a pool-lounger. I'll set off early, while it's
still cool.'

'That sounds incredible.'

'Come.'

One word. So simple. An invitation.

'Oh, I'm not very fit. I'd slow you down.'

She looked at her. 'I'm in no rush, Robyn.'

She didn't know what to say, so chose, 'Okay, then.'

Right there, on the clifftop, Robyn felt the shimmering
heat of her old self, still beating.

~

We arrived on that holiday with baggage.

We packed Grecian sandals and oversized sunglasses, floaty summer dresses and waist-cinching shorts. There were Turkish towels in soft stripes of blush and stone, washbags bulging with shimmering eyeshadows and bronzers and gloss. There were new paperbacks ready to be thumbed, and bottles of sunscreen holding the coconut-scent of summer.

Beneath the holiday trappings were other things, private things, just for ourselves: a sleeve of unlabelled pills tucked into a side pocket; a slim bottle of gin rolled within a towel; a faded photograph of a man with warm eyes slipped inside an envelope.

Oh, and hidden in one of the suitcases, there was a sculpture of the bride. Later we'd see its broken remains carried from the villa – zipped within a clear evidence bag.

6

Ana

Ana checked her phone. No signal. She moved closer to the window, which was set deep into the stone. Still nothing. The absence of those little bars of connectivity made her feel absurdly dislocated. She was a Londoner: unless she was on the Tube there was always a signal.

Must be the thickness of the walls, she decided, pressing her palm to the cold stone. Earlier, while the other hens had raved about the villa's beauty, she'd kept quiet, finding the cave-like architecture stark, and lacking warmth and colour. Nothing like her two-bed flat, which was filled with artwork, bright cushions, and stacks of books.

The twin room she was sharing with Eleanor was at the back of the villa. She stared out into the growing dusk, following the craggy spine of the mountain. It felt impossibly isolated. No villages. No buildings. No traffic. Only a single dusty track winding towards their villa. A trail of goosebumps travelled down the tops of her arms.

'Knock knock!' Lexi called from the open doorway, startling her. 'Just letting you know we're going to have drinks on the terrace.'

Ana rubbed her arms, brushing away the goosebumps. 'Great. I've almost finished unpacking,' she said, returning to her suitcase and removing a jade dress.

'That's beautiful. Is it new?' Lexi asked, entering the room and shutting the door behind her.

Glancing at the closed door, Ana felt a hot prick of panic. It was a familiar sensation, as quick as a reflex. She told herself: *The door isn't locked. You can leave. You are safe.* She allowed the thought to settle, then calmly redirected her attention to Lexi's question. 'Yes, I treated myself.' The dress was vintage, picked up from a dress agency she loved. It was second-hand, but still cost more than she'd usually pay, and felt like an extravagance – much like the hen do. Even though they weren't being charged for the villa, the flights had been expensive and she'd battled with herself over whether to come. She'd spent a lifetime budgeting, checking and rechecking her cash flow so she and Luca wouldn't be caught out. Even though her work was steady, her income secure, she couldn't quite shake her practice of frugality.

Do something for yourself for a change, her sister had signed to her when Ana told her about the hen party. *You haven't been on holiday since Luca was born. Let him stay with me for the weekend. We'll have a movie night and do take-out pizzas and simsim cookies. He could use some Auntie Lenora time.*

Ana had considered her sister's offer, eventually signing a single beat with her fist: *Yes.*

Yet as the hen drew nearer, her trepidation about the weekend grew. It was more than the expense that worried her.

Far more.

She hung up the dress and returned to her suitcase. Lexi had perched on the bed beside it. Ana blinked. Her passport was open on top. Panic flared in her chest. She'd been vigilant about keeping hold of it at the airport, making sure no one had access to it except her.

'I can't believe it's only four weeks till the wedding,' Lexi was saying.

Ana reached towards the suitcase, making as if to unpack a beach towel. With a swift but subtle movement, she slid the passport from sight, tucking it into her pocket.

Lexi didn't seem to have noticed, thank God. She refocused on what Lexi had said. 'Four weeks. Is that all? How are you feeling?'

'Honestly? I'm excited about the evening party, but the formalities of the service, the saying *I do* in front of all those people, fills me with dread.'

'But you've performed in front of huge audiences. I'd have thought you'd be completely at home before a crowd.'

'Yes – *performed*. But on my wedding day, well, that's actually *me*.'

'I get that,' Ana said. She'd always preferred standing at the back of a room, never desiring the spotlight. Not that she was a wallflower. Absolutely not. She'd been brought up to believe that to be taken seriously, she had to work harder, be stronger, be smarter. Be *more*.

'I can't wait for you to see the venue. It's set right on the edge of the river and has this gorgeous deck – if we get good weather.'

Ana knew it would be beautiful, and the weather would be fine, and the simple flowers and strings of lights Lexi had described would be perfect – because everything that Lexi touched turned out right.

Which made Ana wonder: *Is it me who's wrong?*

Ana loved weddings. The joy of the occasion. Everyone so pleased to be there. A feeling of cutting loose. The dancing. The food. The soft glamour and romance of it all. She'd never married – never planned to. There'd been a handful of men over the past few years, but no one who she'd adored, who'd made her think: *Yes, I want to share my life with you.*

She had Luca. She had her sister. She had her work.

She was lucky.

'I'm so happy you'll be there,' Lexi said, smiling openly.

'I can't wait.' Ana had RSVP'd the day the invite arrived in its thick cream envelope lined with tissue paper. Even as she'd ticked the box – '*I'd love to attend*' – noted her dietary requirements, and chosen her favourite song for the evening playlist, she already knew that she wouldn't turn up: there would be an emergency.

7

Eleanor

Eleanor poured the glossy olives into a little wooden bowl she'd found at the back of the cupboard. Everything in this villa was pared back, tasteful. She sensed that Fen's aunt was one of those women who oozed style. She wondered if there was a photo of her. Eleanor always liked looking at people in photos: they couldn't look back, so you had plenty of time to make up your mind about whether you liked them or not, whether you could trust them.

She opened a tub of tzatziki. Inhaled. She dipped a spoon in, then sucked the creamy, garlic-infused yoghurt straight off. She could eat it by the bowlful – slathered on fresh bread, dunked with chips, dolloped on salad: tzatziki worked in a thousand different ways. She dipped the spoon in a second time and when she glanced up, Lexi had arrived at the kitchen counter. She waited for the recrimination, but Lexi only smiled.

She sucked the spoon clean, rinsed it, and then continued fetching the rest of the ingredients. She took half a dozen plump tomatoes from the fridge. (Did Robyn have no clue? Tomatoes should never go in the fridge. Hell, she'd best check what she'd done with the avocados.) She rinsed their bright red skins, then found a sharp vegetable knife and began slicing them into thick rounds. None of the hens had the energy for climbing back into a taxi and heading to a taverna, so Eleanor had quietly begun putting together mezes, shaking roasted almonds into a little dish, arranging stuffed vine leaves on a plate, tearing and toasting pittas ready to dip in creamy hummus.

'Can I give you a hand?' Lexi asked warmly, setting down a glass of something fizzy on the counter. Her soon to be sister-in-law.

She looked at Lexi's wrists. They were so slender. Could you have elegant wrists? That was how she'd describe them. No jewellery, except for the huge diamond on her ring finger that her brother had chosen.

She remembered him announcing, *I've met someone.* He'd been sitting in Eleanor's flat, feet on the table, tie loose around his neck. It was a rare visit and she'd kept glancing at him, wondering why he'd come. There was a lightness in his eyes, a giddiness that made him look less serious.

Her brother, in love.

She'd typed Lexi's name into Google. She didn't even need to hit *search* to know that anyone named Lexi Lowe would be bound for stardom. She wondered what *Lexi Lowe* would do when it came to swapping that rhythmic, alliterative name for their family surname: *Tollock.*

Eleanor Tollock's hiding a bollock.

It was no surprise then when hundreds of images of Lexi

Lowe filled her screen. There were shots of her performing with bands and old clips from MTV of her dancing in a tiger-striped leotard. She'd clicked on a video and had been mesmerised by the way she moved, body like liquid, as if muscles and tendons and bones flowed. Even in a group of top dancers, Lexi stood out. There was something captivating about the proportions of her body, her expression – lost completely in the throes of the music. She'd watched, thinking: no wonder Ed is in love. The whole damn audience is.

When she met Lexi for the first time – dinner at her parents' house, their mother using the best china, her father bringing out bottle after bottle of Châteauneuf-du-Pape and trying not to stare – Eleanor had been surprised to find she *liked* Lexi.

Ed's girlfriends had always been beautiful, but Lexi seemed different. She was able to tease Ed, make him laugh, question his opinions – and he listened. *Maybe with her* . . . she let herself hope.

As she looked at Lexi now, she decided that there was something about the symmetry of her features, the precise straightness of her nose, that made you keep on looking, as if beauty were something mathematical you could work out, solve.

'I'm fine,' she said, declining Lexi's offer of help.

Instead of moving off, Lexi stayed. Eleanor didn't like people talking to her while she cooked. She liked to concentrate on the food, the texture of it in her hands, tasting as she went to find exactly the right balance of seasoning and herbs.

She arranged the tomatoes on a plate with a finely sliced red onion. Then she crumbled over a block of feta, finishing with a sprinkling of fresh oregano she'd picked from a pot on the terrace.

'I'm so pleased you could come on the hen weekend,' Lexi said. She seemed to be trying out the words, to see whether she believed them. 'What changed your mind?'

Eleanor blinked. 'Not sure.'

A lie.

When Ed had told her about the hen party, saying, *You should go. It'll do you good,* she'd responded, 'Anyone who tells you, *It'll do you good,* needs to live their own life.' Ed had looked at her for a moment – she'd felt her shoulders tense, her skin tighten – and then his mouth had broken into a smile as he'd laughed. 'Fair enough.'

But then she'd received Bella's email. It'd popped into her inbox on a Thursday evening after a day sculpting in the garage. Her fingers were numb from the cold and smelt faintly metallic. She'd scrolled to the photos of the villa basking beneath a cloudless sky – and she'd thought, *Maybe.* Then she'd read the subject header: **The Hen Weekend.** She liked that. Not Lexi's Hen, or Plans for the Hen. Just *The* Hen Weekend. Like there was no other.

She'd scanned the names – six of them; a small, select group – and felt, what? Flattered? Chosen? Then she'd noticed something else. Leaning closer, her heart kicked hard between her ribs.

The screen wavered, the words swam. She blinked, wiping a hand across her eyes.

She took a breath. Read it again.

Huh. She'd sat back, arms folded.

And just like that, she was a *Yes.*

8

Ana

Ana could hear the faint drift of voices rising from the terrace. She freshened up, pulling on a shift dress in a soft fizz of lemon that she'd discovered in a favourite charity shop in Kings Cross. She retied her headscarf, spritzed her neck and wrists with perfume, then left the cool of the room.

She passed the kitchen, where Lexi and Eleanor were talking, and made for the open doors leading onto the terrace. There she paused, hovering on the fringes for a moment.

Gilded by the setting sun, Bella and Robyn were buzzing around a long wooden table set beneath the pergola. Moving lightly to the music, Bella was laying out laminated photos, while Robyn lit candles, occasionally glancing towards Bella to laugh or comment on a picture.

In Ana's job as a sign-language interpreter, she was used to reading people and situations, noticing details that others missed: the angle of a shoulder; where the gaze rested; the parts of a body that might be touched unconsciously. The dynamic between Robyn and Bella interested her: Robyn seemed to skirt wide around Bella, her gaze flicking regularly to Bella to check her reaction or approval. There was a wariness in their exchanges, not the easy familiarity she'd have expected between old friends.

Robyn looked up and, noticing Ana, asked, 'Prosecco?'

Ana preferred to drink gin spiked with ginger beer. Prosecco always felt cloyingly sweet, but hell, she'd join in. 'Sure,' she said, sandals clacking as she crossed the terrace.

Bubbles fizzed over the rim as Robyn handed her a freshly poured glass.

'D'you remember this night?' Bella asked, grinning as she angled a photo towards Robyn.

Ana glanced at the photo. Lexi looked to be in her early twenties, her hair bleach-blonde and cut short. The photo must have been snapped in the back of a taxi, Lexi's eyes unfocused, a tiny gold dress riding up her thighs, handbag splayed open on the seat, head lolling towards the window.

'Can't believe you printed *that* one.' Robyn rolled her eyes.

There were other photos: different Lexis, in different places, wearing different clothes. Young Lexi in school uniform, tie worn like a bandana around her head, arms slung around Robyn and Bella. Holiday Lexi riding on the back of a banana boat in a string bikini. Wild Lexi dancing on a podium, body painted silver.

Ana stared at the images one after the other, feeling oddly disconcerted. She didn't know any of these Lexis. The Lexi who Ana had come to know over the past year was a yoga teacher who loved talking about what she was reading or watching; who was happy to trek across London in search of the best pad Thai; who asked her thoughtful, interested questions about her work; who confided that dancing had never been her passion.

Ana had been with Lexi when she'd chosen her wedding dress, giving their fledgling friendship gravitas she'd never expected. They'd been having a lunchtime drink in town at a quirky greenhouse café Ana had discovered and knew Lexi would love. Across the road she'd noticed a pale blue doorway with a sign reading *Vintage Wedding Dresses, by appointment only*. They'd crossed the street and rung the bell. An elegantly dressed man came to the door, a silk handkerchief tucked into the breast pocket of his suit, saying, 'I simply insist you come in.'

It was the first dress Lexi saw – right there at the front of the rail, waiting, as if it had known Lexi was coming for it. A soft champagne colour in French lace. Not fussy and heavy but understated, floor-length, no train, with a deep V at the back.

When Lexi had emerged from behind the heavy curtain, hair loose over her shoulders, the lace falling from all the right points of her body, she'd beamed.

No veil. No tiara. Hair worn long, threaded with a delicate vine of baby's breath, that's what they'd decided, Ana touched that Lexi valued her opinion in matters of style.

'Do you mind if we don't mention this to Bella?' Lexi had asked as they'd emerged from the boutique into late afternoon sunshine.

It was a telling question, and everything she suspected about Bella in the asking of it had been confirmed today when they'd met: the exaggerated swing of her hips as she sashayed through the airport; the loud, throaty laugh as she was patted down by security; the proprietorial arm around Lexi's waist as they boarded. On the plane, just as Lexi had been about to take the seat beside Ana, Bella had tapped the empty space beside hers. Lexi had thrown Ana an apologetic glance and then moved where instructed.

It was interesting to witness the dynamics of childhood friendships playing out into adulthood – but it didn't bother Ana. She was a grown woman. She had a teenager. A mortgage. A career. She wasn't going to sweat over who sat next to the bride-to-be. Let Bella stake her territory.

Taking her drink, Ana moved away from the photos, crossing the terrace. She found Fen standing alone, her gaze on the water. 'Beautiful view,' Ana said, coming to her side.

Fen smiled easily. 'Yes. It is.'

'It's so quiet on the island. So isolated. Quite a sea change from London,' Ana admitted. 'You live in Bournemouth, is that right?' She was trying to piece together the who's who of the group. She knew that Lexi, Bella and Robyn had gone to school together in Bournemouth – and that Fen was Bella's girlfriend.

'I'm from Gloucester, but I came to study in Bournemouth when I was eighteen – and ended up staying.'

'You must have fallen in love with the place.'

'Once you've lived by the sea, it's hard to leave.'

'I bet. Are your parents still in Gloucester? Are they tempted to head south?'

There was a pause. 'Actually, we're estranged.'

'I'm sorry,' Ana said with meaning. 'That must be hard.'

'What must be hard?' Bella asked, tripping towards them with the bottle of Prosecco.

'I was just saying I'm not in touch with my parents.'

'Devout evangelists,' Bella informed Ana. 'Still,' she said, hooking a protective arm around Fen's waist, 'their loss, my gain.'

Fen lifted her beer, drinking deeply, her thumb ring clinking against the bottle.

Ana admired the wide silver-hammered band. 'Beautiful ring.'

'Thank you. Bella had it made at the jewellers where she works.'

'Oh. I thought someone told me you were a nurse?' Ana said to Bella.

'Past life,' she answered with a tight smile. 'Swapped the night shifts and bedpans for retail hours and diamonds.'

Fen adjusted her position ever so slightly, turning her shoulder on Bella.

'Do you miss it?'

'The bedpans?' Bella gave a bark of laughter. 'You've got to be kidding.'

There was a beat of silence. Fen finished her beer. Said she needed another.

Bella watched Fen cross the terrace, a crack of vulnerability caught in the way she pressed her teeth against her bottom lip.

When Bella turned back to Ana, her smile was fixed in place. 'So, what about you, Ana? Lexi's newest bestie. What do you do? How did you and Lexi become such great friends?'

Bella's tone was friendly enough, but Ana understood the point she was making: Ana was the newcomer here and she'd do well to remember it.

9

Eleanor

Eleanor tore open a paper bag to reveal a fresh, stone-baked loaf. She sawed it into generous hunks, breathing in its warm, yeasty scent.

'Have you been to Greece before?' Lexi asked, perched on a kitchen stool.

'Once. With Sam.' There, she'd said his name. It was like she needed to say it aloud several times a day for him to be real. For him to have existed. 'It was the only holiday we took.' It had been beautiful and magical and perfect, and if there was a week in her life – one week that she could relive again and again – it would be that one. A cheap hotel in Corfu. Paper-thin walls. A teenage couple in the room next door who got ragingly drunk every night and took turns to throw up in the windowless en suite. A strip of tavernas that catered to a British palate – burgers and chips and pizzas, with a wisp of Greek salad on the side. But nothing could touch them because they were together.

'I wish I'd met him,' Lexi said. 'I know Ed thought he was great.'

Is that right?

She wanted to tell Lexi that he was more than great. Once, when Eleanor had mentioned there was nowhere to store her sculpting tools, he built her a floor-to-ceiling cupboard that same weekend – and he did it cheerfully, radio on, singing to nineties rock. He loved everything she cooked, often sitting and looking at a meal for the first minute, marvelling and asking questions. Halfway through he'd leave his knife and fork askew on the plate and pause to absorb it. He never rushed. He loved computer games, and when he disappeared into their spare room with his games console, he'd say with a grin, 'Just off to meditate.' He knew himself so completely – and he looked at Eleanor like he knew her too, and still loved her.

'I can't imagine how tough it must have been,' Lexi said.

'Must *be*,' she said, correcting herself.

'He died four weeks before our wedding,' Eleanor said. 'I never had a hen party.'

'Oh. God. I'm sorry,' Lexi said, looking mortified. 'Is it awful for you, being out here?'

Eleanor knew she was being too intense, but sometimes she wanted other people to feel it. It wasn't Lexi's fault. 'It's fine. Anyway, my hen party would've been nothing like this one. Just lunch with my mother and Penelope who lives in the flat below mine. I didn't miss much.' Still, they would have had a good meal at Pinocchio's and she did love their haddock risotto.

She gathered the thick slices of bread and arranged them in a basket ready for the table.

Lexi glanced through the open doors, where the other hens were laughing on the terrace, cast in the soft evening light. 'I'll take the olives out,' she said, sliding from her stool. 'Don't stay in the kitchen too long. Come join us.'

The hens gave a small cheer when Lexi reached them, followed by the clinking of glasses. They all looked so light and happy and in the moment. Everyone else knew how to behave. It was like they'd been taught a lesson on HUMANNESS, and she'd missed the class and never quite caught up.

When she was at school, she'd started each Monday morning with a snake in her stomach, cold and still, shifting occasionally to remind her it lived there – and if she couldn't feel it, it was only because it was sleeping. It didn't take much to wake: a sharp laugh from the back of the school bus; a boy pointing at her across the hall. *There's Eleanor Tollock hiding a bollock!* A teacher asking her to *Speak up so we can hear you!* It was there, wary and fast and poisonous.

Her brother was like the other kids, the ones who simply got it. Life. He'd know the latest bands to listen to, or that yo-yos were cool – and then not cool – or that you needed to wear your jeans low on your hips, not belted at the waist. She'd missed all those nuances. She was looking so damn hard, too. Concentrating, always a little frown line. No one likes people who try too hard, who stare.

People preferred her when she drank. She was easier. Less spiky. People said, 'Hey, Eleanor. You're fun!' as if her funness was of great surprise.

At parties, she felt like a wooden actor who was constantly reading stage directions. *Stop gripping the glass! Put your*

hands in your pockets to look more relaxed. Smile! You're
biting your lip. Smile, for God's sake!

And then she went to that one party where she met him.
'Sam Maine,' she said aloud to the villa.

She'd been washing up glasses at the time. She preferred
a task at a party. It was only twenty minutes till her taxi
was due to whisk her home to pyjamas and mint tea. If she
washed up slowly it would keep her busy until then.

'Want a hand?' Sam had asked.

'No, thanks,' she'd said without even looking up.

'I'm not a fan of house parties either,' he said, leaning
easily against the kitchen side.

When she'd glanced up, he whispered, 'No one does the
washing up if they're having a good time.' He smiled.

She smiled, too.

She took him in properly then, the way his stubble thinned
at the centre of his chin, leaving a smooth patch of pink
skin, and the badly fitting jeans. He told her he worked in
digital advertising but was still mourning the best job of his
life: till boy at Blockbusters. He often said the wrong thing,
told a lame joke, or didn't get the context of what the crowd
was saying. But when he got it wrong, he laughed. That's
what happened – he laughed at himself, like he found it
genuinely funny. When she got something wrong, she felt
shame, humiliation. Her cheeks burned and her gaze lowered.

'How do you do that?' she'd asked him one night when
they got home from dinner with her brother and some of
his friends.

'Do what?'

'Not care what people think.'

'Why would I? You can't please everyone. I reckon you
should only try and please one person.'

She felt like she should know the answer. In fact, she did know the answer. 'Yourself.'

The Wisdom Gun. That's what he fired. Little bullets of truth that seemed so simple when he said them but so hard to find when the volume in her head got too loud. She discovered that most wisdom is hard won. In his teens, Sam had been a carer for his mother, who'd had Parkinson's. He'd talked about how hard it was – but that there was also beauty and darkness and humour and light and love and fear and hope, all of it, because that is life. He'd learned these things from his mother, watching how she lived in those last years, and Eleanor, well she never got to meet her mother-in-law, and that felt like a terrible shame, because she wanted to take her hands, thank her for bringing up a man as wonderful as Sam.

Ten months they'd had together, when they were supposed to have a lifetime.

What the fuck, life? Seriously. What. The. Fuck.

She touched the two wedding bands she wore on a chain around her neck. His and hers. She remembered collecting them from the jewellers, Sam only dead a fortnight, and her standing at the counter, hot-eyed with emotion as she'd studied the inscription he'd secretly arranged. *Always with you.*

There was a loud bark of laughter from the terrace.

Eleanor's head snapped up. She knew which woman the sound had erupted from. She watched the way she laughed with her head tipped back, drink in hand, like the world was there for the taking.

She felt the slow uncoiling of the snake in her gut. Poisonous and deadly.

~

We were all ready for a holiday.

We wanted to surrender our bodies to the hot kiss of the sun. We wanted to idle away evenings in Greek tavernas, mopping up olive oil and oregano with hunks of bread. We wanted to drink cold beers and sip the icy sweetness of Fanta Limon from glass bottles. We wanted the sea, blue and shimmering, with a pebble-white carpet. We wanted to surround ourselves with other women and talk about food and travel and sex – instead of work and children and ageing parents. We wanted to rediscover those parts of ourselves that were freer, sexier, and more fun. We wanted our friends to be our mirrors – to reflect our best, brightest selves.

We wanted it all.

And we deserved it. That's what we told ourselves: We deserve this.

Except one of us was thinking something different. Something darker.

SHE deserves this.

10

Bella

Without spilling a drop of Prosecco, Bella managed to adjust her dress one-handed. It was a strapless canary-yellow number that cinched in her waist and emphasised her bust. She felt sexy in it – and also a little sweaty. Still, give it a few more drinks, and she'd probably strip naked and dive in the pool.

She turned on the spot, taking in the terrace, which was washed rose-gold by the setting sun. Candlelight danced in wide glass lanterns and fairy lights twinkled between the thick tumbling vines woven through the pergola. The hens chatted together, Lexi standing at their centre looking relaxed and at ease.

Bella lifted her shoulders towards her ears, feeling a rush of pleasure and pride. She'd done this! They were in Greece on Lexi's hen do – and she, Bella Rossi, had made it happen. She lifted her glass. 'To you, Lexi,' she called across the group. 'Happy hen party!'

The others raised their glasses. 'Happy hen party!'

Lexi glowed. 'Thank you!'

Bella turned up the music. Madonna: 'Like a Virgin'. She'd collated a playlist called 'The Lexi Years', this track having been on repeat in Bella's teenage bedroom as they'd curled their hair with steaming tongs, her brothers trying to get a peek of Lexi through the open doorway.

She felt a yearning in her chest to cut loose. She wanted music so loud she could feel her blood buzzing with it. She wanted a quick line of coke, just to get glittery. She wanted to slink into a club, feeling a crowd of bodies humming and writhing and moving. She wanted glossy lipstick reapplied in a steaming bathroom filled with women. She wanted to dance with Lexi, eyes on each other, the whole dancefloor gravitating towards them. That. That buzz. That tripping out of the club at two, three, four in the morning and going anywhere . . . wherever the party was . . . taxi rides through London, hotel rooms, minibars. She wanted it all.

Through her twenties, those nights out had given shape to her weeks. She'd been working as a nurse then, living hand to mouth to be able to afford a blowout when she wasn't on shift. Then she'd return to the hospital, rolling in with tales of wild nights that made her patients grin.

She glanced at Lexi, who was standing with a flute of Prosecco in hand, talking to Ana. Lexi may have *said* she didn't want to go clubbing this weekend – but Bella was the maid of honour. She had a job to do – and she planned on doing it *thoroughly*. She'd allow them this first night. Let them have their cosy little mezes, and then she'd step forward.

She fetched another bottle of Prosecco from the ice bucket, giving it a quick shake so that the cork flew off and it bubbled over, causing squeals of delight and the rushing of glasses. They cheers-ed again, glasses clinking, music playing, the night warm against their skin. Yes, this was good.

Robyn approached wearing a navy dress that said *interview candidate* more than *hen party*. In a hushed, organiser's voice, Robyn said, 'Shall we do the presents tonight?'

A fortnight ago, Robyn had emailed the hens suggesting that each of them make a present for Lexi that 'reflects your friendship'.

Bella had rolled her eyes at the screen.

'Sure. If you want.'

'Perhaps now, before we eat?'

Bella noticed how knackered Robyn looked. Kids. That's what they do to you. She'd only met Robyn's little boy once. Jack. He was cute; he had Robyn's big, innocent eyes, and a lopsided grin that hinted at a mischievous streak.

Bella's three brothers were all married with kids. She was an auntie to six nephews and one niece (named Lolita, for God's sake!) who the family spoiled rotten and Bella already saw worrying signs of herself in, like the way she'd check who was watching before performing a pirouette. But Bella didn't want children of her own. It was a discussion she'd had with Fen right at the start. Sperm donors and artificial insemination weren't the problem, it was that she didn't want a baby in her body. No, she liked her body with just her inside, thank you very much. Plus, she enjoyed being Fun Auntie Bella. She didn't want to impose rules and serve healthy snacks. She loved it when her nephews flocked around her ankles, like little vultures, hunting out whatever treats were stuffed in her handbag.

'By the way,' Robyn said, 'I wanted to say thank you for arranging the villa with Fen. It's perfect. Lexi looks so happy.'

'Oh. You're welcome,' Bella said, disarmed by the compliment. She glanced over at Lexi. 'You're right. She does look happy.'

'It's nice to hang out again. All together,' Robyn added.

Bella felt her shoulders softening. 'It is,' she said, meaning it.

A long pause followed. 'I'd best get the gifts organised,' Robyn said, then ducked away.

That was the problem with her and Robyn these days: they ran out of things to say. It was like every conversation stalled to a dead end. Bella lifted her glass to her lips and took another drink.

Chair legs scraped across stone as the hens took their seats beneath the pergola. Candles flickered in jars, light glinting from the long stems of their glasses.

Robyn had artfully arranged the pile of presents in front of Lexi. She stood at her side, hands clasped, saying, 'We all wanted to make you a gift that says something about our friendship with you. You've got to guess who each one is from.'

'But before we start,' Bella said, sliding back her chair to stand, too, 'let's make sure everyone's drinks are topped up.' She produced a full bottle of Prosecco and worked her way around the table, refilling each of their glasses. She paused at Fen's side, leaning close to her ear, whispering, 'You smell divine.'

Returning to the head of the table, Bella said, 'Now for some housekeeping. There are three rules on this hen party.'

'Here we go,' Lexi groaned.

'One, we all drink when the bride drinks.'

Lexi raised her glass into the air, then brought it to her

64

lips, taking a sip of Prosecco. The other hens followed suit.

'Two: the bride-to-be is to have no communication with the groom.' She stared at Lexi. 'Understood?'

With her free hand, Lexi saluted.

'And three,' she said, addressing the rest of the group, 'what happens on the hen party, stays on the hen party!'

'Cheers to that,' Ana said, raising her drink. They all clinked glasses and the night felt full of promise.

'Presents, now!' Robyn called, smiling.

'Okay,' Lexi said, setting down her drink. Her engagement ring glittered in the candlelight as she reached for the first gift. It was wrapped in tin foil. 'Bella's?'

'Busted,' she grinned. 'Technically, it's not something I *made*. More like something I cut up.'

'Intriguing.' Lexi opened the scrunched foil and pulled out a sequined boob tube. 'Ibiza 2010! Space boobs! Our post-exams holiday.'

'Yes!' Bella said, raising her glass. 'We should really be listening to "We No Speak Americano".' They'd danced to that track all summer, first finding it hilariously cringe and then becoming hooked on the catchy beat. 'That was the summer you got the job on the podium. D'you remember?' she said, reaching for Lexi's hand, squeezing.

Lexi nodded, smiling with her whole being, like she could taste another life.

Bella told the others, 'We were only meant to be out there for a week's holiday – a post-A-levels mash-up, we called it – but Lexi got scouted by this club manager and asked to be one of their dancers. You spent most of that summer painted silver wearing space boobs.'

'And you spent most of it drinking my wages!'

'Did you go, too?' Ana asked Robyn.

'No. I couldn't. I had a job at home.' Robyn smiled stoically, before her gaze fell to her lap.

Bella felt the recrimination: it was hardly her fault that the apartment she'd sourced through a mate was one-bedroom. Or that they'd ended up staying in Ibiza for the whole summer. If Robyn had wanted to come badly enough, she'd have worked it out.

'We missed you on that trip,' Lexi said loyally, her free hand reaching for Robyn's.

The three of them used to hold hands all the time as teenagers; wherever they walked, their arms were linked, or their hands were slipped into one of the others'. Bella felt a wave of nostalgia for those school days, when the three of them were inseparable and life seemed simpler.

Lexi let go of them both to pick up the next gift. This one was slim, wrapped in the pages of an old comic book.

'Not something I made,' Ana admitted, chin resting easily on her fist. 'But it's something I thought you'd like.'

Lexi carefully removed the wrapping to reveal a second-hand book. She turned the cover over and the pitch of her voice rose as she said, 'Jack Kerouac. *On the Road*!'

Ana beamed. 'I saw it in the second-hand bookshop on my street. I just had to get it. I love this edition – and I know it's one of your favourites.'

Is it? Bella had no idea Lexi even read books. When they were together, they talked about films and sex and music and parties.

Lexi reached across the table, circling her arms around Ana. It was one of Lexi's yoga hugs: a long, meaningful embrace, probably exchanging connectivity or energy or whatever. 'I love it. Thank you.'

The next present was from Fen, who'd made Lexi a voucher for a one-to-one personal training session. They'd discussed the gift together before the hen, Fen worrying that it wasn't thoughtful enough, but Bella knew Lexi would be diligent about using it – asking Fen questions about nutrition and exercise. Bella loved how easily the two of them had hit it off.

Robyn's gift was next. The elegant cream wrapping and neatly tied chocolate-coloured ribbon were a total giveaway. She suspected Robyn had a dedicated present drawer at home, sectioned with pre-emptive gifts and rolls of wrapping paper and gift tags. Bella took a large swallow of her drink, finishing it.

Lexi gasped as she unwrapped a photo book. Two decades of friendship beautifully printed on good quality cream stock complete with sentimental captions. Typical of Robyn to be so thoughtful and show her up.

'Look at the three of you!' Fen cried, pointing as Lexi flicked through the pages.

Bella angled her head to see a photo of her, Lexi and Robyn in wellies, posing with their fingers in the peace sign.

'Glastonbury,' Lexi grinned. 'We must've been, what? Seventeen?'

Robyn nodded.

Bella remembered driving there, leaving her car in some random field before walking for miles with borrowed rucksacks on their shoulders. When they arrived at the festival gate, they paid a fiver to be let in through a hole in the fence, which a teenager held open with wire-cutters. It was one of the muddy years, and they'd painted tribal mud stripes on their cheeks and worn wellies and denim shorts, nests of flowers woven into their hair, glitter glimmering beneath the streaks of mud.

Bella glanced at the next photo, feeling her heartbeat accelerate. It was taken in a swimming pool, Lexi riding high on the shoulders of a guy from sixth form. It had been edited to include only him and Lexi in the frame – but if the photo had panned out, Bella would've been right there in the pool, Robyn on her shoulders.

She may have been cropped from the photo, but Bella had not forgotten that night. Not a single moment of it. The dull thud of a skull against concrete. The fresh blood on the poolside. The long wait in A&E, her wet bikini soaking through her dress.

She heard a collective gasp and looked across the table.

Lexi was holding the final present. There was a perplexed crease in her brow. 'Wow . . . I can't believe . . . Gosh, thank you, Eleanor.'

Two pink spots of colour rose on Eleanor's pale cheeks. Her voice sounded tight, defensive, as she said, 'The email said to make something . . . I didn't know what . . . these are the only things I make.'

Lexi needed both hands to hold the heavy bronze sculpture. It was a dancer, head tipped back, throat exposed, hair trailing down a slender, muscled back. The expression was one of rapture, eyes closed.

It wasn't just any dancer. The detailing was clear, the expression sculpted with skill and precision.

It was Lexi.

'Ladies,' Bella announced, grinning, 'I think we have a winner!'

11

Eleanor

Eleanor had got it wrong. She realised it immediately. She knew the moment Lexi had opened that first present, a silly slip of sequins harking back to some club night out.

As everyone crowded around the sculpture, she felt her skin flushing hot to the very tips of her ears.

'Wow!' Ana said. 'You made this?'

'I'm a sculptor.'

'It's absolutely incredible. The detailing. Lexi's expression . . . You've captured her exactly. Eleanor, you're so talented.'

She wanted Ana to stop talking. She wanted someone to say, *Hey, come over here and look at the moon. The sea. A gecko eating a cricket.* Anything!

This was the sort of thing she invariably got wrong. At the time, it seemed so obvious. *Make something for Lexi = sculpture.* And since she'd no idea what type of thing Lexi liked, except for her brother, she'd thought, *Dancing!*

She'd enjoyed modelling the clay ready for casting. She'd meant to keep it simple, do the lines of her body, the muscle tone, but then it was all coming together so well and she had that amazing feeling of being lost in her work. It was so nice not to be thinking about missing Sam. To just be working, creating. So she began to work the clay to form the features, the eyes, the full lips, the straps of her leotard. And so it became Lexi.

When she'd finished, she'd looked at it beneath the studio lights and knew it was good. One of her best. She wondered if it would be better given as a wedding present – something she could gift to them as a couple – but then she'd have had nothing for the hen present, so she'd decided to bring it after all. She'd barely managed to fit anything else in her bag because it took up several kilos of her weight allowance. So now she was stuck out here with two changes of clothes and a bronze sculpture of her sister-in-law.

If Sam were here, he'd have kissed her on the head and said something easy like, 'EJ, it's gorgeous. You should be proud.'

But what she felt was shame. It was her default emotion. It's what comes when you're familiar with standing in line at the school canteen and having someone whispering at the back of your neck, *Freak. Move. You're putting me off my food.* Or when you know how it feels to sit alone at the front of the school bus, shoulders rounded, waiting for the pelt of an exercise book, a tennis ball, a shoe, to clunk you in the back of the head. You swallow that stuff whole and tell yourself you probably deserved it.

She lifted her gaze, just in time to see Bella pretending to snog the sculpture.

No. She may feel shame, but she didn't do ridicule. Not

by her. 'I can see you think the sculpture is too much. Perhaps it is. I don't go on hen weekends. I don't know what the unwritten rules are. I've never known the rules. I simply thought it would be nice. I wanted to do something *nice* for Lexi.'

Bella's laughter vanished. She set down the sculpture, looking sheepish. 'Sorry. That was rude of me. The sculpture is amazing, Eleanor. Really. I was only messing around because it's a bit . . . intense.'

There was a long pause. 'I suppose it's lucky I didn't give Lexi the naked version.'

Bella stared at her. And then she laughed. They all did.

Eleanor had remembered one of the rules after all: humour.

12

Lexi

Lexi couldn't sleep. Somewhere close to her face, a mosquito whined. It was hot and pitch-black in the room – so dark she couldn't be sure whether her eyes were open or shut. Beside her, she could hear the slow draw of Robyn's breath.

She could never sleep when she arrived in a new place. She'd read an article about it once. *The first-night effect*, it was called. Some evolutionary throwback to do with the left hemisphere of the brain remaining active so it could be alert to threats or potential danger.

Lexi swung her legs out of bed, pressing her feet into the cool tiles. Her skin felt clammy, her chest tight. She plucked Ed's T-shirt away from her skin, eager to feel a breeze. She caught the scent of his aftershave, a deep citrus note married with something smoked. Saliva pooled at the back of her throat.

She got to her feet, moving silently through the darkness,

fingers splayed like antennae. She reached the shutters, pushing them open. The moon was cloaked in cloud and the night stretched endlessly, nothing to interrupt the black apart from the eerie glow of the swimming pool.

She twisted her engagement ring, missing the lights of London and its comforting orchestra of traffic. Here, there was only the drone of insects, the distant wash of the sea. No streetlights; no houses; no phone signal.

Just them.

She turned away. Her heart was racing. Hadn't settled all day. She tiptoed out of the bedroom door and downstairs, heading for the kitchen.

Opening the fridge, she blinked into the bright interior light, enjoying the blast of chilled air. She removed a bottle of mineral water and poured a tall glass. She sipped it slowly, a hip against the kitchen counter, letting her breathing settle.

Strange to be here. Greece. Celebrating her hen party. It was the pressure that was making her uneasy, she decided. Everyone coming here for *her*.

Or perhaps it was the wedding. A few years ago, she'd been at a friend's wedding reception and found herself sitting beneath a huge oak tree, the moon glimmering between its branches, Bella beside her tipping back a bottle of free wine she'd grabbed from their table.

'Promise me we'll never do that,' Lexi had said.

Bella looked across to the open-sided marquee where a middle-aged woman was dancing hopelessly offbeat, her skirt hitched around her thighs. 'What, dance badly in an M&S two-piece to Lionel Richie? I won't make a promise I can't keep.'

Lexi grinned. 'I mean, promise me we won't get married.'

'Hell yes. That's a promise I can keep. We're not doing

marriage. We're doing partying and adventuring and skipping off to a festival on a moment's notice. These suckers with their mortgages and pension plans, they can read in bed with the same person for the next four decades. I'll keep my credit arrangement with Agent Provocateur, thanks.'

Lexi had rested her head on Bella's shoulder. 'I love you.'

'Course you do.'

Yet now, here she was, four weeks away from saying *I do* to a man who kept reading glasses in his bedside drawer and had a subscription to the *Financial Times*. Yet, she found that maybe she did want it, after all. Maybe she liked going to bed sober, early, with him and a book. Maybe she liked living in his house, where there was always good food in the fridge and clean towels in the bathroom. Maybe she wanted in on that dream of a home, a husband, a family.

But what if the appeal was no more than the trick of novelty? What about a year from now? Three? Five? Still in that same bed. That same man.

She set down her glass, pressing her cold fingertips against her brow.

Her parents' marriage was no blueprint for happiness. Growing up, Lexi's father was often away racing cars and, during those periods, her mother would fall into a slump, wearing the same clothes for days on end, forgetting to food-shop or pack Lexi lunch for school. The bins overflowed with take-away containers and wine bottles, the windows were kept shut, dishes cluttered the side. Then, the day before her father was due back, the house would be frantically cleaned, the windows pushed wide so that fresh air blasted through every room. Her mother would have her hair coloured and her nails manicured. A new outfit would appear. The fridge would be restocked, and she'd cook an elaborate meal that made the house smell like a home once again. Lexi would be made to wear a pretty dress and have her hair brushed, hard bristles scratching her scalp, leaving it pinkened and sore.

Lexi had learned this dance over the years, understanding they must both be sparkly for her father's return. They wanted him to stay, to show him how bright and warm the life they were offering him could be. Lexi needed to be the wild, beautiful girl that he told her she was. They kept up this performance, because when she or her mother were low, or difficult, or cried, her father left the room, left the house, left the country.

Left.

Lexi needed air. She crossed the kitchen, slipping out onto the darkened terrace. A nub of a candle still flickered on the main table, throwing light across the bronze sculpture of herself. She picked it up, feeling the cool weight in her hand.

A dancer. That's who she'd been, once. Eleanor had captured her expression perfectly. When Lexi was in the moment – lost in music, dancing, connecting to the rhythm – that had been her bliss.

The bronze was cool beneath her fingertips as she traced her enraptured mouth. Sometimes she still craved the applause of an audience, the glitter of a stage outfit, the party afterwards, the effervescence of adrenaline sparkling.

Would she crave the feel of a different man's arms, the novelty of a hotel room, the honeyed sensation of desire deep between her legs? Maybe, maybe she would.

'I love Ed,' she said out loud to the night. He did thoughtful things like arranging for a bottle of champagne to be waiting for Lexi and her friends on a night out, or surprising her with a delivery of fresh croissants on a Saturday morning when he was away for the weekend. She loved that he took his mother out for dinner every fortnight, and that he secretly enjoyed watching trashy television to wind down after work.

What was this, then? This creeping fear she couldn't shake? She glanced over her shoulder, where the mountains crouched, black and heavy. She wished they were staying closer to town. She wanted to feel the pulse of other people, see the twinkling lights of tavernas or the boats in the harbour, or hear the passing engines of mopeds.

Out here, they were so isolated. They had no car. No way of leaving. Standing in the empty darkness, Lexi experienced a strange, creeping sensation prickle across her neck: she wasn't alone.

She listened, alert. Cicadas calling. The low hum of the sea.

She turned.

The pool was ahead of her, lit by a greenish underwater glow.

She blinked.

The sculpture slipped from her fingers, clattering against the table.

Floating face down in the pool was a body.

13

Eleanor

Eleanor held herself still, water sealing her nose, pressing against her open eyes, muffling her ears, weighting the cotton of her T-shirt.

The desire for air was elemental, urgent, kicking her in the chest, screaming at her to *Breathe!*

She held firm as her lungs burned.

Suddenly there was an explosion of noise, the water bubbling white, a gargled scream – then pain wrenching at her scalp.

She was being yanked upwards by her hair. Her arms flailed, swinging out. A crash of limbs, of water, of words. She caught her name, before plunging under again, eyes wide to the chlorinated sting.

She managed to find her footing, push to the surface, gasping.

Lexi was in the pool, face stricken, voice shrill as she shouted, 'Eleanor! Eleanor!'

Eleanor jerked away, sucking air deep into her chest.

'Are you okay?' Lexi cried, face ashen.

'Yes . . . I . . .'

'What the hell were you doing?'

'I . . . I was . . . floating.'

Gripping at the roots of her hair, Lexi said, 'I thought . . . it looked like . . . like you were *dead*.'

Oh. Well, yes. Eleanor could see how that might work: her floating in the pool in the middle of the night, face down. 'I see.'

'You're in your clothes!'

She looked down, suddenly aware that she wasn't wearing a bra and her wet T-shirt was clinging rather unflatteringly to the folds of her stomach. She clamped her arms across her middle. 'I don't have a swimsuit.'

'Why not?'

'I didn't think I'd need one. I . . . I can't actually swim.'

Lexi was staring at her as if she were mad. 'But you're in the pool.'

'The shallows. Only the shallows where I can stand up. See,' she said, lifting her arms. 'Standing.'

Lexi looked utterly lost.

The water settled around them, light ripples lapping at their waists. 'Why get in the pool?'

These were all fair questions, but now that Lexi was asking them, Eleanor found her answers were coming out a bit strange. 'I couldn't sleep.'

Lexi stared at her, a frown creasing her forehead.

'I was too hot. I didn't want to run the shower and wake Ana. I overheat.'

'You overheat?'

'I overheat,' Eleanor repeated. Her lips began to curl upwards at the absurdity of this moment. Here they were, both drenched, standing in the shallow end of a pool in the middle of the night. Her nose began to wrinkle, her mouth splitting into a grin – and then she was laughing, the sound bubbling from her chest in a cascade of relief. Her shoulders shook.

And then Lexi was laughing, too, covering her mouth with her hands, her knees bending helplessly.

Eleanor clutched herself, bending double, eyelids creased. Her whole body was shuddering. She staggered to the pool-side, gripping on. She hadn't laughed in so long.

'Oh God!' Lexi gasped through another peal of laughter. 'I really thought you were dead.'

'I know!' she managed. 'You ripped half my hair out!'

'I panicked!' Lexi choked out. 'It looked like you'd topped your—' her laughter stalled.

Eleanor blanched.

There was a terrible, loaded silence.

Lexi looked mortified. 'I . . . I . . .'

'So Ed's told you,' Eleanor said eventually, her voice low.

Lexi hesitated. 'Yes, yes he did.'

A furious burn of shame scorched her cheeks. She imagined him describing the morning he'd turned up at her flat. When Eleanor hadn't answered, he'd fetched the spare key from Penelope downstairs, striding in to find Eleanor slumped on her bathroom floor. She was still semiconscious: aware enough to remember the look on his face – first shock, and then, what? Something else, something uglier.

Had he told Lexi this over dinner one night, candlelight flickering, concerned expressions quickly washed away by another glass of red? How would someone like Lexi – whose life glittered and shone – understand how it felt to lie on that bathroom floor, a slick of vomit damp on your cheek?

'A moment of madness. That's all. There won't be a repeat

79

performance,' Eleanor said, straightening her back, smoothing down her wet T-shirt, and trying to regain some sort of composure.

Lexi nodded. 'You've had such a tough ride, Eleanor. I'm sorry. I'm really sorry for all of it.'

She heard the truth in her words.

'Look,' Lexi said, stepping closer. So close that Eleanor worried she was about to reach out, put an arm around her. 'We might not have known each other for long, but if you ever need to talk, I'm here. Okay? I might not have the answers – but I can listen. I want to listen.'

Eleanor felt a pressure in her sinuses, tightening at her temples. 'Yes. Well. Thank you.' Her voice came out strangled.

There was a long silence. The pool filter hummed.

Eleanor cleared her throat. 'Apologies for scaring you.'

'It's fine,' Lexi said. She looked like she was going to say something else, but Eleanor cut her off, saying, 'I'm going to dry off. Head for bed.'

'Good idea. Me, too.'

Water sluiced from Eleanor's body as she climbed the pool steps. She could feel Lexi watching as she crossed the terrace, and tried to make her stride confident, dignified, although it was difficult when her sodden T-shirt was clinging to her dimpled backside.

Lexi called out, 'It's called the first-night effect, by the way. It's when you can't sleep because you've arrived somewhere new.'

'Right,' Eleanor said with a small nod, which she hoped looked like agreement.

Wet-footed, she disappeared into the darkened villa where the other hens slept, knowing that her wakefulness had nothing to do with arriving somewhere new.

THURSDAY

14

Ana

Ana rotated the handle of the grinder, breathing in the sweet, roasted scent of freshly ground coffee beans. Behind her the kettle steamed, but the rest of the villa was pleasingly silent. She'd always loved being the first awake. It felt like being ahead, like a stolen moment just for herself. And God knows, there weren't many of those.

She spooned the coffee into the waiting cafetière, then poured in the boiling water. A rich, darkly smoked flavour lifted with the steam. Her eyes briefly fluttered closed. She set the cafetière on the waiting tray, beside a small jug of full-fat milk, an earthenware mug and, most important, her book.

Outside, the terrace was still in shade, the sun yet to climb from behind the mountain. *Damn, that's some view!* she thought, hand on hip, drinking in the expanse of the horizon, wisps of morning pink feathering the sky. Last night she'd found the silence in the villa deafening, missing the familiar roll of traffic, the lilting voices of passers-by, the rumble of street cleaners – yet in the fresh morning light, she welcomed it.

She crossed the cool stones, the air perfumed with the fragrance of opening flowers. She set the tray on the low wall, peering over the edge at the sheer drop that plummeted towards fists of rock. Dizzying to be so high.

She poured the coffee, dragged a chair towards the wall, then lowered herself into it and opened her book. Her heart sped up in anticipation of this moment. This – coffee and a book – was her morning ritual, and God help anyone who interrupted it.

She'd started it years ago, when Luca was six months old and she'd felt her life spinning wildly out of control. She'd find herself dragged from sleep, groggy and exhausted, Luca's needs blaring and urgent: *Feed me! Change me! Hold me!* She'd stagger through the flat, eyes barely open, and by the time he was fed and changed, she was already spent. When you're a single mother, and exhausted by seven in the morning, well, a long day lies ahead. So she began getting up *before* the baby. Her mother told her she was crazy – 'Grab every damn second of sleep!' – yet that slice of time, just for herself, was even more precious than sleep, because when Luca did wake, she was alert, rested, ready and eager to feel his warm little body against her skin.

She had kept the routine, even though Luca was a teenager now and didn't wake until mid-morning (unless she physically yanked off his covers, pulled the blinds, and flung open the window).

She checked her watch. He'd still be crashed out on her sister's sofa bed, while Leonora prepared pancake batter for when he woke, caramelising bananas to serve on top with sweet, warmed syrup. Luca's favourite since he was small.

How had that pudgy-faced little boy of hers, who used to beam and shout, 'Mama's home!' hurling himself at her legs the moment she entered the flat, become the same boy who'd fail to drag his eyes from his phone screen when she returned?

Yesterday, the school had rung to inform her that Luca and three friends had been caught smoking marijuana on school grounds and been suspended for ten days. The blood had drained from her head as she'd listened, standing outside a Greek supermarket, the phoneline crackling and distorting. 'There must be some mistake,' she'd said, but the words didn't even ring true to her. She knew the boys he'd started hanging around with this past year. She'd tried to gently steer Luca away, but what say did she have? If she pushed in one direction, he'd pull in the other.

She'd called Luca immediately after. His voice was gruff, unapologetic. Angry. That's what scared her: his anger. He'd always been such a gentle boy, sensitive and caring. He loved books, loved painting, loved spending his weekends at the Natural History Museum – and then, somewhere along the way, he'd grown up, grown apart, and she'd lost him. She wondered if she'd been working too hard, putting her concentration in the wrong place, missed the signs.

She asked Leonora not to tell their parents he'd been suspended: they'd only blame Ana. *That boy needs a father,* her mother was fond of clucking, eyes downcast, head shaking.

Her parents were immigrants from Uganda. When they'd arrived in Brixton in the eighties, they'd done everything they could to *fit*. They bought British clothes, cooked British food, adopted British accents. Ana and her sister were taught not to complain, not to challenge, not to be different.

So that's what they did. Never complained, never kicked back. If they got knocked down, they simply got back up. But Ana wanted something different for Luca. She wanted him to make his presence known. To never apologise for who he was or the space he took up. She wanted him to have the same opportunities as everyone else. To fight for them.

Yet somehow, here he was, fifteen years old, angry, suspended from school, something simmering beneath his skin. She felt a lurch of homesickness – for Luca, for her sister, for her flat with the little kitchen window that faced the laundrette opposite, the smell of soap suds drifting in on a summer's night.

I shouldn't be here, she thought, the sea view mocking her with its sheer, clean beauty. She was on a hen weekend with a group of women she barely knew, spending money that would be better saved, while she'd left Luca to unravel. She was selfish, wanting too much.

She caught herself. *No,* that wasn't *her* voice: it was her mother's. The condemnation; the judgement disguised as self-sacrifice. Ana worked hard. She was scrupulous with saving. She was a good mother. She deserved a break, a holiday, something for herself.

She glanced over her shoulder towards the pristine villa.

But, she thought, wavering, *not this holiday.*

Not these women.

Her gaze travelled over the shutters that sealed off each of the darkened bedrooms, mapping where Lexi would be sleeping.

Somewhere deep in her gut, a voice was telling her: *Go home.* She should take a taxi to the airport. Return to London. Never see any of these women again. Leave Lexi be. The hen party could become a memory – a strange beat in time where she lost her way, if only for a moment.

As the shutters to Lexi's room cracked open, light hitting Lexi's slender forearm as she welcomed in the morning, Ana knew she couldn't leave.

15

Fen

'I'm going hiking,' Fen whispered to Bella, who was sleeping with her arms thrown back, the smooth hollows of her underarms exposed.

There was something softer, vulnerable, about Bella when she slept, like a child who, no matter how obnoxiously they'd behaved throughout the day, was returned to innocence by sleep.

Yesterday's argument still throbbed hotly, but Fen knew the hen weekend wasn't the time to examine it. That would have to wait until they were home. 'You're welcome to come,' she added.

Bella curled onto her side. 'No sunlight till ten a.m.'

Fen grabbed her backpack and slipped from the bedroom, quietly relieved. Bella would only have complained about the heat, the weight of her pack, the length of the hike, and they'd have ended up returning early.

In the lounge, the shutters had been thrown wide, the scent of flowering jasmine breathing into the villa with the morning light. Beyond the pool, she could see Lexi on her yoga mat, walking out her heels in downward dog. Ana had her head in a book, a cafetière beside her on the low stone wall.

As she turned to cross the room, her gaze caught on the framed photo of herself that Bella had picked up yesterday. Her stomach lurched.

No way was she having that. She made herself pick up the picture and study her own image. She was only nineteen when it was taken, still so fresh and inexperienced. She wanted to warn that girl with the full, sunny smile, tell her: *Be careful. You don't know what's coming.*

She felt a tightness spreading across her ribs, a tremble in her fingertips. She gritted her teeth, fighting it down. She didn't need to feel afraid. It was over. In the past. Done. She'd worked through it. She was stronger now.

Yet when she looked at herself, all she could hear was his words: *You disgust me.*

Without pausing to think, she was bending towards the cupboard, shoving the framed picture to the very back. She slammed it shut, then wiped her hands down the sides of her shorts. Fuck him.

She drew a breath.

'Sure you don't mind me tagging along?'

Fen spun around. Robyn was crouching near the door, lacing up her hiking boots. She'd forgotten she'd mentioned the hike to Robyn. In truth, she'd have rather stolen out solo, disappeared into the mountains alone, but Robyn was looking so eager as she smiled, rucksack at her side, that Fen could only say, 'I'm sure.'

*

The morning light was pure, scented with pine. The sun was still behind the mountain as they followed the winding dirt trail, giving them at least another hour of shade before it crested.

The path ascended through shrubs and cypress trees, clouds of dust rising from the tramp of their footsteps. Robyn kept pace at Fen's shoulder, ponytail bobbing, pale knees rising.

In the distance, the faint echo of a bell rang across the mountain. 'Is there a church nearby?' Robyn asked, a little out of breath.

'There's a monastery on the northern side of the mountain. I've only seen it from a distance – women are forbidden.'

'What? Why?'

'Temptation, I suppose. Keep the monks' thoughts pure,' she said with a raised brow. Fen didn't have much tolerance for the rules of the church; her deeply religious upbringing had left a legacy of guilt and shame surrounding her sexuality, which had taken years to unpack.

As the path narrowed, Fen took the lead. Flowering thyme grew from the sun-cracked earth. A lizard scuttled from beneath a rock, crossing their path and disappearing into a thorny shrub.

'Thanks for letting me tag along,' Robyn said. 'It's so nice to walk without stopping every ten paces to pick up a dropped toy, or examine an ant, or to coax Jack with a trail of rice cakes.'

Fen laughed. 'Do you get the chance to hike at all?'

Robyn sighed. 'No. I miss it. I was in the mountaineering club at university. It was every bit as geeky as it sounds – and I loved it. I carried it on into my twenties, disappearing for weekends in the Brecon Beacons. It's so wild up there and the colours in spring are breathtaking. But then I met my husband – ex-husband – and I sort of fell out of the habit.'

'Maybe it's time to make some new habits.'

'It is,' Robyn said from behind her, and Fen could hear the smile in her voice. 'Lexi said you're a personal trainer. Think I may have driven past your studio. It's in Westbourne?'

'Yes, just off the one-way system.'

'Do you have a huge bamboo plant in the window?'

'Two of them.'

'I pass it on my way to work. I live in Branksome.'

'Oh? So you're only down the road from Bella?'

There was a pause. 'Yes.'

Bella rarely mentioned Robyn and when she did, she gave the impression that Robyn was dull company, one of those friends that she'd have long ago let drift had it not been for Lexi.

'Do you train Bella? Is that how you met?'

'We met doing our food shop. Glamorous, right?'

'I met my ex-husband in a chiropodist's waiting room. I'm no judge.'

Fen grinned. 'Makes the canned food aisle feel glamorous. Actually, the circumstances were sad really because we came across a lovely elderly woman, Penny, who was having a stroke. Bella was the first to get to her. She was so calm, so reassuring. Her voice never faltered. She kept talking brightly, calmly. Should've guessed she used to be a nurse.'

'Yes, she was so good at her job,' Robyn said.

Fen glanced at Robyn. Her expression was at ease. *She really doesn't know.*

'When the ambulance arrived,' Fen went on, 'Bella promised Penny that she'd get in touch with her daughter. I knew the street she lived on. It was around the corner from me, so I drove Bella there and waited in the car while she broke the news to Penny's daughter. After that, Bella and I, well, we were just sitting in my car, catching our breath, I guess. I thought she was going to say something about what had happened, and then this nineties song came on the radio. I think it was TLC. I was about to flick stations when she said, "I *love* this song." She started to sing, right there in my car, hopelessly out of tune, but with full conviction.'

Robyn grinned. 'Was it "Waterfalls"?'

'Yes!' Fen tipped back her head and laughed.

'Thank God for the ten-kilo luggage limit,' Robyn said. 'She'd have brought her karaoke machine otherwise.'

'It was one of Lexi's three vetoes: *No veils, cocks or karaoke.*'

Robyn laughed and the sound was loud and deep – a big laugh. Fen liked it.

'How did you get into personal training?' Robyn asked as they continued hiking, the path ascending steeply.

Fen could have given Robyn the party line about being passionate about helping others achieve their fitness goals, but instead, perhaps because she was out here, the rhythm of their walk freeing something, she found herself confiding, 'I went through a pretty rough patch a few years ago.' She glanced briefly across the cliffs, her gaze falling fleetingly on the villa, a dark memory swimming to the surface. 'I lost my confidence. My motivation. I was unfit, eating badly. I still didn't know many people in Bournemouth, so I used to take myself off for these long walks on the seafront . . . just because it was easier than sitting still.'

Fen kept up her pace as she said, 'Gradually, I became fitter, and soon I was putting trainers on, deciding to run a little of the way. I don't know whether it was as simple as releasing endorphins or the exercise getting me out in nature, but I started to feel more like myself again. I lost weight, I felt stronger. Happier.'

The path widened and Robyn joined Fen at her shoulder.

'It got me interested in the body-mind connection, so I began reading up on it, learning about nutrition and the psychology behind creating and maintaining positive habits. I saved up to do my PT training and, after a couple of years working for someone else, I decided to take the leap and rent a studio of my own. You've seen it – it's tiny – but I love it there. I can walk to the beach on my lunch breaks, and my clients are wonderful.'

'What type of people do you train?' Robyn asked, slightly out of breath.

Fen adjusted her pace. 'They're not all gym bunnies wanting to get a six-pack for their Instagram squares. They're mothers, grandfathers, teenagers . . . People who want to get the most out of their bodies.'

Robyn was smiling. 'I love that.'

'Sometimes it feels like modern life sets us up for failure. Most of our movement is outsourced – cars, tubes, escalators, lifts. It can be hard to eat healthily too as every street you pass has a coffee shop or fast-food places. Lots of us live in flats and don't have a garden to move around in, so people start outsourcing their exercise, too, and it becomes something that happens once or twice a week at a gym or a fitness class. I guess I'm interested in helping people look at their habits, their whole lifestyle, and explore how they can build more movement into their everyday routine.' Fen suddenly became conscious of how much she'd talked. 'Sorry, sermon on the mount.'

'It's fascinating. I'm thinking it's exactly the sort of thing I need.'

Fen looked at Robyn. 'Come by the studio some time.'

Robyn smiled, the sun finally cresting the mountain, lighting her face. 'I'd like that.'

Our friends are the people who understand us. They know Marmite on toast is our comfort food, they share our obsession with stationery, they've seen where we keep the emergency supply of chocolate. Our friends know the story of our first kiss, or the song that will pull us onto the dance floor, or why we can't listen to David Bowie without crying.

The biochemistry of our bodies changes when we spend time with good friends. A beautiful cocktail of our happy hormones – oxytocin, dopamine and serotonin – elevates our mood. Studies have shown that friendships can strengthen the positive neural pathways in our brains and improve our emotional intelligence.

You might even say that friends are medicine.

But then any biochemist will tell you that medicine to one person can be poison to another.

16

Bella

Bella floated on a lilo beneath a cloudless blue sky. She loved the sun. She would date the sun. Nothing seemed quite so urgent or drastic when the sun was shining. She had never understood people who didn't like the heat. Robyn had always claimed to prefer winter. What was good about grey skies, bone-clenching cold, or side-sleeting rain?

Bella had great admiration for the Mediterranean lifestyle: daily siestas, wine with lunch, and partying until dawn. 'You got all the Italian,' her father was fond of saying, giving her chin a playful squeeze. He was from a village on the lakes near Verona but had met Bella's mother in London when he'd been working as a hotel porter. They'd fallen in love, married, begun a family, but she could never be persuaded to leave England. Moving from London to Bournemouth had been her compromise: a beach beside a town.

There was a flurry of footsteps along the poolside, close

and uneven, followed by a whoosh of laughter. Bella looked up just in time to see Lexi launching herself into the air, tanned knees hugged to her chest. She bombed into the pool in an explosion of water.

Soaked, Bella squealed as her lilo bucked in the rippling pool. She tried to keep her balance but could already feel the sudden, unstoppable lurch. She tipped in – sunglasses, lipstick, blow-dried hair and all.

Underwater her sunglasses swam free of her face and her legs thrashed madly. She surfaced coughing and laughing. 'You dick!'

Lexi was laughing so hard she could barely tread water.
'My sunglasses!'

'I'll get them!' Lexi dived down, a flash of limbs disappearing into the chlorinated blue. She surfaced moments later with a pair of drenched dark glasses. She swam them back to Bella, propping them on her wet head, the lenses studded with water.

Bella seized the moment to press down hard on Lexi's shoulders, shoving her under, laughing. Silver bubbles rose to the surface, Lexi's hair fanning around her face. When she came up for air, she arced a fountain of pool water from her mouth.

Bella was helpless with laughter. Kids. A pair of kids goofing around in a pool. That's all they were. All she ever wanted to be.

They both swam to the poolside, breathless, giddy. They rested their forearms on the warmed concrete. Bella ran a knuckle beneath her eyes, removing the trails of mascara. 'I'm thinking you should sack off the wedding, and we should live here.'

'We can survive on ouzo and olives,' Lexi agreed.

'Take long siestas.'

'Work really, really hard on our tans,' Lexi added. 'But what would we do for money?'

Bella thought for a moment. 'You'd make an excellent goat herder.'

Lexi laughed, her teeth white against her sun-kissed skin. Bella reached out and touched the bridge of her nose. 'Freckles are out.'

'Already?'

Lexi's freckles made her look young and fresh-faced – the Lexi of her teenage years. Bella remembered moving to a new school in Bournemouth when she was thirteen, pretending to be all tough-girl-London. She'd seen Lexi and Robyn sitting together at the edge of the school field, laughing, shoulders quaking, hands gripped. They looked not only happy but easy together, like they fitted.

Those two, she'd decided in that moment. Those were the two girls she wanted to be friends with.

Lexi slipped from the pool, leaving a trail of wet footprints as she returned to their sun loungers.

Bella followed, squeezing water from the ends of her hair. 'Where's Robyn? I've not seen her all morning.'

Lexi laid a towel over her sun-lounger and settled onto it. 'She went hiking with Fen.'

'Did she?' Bella must've been half asleep when Fen mentioned it. She'd forgotten how much Robyn loved to hike. She had always been the one to suggest an evening beach walk in preference over the pub, stashing a bottle of wine or a few beers in her backpack instead.

Lexi pulled her sunglasses on, then reached for her book.

'*Autobiography of a Yogi,*' Bella said, eyeing the cover. 'Tell me you're not going to swap London for an ashram?'

'Can't see Ed going for it.'

The clack of sandals on stone caused them both to look up. Eleanor was crossing the terrace dressed in tailored, knee-length shorts, a strange tie-dye T-shirt, and a floppy hat that could well have belonged to a great aunt. Her skin looked too pale to withstand the scorch of the Mediterranean heat.

'What do you think, Eleanor?' Bella asked. 'Would Ed be up for living in an ashram?'

'No. His feet would look dreadful in sandals.'

Lexi laughed.

'Ana and I have booked a taxi for the Old Town,' Eleanor said. 'It's arriving in an hour. Would you like to come?'

'I'd love to!' Lexi said.

Bella had planned to lie by the pool and drink cocktails all day, but if Lexi was going, she would, too. Maybe they could find a nice little pavement table in the shade and order cocktails there.

Although perhaps she should stay. Bella wanted to make things right with Fen after the awful argument at the airport. Time together without the bustle of the others was exactly what they needed. 'Think I'll stay behind. Wait for Fen.'

She turned, squinting into the sun, her gaze travelling the muscular flanks of the mountain in search of Fen. But the scorched landscape looked deserted, framed only by unbroken blue sky.

17

Robyn

The midday sun was fierce as Robyn and Fen powered down the mountainside, struggling to find their footing in the loose scree.

A cloud of dust settled around Robyn's legs as she reached the bottom, pausing to catch her breath. She plucked her T-shirt away from her sweat-coated skin.

'Fancy a swim?' Fen asked, looking east along the coastline.

The sea, rippling and sunlit, was tantalisingly close, but there was no obvious access from the clifftop. 'How would we get in?'

'There's a cove just off the path. I used to row to it when I spent the summer here. From memory, there are a few steps further along. Could be a bit of a scramble. Want to try?'

The idea of slipping into cool water was intoxicating. 'Definitely.' She followed Fen with renewed energy, striding out along the arid clifftop, skirting patches of scrub where insects teemed. The detour pleased Robyn who, although exhausted, wasn't ready to return to the villa.

'It's down there,' Fen said, pointing.

A tiny white-sand cove waited temptingly at the foot of the cliffs, crystal-clear water lapping onto its shore.

'Looks like the steps have washed away,' Fen said. Now only a narrow ledge cut steeply to the bottom of the cove. 'Think you can make it down?'

Robyn eyed the path. It looked like little more than a precarious goat track that staggered and lurched towards the beach. If either of them slipped, the drop was at least a hundred feet. Fear prickled at her skin.

Fen was watching her, waiting for an answer.

The sun pulsed against the crown of her head, sweat pooling between her breasts. The sea glittered, teasingly close. She took a breath. 'Yes.'

'We'll take it slow,' Fen said. 'Follow my path.'

They descended in silence, Robyn aware of the tremor in her calves as she placed one foot in front of the other, pulse audible in her ears. A trail of red ants marched from a fissure in the cliff face. She could smell the sea breeze lifting lightly. Thirst roared in her throat.

She refused to look at the drop, concentrating only on the positioning of each foot. Her breath was high in her chest. A halo of tiny flies buzzed too close to her face and she wafted a hand through the air, clearing them.

Suddenly the ground began to move, shift. A chunk of dried earth crumbled to dust beneath her hiking boots. Unbalanced, she cried out, scrambling to stay upright.

Fen grabbed her hand, yanking her onto a firmer part of the ledge. 'Here! I've got you.'

Robyn pressed herself against the cliff, palms flat to the hard stone.

'You okay? We can turn back?'

Robyn shook her head. 'I can do this.'

'I've no doubt.' Fen maintained her grip on Robyn's hand as they moved on, step by step, keeping their shoulders grazing the cliff, eyes forward.

Soon enough, the path began to widen, the trickiest section passed. When they finally reached the beach, Fen squeezed Robyn's fingers. 'You did it.'

They were standing in the tiny cove, shaded by the towering cliffs. Robyn turned to see the path they'd followed. It was high. Ridiculously high. 'Holy shit.'

'Sorry,' Fen said, 'the path was a bit sketchier than I remembered. It'll be easier going up.'

'I definitely need a swim now.' As she said it, she realised she had no swimming costume, and was about to say so when Fen began removing her boots, pulling her vest over-head, and peeling off her underwear.

Fen walked straight to the water's edge, her body tanned and muscular and strong, wading in without hesitation.

Robyn glanced down, wondering if she had the nerve to strip off. She hadn't been naked in front of anyone since she'd had Jack, and was embarrassed by the loose skin on her stomach and the empty slope of her breasts. She'd agonised over what swimsuit to buy for the holiday, knowing Lexi and Bella would be lounging poolside, looking gorgeous and fresh in whatever they wore. Yet she couldn't stand here, fully dressed, baking in the heat.

Fen had already put some distance between her and the shore – and there was no one else watching. *Come on, Robyn.*

She crouched, unknotting the laces of her hiking boots. She

peeled off her socks and wriggled her pink toes. The urge to plunge her hot, swollen feet in the sea was overpowering. With a burst of courage, she flung off her sweat-dampened clothes and underwear, then hot-footed it across the beach.

Cold water splashed around her calves, climbing her thighs, cool and secret. Then she dived under, the salt water sensual and incredible, cooling every inch of her flushed skin.

When she surfaced, hair slicked, water beading her eyelashes, she hooted with delight. She rolled onto her back, floating with her arms wide, nipples exposed to the warmth of the sun – and found she was grinning.

In the periphery of her vision, she was aware of Fen making smooth, clean strokes. She admired her athleticism and strength, and how she seemed to know herself in a way that felt intoxicating to Robyn.

Floating on the sun-dazzled surface, hair fanning around her face, Robyn closed her eyes. The hot orb of the sun glowed orange against her eyelids and when she let in a fraction of light, a rainbow caught at the edges of her lashes. Here she was, skinny-dipping in the Aegean Sea! She floated in this moment of bliss, the mountains rising before her, feeling an opening of something deep in her chest.

Robyn wrung the water from her hair, droplets darkening the sand. She'd nothing to dry herself with, so she stood there naked, letting the sun bake her.

By the time Fen waded to shore, Robyn had pulled on her clothes and was standing in the shade of the cliff, sipping from her water bottle. 'Good swim?' Robyn asked as Fen approached, her skin wet and glistening.

'Glorious.' She pulled on her top, not bothering with a bra. 'Worth the scramble down, right?'

Water droplets were caught in the ends of Fen's lashes, sunlight glinting off the perfect clear beads, making her green eyes look like they were sparkling. Robyn felt a fresh charge of energy in her chest. 'Absolutely.'

The climb back up was easier, toes of their boots stamping dust, fingers reaching for the nooks in the cliff for purchase. Too easy, in fact, because before Robyn knew it, the villa was in sight, their adventure over. She asked, 'Think we'll be in trouble for disappearing for so long?'

Fen shrugged. 'Probably.'

'Thank you for today,' Robyn said. 'I've loved it.'

Fen smiled. 'Me too.'

Robyn felt warmth bloom in her cheeks, heat rising from the very centre of her. Fen's gaze skirted across her face, as if reading something in her expression. Robyn could feel the sun hot against her scalp, hear the gentle lap of the sea at the foot of the cliffs.

Then, echoing from within the walls of the villa, the stillness of the moment was dissected by a scream.

18

Bella

A flare of pain stabbed between Bella's toes as she pulled her foot from her espadrille.

'What is it?' Lexi cried, rushing to Bella's side.

Bella, hopping, grabbed on to Lexi's shoulder. She pointed to a glossy black creature, emerging from the toe of her shoe. 'Scorpion!'

'Shit! How bad is it? Should I call an ambulance?'

A burning sensation was spreading across her foot. Bella sucked in a deep breath. She could handle this. It was just pain. Her heart rate had increased but not dangerously so. Healthy people didn't die from scorpion stings. This didn't mean hospital. It was going to be okay. There was nothing to show for the searing pain except an insultingly small pink mark between her toes.

Eleanor and Ana burst from their room, dressed for town.

'Jesus, are you okay?' Ana asked, clocking the scorpion. 'What can we do?'

'I need to wash the sting,' Bella said.

Lexi helped Bella hobble to the sofa, while Ana filled a bowl with water and Eleanor fetched a towel.

'How's the pain?' Lexi asked, face creased in concern.

Bella brought her foot into her lap to examine it. Now the redness was beginning to bloom outwards. She'd stepped on a weaver fish as a child and this was a similar pain: she wasn't dying, but damn it hurt.

'I'll be fine,' she told Lexi through gritted teeth. She was the girl who, when she went over the handlebars of her cherry-red BMX and needed four stitches in her chin, did not cry. She broke her wrist in two places falling from a trampoline and did not cry. Bella Rossi was the younger sister to three brothers. She did not fucking cry.

Ana delivered the bowl of soapy water and, always the nurse, Bella washed her own foot. Oh God, her toes were already beginning to get all puffy and red, and her espadrilles were new and now she wouldn't be able to squeeze her fat fucking foot into them.

See. She wasn't dying. She was worrying about shoes.

'What about some ice on it?' Ana asked.

'Wrap a bunch in a tea towel. Cold compress.'

Eleanor had caught the scorpion in a glass. She stared at it, head angled, the glass distorting her face so her eyes appeared magnified and strange.

'Go drown that damn thing!' Bella said. 'But first take a photo.'

'I don't think this is an Instagram moment,' Lexi said.

'For identification. In case I go into shock and the hospital needs to see what stung me.'

'What's stung you?' Fen said, breathless, as she rushed through the villa door, Robyn behind her. She shrugged off her backpack and crouched at Bella's side. 'Y'okay? What happened?'

'Run-in with a scorpion. I'm fine.'

Fen hugged her. Her skin smelt of sunscreen and salt, and suddenly Bella didn't want to let go and wondered if, oh dear, she might cry after all.

'Here you go,' Ana said, delivering the ice wrapped in a tea towel.

Fen stepped back while the cold compress was applied by Ana, who was measured and steady. Bella thought, *Yep, she'd make a good nurse.* She often pictured people in a hospital setting, imagining what role they'd be best suited to. Lexi, for example, would be on reception. Customer-facing, good at chatting with everyone, slow to rile. Ana would be in triage. Unflappable, not easily fazed, as comfortable helping a drunk to his feet as she'd be dealing with a head injury. Robyn, she thought, glancing her way, well, she'd be a bloody surgeon, wouldn't she? Confident and boring and nerdy, but exactly the person you wanted to cut through your ribcage if push came to shove. She watched Eleanor taking a photo of the scorpion. Mortuary. Definitely mortuary. And Fen? Well, that was obvious. Gynaecologist – and not just for the fantastic examinations, but because you could talk to her. You could be open and tell her you were scared and she'd hold your hand and you'd believe everything would be okay.

Almost everything.

'Anything you need, babe?' Lexi asked.

'Painkillers.'

'Pills or alcoholic?'

'A cocktail of both,' Bella said, feeling like maybe it would be okay.

Lexi made her a strong rum and Coke, with a couple of paracetamol on the side.

Outside there was the sound of tyres on gravel. Eleanor moved to the doorway. 'Taxi's here for the Old Town.'

'We can't go now,' Lexi said.

'Course you can,' Bella insisted.

'I'm staying here with you,' Lexi said. 'But Eleanor and Ana – you should both go.'

Bella leaned forward and took the cold compress from Ana's hand. 'Really. Go. I'm fine here.'

'If you're sure,' Ana said. To the others, she asked, 'There's an extra space if anyone else wants to ride?'

Robyn was unlacing her hiking boots by the door. She looked flushed and fresh-faced from the walk. How long had they been gone, anyway? It was past lunchtime now. Hours, she decided. They'd been gone for hours. 'Take Robyn with you.'

Robyn's head snapped up. 'I don't want to go.'

'You can see the sights. Visit a museum.'

'I want to have a shower and a drink.'

Bella sighed. 'I'm going to have a lie-down. Fen? Come with me?'

Fen put her arm around Bella's waist and supported her as she hobbled to their room.

Propped up on the double bed, Bella watched Fen's concentration as she resettled the cold compress.

Above them, the fan droned, wafting warm air around the room. Bella took a sip of her rum. 'How's it looking?'

Crouched down, Fen answered, 'Cankle-y.'

'Likelihood of wearing my espadrilles again this trip?'

She thought for a moment. 'You could wear one.'

'Humph.'

'Sure you're okay? We could get a taxi to hospital – get you checked out.'

Bella flicked a hand through the air. 'They'll check my blood pressure, take my temperature, give me paracetamol – and charge me a hundred euros for the pleasure. So I'm fine here with my rum and sea view, thanks.'

Fen unlaced her hiking boots, then peeled off her socks. She pressed her feet onto the cool tiles and sighed.

'Good hike?'

Her eyes glittered as she said, 'It was so nice to be out in the hills again. I'd forgotten how beautiful it is.'

'Didn't know Robyn was going.' She said it as easily as she could.

'Anyone was welcome.'

Bella took a sip of her drink, ice cubes knocking against the almost empty glass. 'You've been gone all morning.'

'I didn't think there was any set plan for the day,' Fen said, picking up her hiking boots, crossing the room and setting them by the bedroom door.

'There isn't. I missed you, that's all.' Bella didn't have any right to complain, but she still felt hurt.

She studied Fen: the nose piercing, the tattoo, those broad shoulders. She was wearing a vest with *Good vibes* printed in rainbow colours across the chest. She always looked so effortlessly cool. Bella followed the curve of her breasts. 'No bra,' she said, thinking how sexy it was seeing her nipples through her top. 'Wait. You hiked without a bra?'

'It's in my bag. I went for a swim.'

'When?'

'On the way back. There's a cove—'

'With Robyn?' Bella stiffened.

'Of course with Robyn.'

'I didn't know you were planning on stopping at a beach. Did you have swimming stuff?'

'What is this?' Fen said, brow furrowed. 'We skinny-dipped.'

'You and Robyn swam *naked*?' Bella whisper-shouted.

'Yes. We did.'

'Fuck.'

Fen opened her hands. 'We've never had issues with things like that. You sleep in Lexi's bed or take a sauna at a health spa with a bunch of naked women. I went for a skinny-dip. Am I not allowed to do that?'

Bella knew the hot, fizzing anger in her chest was too big for the situation. 'I just don't want my girlfriend to disappear for half a day.'

'With Robyn.'

'Yes, with Robyn. I don't know why you'd want to hang out with her anyway. She's so . . . so fucking boring!' There. She'd said it.

Fen glared at her. She didn't contradict Bella, tell her she was wrong, tell her she shouldn't speak about people in that way. It was worse: she looked disappointed.

Bella wanted to say, *Please, stop looking at me like that. I can't bear it. You're everything that is good, Fen. I can't lose you. I need you. I know I get like this sometimes – but it's because I'm scared you're pulling away. And when I'm scared, I fight.* She tried to open her mouth to communicate something of this, but all that sounded was a little humph of indignation.

Fen turned, crossing their room towards the en suite. There was the soft sound of the door closing behind her.

'At least fucking slam it!' Bella yelled.

Out of all the words, those were the ones she chose.

~

We were sharing a villa, sharing bedrooms, sharing beds: talking was our currency. But it was when the whispering began that things shifted.

We caught the hushed tones of arguments meant to be played out in private. We heard the raised voices behind closed doors and pretended that we hadn't. And later, we'd hear other things: a soft cry rippling from an open window, a strike of blame lighting up the terrace, a secret excavated on a clifftop after midnight.

Those whisperings felt like the fourth wall of the holiday being removed. We could no longer suspend our disbelief that all was sun-kissed and easy and light.

We could no longer believe that we were all friends.

19

Lexi

Lexi crossed the bedroom and pulled the balcony doors closed. Bella and her big mouth!

Robyn was pacing the room, cheeks flushed, mouth in a tight scowl. '*She's so fucking boring!*' she repeated.

'Bella didn't really mean that,' Lexi said gently.

Robyn raised an eyebrow.

Lexi reached out, catching Robyn's hand as she passed. She looked directly at her, waiting until she met her eye. 'We both know that whenever Bella feels threatened, she lashes out.'

'Threatened? Because I went for a hike with Fen?'

'You know what she's like. She needs the attention circling her.' It was one of the things she had learned to accept about Bella over the years.

'She's right, though. I am boring.'

'Course you're not!'

'It's true.' Robyn let go of Lexi's hands and sank down onto the bed, shoulders rounding. 'The social highlight of my week is taking Jack to Wriggle and Rhyme.'

Lexi laughed.

'I wish it were a joke. I don't even have a sense of humour anymore, so it can't be. I lost that with my social life. All I do now is go to work. Look after Jack. Eat dinner with my parents. Watch Netflix. Then go to bed. That's it. That's my life. *I'm* bored by it.'

Lexi sat beside Robyn, the mattress dipping. 'How long have you felt like this?'

'For months. Oh God,' she said, covering her face with her hands. 'Maybe even years. Since I had Jack, sometimes I feel like, like I've lost a part of myself. I know that sounds selfish, because I love him so much and I want him to be the centre of my world . . . but . . . what if I'm pouring so much into him that there's nothing left for me?' Robyn looked up and her expression was raw, vulnerable. 'Living back at Mum and Dad's – it's been such a help after Bill, but I don't think it's good for me. I'm still sleeping in my childhood bed, for God's sake!'

Lexi had always liked Robyn's parents. They were kind and caring and dependable – a welcome contrast to her family – but there was also (and Lexi felt disloyal for even thinking this) a sadness that clung to them. Their son, Drew, had died in a drink-driving accident over a decade ago and, God, Lexi knew grief wasn't stamped with an end date, but over the years, she'd also wondered if their sadness had been accepted as the norm, like they were no longer even aiming for anything else. Robyn was their glimmer of light. Her decisions to go to a local university and then take a job in a local firm were made because she knew that, too.

'I need to move out,' Robyn said, rubbing the back of her neck, as if the thought alone caused her muscles to knot. 'But Jack would be so sad to leave my parents' house. And Dad would be heartbroken – he and Jack have breakfast together, spotting the birds on the garden feeder while they share toast. Mum is always saying how nice it is to have the extra noise and bustle in the house, and I'd feel terrible if—'

'Robyn,' Lexi cut in. 'Maybe it's time to think about you – what *you* want – rather than what is best for Jack or your parents.' Lexi maintained her gaze, holding the space for her.

Robyn looked right into her eyes. 'But . . . what if I can't manage on my own?'

'You're the most capable person I know. You're always putting everyone else's needs before your own. I think you're so used to it that you're not even sure what it is *you* need.'

Robyn blinked as if considering this. There was a whorl of salt on her sun-pinkened shoulders, and her usually straight hair was kinked from the sea. 'This,' she said after a long moment. 'I need this. My friends. Sunshine. Meeting new people. Doing new things. I need a break from routine.' She leaned her head on Lexi's shoulder. 'Thank you.'

Robyn smelled pleasingly of sweat and salt, and it made Lexi think of netball games, when Robyn wore her Wing Attack bib, fast little legs nipping around the court. Bella always played Centre, and the two of them had an unstoppable on-court dynamic, shooting the ball away from the defence with speed and silent communication.

'You should let Bella know that you heard. That she hurt you,' Lexi said.

Robyn shrugged. 'No point. She's not going to change her opinion of me.'

'We were all such good friends, weren't we? The three of

us. Sometimes I think I imagined it.' Lexi shook her head. It was easy to forget just how close the three of them had been at school. Their friendship had felt easy and natural, absent of the usual petty jealousies that other friendships suffered. They felt above it – as if their trio were so rich and true that they were untouchable.

'Do you remember how we used to call each other every night after school? I'd sit at the bottom of our stairs – that was as far as the phone cord would stretch – and we'd talk for an hour, while our parents yelled that we'd see each other in the morning.'

Robyn laughed. 'Dad started getting our phone bills itemised. He'd go through them with a highlighter, marking your and Bella's numbers.'

Lexi grinned. 'Thank God you had a paper round to pay it off.'

'We slept over at Bella's every Friday, on that futon she had with the stars and moon throw. And all those posters on her wall: Lenny Kravitz, Tupac, Bob Marley. We used to borrow her eldest brother's CDs, and he'd keep an inventory of which tracks skipped. We'd always make you hand them back as we knew you had more chance of getting away with it.'

Lexi laughed. She could remember the lipstick smell of Bella's room, the clutter of nail polishes and body sprays and lip glosses on her dressing table. They'd experiment with make-up and eyebrow-plucking, and testing fake tans. 'We were close. I didn't misremember it,' she said almost wistfully. 'What happened?'

Robyn glanced down. 'I guess we went in different directions. Bella was in London for a few years. I stayed home.'

'Yes, but she's been back in Bournemouth for ages now. You only live a few miles apart.'

Robyn shrugged. 'We're both busy.'

'Do you ever meet up? Call each other?'

'Not really. We should. I know we should.'

Lexi knew things had cooled after she and Bella spent the summer in Ibiza and Robyn hadn't come. Bella would've usually cajoled – or bulldozed – Robyn into joining them. Only she hadn't. She'd just let her go. 'This hen weekend – it's the longest stretch of time the three of us have spent together in years. I miss us. The *three* of us.'

Robyn smiled at her sadly. 'Me, too.'

20

Ana

Ana followed Eleanor along the shaded alley, Greek music drifting from open shop fronts. Rambling trails of bougain-villea clung to crumbling stone walls and the air smelled faintly of incense.

She was pleased they'd taken a taxi into town. Sunbathing by the villa pool held no appeal for Ana, nor, she suspected, Eleanor. She paused at a pavement stall to admire the local sponges. The material was surprisingly abrasive beneath her fingertips. It would make a nice little gift to thank her sister for having Luca. She checked the price, then took out her purse and paid.

Eleanor had stopped at the stall opposite and was looking at a stand of leather handbags.

'These are beautiful,' Ana said, approaching, the warm resin smell of the leather lifting into the afternoon heat.

'I always wear a backpack. More practical.'

Ana glanced at the grey quilted bag sagging over Eleanor's pale shoulders.

'Suppose it doesn't cut it on a night out.' She paused. 'Not that I go on many of those.'

'Treat yourself,' Ana gently suggested, guessing that Eleanor, like her, probably spent little money on herself. She unhooked a satchel in a deep mahogany. The leather was soft and well oiled, thick buckles closing over a front pocket. 'This would look gorgeous on you.'

Eleanor studied the bag carefully before placing it reverently over her shoulder. The corners of her mouth turned up.

A shop owner emerged from between two rails of scarfs, holding a mirror. 'Here. You see?'

Ana caught the bloom of pleasure on Eleanor's face as she admired the bag. 'Yes, I do like it.'

'Get it!' Ana encouraged. 'Go on! We're on holiday!'

Eleanor studied the bag again. 'It doesn't make me look . . . showy?'

Ana laughed. 'No! It's simple and understated and stylish. It's just right!'

Eleanor nodded. 'Yes. Well. I think I will buy it.' She unhooked it from her shoulder and passed it to the shop owner, who carefully wrapped it in brown paper, tying it with string and a sprig of fresh rosemary.

With their purchases tucked away, they continued wandering along the shaded alleyways, blue flashes of the harbour glimpsed in the distance. They stopped for ice creams, served in wide waffle cones and doused generously with melted dark chocolate, and strolled to the harbour edge to eat them. There, tourist boats were returning after a day of island-hopping or snorkelling, and they watched crowds of holidaymakers with sun-pinkened faces and beach bags hooked over arms filling up the tavernas.

Ana's phone buzzed – the holiday atmosphere dissolving when she saw it was a message about Luca. Her sister said he seemed withdrawn and surly – not his usual self – and refused to talk about the suspension from school.

Luca was fifteen years old – not yet a man, but no longer a boy, lost somewhere between those two worlds, where Ana was unable to reach him. She had a fierce urge to be home, in the cool of their flat, Luca sitting opposite her at their small Formica table. She wanted to be able to look him in the eye. Talk. Find out what was hurting him.

'Everything okay?' Eleanor asked. She'd stopped a few paces ahead of Ana, crumbling the end of her cone into the harbour where a shoal of tiny fish darted across the filmy surface, mouths opened.

'My son's got himself in some trouble at school.' She paused. 'He's been suspended. He's not the sort of kid who gets suspended. Maybe all parents say that. But he's not. My sister thinks he's lost his way.' Ana's ice cream was melting, dripping a puddle of liquid chocolate onto the concrete. She tossed the remains of it into a bin, then sucked her fingers clean.

'What do you think?' Eleanor asked.

'Luca's hanging out with this crowd of friends. He looks up to these boys – but they're not like him. A bit older, a bit tougher, you know? He's not himself when he's with them.'

Eleanor nodded. 'What's Luca interested in?'

'He'd tell you football, computer games, cars – like the other boys – but they're not his passion.'

'What is?'

'I'm not sure he knows yet. He used to love art – he'd spend hours sketching these wild, beautiful pictures of dragons and sea monsters – but I've not seen him pick up his sketch pad in a long while.'

'Maybe he'll come back to it. He's so young.'

'Was your passion always sculpting?'

'No. I only started in my twenties. Wish I'd found it sooner because it gives me a place to go, somewhere to put my mind when everything else feels too noisy.'

Ana realised how much she liked this woman. She was smart. Perceptive. Forthright. 'Tell me about your work. Do you have a studio?'

'Of sorts. It's a garage I rent. I love it though. In summer I roll up the door, let the light flood in. In winter all I need is a gas heater.'

'And thermals beneath your overalls.'

Eleanor's head tipped to one side. 'Yes. How did you know that?'

Ana hesitated. A couple of years ago, she'd read an interview in a magazine about Eleanor's sculpting process, which she'd torn out, keeping it in a private file with a slim collection of other documents. Eleanor had been wearing blue overalls in the profile picture and explained that she layered thermals beneath them so she could keep working in all conditions.

Ana made her face look easy, careful not to give herself away. 'Lucky guess,' she said.

21

Bella

That evening, the hens ate dinner on the terrace, the table filled with bowls of herb-flecked couscous and blistered stuffed peppers. Bella's foot still throbbed from the scorpion sting and, deciding she needed more alcohol on medicinal grounds, she reached for a bottle of retsina.

She glanced about in search of other glasses that needed topping up, but they were all full. She rolled her eyes. There had been a time when she and Lexi would have skipped dinner altogether, voting for alcohol and dancing over food and talking.

If you can't beat them, join them, she decided, stabbing her fork into a slice of grilled aubergine and dropping it into her mouth. It dripped with a sweet, honeyed flavour. 'Eleanor, what magic have you drizzled over this to make it taste like a meadow? A fragrant, smoky meadow.'

From the far end of the table, Eleanor glanced up, as if surprised to be spoken to. 'Seasoning and dried herbs I found in the cupboard.' She shrugged as if it were no big deal – as if the skill of turning a humble aubergine into a magnificent flavour-drenched meal was something that all humans possessed.

'Well, you are officially invited to all future hen parties I attend,' Bella said, forking another piece into her mouth and swallowing.

'Your personal chef. Can't wait.'

Bella blinked. She'd meant it as a compliment. Why was this woman so damn prickly? It was like holidaying with a cactus!

She picked up her drink and took a large swallow. It was important to Bella that people liked her. It was one of her strengths that she could get women – and men – to like her. It was about knowing how to reach them, what was needed to make the connection. It was instinct. Intuition. Some people were born with a natural aptitude for sports, or music, or art – and she, Bella Rossi, was born with the ability to make people like her. (And, if she were being honest, also dislike her. It wasn't that she minded being *dis*liked. It was that she wanted to be the one to choose.)

But Eleanor? She was tricky. Not that she even particularly wanted Eleanor's friendship – after all, the only connecting piece in their lives was Lexi, so they didn't *need* to become friends. She knew Eleanor had lost her partner fairly recently, but she shouldn't have come if she didn't plan to *try* to have a good time.

Her gaze trailed to Fen. She looked clean and fresh from the shower. Bella wanted to run her fingers along the shorn sides of her hair, feel her palms kiss her neck. She wore a blue short-sleeved shirt buttoned to the collar, a fabric badge stitched to the breast reading: *Nevertheless, she persisted.*

This woman.

Bella would persist. She wasn't going to lose Fen.

She couldn't.

At the other end of the table, Lexi was listening to Ana, her eyes bright with interest. Bella watched for a moment, trying to understand Lexi's infatuation with the woman. Sure, they could swap notes on hipster London hangouts, or talk about books, or yoga, or vintage stores, or whatever the hell they both wrote in their gratitude journals – but Ana and Lexi didn't have history. Ana hadn't made her own cigarettes out of tracing paper and a stale pack of tobacco. She hadn't nicked Lexi's mum's stash of vodka and got wasted on a Thursday morning before assembly just for the hell of it. She hadn't crowd-surfed at a Jamiroquai gig beneath a blaze of strobe lights or slept on the beach, shivering beneath a single blanket and a full moon.

Bella stood, tugging down her body-con dress. This outfit looked so much better when she wore it with heels. Still. Soon she'd be too drunk to notice. Barefoot, she limped around the table to Lexi's side. She draped an arm over her shoulder. 'How's your hen party, babe?'

Lexi looked up at her, smiling. 'The best.'

Bella grinned. 'Hope you've noted the lack of veils, cocks, and karaoke?' Then with a wink, she added, 'So far.'

'I called veto.'

'Really? I didn't hear: all that clubbing has given me tinnitus. I do have one small surprise for you.'

Lexi raised an eyebrow.

'All I'm going to say is, I hope you've had enough to eat as you'll want that flat yoga-stomach of yours lined.'

'No drinking games, that's what we agreed.'

'Did we?' Bella said, wiggling her eyebrows. 'I get so forgetful when I've been in the sun all day. Back in a minute.' She turned, limping rather than sauntering across the terrace.

Inside, the villa was cool and quiet. She pushed her sunglasses onto the top of her head. Alone, she felt her smile slipping. A wash of exhaustion broke over her and she leaned her forearms against the kitchen counter, head hanging down. She sighed. What was going on with this introspective mood? She was on holiday!

Outside, an eruption of laughter echoed around the terrace. She glanced sideways to see Ana collapsing against Lexi, their shoulders shaking. Across the table, Fen was smiling too, her skin tanned, her expression easy. Bella felt the hollowing lurch of insecurity: she should be the one making Lexi laugh, or lighting up Fen's expression.

She bit down on her lower lip. She would not cry! This was Lexi's hen party! The sun was setting! The drinks were flowing. She should be having a good time.

Pressing her palms firmly against the work surface, she pushed herself upright. Lengthening her spine, she took a deep breath. She shook out her hair. Right. Time to get this night back on track. She fetched her lipstick and reapplied it using the lens of her sunglasses as a mirror. She pressed her lips together. Pouted.

If Lexi thought she was getting through this hen party sober, she was mistaken. She lined up six shot glasses on a tray, then reached into the fridge for the ice-cold bottle of ouzo. There was no chance that this weekend was going to pass without one blowout.

Ana may have thought she knew Lexi, but all she was seeing was a slice of her. Bella unscrewed the metal cap and began pouring the ouzo. Time to shake things up.

Let Ana get a glimpse of the old Lexi. The real Lexi.

Her Lexi.

22

Lexi

Through the open doors to the villa came Bella, the sunset reflecting off the white-framed sunglasses propped on her head. Her usual hip-swinging sashay was punctuated with a faint limp, but her chin was held aloft, red lipstick reapplied. Lexi clocked the tray lined with shot glasses and a bottle of ouzo.

Oh, crap.

Bella met Lexi's eye and gave an exaggerated wink. Then she set the tray on the table, plunged her fingers into her mouth, and whistled.

Robyn gripped her hands over her ears. 'We're not a pack of dogs!'

'Get your ass up here, bride-to-be,' Bella said, standing at the head of the table. 'It's time for the Mr and Mrs quiz!'

Lexi felt a flare of annoyance: Bella had promised. She knew that Ed would hate this sort of thing. He was a private man, and she respected that. 'You're serious?'

'Hell yeah.'

She looked to Robyn for support, but she held up her palms as if saying, *Nothing to do with me!*

Reluctantly, Lexi moved to Bella's side at the head of the table. Candlelight flickered across the terrace. Eleanor sprayed a cloud of mosquito repellent over her neck and shoulders, the smell of citronella filling the night.

Lexi eyed the shots uneasily. 'I want to remember my evening – not spend it vomiting ouzo over the balcony.'

'Honey,' Bella said, planting a hand on her hip, 'I've seen you do a bottle of Jack straight. I know you're all clean-food and purified-water these days, but that liver of yours . . . it remembers.' She pulled a crumpled slip of paper from her bra. Bella was forever stashing things there: money, a spare tissue, a cloakroom ticket. She unfolded the paper, glossy nails shining, then addressed the hens. 'Ten questions, ten shots. Lexi gets the question right and she gets to nominate someone to take the shot for her. Gets it wrong and she does the shot. Got it?'

'I'll answer the questions,' Lexi said, 'but I can't stomach ouzo.'

'Who are you and what have you done with the real Lexi?'

'I just want to enjoy the night. Go at my own pace.'

Bella placed her palms together in prayer position, and spoke exceedingly slowly. 'This. Is. A. Hen. Party.'

Lexi waited for something further – but that was all: *This is a hen party.*

'Are we all ready?' Bella asked, voice as honeyed as a gameshow host's.

There were no hoots or catcalls in response, only a vague murmur of assent.

'Question one,' Bella began, undeterred. 'What would Ed say is your worst habit?'

'You've spoken to Ed?'

'Have you not heard of a Mr and Mrs quiz? Do I need to give you the basics of how a hen party works? I called your husband-to-be and asked him a series of questions about you, your relationship, and his chequered past. He became embarrassed, then defensive, suggesting that this wasn't his sort of thing – but eventually answered them anyway because even *he* understands the fundamentals of how a hen party works.' She took a breath. 'So, I shall repeat: *What would Ed say is your worst habit?*'

Lexi wiped her palms down the sides of her dress. She needed to get this right. All ten questions right.

What would Ed say was her worst habit? They'd only been living together for five months, so they were still on good behaviour. She'd seen Ed irritated in a restaurant when the service was terrible and heard him taking his frustrations out on his rowing machine after an exasperating call – but he'd never seemed annoyed by her habits.

Bella tapped a fingernail against her watch face.

'Oh, there is one,' Lexi said. 'My worst habit is probably going out and leaving all the windows wide open.'

'Boring answer alert,' Bella announced. 'What about all the other options? The pillow drool. Using other people's toothbrushes when you can't find your own. Eating toast but leaving the crusts.'

'Or putting half-eaten chocolates back in the box,' Robyn chimed in. 'Checking your phone mid-conversation. Picking your split ends.'

'Excellent examples, Robyn,' Bella said. 'Anyone got any more of Lexi's bad habits they'd like to share?'

'I think that's enough,' Lexi said. 'What was Ed's answer?'

Bella glanced down at the sheet and rolled her eyes. 'Ed

said, *Lexi always leaves the windows open when she goes out. It's a security issue.*'

'See!' Lexi laughed. 'Now, about this nominating.' She picked up the first shot and handed it to Bella. 'All yours.'

'Thought you'd never ask,' Bella tipped it back in one movement. She licked her lips with relish, then belched. Bella loved to belch. Despite the immaculate outfits, the full make-up, the perfume-sweetened skin, she belched like a barbarian.

'Question two,' Bella began. She leaned forward – giving everyone a clear view down the neckline of her dress – whispering theatrically, 'Don't worry, the answers get a *lot* more interesting.'

Lexi had to keep reminding herself to smile.

'We asked Ed how many sexual partners you've had.'

Her jaw tightened. 'You asked him that?'

'There's no "*we*" by the way,' Robyn said, palms raised.

Bella grinned. 'Sure did.'

'I can't believe you.' She knew Ed would've hated being asked that. *Brassy* and *outspoken* – those were the words he'd used to describe Bella a few weeks ago, which had prompted their first row.

'Honey,' Bella said, planting a hand on her hip, 'we've not even got into the hard stuff. I mean, I could've asked him how many people you've slept with in *one* night.'

Lexi stared at Bella, who was grinning. She honestly thought this was good fun. Her sister-in-law was sitting at the table, for God's sake. Ed was no wallflower, but Lexi had scrimped on some of the details of her past. The crowd she used to mix with were dancers, which meant supple bodies in tiny outfits, and wild parties, and drink and drugs and sex. Lexi wasn't sorry for any of it. She loved sex. Loved men. But it was in her past.

'I'm not answering that question. I hope Ed didn't either.'

'He answered,' Bella said, raising her eyebrows at whatever was written on the paper. 'You either give us your answer or take the shot.'

A brittle silence crackled around the table. Lexi wasn't about to do either. She wanted to leave the terrace, walk down the stone steps to the beach and sink her feet in the sea. But if she left, it would make things worse – it would show that Bella had got to her. 'Fine. A dozen.'

'That's what you told Ed? Oh, babe, that's hilarious!' Bella laughed. 'But no, I'm afraid your answer is incorrect. Your husband-to-be said, and I quote, *Lexi, of course, was a virgin when we met.*'

Everyone laughed, including Lexi, the tension easing a little.

'There you go,' Bella said, handing her the shot.

The old Lexi wouldn't have blinked. She'd have knocked it back without hesitation.

'Get it down you,' Bella said, challenging her.

Lexi stared at the clear liquid. Slowly, she lifted the glass to her lips, took the ouzo into her throat, felt its hot bite. She held it there while she set down the empty glass. Then, as Bella's gaze returned to the questions, Lexi ducked low and spat the liquid into the cactus behind her.

Bella's head whipped up. 'Er. What was that?'

Lexi straightened, wiping the back of her hand across her mouth.

'You may be a woman who spits not swallows – but *never* with alcohol.'

'I don't want to make this a drinking game.'

'It's one shot.'

'I'm not in the mood for drinking,' she snapped.

'I do not speak your language. Is there a translator anywhere? This woman is saying, *I'm not in the mood for drinking*?'

Around the table, the others smiled uneasily.

'As your forfeit, you can do two,' Bella decided, picking up two more shot glasses and holding them out.

Lexi's hands remained at her sides.

Bella's chin lifted a fraction. The atmosphere stretched taut.

'Here, I'll do the forfeit,' Robyn said, standing quickly.

'You will not!' Bella refused.

Robyn hesitated uncertainly. She looked between Lexi and Bella, then lowered herself back down.

Bella thrust the two shots towards Lexi. 'They are yours.'

Lexi looked Bella square in the eye. Shook her head. 'I said no.'

'What is going on?' Bella asked, genuinely bemused. 'You're not bloody pregnant, are you?'

Lexi held herself very still.

Across the darkening terrace, a moth fluttered towards the candlelight.

She was aware of silence forming around her, except for the thrumming of wings.

Bella's eyes widened. 'Oh my God! You are! You're pregnant!'

23

Bella

Lexi is pregnant. That's all Bella could think, over and over, like a marching beat in her head. *Lexi is pregnant.*

There was silence around the table. Candles flickered in glass jars, illuminating surprised expressions.

When Lexi spoke, her voice was flat and even. 'I'm eleven weeks.'

Bella blinked. *Eleven weeks? Already?* 'Why didn't you tell me?'

'I've only just found out. Ed doesn't even know yet.'

'Oh,' Eleanor said from the other end of the table.

Lexi's gaze lowered briefly. 'He was working in Ireland when I took the test. I want to tell him in person.'

Bella placed her fingertips on the table edge to stop herself swaying. She looked at Lexi, trying to make sense of the news.

Lexi had said that she never wanted children. They'd pass other mothers looking harassed and exhausted and think,

Not us. Soft play was for suckers, that's what they'd always maintained. Snotty playdates and Saturday mornings at the park and lie-in-less weekends – no, thank you very much. They both loved kids – they weren't *monsters* – but they wanted a different type of life. Plus, Lexi had known that you couldn't be a professional dancer *and* pregnant.

But now Lexi wasn't a dancer. She was a yoga instructor (Bella's brain had only just stopped scrambling over that one). She was getting married. She was . . . having a baby?

Fuck.

Fen broke the silence, smiling warmly as she said, 'Congratulations. This is wonderful news.'

Lexi looked at her gratefully. 'Thank you.'

Around the table, the rest of the hens were beginning to chime in.

Bella knew she should say something. That she should hug her friend. Use the word *congratulations*. But her mouth didn't seem to want to move. The quiz questions were hanging limply from her hand. She needed to speak. Everyone's attention was turning to her.

Silence stretched.

Lexi looked at her. Waited.

Bella stared back. Said nothing.

'You know what?' Lexi said. 'I'm tired.' She left the table, her footsteps barely making a sound as she crossed the terrace and disappeared inside the villa.

Bella carried the bottle of ouzo to a corner of the terrace and slumped down on the edge of the wall. Her dress had ridden up around the tops of her thighs and she didn't bother to adjust it. She drank straight from the bottle, her lipstick marking the glass neck.

She was aware of the lethal drop at her back. Didn't care.

She wriggled her right toes and felt the hot throb of the scorpion sting. She knew she should ice it again but couldn't face going into the kitchen where the others were washing up – and probably bitching about her.

A speaker still played a low pulse of reggae. She took another swig of ouzo, then stood, swaying in time to the beat. She wasn't going to end the party. Fuck them all and their stony judgements. She moved her hips, hair swinging.

Robyn strode from the villa with an empty tray, refusing to look in her direction. Bella danced on. Robyn began stacking the tray with used glasses and empty bottles, her movements neat, precise.

See? Surgeon.

When the table was cleared, she moved off. As she passed, Bella found herself calling out, 'We didn't even finish the quiz.'

Robyn stopped. 'It was a shitty quiz. You humiliated Lexi.'

She'd forgotten how punchy Robyn could get with a few drinks under her belt. It was either that, or she'd start swaying against your shoulder, telling you she loved the whole world. 'It was supposed to be fun.'

'Guess I'm too *boring* to know what fun means.'

Oh. So Robyn had heard. 'Sorry,' Bella said sheepishly. 'I was venting. I didn't mean it.'

'Well, it hurt,' she said.

Bella moved towards Robyn. 'Really, I'm sorry,' she said, feeling terrible. 'Forgive me for being an arsehole?'

Robyn looked at her, then rolled her eyes. 'Fine. Forgiven.'

'Thank God for that. I can't handle *everyone* being pissed off with me. You know I'd never have done the drinking games if Lexi had told me she was pregnant?'

136

'I know.' She set down the tray on the low stone wall, then pressed a hand into her lower back, as if it were causing her pain.

'Why didn't Lexi tell us?'

'Like she said – she wanted to tell Ed first. She probably needs some time to get her head around things.'

'I don't think she wants this baby.'

'She does. She said—' Robyn cut herself short.

Bella blinked. 'Wait. You knew, didn't you? Lexi told you she was pregnant.'

'She called because she was upset—'

'When?'

'Last Sunday.'

'Last Sunday? That's over a week ago! She's known all this time and not told me? I'm her maid of honour!'

'Maybe she wasn't sure she'd get the reaction she wanted from you.'

'What does that mean?'

'You didn't even say congratulations.'

'It was a shock.'

'Is it? Lexi's getting married. Everything's different now. She's not the same Lexi you were partying with in your twenties. She's in love with Ed—'

Bella rolled her eyes.

'What does' – Robyn mirrored Bella's eye-rolling, making her look deranged – 'mean?'

'It means *Ed*. She's in love with Ed?' She was saying his name in that way again, like it was a question.

Robyn folded her arms. 'Let me guess, you don't like him?'

She shrugged.

'Name one boyfriend of Lexi's you've actually liked.'

Bella went to the tray of drinks and poured two shots into used glasses. 'The guy with the eagle tattoo,' she said, passing a shot to Robyn.

'*Him?* That's the one you liked?'

She clinked her glass against Robyn's and tipped back her drink in one swallow. 'I liked that he was from Australia and his visa was running out.'

'See! You're impossible!' Robyn swallowed her drink, then grimaced.

'I just want Lexi to be with someone as amazing as her.'

'No, what you want is for Lexi to be single. You're scared that she'll love someone else more than she loves you.'

'Ow,' Bella said. 'Easy there with the truth bullets.'

Robyn pursed her lips. 'Look, I'm only saying maybe this isn't about Ed—'

'Course it is! I don't trust him!' Bella shot.

'Why not?' Robyn asked, her voice piqued with curiosity.

Bella glanced up at Lexi's room. The shutters were closed, a faint glow of light spilling from the slats. She took a step closer to Robyn. Maybe she shouldn't be saying this. If anything, it was Lexi she should speak to. 'You remember the engagement drinks?'

Robyn nodded.

'I was at the bar with Ed and we bumped into a friend of mine, Cynthia. She used to work as a lap-dancer to pay for her nursing training. When she clocked Ed, she had this look on her face.' She tried to replicate it, but Robyn just stared at her blankly. 'She gets it whenever she's out and bumps into a punter. You know, like how a teacher looks when they spot one of their pupils on holiday while they're getting their money's worth at the all-inclusive bar. Like, *Quick! Hide me!* Well, Cynthia did *that* face. Turns out he used to be one of her clients. Had been a regular a while back. For, like, two years.'

Robyn's expression didn't change. 'Lexi probably knows. Her past isn't exactly snow-white.'

'I know that.'

'So what's the problem?'

She hesitated. It was Cynthia's reaction on seeing Ed: her lip had curled with a hint of distaste. Trying to explain it to Robyn felt too loose, unsubstantiated; instead, she said, 'I don't like him.'

'Let Lexi be happy. Don't ruin it for her.'

'Of course I want her to be happy! She's my best friend!'

'Well, your best friend has just told you she's pregnant. You should either be telling her how pleased you are, or, if you can't manage that, maybe you should be asking yourself why not.' Robyn gathered the drinks tray, glasses sliding and clinking, then returned to the villa.

Once again, Bella was alone on the terrace. A chorus of cicadas blazed in the darkness, as loud and unsettled as her thoughts. Inside the villa, the lights were on but there was no invitation in their warm glow.

She returned to the memory of the engagement drinks. When Cynthia had left the bar, Ed had appeared at Bella's side. 'Nice chat with your friend?'

She'd looked him dead in the eye. 'Turns out you know each other.'

'I know a lot of people. Just like I know a lot of things.' He lowered his voice. 'And some things are better left unsaid, don't you think, Nurse Rossi?'

A cold shiver had travelled through her body, as if someone had opened a door in the bar and a blast of icy wind had travelled through.

Then, a moment later, Ed had bumped his shoulder against hers, chummily. 'Come on,' he grinned, 'let me buy you another cocktail.'

His smile was back in place and it was as if the moment hadn't happened. Yet she was certain she'd witnessed it, something unnerving just beneath the surface. Blink and you miss it.

24

Lexi

Lexi perched on the end of the bed, feet pressed together on the cool stone floor. She kept the balcony doors closed; she didn't want to catch the whisperings from the terrace.

Bella and her stupid quiz! This wasn't how she wanted the news of her pregnancy to come out. Downstairs she could hear the clatter of plates in the kitchen, the turning of taps. Voices were dulled by the thick stone walls, but she knew everyone would be talking about it.

She'd found out she was pregnant eight days ago. Ed had just left for Dublin, where he was working on a case. She could've called him, of course she could – he'd have flown back immediately – but she needed time to gather her thoughts, work out what she wanted.

Lexi had never liked voicing things until she knew how *she* felt. Everyone else's opinions crowded in so quick and loud that they drowned out her own.

She'd thought about cancelling the hen, worrying that Bella would never let her get through it sober, but everyone had already paid for the flights and booked time off work and she couldn't pull out at the last minute. She should have told Bella about the pregnancy to take the pressure off the weekend. She knew why she hadn't: Lexi was scared of seeing her own fears reflected in Bella's face.

Instead, she'd told Robyn.

Didn't women always do that: select the friend to share with, subconsciously knowing the reaction they were seeking? She'd called Robyn the evening she'd taken the test, when she couldn't regulate her breathing and her heart was trying to claw out of her chest.

Robyn had listened as Lexi talked and panicked without jumping in with her opinion. Once Lexi finally ran out of steam and remembered to anchor herself to her breath, Robyn had asked one question: *What do you want?*

There was no pause. No hesitation. She'd felt the answer in her body. *The baby. I want this baby.*

Yet the strange thing was, even though she knew that, she still felt terrified. Her heart rate remained raised, her chest constricted. It was like she wanted to run – but didn't know what from.

There was a knock on the door. 'Hey,' Robyn said, poking her head around. 'You okay in here?'

Lexi shook her head.

Robyn slipped into the room, pulling the door closed behind her. She sat beside Lexi. 'Bella's like a sniffer dog when it comes to secrets. I'm amazed you made it to the second night.'

'Me too.'

The bedside lamp cast a long shadow up the wall, where a gecko clung, its body pale and soft. They both looked at it in silence for a few moments, then Robyn asked, 'So, how are you feeling?'

'Terrified.'

'About what? The pregnancy?'

'That's just it – I don't know. I don't understand. I'm barely sleeping. My thoughts feel jumpy, distracted.'

'Maybe it's because you haven't told Ed yet? Are you worried he won't want this?'

'We both said we didn't want children – but Ed, he wasn't resolute about it. I think – I hope – he'll be pleased. Surprised, definitely. But pleased. So, no, I'm not scared that he won't want the baby.' She shook her head, confused.

Robyn thought for a while. 'Do you think,' she began, her voice tentative, 'that this could be about your parents? You know, what your mother said that time?'

Lexi knew exactly what Robyn was referring to. When she was fourteen, she'd overheard her mother talking to one of the ex-professional ballerinas she'd performed with, who now ran a prestigious ballet school. 'You were so smart,' her mother had said into the phone, not realising Lexi was home. 'Me, I did it all wrong. Honestly, getting pregnant was the biggest mistake of my life.'

Crushed, Lexi had left the house and walked three miles to Robyn's house – where she arrived silent and devastated. She knew her mother's ballet career was ended by her getting pregnant – but as Lexi grew up, she also realised that without ballet, her mother's sense of self had vaporised, as if all along the ballet had been the support beam to her identity.

Was she scared that one day she'd turn around, just like her mother, and think, *This baby was a mistake*?

No. Lexi knew unequivocally that she wanted this baby – and she told Robyn as much.

Robyn took her hand, squeezed. 'Good.'

So then, what was it? How did she explain this strange, pulsing unease lodged in her chest?

There was a knock at the door. It opened a crack and Bella poked her head around. 'Permission to enter?'

'Granted,' Lexi said eventually.

Robyn got to her feet, slipping past Bella, saying, 'I'm going to grab a drink.'

Bella took Robyn's space on the bed. She lay flat on her back, boobs bouncing in her dress. 'Sorry I was such a dick.'

Lexi shrugged and lay on her back, too.

They both stared up at the ceiling watching the fan whirl in slow circles.

'I'm pleased for you – about the baby – really,' Bella said. 'It was just a shock.'

'And for me.'

'You told Robyn.'

She nodded.

'Why?'

'Because I was anxious about being here, on the hen do, with no one knowing. I needed to talk to someone.'

'You could've talked to me. I'm your best friend.'

Bella always did that – labelled herself as Lexi's best friend. She thought of both Robyn and Bella as her closest friends. She didn't want to pick. 'I didn't tell you first as I wasn't sure you'd be happy for me.'

'God, I really am a bitch.'

After a moment, Bella rolled onto her side, pushing herself up on an elbow so that she faced Lexi. She smelled faintly of ouzo, the sweetness turning Lexi's stomach. 'I am happy for you, Lexi. Or what I mean is, I want everything for you.

I want you to be happy. And if this is what you choose – a baby and a husband – then I will be happy, too. You know how I am . . . I take a while to *adjust*. That's what was happening out on the terrace. I was doing my adjusting.'

Lexi got it. Of course she did.

'I'm really sorry,' Bella said, eyes glistening with tears.

'It's okay.'

'It's not okay. I'm a shit friend.' Bella sat up fully, wiping her eyes.

Lexi sat up, too. 'No, you're not.' She might have been strident and, yes, a little selfish at times, but Bella would have taken a bullet for her friends.

'Can I?' Bella asked, hovering her hand towards Lexi's middle.

She nodded.

Tentatively, Bella placed her palm there. Lexi could feel the warmth of her hand through her cotton dress.

'There's a small swell . . .'

'Trapped wind.'

'Forever sexy.' Bella didn't withdraw her hand. She kept it there as she said, 'We always said we wouldn't be like the other people. No kids. No saloon cars. No pedestrian life.'

'I know we did. But those other people, maybe they're onto something.'

'Maybe they are,' she said, and in the low light, Lexi wondered if Bella's eyes had filmed with tears.

25

Eleanor

Alone on the terrace, Eleanor emptied the wine bottle into her glass.

She yawned. Checked her watch. There was no point trying to sleep before one o'clock: she'd only lie awake, restless.

That was one of the problems of losing Sam: she couldn't sleep. She missed the warmth of his body in the bed. She missed the way he liked to cast out an arm and place it on her hip, or boob, or waist. He just liked feeling her right there. He always slept in a T-shirt and boxers, and sometimes he wore that T-shirt through the day and she didn't care. She liked it. She even missed the rolling waves of his snoring. Falling in love – it'd ruined her. Better never to know that it was possible for your heart to beat at a different rhythm.

She swallowed another mouthful of wine. A few drinks before bed served as a sort of buffer, a lubrication to oil and loosen the sadness, ease her towards sleep. But that only got her halfway through the night. Then she'd wake around three in the morning, all alone with the silence.

Silence.

Silence.

Silence.

Sometimes she wondered if it were possible to drown in silence. Because that's how it felt – like it was suffocating her. So then she'd drink a little bit more. It wasn't like she even wanted to. All she wanted was to bloody sleep.

You don't need to be a genius to know there's a price to pay in the morning. A tax on that sleep, because her head felt like shit, and her mind was foggy, and all the anxiety and loneliness and sadness and shame was there on amplify mode. So what did she do?

Bingo! Another drink. Congratulations, Eleanor! You are winning at grief!

She knew what Sam would say if he were still here. 'Hey EJ!' (He loved an acronym. Said it made him feel like he was an American high school kid sliding around a corridor with his T-shirt untucked, crashing into her at the lockers.) 'You know you've got to sort this out, right? I'll be your wingman.' And he would've been. They'd have cleared the house of alcohol. He'd have probably made her really nice drinks instead, maybe bought her some herbal sleeping tablets – he had a thing for Holland & Barrett, which was odd as he liked nothing better than a stuffed-crust pizza and bowl of nachos.

God, she loved everything about him.

She finished her wine. Wondered if she could get away with opening another bottle. She didn't want to run the villa dry on the second night. She'd slipped a bottle of gin in her case for emergencies, but Ana was already in their room. She briefly flirted with the idea of crawling her way to the suit-case beneath her bed, but then thought about the possibility of coming eye to eye with a cockroach or scorpion.

Looked like it was just her, an empty glass, and the dark stretch of night. The pool glowed eerily on the terrace. Nope, she wouldn't be floating in there again any time soon. She'd still not got over the shame of Lexi happening upon her and the awkward conversation that had followed. For the rem-ainder of the weekend, she planned to work very hard on not being weird.

There were footsteps behind her and she turned, her chair creaking, to find Ana crossing the terrace carrying a bottle of ouzo and two glasses. 'Want a nightcap?'

Eleanor smiled. 'Thought you'd gone to bed.'

'We're on a hen party, aren't we?'

'Indeed we are.' She pulled out the chair beside hers and Ana took a seat.

She poured them both generous measures, sliding one across to Eleanor. They clinked glasses. '*Ya mas!*'

Ana was a good roommate. Didn't talk too much. Didn't lay claim to the bathroom shelves or dresser. She liked the way she walked, too: steady, confident, shoulders back. Nothing haughty about it: she just walked as if she were in no hurry. Eleanor decided she would practise that walk when she was back home. (She'd only agreed to be less weird for the weekend.)

Ana untied her headscarf, then pushed her fingers against the roots of her braids.

Above them a spray of fairy lights twinkled through the pergola, clambering alongside jasmine and grapevines.

'So, you're going to be an auntie,' Ana said, smiling.

'I guess so.'

'How do you feel about it?'

'I don't know.' She couldn't trust her emotions these days. It was like they'd been knocked off-kilter and where most people felt one thing, she found herself feeling something very different. 'Pleased?'

'*Pleased* with a question mark?'

She shrugged. 'I didn't expect it.'

She'd never heard Ed talk about wanting a family, couldn't imagine him cradling a child. A beat of memory arrived like a shadow: the doll she'd loved as a child, an ear cut off to reveal the horror of stuffing. Ed in his room, face impassive. 'That's awful,' he'd said when confronted by their mother, who was holding Eleanor's hand. 'Why did Eleanor do it?' Ed had asked. Eleanor had stared, confused. Through her tears, she'd seen her mother's gaze flicker uncertainly to her, then felt her grip loosen, let go.

She pushed down the memory and instead thought of the way Ed lit up when he was with Lexi. She imagined visits to Lexi and Ed's home once the baby had arrived. Eleanor would bring over something she'd made in the slow cooker and a cake with freshly whipped cream. It was a nice image. Fanciful, perhaps, since when had she had an invite into Ed's home?

'Do you think Ed will be a good father?' Ana asked.

Eleanor felt a tiny icicle creaking between her shoulder blades. Ana was watching her closely, as if she were reading something written in her expression. 'He'll want to be the best,' Eleanor said eventually.

'Are the two of you close?'

Eleanor was silent for a moment. 'Ed calls every week. Pops in when he can.'

'That must be nice.'

Eleanor wondered if it was. Her face must have shown her doubt – it had a habit of letting her down like that – because Ana asked, 'What, it's *not* nice?'

'They're duty visits,' Eleanor admitted with a shrug. Ed had been good to her when she lost Sam, barely leaving her side in the days after he died, but gradually his concern for her had shifted, changed shape. 'He's usually in a hurry to leave. I don't think he likes being around me when I'm sad.'

Ana's brow dipped. 'Why not?'

'It's been almost a year now. Ed finds it indulgent.'

Ana went very still. 'Indulgent?'

'Yes.'

She blinked. 'He's said that?'

Eleanor felt a thrilling sense of the telltale. 'Yes.'

Ana's back seemed to straighten, vertebra by vertebra. 'A long soak in a bubble bath is indulgent. A second slice of cake is indulgent. Grieving for the person who you planned to spend your life with is *not* indulgent. How dare he!'

Eleanor found herself sitting taller as she pictured herself using Ana's words, repeating them to Ed. She felt a spark of fire in her belly, a heat that she liked.

The interesting thing about a spark, Eleanor thought as she looked at Ana, was that it either burns out, or begins to smoulder – and then flame.

FRIDAY

26

Bella

Bella stood at the bow of the yacht, hair blowing in the wind. Sea spray misted her sunglasses and the air fizzed with salt and ozone. She wanted to do *Titanic* arms to make Lexi and the others laugh, but she didn't trust boats. Two hands on the guardrail at all times, thank you.

She'd announced the yacht trip over breakfast, telling the others, 'Pack your swimwear and sunscreen. We're going on an excursion!'

She adored surprises. She would never understand people who rolled their eyes at the thought of them. What, they didn't like that little kick of anticipation? The sense of letting go? Lighten up!

When the yacht had sailed into their bay, it was even more exquisite than she'd imagined with its varnished wooden hull parting the clear turquoise waters. The six of them had been waiting on the shore, beach bags hooked over their shoulders, sunscreen scenting the air. Lexi had gasped. 'Is that for us?'

'Sure is. We're sailing off into the big blue to snorkel and sunbathe.'

Lexi had thrown her arms around Bella, hugging her so tightly that she'd left behind an imprint of sunscreen on Bella's dress.

This was going to be a good day, Bella decided, turning her face into the sun. After last night's disastrous quiz she needed to get the hen party back on track – and this was the way to do it.

Yannis, their ageing captain, wore a crumpled shirt unbuttoned to the navel, his tanned face peppered with greying stubble. He pointed towards a tiny islet to the east. 'Beautiful snorkelling there.' He steered the yacht into the wind and sea spray lifted over the bow, soaking Bella's bare legs.

Cowed by the breaking waves, Bella picked her way carefully along the side of the yacht. Fen was sitting at the stern, her body turned towards the water, chin resting on her hands. She was wearing cut-offs and a loose vest, the fabric billowing in the breeze. Bella couldn't see her eyes behind her sunglasses, but sensed she was lost in the spaciousness of the moment. She stopped herself from climbing on Fen's lap.

Bella always loved company, noise, a good dose of chaos. Whenever she returned to her empty flat, she'd switch on the radio or television, then throw open a window so she could hear the outside world buzzing by. A chat with Alexa wasn't out of the question. Maybe it was a product of growing up in a big family. Her mother said the only way she could get Bella to sleep as a baby was by putting her Moses basket on the lounge table, amidst the chatter and chaos and blare of the television. 'You've always needed to be at the centre of things.'

But not Fen. Baby-Fen probably fell asleep in a quiet room with blackout blinds and sound-proofed walls. Adult-Fen didn't even own a television (quite how she functioned in the modern world was still part mystery to Bella).

'You okay?' she asked, perching beside her, their thighs brushing. What she really meant was, Are *we* okay?

Last night she'd woken to find Fen's side of the bed empty. Bella had gone to the window and spotted Fen standing alone on the dark terrace, staring over the low wall towards the boneyard of rocks below. There was something perturbing about her stillness out there in the middle of the night. Pulling a T-shirt on, Bella had padded down to check on her, but Fen had crossed her on the stairs, insisting she was fine. *Just getting some air.*

Now Fen echoed that response again. 'I'm fine.' She smiled lightly. The wind had fingered her short hair, so it stood up at the roots.

'What are you thinking?' Oh God. Had she really asked that? Such a sappy, needy question.

'Just how nice it is to be on the water, I guess.'

Of course that wasn't what Fen was really thinking – but what could Bella say? *I don't believe you! Tell me what you're really thinking!* She had some pride. 'Maybe next summer we could come back. Stay for longer. Even if the villa's been sold, we could find somewhere else. I love this island.'

Fen smiled but said nothing.

Bella felt the lurch of dread: there wasn't going to be a next summer. *That's* what Fen was thinking. Wasn't it? All weekend they'd been carefully skirting the subject of what had happened at the airport, as if some tacit agreement had been made to not discuss it until they returned home.

It was Sue's fault. Sue and her big mouth. Was it impossible to go to an airport without bumping into someone from your past? Bella had known Sue since they'd worked nights together at Royal Bournemouth Hospital. She could be warm and funny, but also fantastically gossipy.

'Wave and walk,' Bella had whispered to Fen when Sue began steering her luggage trolley towards them.

But Sue was fast. She'd pounced on Bella, clutching her arm. 'Bella! It's been so long!'

'Oh. Sue. Hi. Great to see you. But, listen – we're running late for our flight, so—'

'I won't hold you up. It's so good to lay eyes on you again! We all miss you! And I just want you to know, Bella,' she went on, lowering her voice, 'we were all so sorry about what happened.'

And then Fen, in her straightforward, unmasked way, had asked: 'What happened?'

There it was. The question laid so straightforwardly that Bella had no choice but to answer.

She had watched Fen's expression cloud with confusion, colour draining from her face.

It wasn't that Bella had intended to keep secrets from Fen. It was just that she'd got so used to lying that it felt like the truth.

27

Fen

Fen felt the crest and fall of the waves. She wanted to close her eyes, drink in the sensations – but Bella was talking to her, her voice fast and bright, fingers squeezing at her arm. She used to find Bella's habit of touching whoever she was talking with endearing, as if her excitement and warmth bubbled out of her body, unstoppable. This morning, though, she needed space.

Her head felt too busy, too loud. Being back on Aegos was far harder than she'd expected. Rationally, she knew there were plenty of happy moments during that long summer seven years ago, but all her body remembered was that one night. It was like spilling red wine on a beautiful new sofa: it didn't matter that the rest of the sofa remained in perfect condition – the only thing you noticed was the stain.

Yannis cut the engine. For a blissful moment, all Fen could hear was the settling of waves and a faint sea breeze clinking a wire against the mast. Light-footed, Yannis crossed the deck, hauling a salt-crusted anchor from the bow. The tails of his shirt lifted as he launched it overboard. A deep splash, then the heavy rope uncoiling behind it at speed.

Beside her, Bella clapped.

She did that a lot – clapped her hands together when anything excited her. Fen used to find it cute, but lately that gesture had begun to irritate her, too. She tried to refocus on the glittering sea because she didn't want to be someone who saw flaws where others saw gifts, but she couldn't fully tune in to the beauty of the day.

The sense of dissatisfaction in their relationship had crept up on her so slowly that she'd barely had a chance to put a name to it. Then, after that awful encounter at the airport with Sue, Fen had wanted to turn around right then, leave. Bella had begged her not to go, promised they'd sort everything out – and then the other hens had arrived, and Fen felt like she had no choice but to see the weekend through.

Bella was nothing like Fen's previous girlfriends, and that had been part of her appeal. She loved her sassiness, the way she blasted into a room in a cloud of perfume and infectious energy. She loved Bella's knack for creating fun from thin air – a boring drive to a homeware store could suddenly turn into an adventure with Bella, who'd demand that they pull over so she could dance to the busker playing a fiddle, or watch a film despite it being ten o'clock on a beautifully sunny Saturday.

She had a gloriously dirty laugh. You could hear Bella laughing three rooms away. And she was sexy as hell, no doubt about that. Fen didn't even want to know where or with whom she'd learned some of the things she knew.

But sex and laughter – as delicious and addictive as they were – weren't enough.

The only thing that was enough was love.

And Fen realised she didn't love Bella.

28

Eleanor

Eleanor let her shoulders sway to the yawing of the yacht as it turned on its anchor. She briefly closed her eyes behind her sunglasses and breathed. The air tasted clean and salt-bright, the faint fragrance of herbs drifting from the land.

Sitting at the stern, she was grateful for the shade of the canopy. Her pale, mole-studded skin wasn't designed for the Mediterranean heat.

Opening her eyes, she saw the Greek flag dancing from the yacht railing in the light breeze. Yannis was gesturing beyond it towards a rocky pinnacle. 'Only for very good swimmers, yes? Long way. But,' he said, a finger poised in the air, 'if you reach the island, if you very good at climbing rock, then you get big surprise.' He smiled widely, his face turning boyish.

'A surprise?' asked Robyn, who was fixing her hair into a ponytail.

Yannis's eyes twinkled. 'Many hidden sea caves here . . . and sea washes in them and makes water hole. Natural swimming pool, yes? Very beautiful.'

'You can swim in it?' Fen asked, stepping out of her denim shorts. She looked every inch the athlete in a simple tankini, her body toned and vital. Eleanor wondered what it would feel like to dive from the side of this boat, to know you could just swim and swim, and your body had the power to carry you wherever you commanded it.

'Dive from rocks – deep water. Twenty, thirty metres, yes? Very good for swimming.' He angled a thick, tanned wrist towards his face, sunlight glinting off his watch. 'You have an hour or two to swim, yes? Then after, back to boat for lunch, okay? No rush, no rush.'

'Sounds perfect,' Bella gushed, hands clasped.

'Would you do my shoulders?' Robyn asked Lexi, holding a tube of sunscreen.

Lexi squeezed lotion into her palms, while Robyn removed her T-shirt, keeping her back to the others. She folded her arms over her stomach.

I know that feeling, Eleanor thought.

From beneath the seat locker, Yannis lifted a plastic tub containing bright flippers and snorkel masks. He doused them with fresh water, then began handing them out, drops of water darkening the sun-warmed deck.

'No, thank you,' Eleanor said when he held out a mask for her. 'I'm staying on board.'

'You must snorkel! Beautiful clear water! So many fish here. Not like the other islands where dynamite ruin the coral. Here the fish are many – and big,' he said, making a space between his tanned hands to demonstrate their size. 'Come, you'll enjoy!'

She liked the lilting, musical rhythm of Yannis's voice, but enthusiasm alone couldn't win her over. 'Not for me.'

'Please come in with us!' Ana said, looping a mask around her neck. 'We don't have to go far from the boat. I'll stick with you.'

'I can't swim,' Eleanor said. She delivered the fact plainly and without embarrassment.

Hearing, the other hens looked at her as if she'd announced she'd just pissed in her shorts. Actually, that was a thought. If she needed a wee, well, then what? She eyed the plastic tub the flippers came in. That would have to do. 'I've got my book for company. I'm planning on having a lovely time staying dry on deck.' She smiled to put them at ease.

'Reading on a boat in the morning sunshine? Sounds awful. I'm not envious at all.' Ana winked.

'Sure you'll be okay?' Lexi asked, wiping the remains of Robyn's sunscreen into her hands.

'Course! Now get in the water and leave me in peace.' She intended it to come out jokily, but Eleanor saw from Lexi's expression that she'd sounded brusque.

Behind them, Bella cursed as she tried to squeeze her swollen, scorpion-stung foot into a flipper.

'Babe, I think you're going to have to go barefoot,' Fen said.

'Bloody scorpion!' she said, flinging the flippers back into the bucket.

'Okay, ladies. We climb down the ladder, here,' Yannis announced, taking Lexi by the hand (rather unnecessarily, in Eleanor's opinion). 'Is better I pass you flippers when you're in the water, yes?' His gaze travelled down her smooth, bikini-clad body. Eleanor didn't blame him. There was something about beauty – male or female – that would always draw the eye.

Eleanor found her gaze roaming to Lexi's stomach, looking for the first hint of a bump. It was hard to believe that Eleanor's future niece or nephew was housed within such a perfect venue. She got a little thrill realising that she knew about the baby before Ed.

'Wait!' Bella called. 'Photo first!' She rummaged through her beach bag for her phone, then pointed it towards Lexi, who smiled gamely from within her snorkel mask.

'Now the rest of you!' Bella said, turning the camera on them.

Ana ducked swiftly out of the shot. Eleanor would have too, had she been quick enough. Who liked a photo in a swimsuit lingering in perpetuity on someone else's camera roll?

The water frothed and fizzed as the rest of them lowered themselves from the ladder, squealing and splashing as they jostled with fins and masks.

Voices quietened as the hens began putting their faces beneath the water, swimming away from the yacht. A peal of laughter bubbled from Lexi's snorkel pipe. The water was so clear that Eleanor could see Fen dive beneath the surface in pursuit of a shoal of small fish.

Yannis tidied up the spare fins and masks, humming gently to himself, before disappearing into the galley to begin the food preparations. Alone on deck, Eleanor felt a little cloud of sadness descend.

Still, she had her book for company. Plus, she'd already spied the cool box where she was hoping an alcoholic beverage or two would be chilling.

Removing her sunglasses, she peered at her reflection,

smoothing down her hair with her fingers. The boat journey had created frizzy volume in all the wrong places, giving her the appearance of a mushroom. She could really use a blow-dry.

Trips to the hair salon were her one weekly indulgence. She block-booked the last slot every Thursday afternoon for a wash and blow-dry. It wasn't that she was particularly vain about her hair (although it was her strongest asset: thick dark-auburn hair, which she wore in a smooth bob to her chin). It was because of Reece. He had sleeve tattoos in intriguing, complex patterns, and when his thumbs pressed gently into her temples, she'd feel her body relaxing, releasing. She'd melt into the leather chair, close her eyes and luxuriate in the warmth of his hands against her scalp.

Once, she'd cried. Right there with her head tipped back in a sink of warm water. She'd decided that she'd have to stop visiting the salon after that, but Reece had been very sweet about it and she'd forced herself to return the following week, despite turning around twice on the walk there.

Every Thursday Reece would ask the same question. 'Off anywhere nice tonight?' She'd pick one of her favourite answers: *Yes, I'm meeting friends for dinner,* or *I'm going to the cinema with my brother,* or even, *I've got a date tonight.* In fact, what Eleanor did every Thursday was return to her empty flat with her good hair, alone. She'd stride into the lounge, pausing in front of Sam's ashes, which were contained in a black urn with a Dungeons and Dragons sticker in the centre. 'Got Reece at the salon today,' she might say, smoothing her freshly styled hair. She'd give a lascivious wink, adding, 'Did a double condition, didn't he?'

She could always feel Sam's laughter in her chest, warm and easy. At first, she'd felt a little self-conscious talking to his ashes, but then it had become part of the routine of her day – telling him what she was doing or asking his opinion. He was like an invisible guide, telling her, *EJ! Course you should go out tonight! Do it! Put on those smokin' jeans I love!*

When she had received Bella's email about the hen weekend, she'd glanced up from her laptop, her gaze resting briefly on Sam's urn. Then, just as swiftly, she'd looked away.

She hadn't asked his opinion about whether she should join the hen weekend, because she knew exactly what he would've said.

Don't. Don't you go.

29

Ana

Ana floated on the shimmering surface, watching a pale-bellied fish dart towards the seabed. After a few seconds, she lifted her face from the water to breathe. She couldn't get the hang of breathing through a snorkel pipe. She'd never snorkelled before. Never been on a yacht. Never been to Greece. There were, she realised, a lot of things she'd never done.

She pulled the mask onto the top of her head, treading water, trying not to think about how far down the seabed was. Her experience of swimming was limited to her local lido, where she was only ever a few metres from its concrete sides.

She wished she were enjoying this – savouring the experience of snorkelling in the Aegean Sea, giddy on sun-drunk holiday pleasures – but instead, a voice in her head whispered coolly: *You shouldn't be here.*

The holiday seemed to do something strange to her sense of time, elasticating it so that some moments felt slower and extended, her senses enlivened with a new clarity – before snapping back smartly, leaving her shocked that she was so far from home, from Luca.

Giving up on snorkelling, she turned and swam for the yacht.

When she reached the stern, she hauled herself up the ladder, water sluicing from her skin.

On deck, Eleanor looked up sharply from her book.

'I come in peace,' Ana said, a hand raised. 'I'd never stand between a woman and her book. As you were.'

Eleanor smiled. 'Actually, it's a terrible read. I'm relieved to put it down. How's the underwater world?'

'The lure of a cold beer proved incomparable,' Ana said, reaching for her towel.

'I happen to know where Yannis keeps the cooler.' Eleanor lifted her feet to reveal the cool box. She opened the lid and pulled out two ice-cold cans of beer.

'You are divine,' Ana said, and meant it. They snapped back ring pulls and clinked cans.

Eleanor crossed one leg over the other, concealing a thick scar that ran across her left knee. Sharing a room with her, Ana had noticed other old scars, too – one beneath her chin, another zigzagging her shoulder. Although curious, she knew better than to ask about them.

Across the water, Ana could see the flash of leopard print. 'Looks like Bella's returning to the boat.'

'Enjoy the peace while you can.'

Ana grinned, taking a seat beside Eleanor. 'D'you think Lexi is aiming for the swimming hole?' She was halfway between the yacht and the rocky island.

Eleanor watched. 'She's fit enough. All that yoga.'

'Maybe I should've kept up yoga. Then I'd be doing swan dives at the swimming hole rather than drinking beers back on the boat.'

'And you'd want that, why?' Eleanor said with a wry smile. 'That's how you met Lexi, was it? Yoga?'

Ana nodded. 'I turned up at the first-ever class Lexi taught. It was my first time, too, and I was very much planning to hide at the back. Turned out I was the only student. I don't know who was more flustered.'

Eleanor shuddered.

'We made it through. Lexi – you can probably imagine – she's a brilliant teacher. Calm. Encouraging.'

Ana had been surprised to discover a releasing that ran so much deeper than her tight muscles and inflexible hips. At the end of class, as she lay on her brand-new mat in savasana, the lights dimmed, there was an intimacy about sharing the silence of a room with another woman, and she'd found herself in tears. Mortified, she'd hurriedly wiped her face on her sleeve, then rolled up her mat.

Skipping that part of the story, she told Eleanor, 'After class, I stopped at this lovely little pizzeria almost opposite the studio.' The smell of wood-fired pizzas and melting cheese was the perfect antidote to fill whatever space the yoga class had opened. 'Guess who joined the queue behind me?'

'Lexi?'

She nodded. 'Our pizzas arrived at the same time, and the place was so packed that we grabbed a table together. We chatted, got to know each other. It was nice. So nice, in fact, that pizza-on-a-Monday became a thing – even after I quit the yoga part!'

Eleanor smiled. 'I like that.'

There, packaged so neatly, it was almost the truth. She hadn't lied to Eleanor because the yoga studio was the first place she and Lexi had *met*. It just wasn't the first time she'd *seen* her.

That had happened outside a tall, stone building, Ana sitting nearby on a bench, palms sweating as she worried the tassels of her scarf. Her heart had pounded a thunderous march, but she hadn't moved. She'd watched and watched as the revolving doors turned people out into the afternoon light. She'd watched until she saw Lexi, a yoga tote branded with a studio name bouncing against her hip.

30

Robyn

Robyn's breath was even through the snorkel pipe, blending with the fizz and clicks of the sea. Shafts of sunlight fell through the surface, flecking the water with gold. Kicking her flippers, she glided fluidly, hands lightly sculling at her sides.

Earlier, when Bella had announced she had a surprise, Robyn had cringed. She hated surprises. They felt like a power trip: *I know something you don't!* But now that she was cutting through the shimmering water, she was grateful.

A cool brush of fingers grazed her shoulder.

Her head snapped around. It was only Lexi, hair billowing around her mask. She pointed upwards.

They both surfaced, treading water. Lexi hooked her snorkel pipe from her mouth to say, 'I'm going to swim back to the yacht.'

'Is everything okay?'

'Great – but I'm getting a bit cold. Let me know what the swimming hole is like.'

Robyn glanced towards the rocky islet, which was still a distance away. A flutter of adrenalin rose in her chest: she wanted to reach it, and Lexi's assumption that she was capable of doing so emboldened her. 'I will. Are you okay swimming back on your own?'

'Bella and Fen are over there,' she said, pointing to where two snorkel pipes broke the surface. 'I'll go with them.'

'Okay,' Robyn said, reassured. Then she replaced her snorkel pipe, dipped her face into the sea, and began to kick.

When Robyn reached the islet, she checked for sea urchins before hauling herself up the rocks. Her skin, pale beneath a thick layer of sunscreen, was studded with goosebumps.

The rubber strap of the snorkel mask pinched as she snapped it off. She removed her fins, then stood, hands on hips, seeing how far she'd come.

The yacht drifted distantly on its anchor. It was so far away that she couldn't clearly see the others on board. Water from her ponytail trailed coolly down the length of her spine. She shivered. *What if I can't make it back?*

Dragging her gaze from the yacht, she squinted up at the craggy crown of rocks ahead of her. A blue arrow had been painted against the face of a boulder, signalling the direction to climb. She began to move, grasping at angular edges or nooks, heaving herself upwards.

Her skin dried in the heat, whorls of salt left behind on her forearms and shins. The soles of her feet absorbed the chalky warmth of the rocks as she pushed on, heart pounding.

After a few more minutes, Robyn arrived, breathless, at the very top. She blinked, a small gasp of surprise leaving her throat.

She was standing on a flat expanse of rock that jutted like a natural dive platform above a smooth pool of deep blue water. Nature's most perfect plunge pool. The water was so absurdly clear that she could see the striations in the rock beneath the surface. She laughed, thrilled by the secret beauty of the place.

She edged forward, drawn towards the enticing blue.

Jump, a voice whispered deep inside her.

She felt the kick of adrenalin in her chest. She could do it – plunge straight into the cool expanse of water.

If Jack were with her, she would be telling him to stand back, to keep his distance, warning him about the dangers of the rocks, of the water, of the sun. When you have a child, you become alert to danger. You notice the speeding car, the poisonous berries, the bee wafting in the long grass. You scan. You tune in. But then it becomes impossible to tune out.

Maybe that extra awareness arrives at a time where you're getting used to a new body. Muscles have loosened, skin has stretched and, suddenly, that brave, lean, tough person that was once you, has disappeared – and for the life of you, you can't remember how to get her back.

Robyn could never quite articulate her feelings about motherhood. It was like a grieving and a becoming in the same breath, over and over. Inhale, exhale.

The loss was vast: the mourning of her old body, of her sleep, of freedoms she'd once taken for granted. Before Jack, when she decided to go for a walk, she would simply pick up her keys, leave the house. Now it was a complicated choreography involving packing snacks, stocking a changing bag, loading things into a buggy, negotiating the wearing of shoes, negotiating the leaving behind of a huge plastic sword grabbed at the last moment to fight dragons, and then finally, finally leaving the house.

She'd walk, hands gripped to the buggy, or else holding his small pudgy fingers when he refused to stay buckled in, and even when she was consciously trying to slow down, take in her surroundings, she was still responding to demands, trying to decipher the small words that bloomed fresh from his mouth each day.

There were a thousand compromises.

A thousand gifts: 'Mama, buzzlebee!'

Yes, baby! Yes!

Standing above the swimming hole, Robyn understood that she'd lost part of her old self when she'd become a mother. She'd forgotten who she really was, what she wanted. It was like those listless days as a young teen, where she'd flop around the house declaring she was bored, only for her mother to ask, *Well, what do you want to do?* And she wouldn't know. Just wouldn't know.

For so long, she hadn't known what she *wanted* to do, so instead she'd chosen what she *should* do.

Standing on the coarse hide of the boulder, she looked down. The water was deep, deep blue. A perfect, bottomless place to dive. How high up was she, anyway? Maybe thirty feet? Forty?

It's only water.

She inched closer to the edge, toes curled. She felt the rough grain of the rock beneath her bare soles, hot and hard. The sun throbbed against her scalp. She looked at that water, enticingly cool, and felt something stirring. It was a yearning, an unpeeling of something. As scary and exposing as it was thrilling.

Robyn took a breath.

Jumped.

*

Robyn's feet peeled up and off the rocks, her body rising, arms reaching.

She felt the moment of suspension when she was neither lifting nor falling. She caught a glimpse of the yacht's mast in the distance; the shimmer of the sea; a white gull, wheeling.

Everything and nothing nearby. Just her. The sky. The sea.

Her body, strong and capable.

A wild roar left her throat – a pure sound of abandon and exhilaration. It reverberated from the rocks, surrounding her in an echo of rapture. Then came the fast, plunging descent. Hair lifting from her head, body plummeting downwards. Then the smack of salt-drenched liquid enclosing her.

Fizzing sound blooming underwater, eyes open to the sparkling dive.

A glorious falling through layers of blue.

The slowing.

The moment of neutral buoyancy. Surrendering. Letting the moment stretch.

Then – a kick of her legs.

The euphoria of rising, eyes focused on the wavering surface, silver bubbles tumbling from her open mouth.

Suddenly she was bursting into the world, gasping, grinning.

She tipped back her head, laughed.

Then she floated on her back, limbs in a starfish position as she was buoyed by the water, by what she'd done.

This was what it felt like to be free.

She lay still, submitting to the sea, to the sun.

Eventually, she turned, began kicking for the rocks. A figure was standing there, lit by the high, bright sun.

Fen.

She blinked water from her eyes. Their gazes locked. Robyn

felt a pulse of energy rising through her chest, warm and stirring.

Fen moved towards the edge of the rocks, her back straight. She lifted her arms and Robyn watched as she dived, her body a smooth arrow as she cut through the sky, hands pointed towards the water, muscles ridged as she pierced the surface with barely a splash.

She felt the water ripple around her as Fen dived beneath her, a moving shadow that eventually rose to the surface and broke through it grinning.

'You're here,' Robyn said.

They sat on the rocks, their skin drying in a blaze of heat. There was no shade and Robyn knew she'd already had too much sun, but she didn't want to end this moment. 'Thought you'd gone back to the yacht,' Robyn said as Fen flicked water from her damp hair, sunlight glinting from her silver thumb-ring.

'Bella and Lexi went together, so I swam on.'

Robyn was pleased. She looked across the shimmering waterhole. 'It's so good to be out here. To step out of real life for a few days.'

Fen squinted into the sun as she turned to look at Robyn. 'What's real life like?'

Robyn shrugged. 'Fine, I suppose. I've got Jack. My parents. It's just . . . well, you know, sometimes it feels a bit . . .' she searched for the word, unsure what she wanted to say. 'Vanilla.'

'Vanilla. I see. What about your job? You're a solicitor, aren't you?'

'Yes. Very vanilla, right?'

'Do you enjoy it?'

Robyn was going to say something about it being flexible and secure, but that wasn't the question. The question was, *Do you enjoy it?* 'No,' she said eventually. 'I don't.' When she left for the office each morning, she felt her heart thundering: the day had become something to get through, pretending that she wasn't torn in two leaving Jack at home while she spent her day dealing with land registry searches.

Fen said, 'What did you want to do when you were a child?'

'Be a photographer,' she answered without needing to think. 'I used to keep a photo diary, picturing everything that seemed beautiful to me.'

'So why law?'

She'd made the decision at eighteen when she was studying for her A levels. Her parents had suggested it, along with a teacher. Her brother, Drew, had been dead for a matter of weeks and everything felt shaken, insubstantial, as if the ground could simply crumble beneath her. His death had hit her with the blunt shock of what life really has the power to do. Loss either toughens you – chin raised, feet planted – so you won't be knocked off your feet the next time, or it makes you watchful, looking out for when that next cold fist might swing again. 'At the time it seemed like a practical choice. My brother had just died. Life was . . . messy, broken. Law felt like something stable. Solid. My parents wanted it, so I agreed.'

Fen nodded slowly. 'I know something about those choices. The ones we make for other people.' She looked at her for a moment and Robyn felt the heat bloom in her cheeks, as if Fen were looking right inside her, seeing her.

'Have you been to the swimming hole before?' Robyn asked.

'Never. I didn't even know it existed.'

Robyn felt pleased at that – as if the place were more special because of their discovering it together. She wished she had a camera with her now. She wanted to capture something about this moment, and yet she knew a photo would never do it justice – the chalky scent of the sun-warmed rocks, the fresh breeze lifting from the sea, a white-winged bird circling, and then Fen, sitting beside her, arms wrapped easily around her knees, spine curved, the silver stud in her nose catching in the sunlight as she turned.

'How come you've not been back to the island for seven years?'

There was a pause before Fen answered. 'Not all the memories are good ones.'

Yesterday, before their hike, she'd caught Fen removing an old photo of herself from the lounge, shoving the gilt frame to the back of a cupboard. She'd wanted to ask her about it – *Why that photo? What does it mean to you? Why don't you want to look at it?* – yet she sensed that the act was private, not meant to be seen.

'I'm sorry,' Robyn said, not knowing what for – only that she was.

They were both quiet for a time.

Then Robyn asked, 'Are you pleased to have come back?'

Fen turned and looked directly at Robyn. 'Yes, I think I am.'

31

Lexi

The yacht drifted lazily on its anchor. A breeze ruffled the sea, sending light waves lapping against the hull.

Lexi lay on her towel, her arms a pillow for her head. Beside her, Bella unclipped her bikini top. 'You can't go topless!' Lexi said.

'I'm sure Yannis has seen breasts before. Admittedly none quite as sensational as these.' She hung the bikini top over the guardrail.

'You'll make the others uncomfortable,' Lexi whispered, reaching across Bella, unhooking her bikini, and flinging it at her. 'On! I mean it!'

'They make *me* uncomfortable,' Bella stage-whispered, glancing towards the stern, where Ana and Eleanor were reading in the shade. She wriggled the bikini back into place, keeping the straps off her shoulders. 'In Ibiza we sunbathed all summer in nothing but thongs.'

'That was Ibiza.'

'God, I wish we were still eighteen and could disappear for a whole summer. I miss that freedom. The lifestyle we had. Don't you? Partying. Dancing through the night. Music drumming so hard in your chest, you think it's your own heartbeat. The roar of a crowd beneath a strobe of lights. That's how we've always done life, isn't it? Hard, fast, together.'

'I know,' Lexi smiled, full of nostalgia.

'And now here you are – engaged, pregnant, a bloody yoga teacher!' Bella laughed.

'Are you ever going to get over the yoga bit?'

'Om-likely.'

Lexi snorted. 'Anyway, nurse to jeweller. You had your own career swerve.'

'We're just getting our mid-life crises out the way early.' Eyeing Lexi's stomach, she asked, 'Will you still be able to teach with a passenger in tow?'

'For a while at least. I guess my body will let me know.'

'Have you had any morning sickness?'

'Not really. A few waves of nausea, but that's it.' She pressed her fingertips to the wooden deck. 'Touch wood.'

'Still planning on waiting till you're home to tell Ed?'

A warming smell of garlic rose from the galley kitchen, where Yannis was preparing lunch. She nodded. 'We've only got two more nights. Then I can tell him in person.' She looked at her hands, the diamond on her engagement ring sending a shoal of light swimming across her legs. She felt that same strange unease tightening her chest.

Her thoughts circled back to the Mr and Mrs quiz, something bothering her. 'Last night when you did the quiz—'

'Still sorry!'

'Y'know that question about my bad habits? It got me thinking about Ed and . . . well, whether he knows all those weird little things about me, like you and Robyn do.'

'You *want* him to know about the pillow drool?'

'It's just . . .' She hesitated, unsure how to explain. 'Sometimes I think Ed has this image of me as being . . . more than I am.'

'We all put our best foot forward in a new relationship.'

Is that it? Lexi couldn't help wondering if there were parts of herself she was keeping hidden because she sensed that Ed wouldn't like them. That they wouldn't fit his image of the Lexi he described as graceful, stylish, classy. Gently, almost without noticing, she was bending into a version of herself that she knew he wanted.

Did everyone do that?

An image popped into her thoughts: her mother flying through the house, nails manicured, wearing a mask of freshly applied make-up, emptying the overflowing bin, removing all traces of herself before Lexi's father arrived home.

She glanced sideways at Bella. 'What do you think of him?'

'Who?'

'Ed.'

There was a pause. 'He's nice.'

'Damned by faint praise.'

'Remember, I'm the sort of horrible, brittle-souled person who never thinks her friends' boyfriends are good enough, as Robyn's pointed out.'

'You and Robyn were talking about Ed?'

'Only in passing,' she said quickly. 'Ed's a lawyer, so he obviously gets the Robyn-seal-of-approval.'

Lexi tried to keep her tone casual as she asked, 'What would award him the Bella-seal-of-approval?'

'No idea. It's never been handed out.'

Lexi realised how much she needed Bella to say, *You know what, I adore him. He's hilarious! He's the best! I can't wait for us to hang out more. You've made a great choice. You're going to be so happy!*

'I want the two of you to get on. It's important to me.'

Bella looked straight at her. Nodded. 'Okay, I'll try harder.'

Lexi sensed Bella was holding something back. 'What is it? What aren't you telling me?'

'Nothing.'

It was the quickness of the reply that caused the flicker of doubt to flame. Lexi reached forward and pushed Bella's sunglasses onto the top of her head. 'Bella?' she said, looking her right in the eye. 'What is it?' As Lexi waited, she felt her heart rate speeding up, as if – all along – she'd been expecting, waiting, to find a problem.

'It's no big deal. It's nothing.'

'What isn't?'

Bella sighed. 'Just that Cynthia – you know my friend who was a lap-dancer? – well, she mentioned that Ed used to come into the club a lot. He was a regular. That's all.' Bella broke eye contact, her gaze slipping to her lap.

'Oh. That,' Lexi said with relief. 'Ed works in the city. They've all got too much money and don't know what to spend it on. He's told me about it – but he doesn't go anymore.' She was surprised Ed's history of visiting lap-dancing clubs would trouble Bella. 'That's all, is it? That was your reservation about Ed?'

Bella resettled her sunglasses. 'All cleared up.'

Neither of them said anything further.

Lexi lay back on her towel, the deck hard beneath her spine as she stared up at the cloudless sky.

32

Fen

Fen swam towards the yacht, heart light. She held onto the ladder as she removed her dive fins.

'We made it!' Robyn beamed, reaching her side. She trod water as she peeled off her snorkel mask, red indents bracketing her temples.

'The wanderers return!' Bella emerged at the stern, bikini straps pushed down, dark glasses on. The Greek flag billowed above her as she leaned over, saying, 'Pass up your fins.'

Fen handed them to her, then climbed the ladder to where the others lounged in their swimwear with drinks.

'How was the swimming hole?' Lexi asked.

'Absolutely beautiful,' Fen said, rubbing salt water from her shorn hair.

'It really was,' Robyn said, breathless as she clambered on deck, dripping. 'It's this perfect azure pool right in the middle of rocks. God, it was amazing! But colder – definitely colder than the sea.' Robyn fished a towel from her beach bag and made a turban of her wet hair.

'You've been gone ages,' Bella said. She stood on her tiptoes, kissing Fen on the mouth, her sun-baked body pressing briefly against Fen's damp skin. Fen felt herself pulling back.

'Was there somewhere you could dive from?' Eleanor asked, a book shading the sun from her eyes.

Robyn answered, 'One of the rocks juts forward like a natural dive platform. It felt so high. I can't believe I did it. It was such a rush!'

'You little thrill-seeker, you!' Bella said.

Fen knew that if Bella had been there, they'd all have had permission to enthuse about the adventure – but since she wasn't, Bella wouldn't want to hear about it.

Yannis called from below, 'Lunch coming in five minutes, okay?'

Everyone murmured their approval. 'Whatever he's preparing smells incredible,' Lexi said.

Sitting in the shade beneath the sun canopy, a book open beside her, Ana said, 'Is there a plan for tonight?'

'I was thinking we should go out for dinner,' Bella said. 'What do you think, Lex?'

'Sounds perfect.'

'We could go to a taverna in the Old Town,' Ana suggested.

'D'you know any good ones, babe?' Bella asked, linking her hand through Fen's.

Fen pictured the Old Town with its cobbled square, the bougainvillea-clad buildings with their crumbling brickwork, the narrow alleys dotted with tiny stalls. Then she focused on that one taverna beneath a fig tree draped in fairy lights. *Lavaros*. Owned by *his* family. A motorbike parked alongside, branded with his personalised number plate. She remembered being introduced to him, seeing the leather band on his wrist, and the way his hips moved to the taverna music, and thinking – he'd know the best places to have fun.

Only she'd got him wrong.

So very, very wrong.

She felt her heartbeat quicken. It was seven years ago. She was no longer the naïve girl who arrived on this island with her soft, doughy body and fanciful ideas about the world. Now she was fit and lean and strong. She ran her own business. She knew herself. She wouldn't be made to feel weak again.

So why the hell was she standing on a yacht in brilliant sunshine, throat tightening, heart racing, at the thought of returning to the Old Town?

'So where d'you recommend?' Bella prompted, squeezing her fingers.

Fen wanted to tell Ana, *Yes, the Old Town is a great idea.* She wanted to support Ana's suggestion. She wanted what had happened years ago to not matter. She wanted to be stronger than this.

She was beginning to sweat. Reflected in Bella's sunglasses, she could see her jaw was clenched, expression blank.

'Babe?'

She swallowed. 'The Old Town can be a little touristy. The harbour area is better for tavernas.'

Ana nodded, convinced.

Fen hated herself for the lie. Her earlier joy slipped away like the sun disappearing behind a cloud. She removed her hand from Bella's, reaching for a towel, wanting her body covered.

When she turned, Robyn was watching her, a perplexed expression creasing her brow.

~

We journeyed from different corners of the country to be there. We came together for her. Because we loved her. In a hundred different ways we adored her. We wanted her light to shine on us. We wanted to make it special for her, so she'd see how much we loved her. At a hen party, the bride-to-be takes on an almost celestial, golden status.

That weekend, she was the celebrity, and we were her fans and paparazzi.

We were the architects of her rise.

And her fall.

33

Ana

That evening, Lexi climbed from the taxi first, a casual olive dress grazing her bare ankles, hair loose over her tanned shoulders. The others followed, chatting and laughing as they gathered by the harbour. A briny scent lifted from the oil-filmed water. Fishing boats and tourist catamarans were tied to dock pilings, decks cleaned and emptied, wooden clapboards set out advertising the next day's snorkelling excursions.

'Let's find a taverna,' Robyn said.

Bella, clasped in a peacock-blue dress, linked her arm through Lexi's, then sashayed ahead. She said something, cinching Lexi's arm tighter, shoulders shaking as she laughed.

Ana followed with Eleanor, feeling a surge of optimism about the evening: sunset beers and delicious food lay ahead. Talk was of the yacht trip, the food they'd order at the taverna, the sunburn on Robyn's shoulders, the promise of finding somewhere to go dancing later.

A church bell rang from within the Old Town. She glanced towards the high white walls dripping with bougainvillea. Two stray dogs bounded across the road in chase, tails between their legs.

'Oh!' Lexi and Bella had come to a halt. 'What a shame!' Lexi said.

The others stopped, following the direction of her gaze. The small cluster of tavernas on the waterside was shrouded by a dark plume of smoke churning from a road-worker vehicle. A gaping hole had been drilled into the concrete and large pipes were being funnelled into the earth.

Ana caught the sulphuric fume of sewage.

'That stinks,' Bella said, covering her nose.

'Plenty of tavernas in the Old Town,' Eleanor said. She was wearing her uniform of shorts and a T-shirt, but Ana was pleased to see her new leather handbag hooked over a shoulder.

'It's just through the stone archway, there,' Ana said, pointing. On impulse, she linked her arm through Eleanor's, and the two of them steered the way.

Flanked by this group of women, and abuzz at being part of something, she felt suddenly giddy with the novelty of new friendships, holiday freedoms, sunshine. She'd never had a circle of women friends or let herself enjoy the easy frivolity of nights out. She wondered how she appeared to passers-by – moving as part of a pack, the click of heels across cobbled pavements, the peal of laughter, the scent of after-sun and perfume lifting from their skin.

Maybe a stranger would be fooled into thinking Ana belonged here. That she was simply one of the girls.

And what would be the harm in that?

The dangerous part, Ana realised, was that she was beginning to believe it herself.

34

Fen

Fen's heart roared in her chest. She knew that when they walked beneath the stone arch, took in the picturesque Greek square with its cobbled stones, the hens would be drawn to the taverna nestled beneath the branches of a fig tree.

The taverna where *he* worked.

Bella was already tottering ahead, veering away from a skinny dog, the fur at the top of its tail rubbed clean off.

'You coming?' Robyn asked, turning to Fen, who had still failed to move.

She reassured herself that it had been seven years since she'd been to Lavaros – he might not even work there anymore. She managed to nod at Robyn. Following the others, she tried to focus on the chatter surrounding her, but she was aware of her flaring heart rate, hard and insistent, a warning deep in her body.

A cluster of mopeds raced past, the petrol scent spiking

the air. She startled back, chest tight. The others continued and she had no choice but to follow, crossing the road, which delivered them into the town square.

The air was cooler, shaded and still, incense drifting from the church, blending with notes of garlic and oregano.

'That taverna looks lovely,' Lexi said, pointing to Lavaros.

'There's a free table right at the edge,' Bella added. 'Fen, have you eaten there before? Is it meant to be good?'

Everyone turned to look at her. She could feel each sinew in her face stretching, moving, as she tried to make her mouth work. It seemed she must have nodded, done something, as they were all walking again, crossing the square towards the taverna.

She glanced down the side alley and saw a flashy white motorbike parked on its stand, a personalised number plate announcing its owner.

It was his.

Her heart felt as if it were lifting out of her chest, drilling in her ears.

She'd hated riding on the back of that thing, with no choice but to press her body to his as they sped along the mountain roads, petrol fuming behind them as he revved into each bend, swinging the bike low so her bare knees almost skimmed the ground.

A young waitress appeared, leading them towards the free table, pulling out chairs, handing them menus, pointing to a board of specials, smiling and talking. Greek music played from speakers, and the taverna was filled with the sound of chatter and laughter.

Fen took her seat, hands clamped beneath her thighs to stop them from shaking.

35

Lexi

Lexi was in a strange mood. A low, hollow feeling of uncertainty trailed her. It was a bit like how she felt a few hours into a hangover, when the physical symptoms had eased, but all those toxins had left a little dent or depression in her mood.

Pregnancy hormones, she decided, taking a sip of sparkling water.

There was a wave of delight from the others as the waitress returned with the food: small white dishes filled with tzatziki, stuffed peppers, Greek salad with a block of feta resting on top, grilled fish drizzled with lemon oil and herbs, glossy dolmades, a bowl of taramasalata sprinkled with dill.

Disappointingly, all Lexi craved right now was beige, bland foods. She tore off a hunk of bread and nibbled the crust.

Beside her, Ana speared a ring of calamari, telling Robyn,

'When Luca was a baby, I remember singing to him, jigging him, pleading with him, making bargains with the universe: *Please! I'll do anything! Just make this baby sleep!* And then, my God, when he did – his little eyelids starting to droop, the tiny fingers going slack in mine – then comes that heart-in-throat reversing manoeuvre, backing away from their cot, carefully, carefully, avoiding the creaky floorboard that twangs—'

'—All without breathing,' Robyn said, her face flushed from the day's sun.

'Yes! The risk of an *exhale*! Then an hour later, where are you?'

'Standing by the baby's cot,' Robyn answered, 'watching him sleep, hoping he wakes again so you can give him a cuddle.'

Ana laughed. 'Exactly!'

The Mothers' Club. Strictly members only, Lexi thought. Her hand trailed to her stomach: *Admittance coming soon.*

She wondered what sort of mother she'd be. When she pictured this baby, she saw herself outdoors, walking, the baby strapped to her chest in a sling. They would take long strolls in all weathers, pointing out the small things they passed – ducks gliding along the river, a squirrel in a high-up branch. She realised how much she'd enjoy the company, someone to share her day with.

She tried to picture their home in London, with its huge sash windows and sparkling granite surfaces, filled with baby paraphernalia. She added Ed into the scene, placed him kneeling on a rug, smiling over their baby, who'd be cooing on a play mat. The image felt faint, too distant to reach. She tried to zoom in, see Ed's expression. But she couldn't make it out. Was he happy? Bored? Impatient?

The first prickling sensation of panic travelled across her skin. She knew this feeling. Had known it all her adult life: a sensation of the walls closing in, stealing the light, the air, her breath. Trapping her.

Her previous relationships had never lasted more than a few months – because as soon as the other person became emotionally invested, wanted her to commit, this feeling of suffocation closed in. She'd begin thinking about all the things that irritated her – building a case file against the poor, unsuspecting man. It was all there, waiting. The negative energy building and building, until she just had to release it by breaking up with them. It didn't matter what they said, how much they cried; she needed to shift them. Afterwards she'd feel the huge emotional relief that it didn't take up her headspace anymore. Then came the partying, the huge blowouts. Over and over, a little cycle of love affairs gone wrong.

She'd hoped that with Ed it would be different. It had been. It was. Until she'd taken that pregnancy test. Standing on the plush carpet of their bedroom, she'd felt the slam of fear as the blue cross emerged. A relationship could be ended. A marriage could be unravelled legally. But having a child with someone was a forever-tie.

There. That must be the precise root of her anxiety, she thought. That's what she'd struggled to verbalise to Robyn and Bella. The pregnancy heightened everything, sealed her decisions. Knowing she could walk away was her emergency button: she wasn't planning on pressing it, but it was reassuring to know it was there.

She already had a mental file of Ed-irritations standing by. She didn't like the way he showered twice a day – it seemed particular. He couldn't laugh at himself easily. He could be surly with restaurant staff. The problem was, Lexi couldn't tell if these doubts were real and worth listening to – or if they were merely her old patterns getting to work on sabotaging her happiness.

She didn't need to see a therapist to know where her fear of commitment stemmed from. When Lexi was thirteen, a woman had come to the door one spring evening, when the wisteria was in full bloom. It was one of her mother's tracksuit days and Lexi had wished it weren't. She watched from the stairs as her mother spoke to this petite, red-headed woman, her lips full and bowed like a heart. Her mother's voice was thin and taut, and she kept touching her hairline, where her hair hung lank and unwashed.

The woman on the doorstep claimed that Lexi's father hadn't paid maintenance for the past year. 'Sadie's eleven now. She's starting secondary school. There are things she needs.'

She expected her mother to say there'd been some mistake, but instead she'd said icily, 'You'll have to discuss this with Eric. He's racing in Argentina right now.' Then she'd closed the door.

'Who was that?' Lexi asked from the top of the stairs.

Her mother swung around, startled, face bloodless. 'No one.'

'Dad has . . . another daughter?'

Her mother stood pin-straight, her chin lifted, mouth tight. Lexi scanned her expression, searching for an emotion she could recognise. After a long silence, her mother simply said, 'Yes, he does.'

Lexi felt an explosion in her head. *Another daughter! My half-sister! Sadie . . . Sadie . . .* 'Does he see her?'

'No.'

'So what, he had an . . . affair?' The word felt strange,

dramatic. Something she heard on television shows, not in her life.

'Not *an* affair, Lexi. Many.' She'd smiled, a cold, awful smile that chilled Lexi to the bone. Then her mother retreated upstairs and Lexi didn't see her again until the following day.

When her father returned from Argentina, Lexi wouldn't look at him, speak to him, be in the same room as him. She left the present he'd bought unopened in the lounge. She stayed in her bedroom, refusing to come downstairs at meal-times. Eventually, he knocked at her door, insisted she let him in. That's when she'd finally spoken. *Sadie, Sadie, Sadie. You have a daughter!*

'She's not my daughter in the way that you are,' he'd said. 'I don't know her. I don't care about her.'

He'd actually thought that was the right thing to say. He thought Lexi was worried about not being the favourite, not being loved enough – when her questions were really about him – what sort of a man he was. And in that response, he'd answered.

Lexi's parents finally divorced when she was eighteen, but she'd already spent a lifetime witnessing her mother crumbling within the walls of their marriage, trying to fit herself into the image of who her husband wanted her to be.

Lexi didn't want that life.

She stood abruptly, knee bashing the table.

Robyn looked up. 'You okay?'

'Fine. Back in a minute,' she said, feeling for her mobile. She needed to talk to Ed.

36

Fen

'Top-up?' Bella said, hovering the wine bottle above Fen's glass.

She nodded. Fen was already on her third drink.

Bella slid her hand beneath the table, settling it on Fen's bare thigh. Her palm felt warm and smooth as she ran it in slow strokes, fingertips trailing to her inner thigh.

Fen didn't tell her to stop. She was grateful for the distraction and the grounding feeling of touch. She kept glancing around, waiting to see him, steeling herself.

'These are the ones you love, aren't they?' Bella said, passing her the vine leaves, filled with fragrant oiled rice and herbs.

'Yes,' she said, although her appetite had vanished. She knew she should eat more. This afternoon, while the others had been taking a siesta, Fen had gone for a run in the mountains. She'd been too unsettled to lounge by the pool, aware of the current of anxiety like a low beat in her chest that she had to march to. So she'd run. Feet pounding across the hard, dusty earth, knees complaining from the impact, sweat drenching her. But she'd welcomed the discomfort. Needed it. The motion outpacing her thoughts, her mind turning welcomely blank, the sensations of her body taking over.

But now there was nowhere to go. Nowhere to run.

'Babe,' Bella said, voice low so the others couldn't hear. 'I really want us to be okay. I'm going to do better, all right? Make it up to you.' Her eyes were wide, lashes painted long.

As Bella was speaking, a second waiter appeared at her side, with a tray of drinks. Fen's gaze travelled his thick forearms, over a gold watch lost in the weave of dark arm hair, upwards to his face. His jaw had broadened from the boyishly high cheekbones she remembered, and there was a scar now in the centre of his chin. The thin wisp of moustache was gone and his face was clean-shaven.

It was him.

Her mouth turned dry. There were only inches between them. She could smell his cloying aftershave.

'How is your food?' he asked the group.

'Delicious!' Bella purred.

His gaze moved across the table. When his eyes skirted Fen, there was nothing, no flicker of recognition. He didn't even remember.

'What a beautiful group of women!' he said. 'Holiday?'

'A hen party,' Bella said.

He drank her in, eyes roaming across her body. Then he smiled, teeth white.

Fen knew that smile. Knew the quicksilver flash as it slipped from smile to sneer. She felt herself go cold, felt herself sliding back seven years, felt the cool press of the terrace wall, the night at her back.

Bella placed a hand on Fen's arm, about to say something. Her touch was like a bridge. Fen gripped on to her fingers, then leant into her, surprising Bella by placing her mouth on hers, kissing her deeply. She tasted sweet and warm, of familiarity and comfort.

'What was that for?' Bella asked afterwards, delighted and a little taken aback. The waiter had already left.

Fen felt a hot flush of guilt. 'I'm sorry.'

'Don't be. I want more of that.' Lips against Fen's ear, she whispered, 'Much, much more.'

37

Lexi

Ed's voice was deep and welcome. 'Lexi! I was just thinking of you!'

There he was. Her fiancé, smiling right at her from the video call. He was sitting at his home desk. She could see the glare of a computer screen reflected in his glasses. 'One moment,' he said, propping the phone against something on his desk, then fiddling with his mouse, blanking the computer screen.

'You're working?' she asked.

'Catching up on a few bits,' he said, turning his attention back to her. 'Look at you. In Greece! You've caught the sun.' He smiled warmly, pushing a hand through his thick hair.

The normality of the gesture felt reassuring. This was Ed. Her Ed. She took a breath, feeling a sense of ease. Keeping the pregnancy from him was exacerbating her anxiety, she was certain. She hated secrets – had grown up in a house full of them. Maybe she should tell him about the baby now. Get it done.

'I wanted to call you,' Ed said easily, 'but you know I'm scared of Bella.'

'We all are.'

'Where are you?'

'In the Old Town, having dinner at a taverna.' She glanced over her shoulder. Bella was leaning close to Fen and hadn't noticed Lexi was missing, thank God. All communication with the groom was forbidden during the hen party.

'How's my sister? Sticking out like a sore thumb, I imagine.' He laughed.

It was a dismissive, old-fashioned turn of phrase, and Lexi felt a flare of protectiveness towards Eleanor. 'I admire her for coming. It must be hard being out here, celebrating someone else's wedding so soon after losing Sam.'

'You're right. It'll do her a world of good. Some sunshine. A few drinks. Company. You're not missing much here – it's rained for two days straight.'

'Has it?'

'God, I miss you, Lex. I was thinking I could pick you up from the airport on Sunday night. Maybe reschedule my Monday morning appointments so we can catch up properly?'

'Sounds lovely,' she said, feeling pleased.

'Lexi Lowe!'

She startled. Bella was coming towards her, a hand on her hip. 'Talking to the groom! You are in breach of hen party rule number two.' She plucked the phone from Lexi's grip. 'Hello, Edward,' she waved into the camera. 'You know you're aiding and abetting?'

'Guilty as charged.'

'And what have you two lovebirds been talking about?' Bella asked, gaze sliding to Lexi, an eyebrow arched.

Lexi shot her a panicked look.

'I was just telling Lexi how much I missed her,' Ed said.

'If you're infiltrating the hen,' Bella said, 'I suppose you may as well get the full tour. Come,' she said, carrying the phone. 'I am hobbling, by the way.' She angled the video towards her foot. 'A scorpion stung me. It was jealous of my exquisite taste in footwear.' She tottered across the square, mouthing to Lexi: *See? Me and Ed: BFFs!* To Ed she said, 'We've just finished dinner at the best taverna in Greece. I daren't pan to my stomach, else you may think I'm expecting.'

Lexi fired another warning glance. *Bloody Bella.*

'Right, here we go,' she said, panning the camera. 'No one can stand. We've eaten our body weight in tzatziki. I think you know most of us. You've not met Fen yet, my incredibly hot girlfriend.'

'Hey,' she said, lifting a hand.

'Hello!' Ed called cheerfully from the screen.

Bella swung the camera around. 'There's Robyn. Robyn is very sunburned, aren't you, Robyn?'

'Lots of liquids!' Ed advised.

Robyn lifted her wine glass. 'That's the part I'm managing.'

Bella moved on, angling the phone towards Eleanor, saying, 'You obviously know this face.'

'Hello, little sis.'

Lexi saw the way Eleanor pasted on a big smile, lifting her drink to toast the screen. 'Edward.'

Bella hollered to Ana, who was making her way inside the taverna. She was wearing her new jade dress, paired with a simple black headscarf knotted in a funky side bow. Lexi watched her turn, waving vaguely in Bella's direction, calling, 'Off to the loo!'

'There. Now you know Ana needs a piss! Well, that's

everyone. But I'm afraid you can't speak to the bride again. She's off limits.'

Lexi rolled her eyes. 'Give me the phone.'

'No can do,' Bella said, holding it out of reach. 'That's all for now, lovebirds. You'll see each other on Sunday. Wave goodbye.' She held up the phone for Lexi to wave.

As Lexi raised a hand, she saw Ed's image on screen. He looked strange, eyes narrowed, brows pulling close, a hand reaching to the back of his neck.

'Ed?' Bella said. 'Aren't you going to say goodbye to wifey?'

38

Eleanor

The waitress set down the extra dish of saganaki Eleanor had ordered.

Thanking her, Eleanor drew the small plate directly in front of her. It was her favourite – graviera cheese fried in olive oil, brought straight to the table with just a squeeze of lemon. It was so freshly prepared that the golden crust still gently sizzled.

Using the edge of her fork, she sliced into the crisp saganaki, which oozed melted cheese. She dropped a corner into her mouth, closed her eyes, chewed. Salty, lightly zested, a hint of a crust. Utter perfection.

Melted cheese was the closest thing to happiness Eleanor experienced these days. It was to be savoured. She popped a second piece into her mouth.

Her mobile trilled, startling her.

No one called Eleanor except her family, and they knew she

was in Greece. It would be some ridiculous PPI call interrupting her cheese moment. She'd enjoy telling them to go fuck themselves because: cheese. That was the sort of person she was these days, someone who quietly enjoyed swearing at strangers.

Her phone was tucked into her new handbag, which hung from the back of her chair. Reluctantly, she set down her fork, wiped her hands on a napkin, then searched for the phone.

She was surprised to see Ed's name on-screen. 'Why are you calling?' she said warily.

'Where are you?' he whispered.

'Greece,' she whispered back.

'I mean, where are you right now? Are you with everyone?'

'Yes.' The other hens were finishing their meals, chatting as they passed around the last plate of calamari.

'I need to speak to you on your own.'

'You are being strange.'

'Yes. I am. But please . . . I need to talk to you . . .'

She eyed the saganaki ruefully – it was only worth having when it was hot. 'Give me a minute.' She took one final, delectable bite, then clambered from her seat. No one asked where she was going, so she didn't say.

She crossed the cobbled square, where tourists milled at the edge of tavernas, studying the menu lecterns. Dusk had given way to night, and the square was lit with lamps and long strings of bulbs, giving a beautifully festive feel.

Eleanor moved towards the church, the waft of incense drifting from the open doors. She stood with her back to one of its towering stone walls, beside an ancient lemon tree in fruit.

'So?' She wondered whether this had anything to do with the news that Lexi was pregnant. Had Lexi told him a moment ago on their video call? Had Bella given the game away?

Ed's voice was low, clipped. 'There's a woman on the hen do.'

'Six of us, actually. It's sort of, like, the point.'

'Ana.'

'Yes, I'm sharing a room with her.'

'Who is she?'

'A friend of Lexi's. They met at a yoga class—'

'Yes, yes. Lexi's talked about her. But what do you know about her?'

'You're being odd.'

'Eleanor. Just tell me what you know,' he demanded, failing to hide his impatience.

'Okay, well, she's from Brixton. She's a sign-language person. An interpreter, that's the word. For her job. That's what she does. Her sister is deaf, so she—'

'Does she have children?'

'Ana? Yes. A son. Luca. He's fifteen. She doesn't look old enough—'

'Oh God . . .' Ed said, his voice strangely distant.

'Ed?'

There was a long silence.

'Why are you asking me about Ana? About Luca?' As she spoke, a memory she'd not thought about in a long time began to rise to the surface.

Ed's voice was quiet. '*Ana* is short for Jul*iana*.'

Eleanor hadn't heard that name spoken in years, and even then it was whispered behind the closed doors of her father's study.

'Oh,' she said, looking across the square towards the taverna. Her gaze fixed on Ana, who was sitting close to Lexi, their heads leant towards one another. 'It's her, isn't it?'

39

Fen

Fen folded her arms across her chest. It had been so long since she had felt this way, as if she were ashamed of her entire body: the boyish haircut; the tattoos; the holes she'd pierced through her ears and nose; her too-broad shoulders; her high, small breasts flattened within a sports bra.

His voice, hissing in her ear: *You disgust me.*

These thoughts were so old, so well-worn, she was surprised they could still hold any power.

That was the thing about fear: avoiding or running from it only magnified it. To overcome fear, Fen knew, one had to face it. It was as simple – and as hard – as that.

She looked across the table at Robyn. Fen replayed the moment she'd come across her at the swimming hole, Robyn standing aloft the rocky boulder, toes curled over the edge. Fen had seen the tremble in Robyn's bare legs, the breath moving high in her chest. Robyn had stared down at the long drop, but she hadn't stepped back.

She'd raised her chin, set her gaze on the horizon.

Jumped.

To overcome fear, one has to face it.

Fen took a breath. Stood.

There was a moment where the ground seemed to sway a little, but she lifted her gaze, set it straight ahead.

'You okay?' Bella asked, brows dipped, a hand rising as if to reach for her.

'I will be,' Fen said, almost to herself. Her legs carried her away from the table, crossing the taverna and delivering her into the dimness of the restaurant. The indoor tables were empty, the bar area clear.

She made herself keep moving. She knew this thin corridor with its open brickwork, stacked wooden crates, and scent of cooking oil drifting from the steamy kitchen. Her heart was beating hard and high in her chest as she allowed herself to feel it, all of it. The fear. The rage. The shame.

She heard footsteps coming from behind her, leather soles against stone. His.

Nico.

Her hands were shaking. Maybe she couldn't do this. Face him. She began to turn, but there was nowhere to go. She caught the scent of his aftershave in the air – felt her stomach turn. She froze.

A tray of cutlery glinted on top of the stack of crates. At the centre was a meat knife with a wooden handle. On instinct, Fen reached for it. The blade glinted silver as she felt the thrilling secret press of metal against her thigh.

Nico, holding a stack of cleared plates, emerged in the

corridor. He needed to pass right by her to enter the kitchen. He changed the angle of his hips, saying, 'Hello, madam,' moving to step around her.

Hot-cold panic flushed through her chest. They were face to face. His body an inch from hers.

He'd almost passed her when she finally spoke. 'Do you remember me?' The question came out like a bark.

He blinked. Cocked his head. He looked as if he were going to shrug, say *No*, but then his gaze lowered, eyes travelling towards her left hand.

The knife.

His eyes widened, registering it.

He looked up, right at her face.

Saw the intensity in her eyes as they burned into his.

Now he remembered.

40

Eleanor

Eleanor placed her fingertips to her temple. She felt dizzy, too hot. The neckline of her T-shirt was compressing her throat.

Her mind skipped back years and years, to when Ed was graduating from university. She remembered overhearing a hushed conversation in their father's study: Ed had got a first-year student pregnant. He'd wanted her to terminate the pregnancy, but she'd refused. Her mother had caught Eleanor listening and redirected her to the kitchen, fingers digging into the top of her arm.

'What's going to happen?' Eleanor had asked. She'd meant to the baby, to the pregnant girl, but her mother had answered:

'Don't worry. Ed will be fine. Your father and he will smooth things out.'

Smoothing was a family speciality. If she remembered rightly, a contract had been drawn up by Ed and her father, agreeing to a monthly maintenance contribution in exchange for Ed's anonymity. Handy to come from a family of lawyers when you needed to cover your own arse.

The girl's name was Juliana. They'd never met, but Eleanor had often found herself wondering about her and the baby. Did she have a boy or girl? Where did they live? Did Juliana ever return to university? Was she happy?

Several years ago, prompted by an afternoon spent with a cousin's newborn, she'd asked Ed, 'Do you ever wonder about your baby?'

He'd looked at her, appalled. 'I've closed the entire thing from my mind. I suggest you do the same.'

And that was that.

Until now.

'I take it,' Eleanor said into the phone, 'that Lexi doesn't know you have a child?'

'No.'

'Don't you think you should've told her?'

'I was scared that if I told her, she'd run.' She caught a rare note of vulnerability in his voice. He really did love Lexi.

'High flight risk,' Eleanor said. That's how Ed had described Lexi. She was wonderful, fun, gregarious, but also had an air of someone who might just disappear, like she was too good to be true. *Pouff!* 'Do you think Ana knows who you are? Who Lexi is?' Eleanor asked.

'It can't be a coincidence. Juliana – *Ana* – knows my name. Lexi will have spoken about me, used my name. She knows exactly who I am.'

Huh. Eleanor looked again towards the taverna. Ana was reaching for a jug of water. She refilled Lexi's glass, then her own. An itchy sensation travelled across her skin: Ana had been lying to her. To all of them.

Eleanor hated liars.

'Has she asked anything about me?' Ed said.

Ana had asked several questions about Ed, like whether he'd be happy about the news of Lexi's pregnancy and what sort of father he'd be. 'Yes, she has. I think she was digging.'

'*Bitch,*' she heard Ed say beneath his breath.

'What do you want me to do? Poison, blade, or gun?'

'Don't joke.'

'I'm not. Why has she befriended Lexi? Why not just speak to you?'

'Money. She gets double the maintenance if there's no contact between us and my identity remains undisclosed until Luca is eighteen.'

Eleanor was quite familiar with the sensation of being appalled by her brother, her family. 'Luca,' she said slowly. 'So you knew he was a boy?'

'Yes, I knew. I have a copy of the birth certificate.'

'Is your name on it?' she asked, but even as she did, she knew the answer to the question. Under the heading Father, it would read *Unknown.* Another condition of Ed's contract.

'I need to talk to Lexi before Ana does. I'm going to get on a flight right now.'

'There are only two connecting flights from Athens and they're on Sundays and Wednesdays. The earliest you'll get out here is the day we leave.'

'Shit.' She could hear him pacing, knew he'd be making tight strides, arms rigid, a knot of tension clenching his jaw. 'Then I'll have to do it when I pick her up from the airport. Tell her face to face. That's the right thing, isn't it?'

'Best you've got.'

'Listen, Eleanor, I don't want Ana to work out that we know who she is. I don't want her saying anything to Lexi, not until I do. And I need you to keep your eye on her. You'll do that for me, won't you?'

She agreed.

'Call me tomorrow. Let me know everything is okay.'

She ended the call and remained rooted to the spot, shoulder blades pressing into the stone wall of the church. Her neck fizzed with tension, mind abuzz.

A Greek woman ascended the steps, a baby swaddled in a light blanket in her arms. She caught the shock of dark hair, the perfectly round head. She remembered the look on Ana's face when Lexi announced she was pregnant. She was surprised, like the rest of them, but there was something else there, too. A hollowed expression, the swallow of her throat, her eyes lowering for a moment. She'd pressed her lips together before lifting her head, smiling, offering up her congratulations. Eleanor had never been particularly good at reading people; she'd assumed Ana was simply surprised like the rest of them – but now she wondered what that expression revealed.

Ana knew exactly who Ed was, so she must have planned this – purposefully befriending Lexi; avoiding situations where she'd see Ed, like the engagement drinks; ensuring she was invited on the hen weekend.

Her lip began to twitch as she thought about how Ana had used her, too: the lovely shopping trip to the Old Town; Ana helping her choose a new handbag; her interest in Eleanor's sculpting; the evening chats over a drink. Her cheeks burned with humiliation. She'd let herself believe that Ana liked her, that they were friends.

Fool.

41

Robyn

Robyn glanced again at the entrance to the taverna. Still no sign of Fen. There was something off about Fen tonight – she seemed on edge, preoccupied, nothing like the relaxed, buoyant company she'd been at the swimming hole earlier in the day.

She waited to see who was exiting the taverna, but it was only the waitress returning with a tray of drinks for another table.

Robyn pressed her fingertips against her temples, moving them in slow circles. She had a banging headache.

'You okay?' Lexi asked from across the table.

'Too much sun, I think.' The pinkened skin on her shoulders and chest was radiating heat beneath her cotton top.

'Have you had enough water?'

'Probably not. I'll get another jug for the table.' The waitress was busy with the adjacent table, so Robyn went inside the taverna.

It was quiet and cool away from the hum of chatter. Yes, she'd just stand here for a moment and enjoy the silence and air-conditioning. A faint pulse of nausea was beginning to churn in her stomach. She wanted to return to the villa, take some painkillers, and fall into bed – but she'd feel guilty abandoning Lexi on their one night out.

Right now, though, she needed water. She was probably dehydrated. Where was the waiter? She made her way towards the kitchen, following the exposed stone wall. Music was playing faintly from the direction of the kitchen. Beyond it, she heard a woman's voice: low, strained.

She followed the corridor, passing a fire exit and stack of empty crates.

She halted.

Fen was standing near the entrance to the kitchen, facing the waiter who'd been serving them. His white shirt sleeves were pushed up and he had a stack of dirty plates balanced along a tanned forearm.

Her expression was steely, a fixed groove in her brow. Her feet were planted wide, head jutting forwards, tendons in her neck exposed.

In Fen's hand, something flashed silver.

42

Fen

Fen could feel the knife in her grip, the cool metal handle, the blade still close to her thigh. 'Seven years ago I came for dinner here.' Her voice trembled with a barely contained rage.

'Is a long time ago. Popular taverna, yes? So many tourists.' He smiled uncertainly. 'I hope you had a good holiday.'

'Let me jog your memory,' she said, blood pulsing in her fingertips. 'I had long blonde hair back then. Was wearing a denim miniskirt. I was here with my aunt. She spoke to your father; he said you and your sister would take me to some clubs, show me around the island. We went to Club Carlos together. Danced. Drank. Your sister left early, so you offered to drop me back at my aunt's villa. It's at the end of the island, on the clifftop.'

His smile slipped. 'Look, I can't remember—'

'No! You don't get to erase what you did.' Fen's eyes blazed as she leaned closer.

There was nowhere for him to turn. He was standing with his back pressed to the wall, eyes shifting from Fen's face to the hand holding the knife. She'd not raised it. Not threatened him. It simply waited at her side, a silent reminder of who had the power. This time.

'You dropped me home and I thanked you. You said you could use a beer – one for the road. You went out onto the terrace and I fetched us both beers. But that wasn't what you really wanted.' Fen's voice was gravelly, raw with emotion, as she continued. 'You drank your beer, then took mine out of my hands and shoved me back against the wall. Kissed me roughly.'

Nico said, 'It's a long time ago. I don't rem—'

'I told you to *stop!* I told you I was attracted to women, not men. Instead of understanding, stepping back – you pinned me to the wall. You put your body in front of mine so there was nowhere for me to go. If I'd leaned back, even by a few inches, I'd have gone over the edge. And you knew that.'

Fen drew herself closer, the blade of the knife grazing her thigh.

'You stood there, arms on either side of me like a barrier, your face right up in mine. You said, *I don't want you. No one will ever want you. Men won't sleep with you because you're fat. Worthless. You disgust me.*'

The plates balancing on Nico's forearm clinked as his hand trembled.

'Now tell me you don't fucking remember!'

'I'm sorry, okay?' His voice was high, urgent. 'It was wrong, what I did. Yes? I'm sorry. I was just a boy.'

How many times had men got away with things under the label of being *just a boy*?

She lifted the knife, felt his eyes following it. There was an oily sheen of sweat lining his forehead. She could hear his breath, shallow and fast. 'Yes,' she said, slowly placing the knife on the top of his stacked plates. 'And I was just a girl.'

Then she stepped back, allowing him to leave.

Nico ducked past her, hurrying away, disappearing into the kitchen.

The moment he was out of sight, Fen slumped against the wall as if her legs had no more energy left to hold her. Her face was pale, bloodless.

'Fen?'

She turned.

Robyn was standing a few feet away. It was clear from her concerned expression that she'd heard everything.

'I can't go back to our table,' Fen said.

Robyn nodded once, then took her hand, squeezing it hard in her own. 'Come,' she said, steering her away from the kitchen.

Along the corridor, a fire door led out of the restaurant onto a side street. Robyn moved towards it, pulling Fen with her. 'We'll get a taxi. I'll text Lexi, tell her I wasn't feeling well.'

They emerged onto a narrow, cobbled road, strung with lights, the night warm and fragranced. Fen hesitated, looking at the white motorbike with thick tyres, a helmet strung over a handlebar.

Beside her, Robyn asked, 'Is this his?'

She nodded, eyes wet with tears.

Robyn walked towards it, placing her hand on the smooth leather saddle.

Nico would've ridden this bike back from the villa that

night, knowing what he'd done. Fen imagined him riding fast, accelerating into the mountain bends, feeling what, powerful? Manly?

Maybe Robyn pictured that too because, with a swift movement, she toed away the metal kickstand, then gave the lightest of shoves. They both watched as the motorbike teetered for a moment, before crashing onto its side in a clang of metal.

Fen looked at Robyn, eyes stretched with surprise.

And then they ran.

43

Bella

It was supposed to be a hen party! If the others wanted to sip one glass of wine and call it a night by ten o'clock, they should go join a book club.

It was no surprise that Robyn would be lame. *Sunstroke?* Whatever. But Fen? Bella knew she couldn't handle alcohol. Her liver was too clean, that was the problem. But to *text* her excuses?

> *Just thrown up in the loos. In a taxi back to villa. So sorry. Fen x*

Fen should've told her in person. *She* wanted to be the one to put Fen in a taxi and take her home. Not Robyn.

Earlier, when Fen had kissed her at the table, she'd been surprised by the intensity of it, the publicness. For a few delicious, wondrous moments, she'd let herself believe that everything would be okay between them.

She blanked the screen, slipped the phone into her clutch, then tipped back her glass of wine. Belched.

Two down, four still standing. It'd have to do. She stood teetering on her heels. 'Onwards, to the bars!' Bella war-cried.

They found a bar a short walk from the taverna, where a DJ in a raised booth thumped out Euro pop. Jesus, she didn't even recognise any of these songs. Looking at the girls grinding to the beats in their tiny dresses and the boys in their thigh-hugging shorts, she was wondering why *they* weren't in bed at ten o'clock, because surely they were only twelve years old?

'Here we go,' Eleanor said, returning from the bar with a tray filled with shots.

'Yes, Eleanor!' Bella said, impressed. 'What've we got?'

'Tequila and Aftershock,' Eleanor shouted above the music. 'Keeping the vibes nineties. Like it.'

'I got you two shots of lemonade,' Eleanor told Lexi. 'I didn't want you to feel left out.'

Lexi laughed and squeezed her arm.

'Tequila first,' Bella said, handing them out. 'Lemonade for Lexi.' The four of them clinked glasses.

'To Lexi,' Ana said, raising hers in toast.

'To Lexi!' the others chimed, Bella irked that Ana had jumped in to lead the toast.

They tipped back the shots, following them with a chaser of Aftershock. Bella sucked in air through clamped teeth, grimacing.

A group of men in short-sleeved shirts were eyeing them from the other side of the bar. Bella winked, lifting an empty glass as a suggestion. One of the men, who wore a tight pink shirt, nodded, then waved over the barman.

'Wink equals drink,' Bella said to the rest of the hens. She loved flirting with men. They were so easy, so uncomplicated. 'Come on, Lex,' she said, grabbing her hand. 'Let's show these kids how to dance!'

'In a bit,' she said easily. 'I'm just chatting.'

To Ana.

Bella wanted to dance. She needed movement. Wanted to loosen up the night. She could pull Eleanor onto the dancefloor, but that would be weird, like dancing with an aunt.

She swayed on the spot, pushing a hand into the roots of her hair giving it extra volume. Her foot was throbbing and if she didn't do something fun right now, she was in danger of jumping in a taxi herself.

She glanced back at the bar. The group of men was being served, a tray set out with more glasses. This was good. They'd come over, bringing alcohol, and fresh chat. Maybe she'd try to set up Eleanor with the one at the back who was wearing an oversized Hawaiian shirt. There, that would be her good deed for the night.

Ana and Lexi were talking, heads bent together, but she couldn't hear above the music. She sighed, looking around, bored. God, this music. It was like listening to a yapping dog on speed.

'What are you talking about?' she said, leaning forward, interrupting Lexi and Ana's conversation.

'I was just saying I'm worried that I'm not going to fit into my wedding dress. The wedding is still four weeks away and the bump is starting to show.'

'It'll be easy to adjust the dress,' Ana said. 'If you think about that panel at the front, all the seamstress would need to do is add a strip of fabric on either side of it.'

'I thought you were keeping the dress a surprise?' Bella

had been to the first fitting and when she'd seen Lexi step from behind the velvet changing curtain, her eyes had welled with tears. She'd stared at Lexi, saying, *You're getting married, Lex! You're a bride!* And then she'd burst into tears. 'Has Ana seen it?'

Lexi glanced sideways at Ana. 'We went for lunch one day and . . . well, it was an impulse thing . . . we saw the bridal shop and decided to have a quick look in.'

'What, *after* I saw the dress?'

There was a pause. 'Before.'

'Before?' Bella repeated, trying to understand. 'That's when you *chose* the wedding dress? With Ana?'

She nodded.

'You said you'd found the dress on a whim, walking into the dress shop without an appointment.'

'That is what happened,' Lexi explained, 'except Ana was with me.'

Bella felt duped. She'd thought she was the first person to see Lexi in her wedding dress. They'd drunk the free glass of champagne, squealing at Lexi's reflection in the long, ornate mirror. Yet Lexi had omitted the one important detail – that she'd taken Ana with her to choose it. 'Why didn't you tell me?'

'I thought you'd be upset.'

'I am upset.'

'Exactly.'

'I'm upset because you lied! You pretended I was the first person to see you in it.'

'God, I'm sorry. You're right,' Lexi said, shaking her head as if it had been no more than a misunderstanding. That was the thing about Lexi. She never realised how hurtful her actions could be. How important she was in Bella's life. 'I should've told you. You should've been with me that first time.'

'Yes. I should have.'

Ana rolled her eyes, as if Bella's emotions were tiresome. 'Lexi, you don't need to apologise for how you decide to get your own wedding dress.'

'I'm the maid of honour! The maid of honour always accompanies the bride when she chooses her dress.'

There was silence, her complaint hanging there like a stamp of a foot.

'I can't wait to see you in it properly on the big day,' Ana added.

'You'll be there, will you?' Eleanor said.

Bella turned. They all did. The question was asked so sharply it was like it had been fired from a rifle. Eleanor was glaring at Ana, an eyebrow arched. Her cheeks were flushed from the alcohol.

'At Lexi and Ed's wedding? Of course!' Ana smiled nervously.

'So you've RSVP'd?' Eleanor pushed, eyes glittering.

Bella looked between the two women, intrigued.

'Yes, ages ago.'

'Everyone on the hen will be there,' Lexi added, trying to ease the tension.

Eleanor nodded, but as she turned away, Bella caught her whisper, 'If you say so.'

If you say so? Fetch the woman more alcohol!

At that moment, the man in the pink shirt appeared, holding aloft a tray lined with shot glasses. 'Ladies,' he said, lowering it in the centre of them. 'More drinks?'

44

Robyn

When the taxi pulled up outside the villa, Fen blinked, as if startled to see they were already back. She stepped out, the headlights illuminating streaks of dried mascara on her cheeks.

'Let's have a nightcap,' Robyn said. 'I'll bring them out to the terrace.'

Inside the villa, she kicked off her sandals, then rooted through her bag in search of painkillers. She swallowed two with a tall glass of water. She fetched a couple of ice-cold beers and carried them out to the terrace.

Fen was sitting on the spread of cushions by the low stone wall. Lanterns dotted the ground, and Robyn settled beside her, handing her a beer. She pressed her lower back into the warmth of the stone, sighing as she felt the stretch of her spine. 'Want to talk about it?'

'You heard it all,' Fen said, eyes shining in the moonlight.

'You said not all memories here are good ones. He's the memory?'

She nodded. 'Pathetic, isn't it?'

Robyn's beer bottle clanked against flagstone as she set it down. 'No. Not pathetic. What he did – what he said – it was awful.'

'He didn't hit me. He didn't rape me. He just used words.' Her head shook lightly as she said, 'There was nowhere to put them, so I swallowed them whole. They never digested, just sat there, growing heavier and heavier.'

Robyn held her eye steadily.

'He didn't even remember me at first. Isn't it mad that I hadn't registered in his world – yet he took over mine? Those things he said, I let them worm into my head for years.'

Robyn reached for Fen's hand. 'What he feels or remembers isn't important. You can't control that. All that's important is what *you* feel.'

'I hate that he could still make me feel afraid, even now. I thought I was stronger than this.'

'You are strong, Fen, but that doesn't mean you can't also be vulnerable. You don't have to be one thing all of the time.'

The cicadas filled the silence.

'That photo of you in the villa . . . why did you hide it away?'

'You saw?'

Robyn nodded.

'It was taken the evening I met Nico. I can't look at the girl I was then without hearing his voice. Seeing her as he saw me. *Disgusting*. It was an echo of everything I'd heard from my parents . . .'

'Oh, Fen.'

'So I hid the photo. Hid the shame.' She shook her head.

'That hiding, though, it gave him power again. And it's crazy because I know the things he said to me aren't true. I've done the work, y'know? What happened forced me to look myself in the eye. I had to overcome body hang-ups. Self-worth issues. Get my exercise habits in check – because I went from doing almost nothing to overcooking it, using it as an escape.' She hugged her knees tighter to her chest. 'Then I come back out to Greece, and suddenly all this shit rears its head again. And I'm angry – furious at myself for not feeling the way I want to feel.' She shook her head sharply, agitated. 'Sorry. I doubt that makes any sense.'

Robyn smiled. 'More than you know.'

Fen raised her head, eyes locking on Robyn.

There was a shift in the air between them.

'You know, when I confronted him – I thought about you standing on the rock at the swimming hole. How you'd deliberated – but then leapt anyway.' She paused. 'Why did you jump?'

Robyn thought for a moment. 'Because I'm starting to wonder if the things I'm afraid of are the very things I should be doing.'

As Fen looked at her in the darkness, Robyn felt that slender, beating sensation at her centre, warming her like a flame.

45

Eleanor

Eleanor rode in the back of the taxi, sandwiched between Bella and Lexi. The air smelled of warmed perfume, alcohol, and the faint hint of olive oil caught in the fabric of their clothes. She could feel the heat of Lexi's bare arm against her own. As the taxi rounded a bend, Bella swayed into Eleanor, head lolling.

In the front seat, Ana was talking in a low voice to the driver, their conversation mellowed by the drone of the air conditioning. Eleanor wondered if this was what it would be like to have a group of girlfriends, a band of women to go out dancing with, or whom you could call on the weekend because you were feeling glum, or who you'd meet for a mid-week dinner as you had nothing in the fridge.

She felt the gentle slope of the mountain road, the change in terrain as tarmac switched to dust and gravel, ascending towards the villa. She was sorry the journey was over.

Ana paid the fare with money from the kitty.

Arm hooked through Bella's, Lexi crossed the drive, saying, 'Thanks for organising everything today. The boat, the meal out – it's all been perfect.'

Bella swayed lightly against her, espadrilles dangling from a fingertip. 'Sorry I made you go bar-hopping pregnant. I'm a shitty maid of honour. I even packed a veil,' she said, pulling it from her sequinned clutch with a small flourish. 'I was going to make you wear it, but I drank too many tequilas.'

Lexi took the veil from her, slotting the comb of it into her hair. She twirled on the spot, the veil lifting around her shoulders like a ghostly shroud. 'If you've got a pink sash or L-plates stuffed in your handbag, now is your chance.'

Eleanor watched, sensing that Lexi was making up for her slip with the wedding dress.

Bella laughed, saying, 'That's all the hen paraphernalia I could fit in my carry-on bag.'

Lexi threaded her arms around Bella's neck and kissed her tenderly on the forehead. 'Good night,' she said, then slipped into the villa, quietly ascending the stairs in her veil.

Eleanor walked with Bella and Ana onto the terrace, which was bathed in moonlight. Bella paused by the low seating area, taking in the empty beer bottles and the soft lantern light.

'Looks like the early birds got a second wind,' Eleanor noted, a touch unhelpfully, she had to admit.

Bella pursed her lips. 'I'm going to bed.'

Eleanor almost felt guilty as she watched Bella limp into the villa, shoulders rounding.

'Nightcap?' Ana asked.

It had become their evening ritual on the hen weekend, a final drink shared on the terrace while the air was still cool and the volume of the other hens had been lowered. She fancied one more drink to ease her towards sleep, make sure she drifted off. Yet she could hardly sit out here with Ana after learning Ed was the father of her child. 'No, thank you,' she said primly.

'Thought you never slept before one o'clock?'

It was true. Eleanor was dooming herself to lying on the mattress, locked in a cycle of dark thoughts. No, she didn't fancy that one little bit. Maybe she would have one more drink. Anyway, she needed to work out what Ana was up to. 'Go on, then.'

Ana smiled, a wide genuine smile, and Eleanor thought, *It's such a shame you're lying to us all, because I liked you.* Eleanor had let herself imagine a friendship with Ana that stretched beyond the hen weekend. She'd pictured the two of them sharing a pew at the wedding. Ana would have squeezed her hand in silent acknowledgement that the wedding would be hard because of Sam, and Eleanor would've smiled stoically. So many fantasies, so quickly built, and so quickly lost.

She lowered herself onto the cushions, then undid the top button of her shorts. Ah, better! A fitted waistband and saganaki were never a good mix.

She heard the opening and closing of cupboards from within the villa as Ana made the drinks. *Juli*ana, she corrected herself.

She thought back to the soured atmosphere at home when Ed was twenty-one and, instead of going to the pub for their usual Christmas Eve meal, Ed and their father were drawing up contracts in the study. She remembered catching a smug comment from Ed and didn't need to have studied law to understand the gist of what was happening: they were paying the girl off.

'Here you go,' Ana said, returning. 'I went with espresso martini.'

She even made delicious drinks.

They clinked glasses and Eleanor took a small swallow. Only this morning she had been thinking how much Sam would have liked Ana. There was a lack of artifice – like earlier in the bar when she'd refused to apologise to Bella for helping choose Lexi's wedding dress. Why should that be a secret?

And yet, she'd been keeping her own much bigger secret this entire time.

Ed had specifically instructed Eleanor to say nothing, and he was right: better for Lexi to hear the truth from him. She didn't want to blow everything apart, not out here.

The problem was, Eleanor thought, taking another swallow of her drink, that sometimes she didn't have a filter. People said that about her, as if it were a bad thing, but Sam had always liked it: 'You say what you think, EJ. More people should try it.' Right now, she was trying very, very hard to filter, to not say every single thought that came into her head.

Ana, you're lying to me.

You and Ed have a child.

He is my nephew.

I would've liked to have had a chance to be an auntie.

Why did you hunt out Lexi?

What do you want from her?

What are you really doing here, Juliana?

See? She was doing well with all the filtering. All she needed to do was keep up the good work for another twenty-four hours, and then they'd return home and Ed could sort out this mess. Meanwhile, she'd be watching Ana closely.

Ana took a sip of her drink, then tipped her face towards

the stars. She looked peaceful, relaxed, like she hadn't a care in the world.

Eleanor had no idea what her game was, but she planned to find out.

But then, she thought darkly, *I suppose we've all got a game.*

Eleanor finished the second espresso martini. She was just about drunk enough to sleep – although the caffeine probably wasn't her most brilliant idea. As she stood, she felt the ground move with her.

'Think I'm done, too,' Ana said, picking up their empty glasses and following Eleanor through to the kitchen. She set the glasses in the sink, then opened the fridge. 'Shall we apologise to our liver with these?' She held out two bottles of water.

'I make my apologies with carbs.'

Ana smiled warmly. 'It's been really good meeting you on this hen weekend.'

See? Friends. We could've been good friends. Why did Ana have to go and ruin it?

'I'm looking forward to meeting Ed, too,' she said.

No. That was enough. She didn't take bare-faced lies. 'You've already met Ed.'

A tiny line of confusion nestled between Ana's brows. 'Sorry? I'm not sure what you're talking about.'

'I cannot stomach liars. So I'll ask you a question, and I hope you're not going to piss me off by lying.'

Ana smoothed down the sides of her dress, then clasped her hands together.

'Is Ed Luca's father?'

Her eyes widened, then blinked. She said nothing.

'Well?'

Ana turned on the spot, moving towards the exit of the villa.

'Where are you—'

'We can't have this conversation here,' she said in a low, calm voice, reaching the front door. She held it open, indicating that Eleanor should follow.

'I've a feeling,' Eleanor said, folding her arms, 'that this isn't a conversation that works well anywhere.'

～

The real problems began when we discovered we were being lied to. No one likes to be made a fool of.

That sort of thing, well, it couldn't go unpunished, could it?

46

Bella

Bella couldn't sleep.

She loved the heat. Really, she bowed to the sun in all its life-giving glory, but at night, she'd have loved the heat to piss off. Fen preferred not to use the air conditioning on environmental grounds and, as Bella was trying very, very hard to be nice, she was not going to switch it on. Instead, the fan wafted warm air around the room, while Bella lay naked on top of the covers, sweating.

Maybe she'd sweat out the alcohol and wouldn't be hung-over tomorrow. Silver linings and everything.

She didn't sleep very well these days. Hadn't done in almost a year. The problem with night was that all the things you avoided thinking about during the day gave you a knowing wink – *See you tonight, then!* – and there they were, as soon as you closed your eyes. Except at night it was even worse, because by then you were too tired to think rationally and everything became magnified, distorted.

The nights she slept alone were the hardest. There was a comfort when Fen stayed over and she could sleep with a hand on her chest, feeling the firm, strong rhythm of her heartbeat beneath her palm. Tonight, Fen had rolled onto her side, bunching the sheet around her waist.

Bella sat up. No, she would not lie here, sweating.

Naked, she crossed the room, then padded downstairs. She poured herself a glass of water and drank it too fast, giving a little shiver as the water chilled her insides. She meandered onto the terrace. The lanterns were still glowing and the air smelled faintly of herbs and chlorine.

She moved towards the pool, lowering herself onto the edge and slipping her feet into the cool, uplit water.

One day and one night left. That was it, then it'd all be over. The hen party had been a beacon for weeks now – that one golden thing in her diary, underlined three times and surrounded by a cluster of biro stars. Whenever she was having a crap day, she'd remind herself: *Greece! Sun! Lexi's hen! Keep going!* But now the hen was nearly at its end and she would soon be returning home to a rented flat, and a job at a jeweller's that left her unfulfilled.

She missed being a nurse. No matter how she dressed it up – *I was ready for a change. The shift work was relentless. I've always wanted to sell jewellery* – the truth was she missed nursing. She missed her colleagues. She missed the satisfaction of being good at her job. When you work out that a patient presenting with a fever in fact has meningitis and you manage to get them on the right medication before permanent damage is done – now that means something. Yet she'd swapped that for selling silver bangles. *Another great life choice, Bella!*

See? Middle of the night. Who wants to be awake then?

She slipped her legs from the pool and stood. Maybe she should take up reading . . . find a good book to keep her company in the middle of the night. Fen's aunt had a well-stocked bookshelf. She'd pick one. Begin tonight. That could be her thing: she'd become a reader. Maybe she'd start her own book club. That'd knock Ana from her literary throne!

She left a meandering trail of wet footprints as she headed for the villa. Then paused.

Voices.

Who else was awake?

She listened, ears pricked.

Yes, a low whisper was coming from behind the villa. Strange. Why would anyone be out there? She felt a strange beat of unease. She followed the voices, moving gingerly across the terrace, her nakedness suddenly making her feel exposed as she tiptoed along the floodlit path.

Ahead, she could just make out Eleanor's broad frame, arms folded across her chest. She was standing beneath a lemon tree, the limb-like shadows from its branches cross-hatching her face. She was talking to Ana, who had her back to Bella. Her hands cut sharply through the space between them. Their voices were low, hushed.

She caught Lexi's name being whispered.

Bella pressed her naked back flat to the wall, listening.

47

Eleanor

Eleanor stood beneath the lemon tree, the scent of its fruit leaving a citrus kiss on the night air. She suddenly felt very sober.

The floodlight cast strange shadows across Ana's face. Her voice was low, strained, as she finally answered. 'Yes. Ed is Luca's father.'

Eleanor felt the shifting of something deep in her body as the confirmation settled. Her folded arms tightened, fingers gripping the fabric of her top. She studied Ana's face, searching for something she could understand in her expression.

Ana was rooted firmly. 'How did you find out?'

'Ed video-called at the taverna. He saw you.'

Ana ran her tongue over her top teeth, nodding once.

'You've been careful, haven't you? You weren't at their engagement drinks. Or Lexi's birthday.' Now she thought about earlier in the day when Bella had taken a photo on the yacht, and Ana had quickly turned away. 'You've managed to duck out of all the photos this weekend, haven't you? You couldn't risk Ed seeing them.'

Ana said nothing.

She could feel her anger building. 'I'm guessing there'll be an excuse about why you can't make the wedding, too?'

Still, she remained silent.

'What the hell are you doing here?' Eleanor burst out. 'You're at Lexi's hen party! We're here to celebrate her *marrying* Ed! I assume you know that Lexi has no idea he already has a child?'

'I guessed, yes.'

'What are you trying to do? Sabotage their wedding? Is that it?'

'No.'

'Then, why? Why are you here?'

Ana remained very still, as if her body had been sculpted into the stone. 'Are you going to tell Lexi who I am?'

'Ed is.'

Ana shook her head. 'I need to speak to her. Explain.'

'Explain what exactly?' Eleanor demanded. In the glare of the floodlights, she could see Ana's expression was steely. 'Are you obsessed with my brother? Is that what this is about?'

'I don't know what to say.'

'You use words. Put them in order.'

Ana took a breath, her chest rising, chin lifting. 'I've always tried to be honest with Luca. He knows I wasn't in a relationship with his father. He knows the pregnancy was a surprise. He knows his father made it clear that he didn't want children. Luca had always accepted that. But then, last year, he started asking more questions. Told me he wanted to meet his father.'

'And you didn't want him to meet Ed because of the contract? Because the money suited you?'

Ana startled back as if she'd been slapped. 'It was never about the money. Is that what you think? Your family . . .' She shook her head.

The way she said those words, *Your family*, caused a shiver to travel down Eleanor's spine.

Ana's gaze moved across her face. 'I didn't know if I wanted Luca to meet Ed.'

'Why?'

There was a long pause. 'Luca is *everything* to me. I wouldn't do anything that risked him getting hurt.'

Somewhere behind them, Eleanor heard a strange sound, like a scuff. She glanced around, peering into the darkness. She waited, listening.

There was nothing further, only the rustle of wind carrying the calls of cicadas. Still, she'd better check. She passed Ana, moving along the stone pathway towards the edge of the villa.

'Is there someone there?' Ana asked, voice low.

Eleanor peered around the corner.

The floodlit path was empty.

'No one.'

Then she looked down. There on the shadowy stone was the faintest trail of wet footprints.

48

Bella

Bella tiptoed naked along the flagstone path, an arm clamped over her breasts to stop them bouncing. She ducked through a doorway into the darkened villa, then hurried up the stairway, slipping quickly into her and Fen's bedroom.

She closed the door softly, then stood with her back against it, mind racing beneath the slow whirl of the fan.

Ed is the father of Ana's child.

Lexi has no idea.

She knew there was something off about Ed! Hadn't she glimpsed an edge to him? It was impossible not to feel a thrilling burst of pleasure at being right, a sort of quickening of her heart rate at the shock and drama of the discovery.

Then she immediately thought of Lexi. Oh God, poor Lexi! She'd be devastated.

Eleanor had said that Ed wanted to tell Lexi the truth

when she returned from the hen weekend, but fuck that! Bella wasn't going to let the family close ranks, slime their way out of the betrayal. Absolutely not. Bella would be the one to tell Lexi. She was her best friend. Her maid of *honour*!

Her fingers reached for the door handle – then she paused.

Was it right to wake Lexi in the middle of the night? Best to have the conversation in the morning, when Lexi was rested, fully awake. Perhaps Bella would suggest the two of them take a walk. She'd break the news gently. But then Lexi would be stuck in Greece, on her hen weekend, with nowhere to put this knowledge. She'd be distraught. All she'd want would be to go home, speak to Ed.

No, perhaps she should wait. It would be better for Lexi to hear this from Ed. It was his mess, after all. Instead, Bella would be there, ready for when Lexi needed her.

Lexi could move back to Bournemouth and crash in Bella's flat. It'd be just like old times, the two of them together. Lexi could even have the baby there. Bella would give them her room, and she'd sleep on the sofa. It'd be a squeeze, but it could work.

A wave of anger seized her as she thought about Ana. The bitch. All that controlled energy; the forthright, uncompromising tone. She wouldn't have known real friendship if it smacked her in the face. In fact, Bella would have quite liked to smack her in the face right now. Although she suspected Ana would hit back. There was a strength about Ana that was a little threatening, if she were honest. Still, Bella didn't grow up with three older brothers without learning how to throw a good punch.

Anyway. No one was going to get punched.

She stood in the dark, scratching a fresh mosquito bite.

Let Ana and Eleanor keep their secret for another twenty-four hours. Then she'd be ready to support Lexi when the time was right.

There, Ana, she thought. *Who's the good friend now?*

SATURDAY

~

The strangest thing about the night of the beach fire was how ordinarily the day began. The bright blue sky, clean of clouds, and the whitewashed walls reflecting the heat back into the startlingly clear day.

The atmosphere felt holiday-ish, bright and shiny as a freshly minted coin.

Too good to be true.

Perhaps that should've been the clue. But we missed it.

For all the mistakes we made, we couldn't have known then – in the blazing heat of morning – that hours later, one of us would kill.

49

Eleanor

Eleanor sliced the tops and bottoms from the blood oranges, releasing their deliciously sweet citrus scent. They glistened like jewels as she peeled off the rest of the skin with a sharp vegetable knife, slicing through the segments. She laid each carefully on a platter.

A final segment remained on the chopping board. She could pick it up, drop it into her mouth, taste the nectar-like sweetness – but there was pleasure in waiting. Anticipation was so undervalued these days. The wait, the build up. People wanted immediate gratification, and it bored her, that tireless appetite for the next thing, for more.

She speared the segment of orange and placed it on the platter with the rest of the fruit. She, Eleanor Tollock, was a woman who could wait.

From the fridge she removed a tub of thick Greek yoghurt and began spooning it into a stoneware bowl. If she lived here, she could eat like this all week long – fresh fruit with creamy yoghurt and a swirl of honey for breakfast, and in the evenings a big salad with tomatoes so ripe and sweet they balanced the salty tang of the feta. At home in winter, when it had rained all afternoon and was dark by four o'clock, who wanted a salad, no matter how plump the tomatoes? You needed a pie, or a stew with dumplings, or a thick bowl of soup with crusty bread warm from the oven. It wasn't only about eating with the seasons, but eating with the climate, that's what Eleanor thought.

And she thought about food a lot. Even though she was cooking for one at home, she never cut corners. She wouldn't buy the curry paste, she would rather make it fresh. (Once you had a spice cabinet, all it took was a little measuring and a pestle and mortar. Why not invest an extra five minutes and have a curry that tasted fresh and honest, rather than overly salted with the lingering aftertaste of preservatives? Again, this obsession with speed!) One of the things she disliked most about grief was it dulled her tastebuds. Honestly. Nothing tasted quite as good as it once had. It was like Sam had gone to his grave – well, urn technically – and hauled half her tastebuds with him.

The other thing was recipe serving sizes: she always had to take the quantities and divide the 'serves 4' into 'serves 1'. She could, of course, cook the full amount and freeze portions, but then what would she do with her evenings? Some people liked to come home and put the television on for company; Eleanor liked the sizzle of butter in a pan, the smell of garlic and shallots warming in oil, the steam lifting from a joint of beef – that was her company.

Next week, she and Sam should have been celebrating a year of being married. Paper, that was the totem for the first anniversary. She would have done something special, like bought him tickets to a comedy show he liked, or maybe found a vintage comic from his childhood. But she couldn't think about all the would-haves and should-haves. In fact, she didn't want to feel anything, because all of the feelings were too hard. Happiness was an absurdly unreachable notion – but *distracted*, *busy*, those she could do.

Right. What next? She would slice the bread at the last minute, so it was fresh and moist. The butter was already softening at room temperature, the jam warming, too. She'd lay it all out on the table, with a few sprigs of lavender in a glass jar. The coffee was on. A jug of iced cucumber-water waited in the fridge.

She lifted a watermelon from the fruit bowl. Steadying it between her hands, she felt the perfect curve, the dense weight as heavy as a human head. Finding a knife, she pressed its cool tip into the skin, pushing deeper, feeling the moment of give when the knife slid easily into the flesh, splitting it open like a red wound, juices leaking. She made a second incision, removing the wedge, which looked like a grinning, bloody smile.

'Morning,' Bella said, emerging from her room in a tiny sundress.

Eleanor's skin tightened; Bella Rossi was the last person she felt like talking to.

Bella glanced beyond her, looking through the open doors onto the terrace. 'Where is everyone?'

'Lexi's doing yoga. Fen is swimming. Robyn's in her room. Ana's walking.'

Bella sank down onto a stool, clearly disappointed that she'd have to make do with Eleanor's company. She yawned, showing the deep opening of her throat, not bothering to cover it with a hand.

'Tired?' Eleanor noted curtly.

'I was up late.' There was a pointedness to the reply, which made Eleanor hesitate. 'You were, too,' Bella added.

Eleanor could feel the press of the watermelon as she held it steady, juice leaking between her fingers. She kept her face blank.

'You had a nightcap with Ana,' Bella said.

Eleanor's spine stiffened as she remembered the trail of wet footprints. 'Thought you'd gone to bed.'

'I'm a light sleeper,' Bella said, eyeing her.

Eleanor stared back.

There was silence.

A warm wind drifted in from the terrace, carrying a briny, almost sulphuric scent of the sea. It smelled odorous, like something was turning in the heat.

Finally, Eleanor shrugged. She wouldn't allow Bella the satisfaction of getting beneath her skin. If she had something to say, let her say it.

She resumed slicing. Funny thing with knives was that one minute they could be a benign kitchen implement, and the next a weapon. The knife itself didn't change, only the intent of the person holding it.

She glanced sideways at Bella, who was picking at a split end. *I could reach out and put this knife in your chest. In one flash. It doesn't even have to be you. It could be anyone. Whoever walks into this kitchen next. That's what I could do.* She wouldn't, of course. That would be crazy. She knew she wouldn't. But the thought alone gave her a little thrilling jolt.

Bella plucked a segment of orange from the waiting platter. She held it between her glossy nails, like a taloned bird carries its prey, then dropped it into her mouth. Eleanor gritted her teeth. Bella sucked her fingers clean, without making a single sound of appreciation. When Eleanor ate, the pleasure of the flavours travelled through her body – a shiver of delight, a squeezing of her shoulders, a murmur in her throat.

As Bella went to take another piece, fingers glistening with saliva, Eleanor couldn't help herself. With a sharp, swift movement, she reached out and slapped the back of Bella's hand.

'Ow!' Bella clutched her hand to her chest.

'Don't you have any manners?'

'You slapped me!'

'I'm preparing breakfast for us all. You should wait.'

Bella glared at her, shocked.

'I just want it to be nice for Lexi,' Eleanor said. 'For everyone.'

Bella slid from her stool. 'You do know,' she said, pausing in the doorway before she left the kitchen, 'that Lexi only invited you on the hen party because Ed begged her to. I imagine she felt sorry for you.' She delivered the bitter little missive with a smile, then sauntered off.

Eleanor stabbed the knife into the remaining flesh of the watermelon, feeling the release as it split apart.

50

Bella

Bella strode out onto the terrace. What was with that slap on the knuckles? Eleanor was as mad as a box of frogs. Was that gin she'd caught on her breath? Did she fuel up before breakfast?

The comment about Lexi's pity invite had been a spiteful retaliation. She was always bitchy on a hangover. Eleanor would probably spit in her breakfast now.

At the far edge of the terrace, Lexi was lying on her yoga mat, arms at her sides, eyes closed. *And people claim yoga is exercise!* Best Lexi absorbed all the good vibes while she could.

Bella's blood simmered with anger on behalf of her best friend. Ana had better keep away from her today, else Bella would be in danger of igniting.

She perched on the terrace wall then, glancing down at the sheer drop onto rock, quickly stood again. Jesus, that vertical fall-away was enough to make anyone nauseous, hangover or not.

She could really use a coffee. Eleanor had the pot on the stove, but she didn't fancy returning to the kitchen to grovel. No, she'd hang around out here, wait for Lexi to finish yoga, then task her with fetching the coffee.

The stone was already beginning to warm underfoot. There was barely a breeze and the air buzzed with insects. In the cove, a pile of driftwood was stacked for tonight's beach fire. Beyond, the sea shimmered, glistening scales wavering beneath a wide, clear sky. Fen's lone figure glided, arms cutting through the crystal-clear water. She made it look effortless.

Despite the blue sky, Bella felt a dark mood rolling closer like a thunder cloud. She was still hurt that Fen had bailed on them last night – and let Bella know by *text!* She could either dwell on the situation, stirring up her own mood until it was darker and spikier, and then confront Fen the moment she swam in, or, Bella thought, experimenting with drawing a calming breath deep into her diaphragm, she could let it go. She could be one of those good, generous people who accepted everyone was human and flawed and made mistakes. Rather than confronting Fen, Bella would go down to the shore and join her for a swim. Yes! That's what she'd do. They needed some time together, just the two of them. See? That's how you turn a thunder mood into sunshine!

She trotted back into the villa to change. *Jesus, the smell of that coffee,* she thought, passing through the kitchen. It was all she could do not to elbow Eleanor aside and glug the scalding liquid straight from the pot. But no, a swim first. Coffee would be her reward.

In the bathroom, she unhooked her damp bikini from the door handle. As she peeled off her dress and wriggled from her underwear, she caught her reflection in the mirror. At first her gaze skated over the planes of her face, checking her hair, her tan, her lipstick, but when she looked closer, she could see the dark shadows beneath her eyes. She blinked, trying to widen them. Maybe she needed more mascara. Or perhaps she should get some of those lash extensions. She fluttered her lashes again, wondering if that would help.

But it wasn't her eyelashes, or the shadows, that were the problem. It was what lay deeper. Her eyes looked flat, dull.

She moved closer, looking right at herself. A voice inside her, quiet and firm, asked: *Who are you?*

She swallowed, finding herself desperate to turn, look away.

She was due on tomorrow. That's what this was. Not a hangover thunder cloud, but a premenstrual hormone hurricane. Had to be. She tried to pull her gaze away, yet even while one part of her brain was intent on dismissing the question, brushing it aside, the other part, somewhere deeper – maybe not even in her brain, but somewhere in her body – was asking her to stay still, to look at herself, to see.

Eyes burning, she faced herself.

Bella felt the sting of tears as her vision began to blur. Images flashed across her thoughts: the squeak of plimsolls along a corridor; the shrill ring of a ward alarm; wide, panicked eyes; mottled lips; a hand clutching a throat.

She blinked. The tears fell onto her cheeks, plump and heavy.

Standing naked in front of the mirror, Bella found herself sobbing.

51

Fen

Fen cut through the water in a front crawl. She kicked hard, breath even and regular.

Nearing the shore, she slowed, lifting her head. Water dripped from her chin as she set her gaze on the salt-white villa high on the clifftop. There. That's where it happened. Nico pinning her to the terrace wall, his insults hot in her ear. She held her gaze steady. Refused to look away.

Last night she'd faced him. Literally stood in front of him and called him out on what he'd done. This morning, she'd woken feeling physically wrung out, as if her skin were bruised, tender. Yet there was also another sensation emerging from somewhere deeper: one of quiet strength, which had nothing to do with how quickly she could tear through the water.

Reaching the shelf of tiny white pebbles, she lowered her feet and waded towards the shore, shaking the sea from her hair.

At her feet, she reached for a piece of gnarled driftwood, tinder-dry. Turning it through her fingers, she lifted the wood to her face, breathed in. Earth and salt and wood. She tossed it on the growing pile ready for tonight's beach fire, then turned towards the villa.

Bella was descending the steps in a bikini and sunglasses, waving at her. Guilt wormed into her chest. She shouldn't have deserted Bella and the others at the taverna, but she hadn't had the capacity to return to the table, explain.

She wondered why she'd not confided in Bella about Nico. Perhaps it was because she'd thought she wouldn't understand: if a man had said those cruel things to Bella, pressed her up against a wall, Bella would've kneed him in the balls and got on with her day.

Bella was a beautiful whirlwind of vibrant, infectious energy, and God, Fen loved spending time with her, she really did. Yet deep down, she also knew that their relationship wasn't working. Doubts had been building for a while, but this hen weekend had solidified them. A leaden feeling settled in her middle: once they were home, they'd need to talk.

'I was just coming to join you! I even put my bikini on damp,' Bella said, plucking at a wet strap. 'Do you want to go back in the sea?'

'Oh, sorry – I've finished,' she said, picking up a towel and knotting it around her waist. Seeing Bella's disappointment, she added, 'Later, though.'

As they climbed the steps to the terrace, Bella slipped her small, warm hand into Fen's – as if sensing that she would need to hold on tightly.

52

Robyn

Robyn scooped rounds of deep-green kiwi, sweet oranges, and jewelled pomegranate seeds into her bowl. My God, the joy of being able to sit and eat breakfast at leisure, not needing to negotiate with a toddler, or reach for a lobbed beaker, or wipe smeared banana from a high-chair tray.

'Thank you,' she said to Eleanor, who was sitting adjacent to her, hair neat beneath a white cotton sun hat. 'This is such a treat.'

Eleanor smiled, pleased.

Fen and Bella emerged on the terrace, taking seats together on the opposite side of the table. Fen looked lighter this morning, the tension smoothed from her brow. She caught Robyn's eye and smiled.

A burst of warmth moved through her chest.

'Anyone seen Ana this morning?' Lexi asked.

'I think she went walking on the cliff path. Probably ringing Luca,' Robyn said.

Pouring a mug of coffee, Bella asked, 'Who's looking after him while she's on holiday? His father?'

Eleanor looked up sharply.

'No, he's not in the picture,' Lexi explained easily. 'Luca's staying with Ana's sister.'

'I see,' Bella said with a strange arch of her brow.

Had Robyn missed something? Growing up, her parents rarely argued, so she'd learned to read tension in its more subtle manifestations: the clenching of a jaw, the stiffening of a spine, a mug set down to punctuate a sentence. It put her on edge, scanning for the first hint of unease. No, she'd rather an argument, get it over and done with and clear the air.

'How was the rest of your night out?' she asked Lexi. 'Sorry to leave early. I was whacked. Too much sun.'

'We went to a couple of bars in the Old Town. Did you get back okay? How are you feeling?'

'Fine. Just needed a good night's sleep.'

'Went straight to bed, then?' Bella asked.

Robyn looked up. Bella was staring at her from behind her sunglasses. 'We had a drink first, then yes, called it a night.'

'A second wind,' Bella said.

'Guess so.'

Bella plucked a piece of fruit from the serving bowl and dropped it into her mouth.

Eleanor glared at her across the table.

What is with everyone?

'How was Ed when you spoke last night?' Robyn asked Lexi brightly. 'I bet you're missing each other.'

Lexi's expression was remote, her thoughts somewhere else. As the sun hit the side of her face, Robyn noticed her skin looked sallow despite the holiday, purplish shadows settled into the sockets of her eyes.

'Lex?'

She glanced at Robyn. Blinked. 'Missing each other? Yes.'

Robyn was reminded of an earlier conversation, Lexi confiding that she wasn't sleeping well, felt anxious. Was it about the pregnancy, or the wedding? She couldn't recall whether Lexi had said. She made a mental note to find a moment to check in with her.

'Still in the mood for a beach fire tonight?' Robyn asked the others enthusiastically, trying to shake the strange atmosphere. 'I was thinking we could take lanterns and blankets down to the bay, plus there's a big cooler in the pantry we could stock with drinks.'

'Sounds great,' Fen said. 'There's plenty of wood set to burn. It'll be blazing all night.'

Bella's gaze travelled to the cove below, eyes glittering. 'Let's make sure it's a memorable end to the hen weekend.'

53

Lexi

After breakfast was finished, Lexi found Eleanor in the narrow courtyard at the back of the villa, hanging tea towels on the washing line. Her movements were careful and precise, strong hands smoothing each towel, straightening the edges. She wondered if it was agony to be out here, forced to celebrate someone else's upcoming wedding.

'Hey,' Lexi said, stepping forward.

Eleanor startled. She adjusted her hat, keeping the glare from her eyes.

Lexi said, 'I was thinking of taking out the rowing boat this morning. Exploring the next bay along. Fancy coming?'

She saw Eleanor's hesitation, the way her eyes slid to the side as if searching for an excuse to refuse. 'I was going to prepare lunch . . .'

'We've not long finished breakfast. Anyway, I'm taking care of that. You've been working too hard on this trip. If you do one more thing in the kitchen, I'm going to have to start paying you. Please, come. There's no wind and it'll be gorgeous and calm.'

A bee thrummed in the bougainvillea that trailed over the wall, a fragrant scent lifting in the heat.

'Yes. Fine.'

Pleased, Lexi took a damp tea towel from the pile and smoothed it over the line. It would be nice for her and Eleanor to spend time together – she worried she'd been neglecting her this weekend. Plus, it would give her a chance to talk about Ed. She wasn't sure what she wanted from Eleanor. Reassurance? To hear Ed was besotted with her? She just knew she needed *something*.

Eleanor turned, staring over her shoulder. Lexi followed the direction of her gaze and saw Ana returning from her walk. She was looking uncertainly between Lexi and Eleanor.

'Nice stroll?' Lexi asked.

'I went up the cliff path to get a signal so I could call Luca.'

'You must be missing him.'

'Can't say it's mutual,' Ana said as she reached them, positioning herself in the shade. 'He was desperate to get me off the phone so he could get to the skate park.'

'Lexi and I are taking the boat out,' Eleanor said, folding her arms across her chest. 'It'll be a nice chance for us to talk.'

Ana's eyes darted across Eleanor's face. There was a light sheen of sweat across her forehead. 'Great,' she said, smiling tightly.

It was strange being the bride-to-be on a hen weekend, Lexi thought. Whenever she entered a room, it felt like everyone was polishing their smile, ready to tell her what a wonderful weekend they were having. 'Is everything okay?'

A fly buzzed in the still air, the scent of warming stone lifting from the villa walls. A gecko watched from the shade, eyes like black glass beads.

Ana looked at Eleanor. 'Couldn't be better.'

~

When we first arrived at the villa and caught sight of the blue rowing boat pulled up on the shore, it seemed so gorgeously quaint, evocative of the perfect Greek holiday we were anticipating.

Strange how that same boat now evokes different memories. The sound of frantic splashing and the panicked scratch of fingernails clawing at the hull. The hot-eyed sting of tears, oars gripped in fists. The scrape of wood against pebbles as two pairs of hands dragged it up the beach in the dark.

54

Eleanor

The blue rowing boat waited on the shore, varnished oars tucked at its sides.

'Ready?' Lexi said, gripping the boat, a casual straw hat keeping the sun from her eyes. A light breeze lifted the hem of her summer dress.

On the count of three, they heaved it towards the shore, the hull dragging across the pebbles. 'Not sure lugging boats while pregnant is on the recommended list,' Eleanor said.

'Probably not,' Lexi said, breathless. 'There!' She wiped the back of her hand across her forehead.

Eleanor wore long shorts, the cotton darkening as she waded into the shallows, and a plain white T-shirt and a cotton hat. She probably looked like she'd dressed for summer camp. She held the boat steady while Lexi climbed in, hooking the hem of her dress in one hand and swinging a leg over the side.

Eleanor followed, clunking her knee on an oar and stumbling in, causing the boat to rock chaotically.

'Sorry, there aren't any life jackets,' Lexi said, picking up the oars. She'd searched the villa on Eleanor's behalf. 'Are you okay being out on the water?'

'It's fine. I'm not intending to fall in.'

Eleanor didn't want to go rowing. It wasn't because she was afraid she couldn't swim. It was the space: too small. Couldn't get off. Far too intense to be sitting opposite someone with nowhere to go. She'd have preferred to be the one rowing; at least it would give her hands something to do. She never knew where to put her hands when she talked. How did other people not think about them? Hers were like these two drunken idiots who kept lurching with overexaggerated movements. She was forever thinking: *My hands! Look what they're doing now!* And then she'd lose the thread of the conversation.

She shoved them under her thighs. There.

'The last time I rowed was when I was a teenager,' Lexi said, dipping the oars into the water, propelling them forwards. 'Bella, Robyn and I would rent these little wooden motorboats and take them downriver, packs of cigarettes stuffed in our bags. We'd cut the engine and drift into the reeds. We'd lie there and smoke and drink and look at the clouds.'

Eleanor felt the boat glide across the surface, picturing the three of them in their teens. She envied Lexi, having that bond. Friends who journeyed with you throughout all the stages of your life.

'Once, we couldn't restart the engine,' Lexi continued, 'so we had to row back. It took us two hours to get upriver. The owner yelled at us for going too far and running down the petrol tank. Bella insisted the engine was faulty and demanded our money back. When the owner refused, she told him exactly what he could do with his boat – and that was the end of our summer on the river!'

Eleanor knew she should respond by laughing or smiling, but she felt no cheer towards Bella.

Lexi looked at her from beneath the rim of her hat. 'I know Bella can come across as a bit . . . feisty, but there's another side to her. She's one of the most caring people I know. Generous, too. Bella would do anything for her friends.'

Friends, yes, Eleanor thought. *But what about the rest of us?* 'Why did you invite me on this hen weekend?'

Lexi blinked, as if surprised by the non-sequitur. 'Because I wanted you to come.'

Eleanor's hands had freed themselves again and her fingers had started scratching her forearm. 'Or because you felt sorry for me?'

Lexi paused from rowing. 'I feel sorry that you've lost Sam. I'd feel terrible for anyone who'd lost their fiancé. But no, that's not why I wanted you to be here. I invited you because we're going to be sisters-in-law. Because I want us to get to know each other. Because we're going to be family.'

It was a good answer and Eleanor was pleased with it.

'Why would you ask me that?' Lexi said.

'Bella said you invited me out of pity.'

Lexi's eyes widened. 'What? I *never* said that to Bella. She had no right to say otherwise.'

Eleanor shrugged. She glanced at the oars hovering above the glimmering sea. 'You're not getting us very far. Want me to have a go now?'

*

The boat skated gently across the surface, a lengthening wake stretching behind them. The visibility was so clear that Eleanor could still see the round white pebbles of the seabed.

She rowed them towards the cliff line, submerged rocks wavering beneath the surface, studded with sea urchins. She was grateful for the light breeze cooling the sweat lining her back.

'Eleanor,' Lexi began. 'I don't want you to think I was being secretive, not telling Ed about the baby. I'd hoped to talk to him before anyone else found out.'

She shrugged. 'I know.'

Lexi pressed the heels of her hands into the wooden seat. 'Do you think he'll be happy?'

A little frown appeared between Lexi's brows as she waited for Eleanor's answer. 'I'm sure he will. He adores you.' There. That was something that was true. God, this boat was tiny. She pulled harder at the oars to keep her mind focused.

'Were the two of you close growing up? I've always envied people with siblings.'

'Have you? Well. There was a three-year age gap between us,' she said, as if that were an answer.

Lexi waited, evidently expecting more. When Eleanor offered nothing further, she asked, 'So, what was Ed like?'

Is she fishing? Perhaps this was why Lexi had invited her out on the boat. She needed to pick her words carefully. Filter. 'He was sporty. On all the teams – football, cricket, rugby. He worked hard. Liked to do well.' Maybe she could just get a CV printed.

'Did he get on well with Sam?'

Tension fizzed down the length of Eleanor's neck. She thought of the two of them in the same room together, the way it made her skin feel too hot, her clothes too tight, like she couldn't get enough oxygen. She ploughed the oars into the water. 'Ed and Sam were very different.'

'I know Ed worries that he can't help, that he isn't doing enough.'

'It isn't a problem you can fix with a credit card.'

Lexi baulked.

Eleanor's filtering clearly needed work. Still, she didn't have the patience for dealing with other people's sensibilities, not when she could still remember being led into a private room in the hospital, told to wait there for the doctor. She had paced, eyes to the door, watching for whoever was coming. Finally, a woman in scrubs entered, her hair pinned back in a low, neat bun. She wore frameless glasses and Eleanor wondered if they slipped down her nose when she operated, and whether contact lenses might be more suitable. The doctor clasped her hands together as she spoke and Eleanor noticed how dry the skin on her knuckles was and decided it must be from all the washing. She was still looking at the cracked skin at the edges of her thumbs, and wondering whether the woman had ever tried using Neutrogena, because Eleanor suffered with dry skin in winter when the studio was cold, and she'd tried just about every hand cream and it was the only one—

'Miss Tollock?' the doctor was saying. 'Do you understand?'

Eleanor had looked up, right into her eyes. 'Sam is dead.'

'Yes. I'm so sorry.'

Later she was told that she could see his body if she wanted to, and she did want that. She needed to see him because this big, terrible thing was happening, and she needed to tell him about it, and hold his hand because that's what she did when everything was too much – she held his hand. But of course his hand felt all wrong – cold, unyielding, not his big bear grip, just a flaccid, empty hand. She kissed the back of it, but it even smelt wrong – antiseptic, sterile – and her lips brushed the bee-sting mark where the IV line had been. Then she'd clamped her teeth around a few hairs. She ground them between her teeth, then swallowed. She couldn't say why she did it. She knew it was odd, but she didn't care. She would have swallowed him whole if she could, because she knew that was the last time she would ever see or touch or be with him.

Now she looked up and found Lexi staring at her expectantly. Had there been a question she'd missed?

She couldn't say any of what she'd been thinking. You don't tell people the ins and outs of death, the same way women don't tell other women the full horrors of childbirth because, what's the point? People will still die. Children will still be born. Let's just say it's hard, and then focus on all the other stuff that happens in between.

Lexi said, 'Ed tries his best. I think it's hard for him to understand fully because he hasn't been through it.'

Eleanor stared directly at Lexi. 'Actually, it's quite simple: it would be like you – right now – dying. And Ed being expected to carry on. That's what it would be like.'

55

Bella

Bella pushed her fingers through the roots of her hair, tousling for added volume. She licked her lips, then sauntered into her bedroom.

Fen was reading on their bed, one arm pillowing her head, the pale hollow of her underarm exposed. The shutters were thrown open, filling the room with light and welcoming in a faint sea breeze.

'Hey,' Bella said, coming to Fen's side and perching on the edge of the bed. 'Want to come float on a lilo with me?'

'Thanks,' Fen said easily, placing down her book, 'but I'm going to stay out of the sun for a little while.'

Bella peered at the cover of Fen's novel. '*A Theatre for Dreamers*. Any good?'

'Yes. It's about this group of bohemian artists and writers who live on a Greek island in the sixties. One of the characters reminds me a little of my aunt.'

'Maybe I could borrow it afterwards? I want to get into reading.'

Fen looked surprised.

'No more scrolling for me. I'm going to become one of those people who whips out a book in every free moment – a doctor's waiting room, a train journey, a queue.' She made a martial-arts-style movement, demonstrating the whipping out of a book.

Fen smiled.

'So, what do you fancy doing for the rest of the day? Pool? Beach? Town? Mountain?'

Fen sat up. 'I'm happy having a quiet one around the villa. Save our energy for the beach fire tonight.'

'Sure.' She reached for Fen's hand, turning her silver thumb ring between her fingers. It was the first piece of jewellery Bella had bought from the boutique, knowing it would look sexy as hell on Fen. 'Our last day.'

Fen drew back her hand, pushing it through her hair.

Bella felt the cold, hollowing sensation of Fen withdrawing. They both knew something had changed during the argument at the airport. Bella had promised herself that she wouldn't bring it up during the hen weekend. Her strategy was to be so much fun, such magnetic company, that Fen could do nothing but love her. That was the plan – and yet now, she found herself asking, 'What's going on? Is everything okay?' Her voice seemed to shrink. 'Last night you . . . you just left me at the taverna.'

Fen winced. 'I know. I'm sorry. That wasn't fair.' Her gaze drifted to the window. 'There are some difficult memories for me out here. I . . . I saw someone at the taverna who I needed to face.'

'What? Who?' Bella said, straightening, an instant flame of protectiveness lighting in her chest.

'A waiter called Nico. It's not important. He's not important—'

'What did he do?'

'Look, I—'

'I knew something was off! You haven't been yourself. Oh,
babe, I'm sorry, I should've realised something was going
on!' A shot of relief flooded her body. The problem wasn't
their relationship! It was this waiter! A bloody waiter! 'Tell
me, what did this arsehole do?'

'I'm sorry, but I'd rather not go into it. It's over with now.
I just wanted you to know that's why I went home early.'

'With Robyn.' Her name slipped out like a bitter pip.

'Yes. With Robyn.'

'Why didn't you talk to me? I should've been the one who
took you back to the villa.' *Where the hell is fun, magnetic
Bella?*

'It's Lexi's hen. I didn't want to spoil the night. You're the
maid of honour – you needed to stay out with Lexi.'

Outside there was a splash as someone dived into the pool.
Bella wanted to be down there, having fun, swimming with
Fen. 'Do you regret coming on the hen weekend?'

Fen thought for a moment, then shook her head. 'No.'

Bella reached again for Fen's hands, interlacing her fingers
through them. Fen let her – but didn't respond to the intimacy.

Looking down at their joined hands, Bella found herself
saying, 'It's more than just the waiter, isn't it? It's us.'

Fen got to her feet, hands separating from Bella's. She placed
her book on the bedside table, then pushed her hands into
the pockets of her shorts. 'We should just enjoy the last day—'

'You're pulling away. You've barely been able to look at
me all weekend.'

'That's not true.'

But it was. 'When we get back, it's over, isn't it? You're going to break up with me.'

Fen kept her eyes lowered. 'Let's talk about it when we're home.'

Bella could see it all right there in Fen's pained expression. Her stomach lurched. Her hands began to tremble. 'Please. Just say it. Twenty-four hours won't make any difference. It's worse, being here with you but already feeling that distance. Be straight with me, Fen, otherwise we're both just pretending. I'm pretending to be okay – and you're pretending that you still care about me.'

Finally, Fen lifted her gaze, looked right at her. Those beautiful, bright green eyes pinned on Bella.

Bella squared her shoulders. Swallowed. 'So. Are you breaking up with me?'

Fen's face creased with emotion, eyes swimming with tears as she nodded. 'I'm so sorry . . . I just . . . I think we're so different . . . and . . .'

Bella's head shook fiercely. 'Our differences – those are what make us work!' Heat flooded her cheeks. 'Say what you really mean! This is nothing to do with how different we are. It's because . . .' Her throat constricted, her voice becoming strangled. 'It's because of the conversation at the airport, isn't it? What I did?'

The room fell silent. Bella felt pressure building at her temples, in her sinuses.

Outside, the distant sound of laughter drifted up from the pool.

'It's not what you did,' Fen replied. 'It's that you lied to me. It made me realise that I don't really know you, Bella. You keep so much of yourself locked up.'

Blood roared in her ears. 'I'm sorry. I . . . I was scared you wouldn't love me if I told you . . .' Her voice cracked. 'We can talk about it though, can't we? Work through it . . .'

Fen looked at her sadly. 'I'm sorry, but I don't think things have been right for a while. I just . . . didn't see it clearly before.'

Bella clamped both hands to her chest. 'So this is it. You're breaking up with me?'

'I'm so sorry,' Fen said, head shaking, fingertips touching in prayer. 'This shouldn't have happened out here. But, yes. I am.'

Bella's eyes filled instantly with hot tears. 'Wow. There it is.'

'I want you to know that I really do care about—'

'Don't!' Bella held up both hands. She could feel a racking sob moving through her chest, surging into her throat. She couldn't do this. She needed to get out. Yanking down her sunglasses, she stumbled towards the door, her whole body shaking.

She burst from the room, face collapsing, knowing she'd ruined the one bright, beautiful thing she had left.

56

Robyn

Robyn lengthened her strides, enjoying the force of her heels striking the hard, dusty trail. The heat was fierce, splintering the dry earth and lifting the scent of rosemary and wild thyme.

She experimented with pumping her arms, raising her chin a fraction. A pleasing layer of sweat was building at the waistband of her shorts. She wanted to fit in a final walk, have some space to think, breathe. It was quiet out here, alone, just the light hush of a breeze through thin cypress trees and the occasional, distant bleating of a mountain goat.

She startled at the sound of her mobile ringing. Pulling it from her pocket, she saw her parents' number.

'Hello?'

At first there was silence. Then she heard her mother whispering encouragingly in the background. 'Go on, Jack!'

'Mama? Hello! Mama!'

Her heart contracted. 'Oh, baby. Jack! I miss you! Are you having a lovely time with Nana and Grampie?'

More whispering: 'Tell Mummy about the treasure map. What you found at the beach.'

'Tresher! Tresher!'

Robyn smiled. 'Did you find treasure, baby?'

There was no answer, only the pad of feet.

'He's gone to fetch it,' her mother explained. 'It's over there, Jack. By the basket! Yes, that's it!'

Robyn settled herself onto a sun-warmed rock at the side of the path. Closing her eyes, she pictured them all; her parents sitting on the sofa with the Saturday papers spread across the coffee table, the dog curled on the floor in a splash of sunlight, and then Jack, perhaps kneeling by the toy garage, his cars parked in neat formations. Robyn's father never tired of raising and lowering the car lift, as Jack didn't yet have the dexterity for the winch. God, Jack's pudgy little hands. She wanted to press them to her lips this very moment, to pull him onto her lap, kiss the nape of his neck.

She often wondered how a parent's love shifts and readjusts constantly: right now, all she wanted was to hold Jack, carry him, kiss him, stroke him. But as he grew older – became a teenager – would that urge naturally leave, or is it always a battle to stop yourself reaching for them? Did her own parents feel that about her, even now?

'He's showing you the treasure,' her mother said. 'Lovely gold coins, aren't they, Jack?'

'Chocolate tresher!'

'Did you find chocolate—' Robyn began.

'For me? Chocolate, for me?'

Robyn's mother sighed fondly. 'Go on, then. Just a few. Ask Grampie to unwrap them.'

Her mother must have removed the speaker setting as she was close to the phone now and Robyn caught her footsteps across the tiled kitchen floor. 'Sorry, darling. I think that's that.'

'God, I miss him,' Robyn said, realising she was ready to go home now.

'How's Greece?'

Robyn looked up over the huge, sweeping vista, the sea shimmering in the distance. 'It's so beautiful here. The villa is amazing – it has a private beach and there are no other properties for miles. Right now, I'm on a mountain trail and Mum, there's no one in sight. It's incredible.'

'Your dad and I could use a break somewhere like that.'

'Last night I slept for ten hours straight. I can't even remember when that last happened.'

'Lucky for some. Jack was in our bed by five thirty.'

'Oh, sorry,' she apologised instinctively. Her mother always did this, made Robyn feel guilty when she was having a good time. It would be nice if, just for once, she could celebrate Robyn's happiness. 'It's been really good for me coming here.'

'Enjoy it while it lasts because you're going to be busy when you get back.' A pause. 'You've had some post.'

'Oh?'

'From the solicitors. I think it's your divorce papers.'

Her stomach fell. She didn't want to think about her divorce out here. She wanted to feel the soaring freedom of the mountain air, the expanse of the horizon. She wanted to feel like the old Robyn. The memory of her was intoxicating – glimpsed like a fleck of something lost, sparkling in the sand. She just needed to dig, to go a little deeper, to pull it out into the light and remember.

'I'll deal with that when I'm home.' *Can't I just enjoy this?*

'Your father and I were talking . . .'

This call was never about Jack's treasure, Robyn realised, tipping back her head.

'. . . and we think you need to have a long, hard think about whether this really is the right thing for Jack.'

Her mouth fell open. 'For Jack? What does that even mean?'

'Do you want him growing up in a single-parent family?' her mother asked, lowering her voice as if there was something shameful about the very notion of it.

'I want Jack growing up with a happy mother. Have you forgotten that Bill *cheated* on me?'

'Robyn, he's not the first man to make a mistake.'

'It wasn't a mistake! He was sleeping with other women before we even got married, for God's sake!'

'Don't use that tone with me.' Her mother's voice was calm as she said, 'I know he hurt you, but he has apologised and wants to try again.'

Yes, he'd apologised, and yes he'd asked her to come back – but only because his current relationship was crumbling.

Her mother went on. 'I want you to be sure you're not cutting off your nose to spite your face. Bill isn't perfect, but he's a good man.'

'I don't love him.'

I never loved him, she realised, in a startling flash of perfect clarity.

I. Never. Loved. Him.

The knowledge sat there, echoing in the quiet chamber of her mind. She had never loved her husband. When she'd discovered he'd cheated on her, she'd felt angry and deceived, but she hadn't felt a bone-shattering loss. She'd felt indignant because he'd broken a promise. She'd felt humiliated. Never heartbroken.

I never loved him.

She had an overwhelming desire to say those words aloud, see how they fit. 'I never loved him, Mum,' she whispered.

'What did you say?'

She took a breath. 'I never loved Bill.'

'Don't be silly! You married him.'

Silly.

Robyn was always *silly* if she felt anything that was not what her mother expected her to feel. It reduced her emotions, made her tidy them up neatly and store them away.

'I never loved him,' she repeated, louder, firmly.

So why did I marry him? she wondered now. Because they'd been together for three years and she was getting to that age when women start marrying? Because he ticked all the boxes that she thought needed ticking: handsome, kind, good career prospects? Because he'd asked her? Because she didn't want to look at what she would do, who she would be, if she said no?

'Your father and I just wanted to check that you were sure the divorce was the right thing. You're telling us it is, so it is.'

Her mother couldn't abide confrontation. She might be the first to stick the knife in, but she'd pull it out so swiftly that you'd only realise later you were bleeding. Right now, Robyn could feel the hot drip of blood, could feel anger bubbling to the surface. 'Why did you call to tell me about the divorce papers? It could've waited until I'm home,' she said, flicking a black ant from her shin.

'I saw the envelope on the side and it popped into my head. I'm sorry, I didn't realise you'd be so sensitive.'

Her teeth clenched. She hated it when her mother masked an insult by beginning it with an apology. Robyn would not be made to feel guilty. 'I'm not sensitive. I'm on holiday. I wanted to enjoy a few days with my friends. Couldn't you have let me have that?'

'Of course we want you to enjoy yourself.'

Then why are you making me feel so guilty? Or maybe it wasn't them at all. Maybe Robyn was just an expert in guilt. She felt guilty for getting a divorce. Guilty for moving back in with her parents. Guilty for going to work. Guilty for taking a holiday. Guilty for—

She silenced the next thought.

Her mother's voice was an octave higher. 'It might have been nice if you'd asked us how *we* are. It's tiring, you know, at our age, looking after Jack.'

'You said you wanted to look after him. We talked about it! He could've stayed at Bill's, but you said—'

'All I'm saying,' her mother interrupted, in her I'm-being-incredibly-calm voice, 'is a "thank you" wouldn't go amiss.'

Robyn could feel the tendons in her neck seething with tension. She should just say thank you, end the call. It would be forgotten by the time she was home. They were always so polite. So awfully, awfully polite. No one in her household swore or shouted or raged. They just gently, carefully, put their message across.

'Thank you,' Robyn managed.

'You're welcome,' she said. 'You know we love him. We love you.'

She swallowed down whatever was simmering inside her. 'I know.' And she did know. Her mother and father were always telling her how proud they were, that they loved her. What was Robyn's problem? 'Sorry,' she said, with feeling this time. 'I didn't mean to be so waspish.'

'Don't you worry,' her mother said, a smile returning to

her voice. 'Reminds me of teenage Robyn. You always get a bit like this when you're with Lexi and Bella.'

'Like what?'

'Feisty.'

'Do I?'

Her mother probably meant it as a criticism, but Robyn saw it as another glimpse of glitter in the sand. 'I like how I am when I'm with my friends. It reminds me of who I really am. Maybe I've not been feisty enough for a long time.'

'You're a mother now, Robyn.'

'I am, and I love being Jack's mother. But that's not all I am.'

'Of course it isn't. You have a career and friends. And that's right.'

'But this,' she said, standing, 'being away – I need this, Mum. I'm hiking again. Laughing. Diving into water holes.'

'Good for you. It's a holiday. But life isn't like that when you're home.'

'Why?' she asked, moving towards the edge of the cliff, gazing down at the water below.

'You've got responsibilities. We'd all like to be cavorting about in the sunshine—'

'Then why aren't you? You're retired. You've got money. What's stopping you? You could rent a villa and come to places like this. You can do what you want, Mum.'

'Your father wouldn't—'

'What *you* want.'

'*We* want the same things.'

There was a long, weighted pause.

Then her mother's voice was a low whisper, close to the phone. 'Have you had a bump to your head?'

Robyn froze.

Those words. She knew exactly what they meant, what her mother was referring to. Her thoughts pinwheeled back years and years, to when she was eighteen years old, waking in her bedroom, her body curled into the groove of another. She'd seen her bedroom door was open a crack, when she was sure she'd closed it. *She knew.*

She had slipped from the bed, gone downstairs. Her mother was standing at the sink, her stony-faced expression reflected in the kitchen window. Robyn began telling her about the accident the night before, the hours spent in A&E. She pulled her hair apart and showed her the glued section of her scalp.

'A bump like that can make you do . . . strange things.' Her mother had looked her in the eye. 'I'm glad you're feeling yourself again this morning.'

Now Robyn felt her voice grow very cool. 'There's no fucking bump. I'm thinking clearly. More clearly than I have in a long time.'

'Don't use that language.'

'I'm a grown woman and I can say what the fuck I like.' Then she hung up.

57

Lexi

When Lexi and Eleanor rowed to shore, Robyn was sitting on the beach, arms hooked over her knees, shoulders rounded.

Lexi lifted her sunglasses. *Is Robyn crying?*

The moment they beached, Lexi went to her. 'Robyn?' she asked, crouching on the warm pebbles. 'What's happened?'

Eleanor looked between the two friends and said something about needing shade before making for the villa.

'I've just told my mum that I'm a grown woman and I can say what the fuck I like.'

'Robyn Davies – about time!' Lexi laughed.

'I've never sworn at my mum.' Robyn looked mortified – and a little elated. 'She tells me off for saying *knackered*.'

'You know I adore your parents, but they toe a pretty straight line.'

She nodded. 'Maybe it won't hurt to show them not every path goes in the same direction as theirs.'

'Exactly!' Lexi hugged her.

'God, I've missed you,' Robyn said, face pressed against Lexi's. 'I want you in my life more.'

'Me too.'

When they let go, Lexi sat beside her, the two of them looking out over the calm water.

'You know what else I want?' Robyn said. 'I want to be able to do this – come away more, remember the old me. I want to have time to hike, get outdoors, be with my friends.' She paused. 'Do I want too much? Is that the problem? That our generation of women, we want everything? The job, the baby, the adventure, love . . .'

'It's not the wanting that's the problem. It's the permission-seeking.' Lexi scooped up a handful of pebbles, rolling their smooth warmth in her palms. 'We're always doing things because we think we should, or because it's the right thing.'

'Not you. You never did. You've always been brave. Wild.'

Lexi let the pebbles fall through the sieve of her fingers. 'I've not been wild in the way you mean: *free*. I just partied too hard. That wasn't being wild, it was hiding.'

Robyn's brow furrowed.

'All that stuff in my twenties – the drinking, the drugs, the sex, the parties – they were just fillers, numbing all the things I didn't want to look at.'

'You were unhappy?'

'For a long time.'

Robyn blinked. 'I'm so sorry. I didn't realise. I . . .'

'Don't be sorry. I hid it well. I'm pretty good at that.' Lexi smiled, showing Robyn it was okay. She had *wanted* everyone to think she was happy, living her best life, because she needed to believe it, too. 'I enjoyed dancing, but the lifestyle that came with it wasn't good for me. I didn't see that for a long time. If I hadn't fractured my tibia, I'd probably still be doing it now.' Lexi had always let life buffet her in one direction and then another, never plotting her own course.

Robyn said, 'Isn't it strange how sometimes the worst things that happen to us end up being the best.'

'You're right.' She'd sunk into a dark place after the injury, losing all sense of purpose. 'You were the one who suggested giving yoga a try.'

'Only to stay supple while you were rehabilitating. I didn't know you were going to retrain and become an instructor!'

'I remember going to that first class thinking I'd hate it. Too slow, too much *om*, as Bella would say.'

'But you loved it.'

'The teacher said something that really resonated. He said, *Yoga isn't a performance. It's only for you.* Dancing was always a performance. My whole career was about imagining how the audience would see me. But yoga is the opposite. It's only for you. It took time to really understand that. You know what I'm like – I wanted to be the best, bend the furthest, hold the posture for the longest.'

Robyn laughed.

'Then I started taking a daytime class, and the other people were mostly retirees. I think it helped me lose my inhibitions about how I looked, or whether I was doing it right. It was just me and the mat.'

'I've never heard you say that before.'

'You know the pose at the end, Savasana, when you lie still? That's my most challenging posture. The first few months, I'd lie there thinking about how hungry I was, or how my skin itched, or I wanted to fart, or what I'd watch when I got home.'

Robyn laughed again.

'But then slowly, I guess my thoughts began to quieten a little, long enough for me to start following my breath, being still. It's liberating, Robyn. Doing something for you. Not for other people. Not for an audience – whether that's a paid audience in a dance show, or your family, or your friends, or society, or whoever it is you decide you are performing for.' She paused. She looked closely at Robyn. 'Maybe we all need to stop trying to meet everyone else's expectations – and just meet our own.'

'Thank you,' Robyn said with feeling. 'That's exactly what I needed to hear. Hey, and Lex? For the record, I'm really pleased that you're happy now. That you found yoga.'

Lexi smiled.

'And found Ed.'

She kept smiling. Made sure she did.

Sun flared from the whitewashed steps as they climbed towards the villa. A wave of tiredness rolled over Lexi. Her head felt busy, unsettled; she wanted to retreat to her room, alone. Think.

'There you both are!' Bella said, raising her head from the sun lounger, oversized sunglasses balanced on her nose. 'Come! Sit with me! I've been on my own all morning. I have drinks!' She reached down to raise a jug filled with something alcoholic.

Lexi felt herself quietly groan. All she wanted right now was some time alone, but she knew Bella would feel neglected if she didn't join her. 'Sure,' she smiled, then opened the sun umbrella on the lounger beside Bella's. Robyn disappeared into the villa saying she'd fetch them drinks.

Bella topped up her own glass, giggling as it spilled over the side. She was drunk, Lexi realised. Course she was. Her smile got that bit bigger and brighter, and there was a loosening of her movements, something more expansive.

All those nights they'd got ready together in one of their bedrooms, music playing, make-up tumbled across the carpet, applying thick flicks of liquid eyeliner, the burned-hair scent of their straighteners mixed with hairspray. She could almost taste the cheap slide of lipstick and vodka. There were moments, so many, that were strung through with gold. She didn't regret that time – and yet, she couldn't help wondering why, in all those nights out, she'd never once turned to Bella and said, *You know what, I don't want this. I'm sad all the time. Something feels wrong inside me.*

Why hadn't she? Because she'd assumed Bella would've said, 'I've got just the solution,' and produced a bottle of spirits or pack of pills with a magician's flourish. But as she looked at Bella now, she wondered, *Maybe you're not happy. Maybe you don't know how to tell me.*

She squeezed Bella's hands and said, 'Babe, is everything okay?'

'Absolutely fan-fucking-tastic! Fen and I have just broken up!'

Robyn, returning with the drinks, halted. 'Oh, Bella!'

Bella laughed. 'It's fine! Relax! We're both cool about it.'

Lexi said, 'I'm so sorry—'

'Nope. We're not doing pity. Or break-up therapy. It's the last day of the hen weekend. All I want to do is have a good time!' She raised her glass. 'Understood?'

Robyn and Lexi exchanged glances. 'Understood.'

They sipped their drinks in silence.

'Eleanor!' Bella called moments later, seeing her emerge onto the terrace to clear glasses. 'What is on the menu later?'

'Bella!' Lexi hissed. 'Eleanor, join us for a drink?'

'No, thanks,' she said, her gaze flicking coolly to Bella, before she returned inside the villa.

Lexi remembered what Eleanor had said out on the water. 'You told Eleanor I only invited her on the hen do because I feel sorry for her.'

Bella shrugged. 'Well, you do, don't you?'

'I wanted to get to know her better. We're going to be sisters-in-law. You should make more of an effort with her. She's had a rough time.'

'Yeah, I know, you said. Her boyfriend died.' Her breath smelt alcoholic as she stage-whispered, 'Have you checked she didn't bump him off?'

'Bella!' Robyn said.

'What? There's something creepy about her, you've got to admit.'

Lexi stood. She knew Bella was hurting over the break-up, but it didn't excuse cruelness.

'I'm only messing,' Bella said, rising to her feet and sauntering towards the pool. She slinked down the steps, giving a shiver as the cool water met her skin.

'It wasn't her boyfriend who died,' Lexi said as she passed the poolside. 'He was her fiancé – and they should've been celebrating their first wedding anniversary in a few weeks, so try to be nice.'

But Bella had already dived under, her body a shimmering vision beneath the surface.

~

We wanted the last night of the holiday to be memorable.

We pictured ourselves partying at the hem of the ocean beneath a blanket of stars, wood smoke in our hair and alcohol warm in our throats. Looking back – even knowing what happened – there were some beautiful moments that evening, happy ones, the six of us, together.

It's just they get forgotten, buried beneath the darker memories: the crack of a hand across a cheek, swift and violent; a blood-red wisp of fabric falling through the night; the urgent screech of sirens echoing off the dark mountainside. And all the while, the fire ablaze on the shore.

58

Fen

That evening, Fen knelt on the beach, stones pressing against her bare knees. She thumbed a lighter, holding it to the scrunched newspaper nestled beneath a tepee of driftwood. After a few seconds, the paper caught, flames licking at the smallest twigs. Leaning closer, she blew into the fire, feeding the heat with oxygen, watching the flames stretch and grow.

'Fire starter,' Eleanor said, sitting nearby, a bottle of beer between her knees.

Fen reached for her beer, twisted the cap free, and stretched across to clink it against Eleanor's. 'Cheers.'

The night gathered close, the air smelling of salt and wood smoke.

They'd amassed a good pile of tinder-dry wood, enough to keep the beach fire stoked long into the night. Eleanor had dotted lanterns around the beach and laid blankets and cushions around the fire, while Fen had hauled down a cooler of drinks and set a speaker on top. Now a chilled playlist was washing across the cove.

Fen had enjoyed setting this up with Eleanor. Plus, it had given her something to do: she'd been trying to keep a low profile all afternoon, staying out of Bella's way. She'd taken a long walk in the solitude of the mountains and been content to sit in the shade, watching a lizard bask in a streak of sun, while birds dusted their beaks through the dry earth in search of insects.

When she'd finally returned to the villa, she'd found Bella sitting beside an emptied cocktail jug tide-lined with browning mint, and a finished bottle of Prosecco bobbing in a bucket of melted ice. She'd wanted to go to her, check she was okay, but Bella had hooked her sunglasses on and snapped her head in the other direction.

Fen understood. Bella was barely holding herself together. She needed to get through the hen weekend. Talking, unpiecing things – all of that was for later. Even a shard of kindness could crack open everything she was desperate to hold in.

'The final night of the hen weekend,' Eleanor said, picking up a pebble and turning it through her fingers. 'Are you pleased to be going home?'

Fen thought about her answer. Returning to Aegos had been far harder than she'd anticipated – and coupled with the break-up, she felt emotionally wrung out. 'I am. Maybe this sounds odd, but I'm looking forward to getting back to work.' She missed her little studio with its family of indoor plants. It was a space she'd created, tended, loved. The rent was more than she could really afford, but she liked being able to walk to the beach on her lunch break, or drink coffee in the sunshine at a pavement table opposite the studio. 'How about you? Will you be pleased to get home?'

Eleanor's voice was flat as she said, 'Home to what?' She launched the pebble into the sea. 'Sometimes I like imagining what I'd be doing in a parallel universe, if things had worked out differently.'

Fen nodded. 'Tell me. I want to hear. What would you have been doing today – Saturday – if Sam were alive?'

Eleanor turned to face her. 'Thank you – for remembering his name. For saying it. *Sam*. People never say his name.' She smiled. 'Saturday was always table tennis day for Sam.'

'Table tennis?'

'Think of how passionate people are about, say, football. Sam felt that way about table tennis. It was like he was a different person when he played. At home he could be sedentary – yet playing table tennis he was so light and quick on his feet. The *Ping-Pong Ninja*, I called him.'

Fen grinned. 'I love that.'

'Sam used to run table-tennis classes at this retirement home at the end of our road. Every Saturday. Never charged. Just a volunteer thing. Some weekends I went with him – and wow, these men and women, they *adored* Sam. He'd remember everything about them, asking how someone's daughter in Spain was getting on with her house renovations, or whether a grandchild had passed their mocks, or whether Marley the cat ever came back from the vet's. Sam remembered it all because people were important to him.'

'He sounds wonderful,' Fen said, pleased by the glimmer of light that returned to Eleanor's eyes as she talked about Sam. 'Do you ever visit the retirement home now?'

She shook her head. 'I know I could still go. I could sit with them, talk, play table tennis, but . . . it's too hard.

Wouldn't be the same without him.' She watched the flames. 'That's how my whole life feels: like nothing will ever be the same without him.'

High up at the villa, a screech of laughter cut across the night: Bella. The sound felt abrasive, echoing down the solid shoulders of the cliffs.

Eleanor flinched.

'I'm sorry,' Fen said, not sure whether she was sorry for the interruption of laughter, for Eleanor's loss, or for not being able to make any of this better.

'When I was younger, I never thought I'd get married,' Eleanor said, voice lowered. 'Couldn't picture it. Couldn't see me in a white dress, walking down an aisle in front of a crowd of people. And then I met Sam – and, foolishly, I let myself believe it was all going to happen. A wedding. A home. Maybe even children.' She shook her head. 'But I never made it down the aisle. There was no fairy tale, after all.'

Fen was aware of movement as the other hens began to descend the terrace steps, lanterns in hands, voices charged and bright. In another minute they'd be upon them.

Eleanor had turned her gaze towards the villa, too. She silently watched the procession of hens, led by Lexi, who was wearing a crown of flowers.

'Still, it'll be different for Lexi and Ed,' Eleanor said, her expression unreadable. 'They'll get their fairy tale.'

59

Ana

Lexi led the way, a lantern dangling from her hand as she descended the stone steps, barefoot. Bella and Robyn followed, their voices rising and falling, punctuated by bursts of laughter. Drifts of their perfume infused the salted night.

The cove was lit by the glow of the beach fire, orange sparks quivering. The surrounding cliffs shouldered together, eerie in the light-leached shadows.

Ana's feet met the warm give of pebbles. The intensity of the day's heat hadn't abated, and the air felt thick with it. She moved towards the flames where the women gathered, drinks being pulled from an ice chest and passed around, bottles clinking. Fen handed her a beer, and Ana twisted the lid free, drinking deeply, cool bubbles fizzing in her throat.

'Here we go, people!' Bella hollered, commandeering the playlist and dialling up the volume, while Fen watched silently. Ana could feel the bass thumping in her chest.

Robyn uncorked a bottle of Prosecco, a stream of bubbles pouring silver in the moonlight. The flames licked higher as the evening unspooled, moods loosening.

Beneath the bursts of laughter and pounding music, she felt the impending sense that the celebrations were off-kilter, sparks of tension crackling in the moonlit dark. Eleanor was standing on the fringe of the shore, gaze lost to the sea. Bella whirled alone to the music, hair swaying at her back. Lexi watched, a fingertip soothing the clavicle of her throat. Robyn and Fen stood close, cinders swirling towards them.

Someone pointed a phone camera at Ana. She raised a hand to block her face, but not before the brilliant white flash blinded her. Distorted white images imprinted behind her eyelids. When her vision finally resettled, she found Bella staring at her, eyes narrowed, before she spun away, weaving towards Lexi.

Smoke filled her throat and she took a wary step back from the flames. Ana wished she were anywhere but here. She wanted her London flat. The familiarity of the street beyond. Luca. She'd been foolish to allow herself to sink into the weekend, lowering her guard, feeling the joy of being part of a group that was never hers.

She turned, staring up at the empty villa. It stood in darkness on the cliff edge, watchful. She wouldn't go back there alone to wait in the heavy silence. Moving instead towards the light of the fire, she settled herself on a thick blanket. One more night and then it'd be over.

Lexi joined her, sitting cross-legged, the crown of white flowers, woven by Robyn, glowing ethereally. The flames blazed, casting changing shadows across her face. As she studied Lexi's profile, a dark-shelled insect emerged from behind a petal. Black legs crawled slowly into Lexi's hairline.

Instinctively, Ana reached out, knocking the bug away. Her nail caught on one of the flower heads, tearing it.

Lexi startled as loose petals drifted like ash to the ground.

'There was an insect,' Ana explained, drawing back.

Lexi touched a hand to her slipping crown.

'It's gone.'

Lexi looked uncertain, her gaze searching the ground between them, but there was no sign of the insect.

The fire hissed.

'Our last night,' Lexi said eventually.

Yes, Ana thought. *It really is.*

Because everything was about to change.

60

Robyn

Robyn bent unsteadily towards the speaker and turned up the volume.

Across the fire, Bella whooped.

The hem of Robyn's summer dress skimmed her thighs as she moved her hips to the beat. Damn, it felt good to dance, to sway, to feel. She tipped back her head, looking up at the night sky.

Yep, definitely drunk. She giggled. This – this was exactly what she was supposed to be doing. She was at a hen party. She was child-free. She wouldn't be woken at six a.m. by Jack parking a toy car on her forehead. She lifted her beer to her lips and then laughed because the bottle was already empty. She had an urge to launch it into the sea just for the hell of it. But didn't.

Clearly not drunk enough.

Robyn wandered towards the cool box, tiny pebbles

sticking to the soles of her feet. She hooked out another beer, snapped off the lid, and took a long drink. It was cold and pleasantly yeasty and she thought of her ex-husband and how, when they first met, he used to like it when she'd drink beers straight from the bottle. But then when they were married, he'd reminded her – politely – to use a glass.

She let the bottle clink against her teeth as she swallowed. The track changed. 'Rehab'! She loved this one. Robyn had been at Glastonbury years ago when Amy Winehouse played the Pyramid Stage, Robyn dancing in the heart of the crowd, moving and rocking as if they were all part of some huge writhing beast. That's how music could make you feel, wasn't it? Alive and elemental. She needed more music in her life.

The others were sitting around the warming glow of the fire, Fen feeding more wood into the flames. Lexi had a red cashmere wrap draped over her shoulders, long legs stretched towards the fire. Bella danced towards her, snaking low, hair trailing down her back. She swung her hips, reaching a hand towards Lexi, who smiled and mouthed something like, *Later*, then carried on talking to Ana. Bella pouted as she danced on, twisting her hands into the air.

Robyn turned away, only wanting music and the warmth of the night against her skin. The sky was sprayed with stars. Smoke curled into the breathing night.

She heard a *whoop!* and turned to see Bella moving towards the shallows, peeling off her dress and tossing it onto the shore. Course Bella would initiate the skinny-dipping! She unclipped her bra and twirled it around a finger, then flung it towards the beach. Her breasts were full and high, pale in the moonlight from her tan lines. It seemed miraculous to see breasts so real, so unmarked by pregnancy and breastfeeding.

She felt the tug of nostalgia for their teen years, those wild nights with Lexi and Bella, Robyn always feeling like she had to hold herself back – that someone needed to, otherwise things might go too far.

'Robyn!' Bella called above the music. 'Come swimming!'

'I'll watch!' she shouted back.

'Course you will.'

The edge to the remark caught her off guard. She turned to see if anyone had noticed, but the others were still talking around the fire.

Bella wriggled out of her thong, then sashayed into the water, squealing at the cold. She dipped briefly beneath the surface, then rose again, dark hair slick against her scalp. She howled with delight, then rolled onto her back, arms wide.

Bella Rossi. They used to be so close, once.

Lexi had asked what created the distance between them. Robyn could've cited so many things: the hurt she felt when Bella didn't invite her to Ibiza; the tears she sobbed when Bella blanked her in Circle Club; that she didn't send a card when Jack was born, or visit until he was six months old. There were so many small moments, cuts and nicks to their friendship, but the root of it went far deeper.

She remembered the night. Would always remember.

They were celebrating the end of sixth form and their friend, Andy Chrisler, threw a house party. He was the only boy in their school whose parents had a swimming pool. It all felt so Californian – the summer evening, the fancy pool, the parents away for the night. Boys in boardshorts swam in the pool, while the bikini-clad girls gathered around the edges, sucking in their stomachs and pushing out their chests. It hadn't taken long for them all to get in the water together – a bunch of seventeen- and eighteen-year-olds knowing that their school days were done and nothing but the big wide world waited for them.

Robyn felt differently. To her, the long summer stretched like a void, a marker-less expanse of time filled only with the quiet sorrow that clung to her house. Her brother had been dead for four months by then. It amazed her that they no longer specified the time in days or even weeks, but months. He'd been gone from their lives for *months*. It didn't feel possible. She still rushed her showers, waiting to hear the rap of his knuckles on the bathroom door, telling her to hurry, or she'd listen for his loping footsteps as he took the stairs two at a time. She missed the way he'd stand in the doorway of her bedroom when she had friends over, his eyes lingering a beat too long on Lexi. She missed the easy way he'd tease their parents over dinner, his quick banter lightening everyone's moods.

So Robyn had stood on the side of the pool, watching as the other boys – who were still alive, still had hearts beating in their hairless chests – coaxed the girls to ride on their shoulders.

Thomas, a handsome boy from her English Lit class, called to Lexi, 'Jump on!' He'd dived down, ducking his head beneath Lexi's legs, then rising up with her like a prize on his shoulders. Her body dripped with water, skin golden, limbs long. Thomas held onto her smooth calves and Robyn had looked at them both, wishing it were her brother. That he could have this moment in the pool.

'Robyn! Get on!' Bella had called from the water. 'We can take down Lexi!'

'You can't lift me,' Robyn protested.

'Small but deadly, remember? Climb on!'

Robyn moved to the pool edge, climbing carefully onto Bella's wet shoulders. She was pleased she wasn't wrapping her legs around one of the boys as she had goosebumps, which made her leg hair feel like iron filings.

Bella gripped her hands around Robyn's calves as they squared up to Lexi and Thomas. Eye to eye, Lexi and Robyn grinned as they half-heartedly fought, each lacking the competitive spirit to bring the other down.

Bella had other ideas. Letting go of Robyn, she used both hands to shove Thomas square in the chest. He staggered back, but it was Robyn who was left unbalanced. She felt her thighs, slick with water and sunscreen, slipping. There was nothing to hold on to and she heard herself scream as she went over backwards. She saw the concrete lip of the pool coming towards her, unstoppable. Felt the crack of her skull connecting with it, followed by darkness.

Now Robyn looked towards the sea, her gaze searching out Bella.

She scanned the water, eyes travelling from one side of the bay to the other.

Moonlight danced silver, but not a ripple of movement broke the surface.

61

Bella

Bella thought she was meant to feel something liberating about floating on her back, naked in the sea. Silky and freeing, perhaps? What she actually felt was cold and fearful that some small, fish-like thing was going to swim up her vagina.

She rolled onto her front, deciding swimming would be better. So much easier to do with a few drinks inside her. She was practically gliding right now. From the beach, she could hear the distant wash of voices and the drift of music. She imagined the others talking about her, dissecting her break-up with Fen.

Well, let them!

All weekend she'd felt like something was out of balance, as if there was a tension rippling beneath the surface of the group. But as she swam through the dark, silent water, skin puckered with goosebumps, she began to realise it wasn't the hen party that was off-kilter: it was her.

A fist of despair slammed into her middle as she thought about losing Fen. She wanted to curl into a ball, sink to the ocean floor. Without Fen, she had nothing to go back to. Fen was everything golden in her life. She'd always known that Fen was too good for her and that, one day, Fen would realise it.

Bella pushed her face beneath the dark skin of the sea, water filling her ears and nose. She screamed. The sound was gargled, terrifying. Her pain distorted to something even more wretched and desperate.

She snapped her head back up, gasping, panicked. Salt water coated her mouth. What the hell was she doing? She didn't want to be out here, naked, alone. She was suddenly scared. Cold. Tired.

She lowered her feet and disappeared beneath the surface, the black water sealing above her head.

No seabed! No air in her lungs!

She thrashed her legs madly – and broke through the surface, gasping. Her pulse roared in her ears. She swivelled around, clawing at the water.

Her gaze landed on the beach fire in the distance, so very, very far away.

62

Robyn

Robyn stared into the dark bay, searching for Bella.

Inky and still, the sea gave up none of its secrets.

Robyn was reminded of how she'd felt as a teenager, always the one needing to be responsible for Bella – turning down the extra drink so one of them was sober enough to get them home safely, or keeping enough money aside to pay for a taxi so that Bella didn't weave home at three in the morning, alone in a shimmering dress.

But not tonight.

She was done keeping an eye out for Bella Rossi.

Behind her, the music drummed on, the voices of the others rising and falling. Someone threw another branch on the fire, fresh sparks swirling into the night.

Another beer, Robyn decided. That's what she'd do. Drink, dance, enjoy herself. She weaved barefoot along the shoreline, feet sinking into the bed of tiny pebbles. A burst of laughter erupted near the fire.

Ahead, something dark was puddled on the shore. She reached down and touched the fabric: Bella's dress.

Robyn's gaze swung to the sea. There was no breeze and the water looked still, unruffled. Surely she should hear splashing, the light rippling of Bella swimming?

Something didn't feel right. Heart quickening, she edged forward until her feet were in the shallows. Bella had been drinking hard all afternoon. She wasn't a strong swimmer. No, Robyn didn't like this. She needed to let the others know she was missing. She turned—

'Boo!'

Robyn screamed.

Bella was in front of her, naked and grinning.

'Christ!' Robyn said, a hand pressed to her chest. 'I thought you were still in the sea!'

'None of those other fuckers noticed. God knows how I made it back.' Wet hair hung down her back, her body beautiful in the moonlight.

'You shouldn't have gone out there!'

Bella slipped an arm around Robyn's waist. 'My complicated little Robyn. Still looking out for me, aren't you?'

'You're wet,' she said, shrugging her off, annoyed. 'Here,' she said, shoving Bella's dress at her.

She pulled it on obediently, like a child. 'We've not been close for a while, have we?'

Robyn didn't want a conversation like this. Not tonight.

'We never talk about it,' Bella persisted.

'About what?'

'What happened that night.' Bella reached out, placing her

damp fingers at the base of Robyn's skull where a scar weaved through her hairline. 'You remember.'

She did.

The crack of her head against the side of the pool.

Darkness.

Followed by Bella looming over her, calling her name, face washed white with fear.

Bella had been the one to take her to A&E, apologising over and over as she drove, a dream catcher swaying from the rear-view mirror.

They waited for two hours to be seen, Robyn shivering in a damp towel, her skin smelling faintly of chlorine. The doctor who finally saw her glued the gash in her head and handed her a leaflet about concussion. 'Have you got someone to stay with you?'

'Me,' Bella had said. 'I will.'

So they'd returned to Robyn's house, her parents already asleep. They ate Marmite on toast in the kitchen and sipped on glasses of squash, and Robyn had felt like she was both a child and an adult in the same skin.

Later they had crept upstairs to Robyn's room. Usually, she'd set up the futon for friends, but there was no spare bedding and she didn't want to wake her parents. 'All right sharing?' she asked, pointing to her single bed.

'Course.'

Bella borrowed one of Robyn's T-shirts, sitting on the end of her bed, removing her make-up with a face-wipe, revealing glittering, fresh eyes.

'Sorry you're missing the party,' Robyn said as they climbed into her bed, the mattress bouncing.

Bella shrugged. 'We've just left sixth form. The next decade is for getting wasted and partying.' She grinned, her smile smelling of toothpaste.

Robyn stretched across and turned out the light. The room fell dark, quiet. Tentatively, she lay back, feeling a hot throbbing in her skull.

'How's the head?' Bella whispered.

Robyn adjusted the pillow, rolling onto her side. 'Better if I lie like this.'

She was facing Bella. She opened her eyes and could see her silhouette inches from her face. Her eyes were open too.

Bella's voice was quieter when she spoke again. 'I'm really sorry. I should have been holding onto you.' She reached out, her hand finding Robyn's, fingers interlacing beneath the duvet.

Robyn could feel the heat of Bella's hand, the pressure of their skin touching. The atmosphere became charged. She wasn't sure if it was just her who felt it or Bella, too. She was aware of a surprising, pulsing heat in her groin. She was dizzy, almost breathless.

Bella's thumb gently stroked the back of her hand. Somehow their faces seemed closer. She could feel Bella's minty breath against her cheek. Then she felt the brush of her lips – tentative, exploratory at first – and then fuller, melting against her own.

Bella's lips were exquisitely soft and full. Robyn had kissed lots of boys. That was not what kisses were supposed to be like. They were harder, urgent. Bella's mouth was cushiony and sweet; she wanted to sink into it.

Beneath the duvet, Robyn felt her hand being drawn down the length of Bella's body, trailing over the soft skin of her stomach, being guided lower still.

She blinked, trying to free the memory, but the sparks of it burned, red-hot.

'We both remember,' Bella said.

63

Bella

Every detail was vivid in Bella's mind: their fingers entwining as they kissed; the smooth warmth of Robyn's thighs sliding against hers; the faint chlorine smell that still lingered on her neck; the press of her knees into the crook of Robyn's as they'd fallen asleep, curled together.

What she also remembered was waking in the morning, alone. She'd pulled the duvet close to her chin, waiting for Robyn to return with a cup of tea and packet of biscuits – their usual post-sleepover pick-me-up – yet the bedroom door never opened.

Eventually, Bella had slunk downstairs, barefoot, wearing the previous night's dress, the gold fabric feeling cheap and glitzy in the unforgiving morning light.

Robyn was sitting at the kitchen table, flanked by her parents. Her face was washed clean, hair brushed straight, eyes shadowed. 'Hey,' Robyn said, without meeting Bella's eye.

'Good morning, Bella,' Robyn's father welcomed. 'We hear you took Robyn to A&E last night. Thank you very much.'

'It's fine,' Bella said, trying to rearrange the too-low neckline of her dress. She made fists of her hands, the red nail polish feeling garish in their quiet, grief-filled home. She had the unnerving sensation that she'd walked into a funeral service wearing fancy dress. She glanced at Robyn for reassurance, but her gaze was lowered to the kitchen table.

'Quite the bump on the head Robyn had,' her mother said, something sharp in her tone.

'It was,' Bella agreed. 'How are you feeling this morning?' She crossed the kitchen, about to take a seat at the table – but Robyn stood.

'Exhausted. I could use a bit more sleep. You okay getting home?'

'Oh. Sure. I need to head back. I've got the car, so . . .' Bella didn't have any belongings with her, so she simply gathered her shoes and car keys, and moved into the hallway.

Robyn opened the front door, eyes still lowered.

Barefoot on the front step, faux-leather heels dangling from her hand, Bella asked, 'You okay?'

Robyn touched a hand to her head. 'Turns out alcohol plus a concussion aren't a great mix. Can barely remember a thing.'

Bella's face flamed. 'Right.'

A long, awkward silence followed.

'I guess I better go then,' Bella said.

'Sure. See you,' Robyn had said, gaze trailing to the ground in front of her feet.

Humiliation stung Bella's cheeks as she hurried across the cul de sac in her glittering dress. She slung her shoes on the passenger seat, stabbed the key into the ignition, then stalled the car twice. Finally, she roared away with a screeching, over-revved gear change. Stereo volume dialled to max, the bellow of music drowned the smack of her palm as she slammed it into the steering wheel.

Now, standing on the beach, she faced Robyn. 'I remember everything about that night – and I know you do, too.'

In the darkness, Robyn held her gaze.

What was it she wanted: an apology? An admission? Or simply an acknowledgement that it'd happened at all?

'I'm so sorry,' Robyn said eventually, before dropping her head, skirting Bella, then disappearing into the shadows.

64

Eleanor

Laughter and wood smoke curled into the night as Eleanor slipped away from the beach fire.

They'd tried, the others. Fen listening as she talked about Sam. Robyn always checking she had a drink and asking her opinion on the playlist. Lexi making space for her by the beach fire, wanting to chat. But Eleanor couldn't pretend any longer. She was exhausted by it all – the smiling, the talking, the saying one thing but thinking something entirely different.

She wrapped the bottle of vodka within a blanket and placed it in the foot of the rowing boat. Shielded by darkness, she dragged the boat towards the shoreline, keeping her distance from the fire. She hoped no one would notice, asking why she was going out rowing alone, at night. What would she say? That she couldn't bear to be in her own skin a moment longer? That she'd survived three nights of the hen weekend, watching one woman glowing at their centre, and couldn't do it anymore?

She wasn't even sure what this was – rowing out into the night with a bottle of spirits. Or maybe she did know. After all, she'd woken months before on her bathroom floor, cheek pressed to the linoleum, vision blurred. She remembered that place. The terrifying truth was that she was only ever one twist of a pill bottle away from it; one step from a cliff edge; one dive into the deep.

She splashed through the shallows – the party loud enough to swallow her escape – then hauled herself over the side of the boat. Grappling with the oars, she began to row. At first, she moved jerkily, with short, uneven strokes, but soon enough a pleasing rhythm mellowed through her arms, water dripping silver from the oars. She watched the glow of the beach fire and the silhouettes of the others fading in her wake.

She rowed for some time, the moon lighting a path that led her away from the cove.

When her arms began to tire, she set down the oars. There. She'd drift, let the currents decide.

She lifted the bottle of vodka to her lips and took a heavy gulp, the alcohol burning her throat. Then she laid the blanket across the foot of the boat and arranged herself on top, making a pillow of her arms.

The stars. All the stars.

At home, if she woke in the middle of the night and couldn't get back to sleep, she'd step out onto the little balcony of her flat, tip her head to the sky, searching for the few stars that the city lights hadn't muted. It made her problems feel small. Life and the universe and all of it so large and looming, while she – with that black stone of sadness lodged in her chest – was so small.

Exhaustion crashed over her. It was so tiring to pretend. Sometimes when she was at the supermarket or waiting in a traffic jam, she'd look around her and think: *How many of you are pretending to be happy, to feel normal, right now? Or is it only me?* She was out in the world walking and talking and cooking and eating and showing people in a thousand different ways that she was okay. But she wasn't.

Ed had told her she was depressed. His solution was a gym membership – as if her sadness could be physically exercised from her. Then, after the sleeping-pills incident, he insisted she see a doctor. She went through the motions, taking the prescription for antidepressants to the pharmacy, knowing those pills wouldn't touch her lips.

A drug couldn't make her happy.

Only Sam.

Out here in the boat, she was free to think about him. She liked to save her memories throughout the day, storing them up, like the way she'd save chocolate as a child, wanting to enjoy the sweet, creamy flavour alone.

Now, she let her mind roam towards him. She thought of his fondness for stopping in the street to talk to other people's dogs, crouching as he rubbed behind their ears, saying, 'All right there, mate? That good?' She thought of how he liked to wear socks in bed, even in summer. *My feet like cosy.* She thought about his love of board games. Not just Monopoly and Scrabble but old games, ones she remembered vaguely from childhood, like Mouse Trap and Operation.

She was smiling as she remembered how Sam would arrange the games on their coffee table, a second stool pulled close to house retro snacks: cheese and pineapple on sticks, Frazzles, Bombay mix. He wasn't a man for olives and hummus – and yet Eleanor, for all the joy good food gave her – relished the synthetic hit of a Frazzle, the way it melted and clung to your tongue. Other couples enjoyed going out for dinner, hosting kitchen suppers, watching live theatre, but they liked games and snacks. And that was precisely what she missed about Sam – how he made the ordinary feel extraordinary.

She lay in the boat, feeling it rock beneath her, knowing there was a bottle of vodka to drink, a thousand memories to lose herself in. The warm glow of the beach fire had slipped from view altogether, so now it was only her and the sea.

65

Bella

Bella reached into the cooler, her dress clinging to her damp, salt-licked skin. She pulled out the first thing she found: a bottle of ouzo. She untwisted the cap and pressed it to her lips. The hot, menthol hit of aniseed washed down her throat. Yep, much better.

She tucked the bottle under her arm and weaved towards the beach fire, where Lexi was sitting with Ana. Always Ana. She was like Lexi's bloody shadow. She was wearing a striking red dress, braids loose over her shoulders. She had some nerve to be here when Bella knew her sordid little secret.

Bella flopped down on Lexi's other side, grinding the base of the bottle into the tiny pebbles. Her hair hung wetly at her back, seeping into her dress. She shivered.

'You're freezing,' Lexi said, unwinding the red wrap from her shoulders and draping it around Bella.

'Thank you,' she said, pulling the soft fabric close to her skin, breathing in the scent of Lexi's perfume. She scanned the dark beach, lit by flame and moon. 'Where's Fen?'

'Not sure. Perhaps she's gone back to the villa?' Lexi suggested.

Bella looked up at the jagged cliff line, the villa crouching in darkness at the crown. A few lanterns flickered across the terrace, but no lights were on inside those cold stone walls. Had Fen already gone to bed? Would they still sleep on the same double bed tonight, curled at their separate edges? A heavy feeling of gloom spread through her middle.

'What was that with Robyn a moment ago?' Lexi asked, glancing over her shoulder in the direction that Robyn had left.

Bella shrugged. 'Just being her usual uptight, prissy little self.'

'Don't say that.'

Ah. Sober, she remembered. Normally Lexi would've laughed, wouldn't she? 'She is though.'

Lexi sighed as if Bella were an exhausting child that she didn't have the energy to admonish.

'Don't tell me you're pissed off with me, too?'

'I'm not pissed off with anyone. I just want to keep the vibe easy.'

'As opposed to what? My *vibe*?' When did Lexi even start using the word *vibe*, for God's sake?

Ana reached for a piece of driftwood and fed it to the clamouring flames. Bella glared at her. How brazen to be sitting beside Lexi, pretending to be her friend, when Bella knew the truth. She shook her head, disgusted. Reached for the ouzo.

'Maybe you should slow it down.'

Bella arched a brow. 'The Lexi I used to know would be fetching us both more drinks.'

She sighed. 'I'm tired of hearing about this Lexi you used to know. You're always holding me to account. It's like you'll only accept one version of me.'

'I liked the old version better.' Bella didn't know why she was behaving like this. She was aware of Ana gazing studiously into the flames.

'Well, I'm sorry, but I grew up,' Lexi said, hugging her knees to her chest. 'Who I was in my twenties isn't who I am right now. And who I am right now probably isn't going to be who I am next year, or even next month. I don't have to be one thing the whole time. Right now, I'm someone who is engaged, pregnant, sober – and I like all those parts.' She faced Bella. 'I want you to be happy for me.'

'I am! I'm your best friend, of course I'm happy for you! I care about you, more than anyone.'

Across the fire, Ana rolled her eyes.

The gesture caught Bella like a flame. She leaned forward. 'What the fuck was that?' Her whole body was thrumming with tension, her mind jittering. She could feel the racing beat of her heart – needed that energy and anger to go somewhere.

Ana's voice was calm. 'Other people care about Lexi, too.'

'You?' Bella laughed, the sound sharp as a knife. 'What a joke!'

Lexi's head snapped around. 'Bella!' She took a breath, as if consciously trying to remain calm in the face of Bella's childishness. 'I know you're hurting because of Fen, but please, don't take it out on everybody else.'

'You don't even know Ana!'

'Right now, it feels like it's *you* I don't know.'

She felt the blow in her middle. Her gaze swung like a metal hammer towards Ana. She was sitting there, so calmly, so regally, pretending to be this grounding influence in Lexi's life – when everything about her was a lie!

'Ana's not who you think she is,' Bella said to Lexi, her tone lethal.

Lexi didn't respond. Just looked exasperated.

Bella's gaze travelled to Ana, who'd turned rigid. 'Lexi hasn't a clue who you really are, has she?'

Ana's eyes widened – but only a fraction. She shook her head once in a silent plea. *Don't!*

'Apparently Ed wanted to be the one to tell you, Lexi,' Bella said in a low growl.

Lexi's expression grew wary. 'Tell me what?'

An ember burst from the fire, landing in the space between them. Bella's gaze followed it, watching as it cooled to powder-grey ash.

She looked up, meeting Lexi's eye. 'Ed and Ana have already met.'

66

Lexi

Despite the heat of the flames, Lexi felt her skin cooling. She looked at Ana. 'You've never met Ed.' Slowly, her brow began to crease. 'Have you?'

Ana's palms came together as if in prayer. 'I'm sorry.'

For what? Lexi thought, aware of her quickening pulse.

A flaming branch crumbled, sparks dancing into the night.

Ana set her hands on either side of her, as if trying to balance. 'We met a long time ago. At university.'

'What?' Lexi said, with a shake of her head. 'Why didn't you tell me?'

'I told you that I left university because I fell pregnant with Luca.' Ana drew a breath. Looked straight at Lexi. 'Ed is his father.'

Lexi wanted to laugh because it was absurd! *No! Not true!* She waited for Bella to shoot down the wildness of the

claim, but there was only silence, Ana's statement smouldering in the heat of the flames.

She turned to Bella, needing her to translate. 'Is this true?
My Ed?'

Her face was set, grim. 'Yes.'

Lexi stumbled to her feet. 'Oh God!'

'I'm sorry,' Ana was saying, rising too. 'I didn't want you
to hear like this. I wanted to talk to you properly. I know
this is a terrible shock.'

'Does Ed know about Luca?' Lexi asked, her voice small.
'He can't know, can he?'

'I told him when I found out I was pregnant. He didn't
want to be involved. He – he pays maintenance, but he and
Luca have never met.'

Ed knows about Luca? The pebbles beneath her bare feet
seemed to shift, slide away. Her head spun, thoughts whirling.
Nothing made sense. 'But I've talked to Ed about you. He
knows your name. Knows you were coming on the hen
weekend. He would've said something! Told me!'

'You call me Ana – but Ed only knows me by my full
name, Juliana. He wouldn't have realised.'

'But *you* did,' Bella said, chin jutting forward, red shawl
cloaking her shoulders. With her finger pointed at Ana, she
said, '*You* knew perfectly well who Lexi was. You chased
down her friendship. You made sure you planted yourself
right at her side. You knew who she was – and who she was
marrying – when you agreed to come on her hen weekend!'

A deep trembling had overtaken Lexi's body. She stood
on the dark beach staring at Ana, a woman she'd admired,
respected, trusted.

Ana tried to appeal to Lexi. 'You *are* my friend. That part
is real.'

Lexi's voice was shredded with confusion as she asked, 'When you came to my yoga class, did you know who I was?'

Ana held her gaze. 'Yes.'

Lexi let out a sharp exhale, as if she'd been punched. She clasped her arms tight to herself. A drift of wood smoke weaved between them, stinging her eyes.

Beside her, Bella seethed, 'I never trusted you.'

'This has nothing to do with you,' Ana said.

'It's got everything to do with me. Lexi is my best friend.' Bella took a step closer. 'You need to pack your bag and get the fuck away from us.'

'Lexi, please!' Ana said, appealing to her. 'Let's go up to the villa. Talk.'

Lexi felt strangely disconnected from her body, as if she were observing herself, watching the three of them standing on the beach, lit by the fire. Her thoughts were rushed, impossible to grasp. She needed space, distance, silence. She looked at Ana. Shook her head. 'No.'

'Please, if you just give me a chance—'

'You heard!' Bella cut in.

Ana swung around. Her expression had changed, her face hard, eyes narrowed. 'Keep out of this! You're not Lexi's bodyguard!'

'I'm protecting her!' Bella's eyes glittered, her word endings slurred.

Lexi felt her hands rising to her head, squeezing the sides of her skull. The volume. There was too much noise. Too much everything.

'You think that *this* is protecting her?' Ana shot back. 'Slamming her with this news out here?'

'You're lecturing me on friendship?' Bella cried, incredulous.

Lexi's voice was low, shaken. 'I can't do this.'

'See!' Bella said to Ana, triumphant. She hurried to Lexi's side, staggering as she hooked her arm too tightly around her waist. Lexi caught the alcoholic tang of her breath. Pulled away.

'Let me help you, babe.'

Lexi stared at her, eyes shining with tears. 'You've done enough.'

67

Robyn

Robyn picked her way along the narrow cliff path. She had no torch but the moon was high and bright, bathing the mountain in a silvery wash. She felt dust and stone beneath the press of her bare feet.

She was beginning to sober up, could feel the faint retreating of the alcohol in her system, her body absorbing it, breaking it down. She wondered vaguely if she'd be able to do that with her thoughts . . . all the noise in her head, just push it down, swallow it, let her body absorb it.

Or maybe that was exactly what she'd been doing for years.

Like that night with Bella.

She swallowed. How could she have done that to her? Pretending not to remember a thing. Shutting the front door and retreating inside to her parents. Needing to be the good girl because her parents couldn't cope with anything else.

Staying on the straight and narrow. Studying hard. Going to university. Securing a training contract. Working at a solid law firm. Meeting a nice man. Marrying him. Having a baby.

Ticking every damn box.

But that was the problem right there – she was putting herself in a box. She was containing her feelings and dreams in small, square shapes that had been drawn by someone else.

Now she wondered: *What happens if I open the lid?*

'Robyn?'

She was sitting on a boulder set back from the cliff edge and hadn't heard Fen approach.

The moon bathed Fen in a natural glow, so her skin looked porcelain.

'What are you doing up here?' Robyn asked.

'I saw you leave the cove. You looked upset. Is everything okay?'

'Bella and I had a few words. Not a fight, exactly. Just . . . something I needed to hear.'

Fen was quiet for a moment. 'Bella's having a rough day.'

'I know. She told me the two of you broke up. I'm sorry.'

'I didn't mean for it to happen out here. Not on Lexi's hen. It's all such a mess.'

Robyn said, 'Sometimes there isn't a right time or place.'

Fen moved towards the boulder where Robyn was sitting and lowered herself down. 'Can I ask you something?' Fen said, turning to look at her. 'Why did you and your husband separate?'

The question surprised Robyn. 'He cheated on me.' It was such an easy, neat answer. She'd said it a hundred times: *My husband cheated*. And people would squeeze her arm in sympathy, or call him a bastard, because they understood her hurt and anger and betrayal.

What they wouldn't have understood so easily was that when Robyn had discovered he'd been having affairs, she had felt relieved. It gave her a way out. It was clear and obvious and understandable. That was way she'd always liked her emotions to be.

Neat. Neat. Neat.

She found herself admitting to Fen, 'I was *pleased* he cheated. I felt relieved.' She took a breath. 'I wasn't in love with him. I don't think I ever have been.'

'No,' Fen said quietly, that single short word containing a truth that she felt Fen had somehow known.

'If he hadn't cheated, I think we'd still be married. Even though I don't love him. God, that's a terrible thing to admit. I'm so weak,' she said, her head shaking. 'I would still be married to someone I never truly loved because I'm not brave enough to make another choice.'

All around them, cicadas sang. Fen sat quietly at Robyn's side, waiting. Leaving space. And so Robyn found herself opening into it. She told her about losing her brother when she was a teenager. How she'd watched her parents shatter, as if their hearts were only ever made of glass. 'I just want life to be easy and good and gentle on them, because they can't take any more. And tonight . . . tonight I swore at my mum, and she's at home looking after my baby and I should be grateful, but instead I was mean and spiteful, and I know she doesn't sleep well and she'll be worrying about this and—'

Fen placed her hand over Robyn's. 'Breathe.'

One word.

She filled her lungs with air, allowing her diaphragm to expand. Then she exhaled slowly, shoulders releasing.

She drew in another for good measure.

She was acutely aware of the heat of Fen's hand over hers. Something in the air shifted, became still. Her heartbeat quickened in her chest.

Neither of them spoke.

Robyn didn't want to stir, or move, or speak, or do anything to alter the feeling that was lighting her whole body from within.

Fen kept her hand on Robyn's as she asked, 'Did you say anything to your mum that wasn't the truth?'

Robyn thought for a moment. Shook her head.

'Then perhaps that was what's needed?' She posed the question so straightforwardly that Robyn found herself thinking she might be right.

After a lengthy silence, Fen asked, 'What do you want?'

It was such a simple question. She was asked it every day – in a café, or by her mother, or even at work – but right now, Fen's gaze square on hers, the question seemed like the biggest and hardest thing she'd ever need to answer.

Thought and logic, which were her language, seemed to dissolve, and all she could feel was something deeper within herself, a heat burning at her core.

She sensed the whisper of an answer. But it was a ludicrous one. She couldn't say it. Shouldn't even think it. It was absurd.

And yet, when she had first seen Fen on this cliff, she had felt something cleave open in her chest, an expansion, a need, a desire. And she was sure that Fen had felt it too, was feeling it right in this moment.

Robyn's hand was still beneath Fen's. She wanted to look down at them and memorise the places where their skin touched – yet she didn't want to break Fen's gaze. Their eyes felt locked.

She turned her hand within Fen's, palm to palm. Felt the slide of their fingers, like roots searching, linking together, enclosing. She squeezed. The answer was clear and bright.

You. I want you.

Robyn didn't know if she was straight, or gay, or something outside of a box meant for ticking. She only knew, like some deep oceanic roar in her blood, that she wanted this.

She leaned towards Fen, eyes open, never looking away.

Their lips met. She felt the soft give of Fen's mouth. She tasted of night and stars and pine. Their lips and tongues and mouths moved together in a slow dance, her body alight with desire. This kiss was the warmest, deepest pleasure Robyn had known.

Her fingers moved to the nape of Fen's neck, feeling the brush of her shorn hair, and lower to the smooth glide of her skin.

The whole world fizzed. Kissing Fen was like sinking beneath the surface of the sea, but instead of it being airless and dark, it was lit with phosphorescence so luminous that she knew she'd never see the world the same way again.

68

Eleanor

Eleanor lay in the bottom of the boat, the vodka bottle half-empty, listening to the wash of water against the hull.

Memories of Sam were swimming close, then pulling away, like the tug of waves – blanketing her, then exposing her. She only wanted the warm memories, yet a current of other images was dragging her towards a darker place: a call from a hospital; her hands gripped to the sides of a plastic chair as she waited; a surgeon removing her glasses, pinching the bridge of her nose.

Two words kept surfacing in her thoughts. *Human error.* Someone made a mistake.

We all make mistakes! Oh, well! Never mind!

But he was dead. One human error – and Sam was dead. His life over. Her life over.

She had read every detail of the disciplinary hearing. She'd read that Sam had been given the wrong drug, one that contained penicillin, which he was allergic to. Co-amoxiclav instead of co-trimoxazole. A few letters' difference. A different blend of chemicals. That was all it took to make his blood vessels leak, his throat constrict, his body tip into anaphylaxis.

Eleanor knew all about this. She'd read the report so often that the staple at the corner had rubbed loose. She knew it was an accident. She'd memorised the name of the senior nurse who'd made the mistake. On a Tuesday afternoon when she'd failed to sleep for the third night in a row, she'd driven to the Royal Bournemouth Hospital, hands trembling on the wheel, her vision swinging. She'd wanted to look the nurse square in the eye and ask, *Do you have any idea what you've done?*

But the nurse no longer worked there. *Got a new job,* the receptionist had told her cheerfully. Eleanor pushed her fists deep into her pockets. She didn't ask where or doing what. That was where she had left it, there on that ward. She didn't want to track her down. What was the point? Sam was gone.

And then, all those months later, she had been sitting in her flat, eating her one-person serving of shepherd's pie, trying so hard not to ruminate, to move forwards – when that nurse's name popped right into her inbox.

An invite to a hen weekend.

Four nights in Greece.

Just six of them chosen.

Signed:

Kisses and love from the Maid of Honour,
Bella Rossi

69

Bella

The bottle of ouzo swung in Bella's hand as she lurched on, the dusty ground hard beneath her bare feet. She was navigating the cliff path by the torch on her phone, boulders and shrubs rearing from the shadows.

She staggered, weaving dangerously close to the edge. The torch's beam slipped over the cliff, shining through the night, down, down towards the dark mouth of the sea.

'Careful,' she said aloud, enunciating both syllables, as if demonstrating to herself that she was perfectly sober. She pulled back her shoulders. Raised her chin. Snatched a breath. Yes, she was fine. Completely competent.

She stalked on, dress riding around her thighs, hair drying in salty tangles. Lexi's red wrap was trailing from her shoulders, one end dusting the earth.

She was sure telling Lexi about Ana was the right thing. Almost sure. Someone needed to tell her. Ana couldn't be allowed to get away with it. Then she remembered the way Lexi's face had crumpled, as if she couldn't physically support the weight of her shock.

Maybe she shouldn't have said it quite like that. She'd always been hot-headed. Maybe the right thing would've been to pause. To think about the impact of her words. Her big announcement wasn't about Lexi, she realised, staggering to a halt. It was about proving a point to Ana.

There was something wrong with her. Something broken. She kept hurting the people she loved.

She unscrewed the cap from the ouzo. Brought the bottle-neck to her lips. The glass clanked against her teeth as she took a gulp, a dribble spilling down her cheek. She wiped her mouth against the back of her hand, grimacing.

His face loomed suddenly into her thoughts. The large eyes stretched with fear, lips mottled, fighting for breath. She'd been joking with him earlier in the shift, hearing about the accident on his stag do that had landed him in hospital.

Sam Maine.

She'd liked him. Teased him.

And then . . .

She'd killed him.

Bella pulled the wrap tighter around her shoulders, the torch on her phone swerving haphazardly as she stumbled on.

She'd not told any of her friends the truth about why she'd left nursing. Instead, she'd repackaged it as a lifestyle change: 'Swapping bedpans for diamonds,' delivered with a beaming grin. What bullshit! She'd *loved* being a nurse. It was more than a job – it was part of who she was, how she felt about herself.

Ahead, she caught the distant lilt of a voice. She peered along the path as it ascended towards the highest point of the clifftop. She climbed further, a sharp stone pressing into the base of her heel.

As she emerged at the top, she could see Robyn sitting on a boulder near the cliff edge.

Little Robyn.

Even now her heart did something complicated when she saw her – part flutter, part sinking.

Robyn was looking away and, as she moved, Bella saw she was sitting with someone else.

Fen.

In the darkness, neither of them had seen her approach. Bella turned off the torch on her phone. Watched.

They were sitting close to one another, their heads dipped low as if in urgent, private dialogue.

She wondered if they were speaking about her. She hated that feeling of entering a room and voices being lowered, a flick of eyes in her direction. She would join them, she thought, make her apologies. If Bella was good at one thing, it was saying sorry. Quick to fire, but quick to cool, that was her saving grace. She'd always seen the value of a good apology. She'd start right now with Fen – try at least to salvage a strand of friendship.

She walked towards them, beginning to feel a little more optimistic, when she noticed something about the way they were sitting. Their hands were linked.

Why would they be holding hands?

Her gaze rose to Robyn's profile. Her chin was tilted, gaze locked on Fen's.

An icicle of dread pierced between her shoulder blades.

No . . .

She was frozen to the spot, watching. Waiting.

They leaned towards each other – and kissed.

70

Robyn

Robyn was so deep in her body that she was flesh and sinew and blood and heat and movement.

No thinking.

Just feeling.

Being.

A low exhale of pleasure slipped through her lips. She pulled back for a beat – only enough so that she could look at Fen.

Fen was smiling, moonlight catching in her eyes. 'Wow.'

Robyn grinned, heart soaring.

The moment stretched and widened, the two of them held by the night, something expansive opening in her chest.

She couldn't stop grinning.

Somewhere behind Robyn's shoulder, there was the slide of earth beneath a foot. She was pinned so firmly in the moment with Fen that she didn't notice. Didn't register the shape of someone else on the clifftop, watching them.

'How could you?'

Robyn's head whipped around, smile sliced from her face.

Bella was standing there barefoot, a blood-red wrap cloaking her shoulders. Her face looked pale, lips dark and wide. Sand and dirt streaked her shins.

Robyn shot to her feet at the same time as Fen. 'Bella!' they both said, with stinging synchronicity.

Then silence.

The sea licked coolly at the foot of the cliffs. Silver stars knifed from the sky.

Three women standing on a clifftop in the dead of night.

'How could you?' The quiet disbelief in Bella's question sent a chill through Robyn.

Bella's wide, shocked gaze slid to Fen. 'This morning . . . We only broke up this morning!'

Fen said, 'I know. Shit. I'm sorry.'

'I'm in love with you. How could you?'

'Bella . . . I'm so sorry. I've hurt you.'

Bella looked unsteady, as if her legs were threatening to buckle. *The edge,* Robyn thought. *She's too near.* 'Bella—' she began.

Bella's attention cut to Robyn. 'You!' Her lips pulled back in contempt, her entire posture shifting, drawing up. 'You fucking bitch!'

She deserved it. She knew she did. She shouldn't have kissed Fen – yet every cell in her body had been driving her on. She opened her mouth to say something, to apologise, to try to explain, but Bella was speaking: 'Straight little

Robyn. That's what you've always wanted people to think, isn't it? But I knew! I fucking knew!'

'I didn't—' Robyn tried.

But Bella was already finished with her, turning towards Fen. 'Is little Robyn here pretending she's never kissed a woman before? Do you think she's *fallen for you*? Because it isn't the first time – is it, Robyn?'

Heat burned in her cheeks. She could feel Fen's focus turning towards her.

'Robyn and I have history. She told you about that?' Bella demanded. 'Has she?'

Into the silence, Fen said, 'No.'

Bella looked square at Robyn as she said, 'Robyn is the first woman I slept with.'

Robyn's eyes startled wide. *First? No, that couldn't be true*. Bella had always been so open, so bold about her sexuality. Robyn had thought there'd been numerous others before her. 'I . . . I had no idea . . .' she whispered, her voice wavering.

Bella stared right at her, voice cracking as she said, 'I was in love with you, Robyn.'

Robyn was completely still.

'You claimed you were drunk, concussed. That you didn't remember.'

Guilt scorched her. Robyn hadn't known how to handle it. Hadn't understood what had happened or how she felt, so she had closed it out.

'When you said that, it made me feel like . . . like I'd taken advantage of you. That beautiful thing that happened – became something broken, dirty.'

To Robyn's horror, she saw tears trailing down Bella's

cheeks. She'd had no idea that was how Bella had felt. When she'd seen her a few days later, Bella had been her usual self – smiling, joking, breezy, the life and soul.

I was in love with you.

'Bella,' she began, stepping towards her. 'I'm so, so sorry . . .'

'Don't,' Bella said, lurching dangerously close to the cliff edge.

'Careful,' Fen warned.

Bella swung around, the red wrap lifting in the night.

Robyn sensed danger, like something metallic filling the air. She kept her voice low, careful not to startle Bella, as she said, 'You're too close.'

With her back to them, Bella said, 'What do you care?' There was a change in her tone, a raw sadness to it.

'Please, Bella, take a step away,' Robyn pleaded.

'No one cares what happens to me.'

Robyn knew that attention was Bella's oxygen, but this – this felt different. There was something about her, a defeated rounding of her shoulders, a worn edge to her voice.

'That's not true,' Robyn said softly. '*I* care about you.'

'You're lying!' Bella let out a growling roar, an animal sound of pain and frustration, as she launched the bottle of ouzo over the cliff edge.

Robyn watched moonlight catching the bottleneck as it turned through the night, liquid glinting like mercury.

Maybe Bella had been watching it too, not concentrating, because as she stepped back, the movement unbalanced something.

Robyn saw it happening in slow motion: the loose stone beneath Bella's heel, the instability of her foot from the

341

scorpion sting, the tip of Bella's body towards the cliff edge, the billow of the red wrap.

Robyn lurched forward, reached out, tried to pull her back. But her hand met only air.

~

Not one of us thought it would end the way it did. The sea – one moment, so alluring in its shimmering glory, and the next, dark, bottomless, and deadly. It was like it had been lying in wait, biding its time. Watching it all, unmoved by our screams.

71

Fen

Fen lurched to the edge of the cliff, falling to her knees. She dug her fingertips into the dusty earth as she stared over the edge.

A dark swathe of unbroken night.

She glared through empty space, which fell away towards the dark lip of the sea.

There was nothing there, only water, air.

Blood roared in her ears. The drag of her own breath.

At her shoulder, Robyn was deathly still. Her legs glowed white in the moonlight. Her face was wiped clean of any expression she could recognise. Winded by shock, Robyn stared back at Fen, eyes wide with terror.

And then she began to scream.

'Bella!' Robyn yelled, her voice fierce and heavy, as if she could yank Bella to the surface with a rope of sound.

Her name echoed off the cliff face, lonely and desolate, without an answer.

'Bella! Bella!' Robyn screamed, the sounds streaking together, knotted and broken. 'I can't see her! I can't fucking see her! Bella!'

Her hands were moving, fast gestures cutting through the night, feet pacing on the spot, thoughts firing into words. 'We need to get to her! How high are we? Eighty feet? More? Is it deep? God. Oh, God. We need help. To get help! The police! The coastguard! My phone – it's in the villa.'

Fen couldn't process the rush of words. She kept staring into the black water below, desperate to see something. Hear something. She forced herself to take a breath. 'Run to the villa. Call the police. Then take out the rowing boat. There's a torch in the lounge cupboard.'

Robyn nodded rapidly.

'I'll try and get down to Bella.'

'How?'

'That path to the hidden cove – it's a couple of minutes away. I'll climb down, swim out.'

'It's too dangerous! Even in daylight we—'

'Go, Robyn! Now!' Fen yelled, before turning on her heel and sprinting along the cliff edge, dirt loosening beneath her feet.

72

Eleanor

The sea washed against the hull of the rowing boat. The sound was soporific, the warm breeze brushing over Eleanor's skin, as she drifted and drifted . . .

Far off in the distance, she heard a voice.

Let it wash away, too, she thought, concentrating on the slow rock of the boat, the sensation of being lulled to sleep.

But the voice was insistent. Shouting.

At the edge of her awareness, she caught the shape of the word. 'Bella!'

She opened her eyes, looking up at the black sky pricked silver with stars.

A dream?

'Bella!' The name was shouted again.

This time, she sat up, head spinning. On the clifftop, she saw the distant outline of a person. Wait, two people. She rubbed her eyes, salt stinging at their edges. Then the people began to separate, move, running in opposite directions.

Dizzied by the strangeness of the night, she looked around, uncertain. Moonlight bathed the sea silver, but her rowing boat drifted in the cliff's shadow, dark and unseen.

She caught the distant sound of splashing.

Her gaze swung across the water. Was someone out here?

She grabbed the oars, hauling them deep, head turned over her shoulder, searching.

There was more splashing, like something flapping on the surface of the sea. Then a voice. Definitely a voice. 'Help!'

There! She saw something raised from the water. A hand! A silver bangle caught in the moonlight.

'I'm coming!' she called, rowing hard.

Someone was clawing at the surface. Dark hair slicked to a scalp, head scarcely above the waterline, eyes panicked.

'Bella Rossi.'

'Help me!'

For a moment, she was unsure: real, or dream? Was this simply an imagined scenario, like the ones she toyed with during sleepless nights, planning all the ways she could make Bella suffer?

Eleanor tightened her grip on the wooden oars, while all around her the sea and night wavered, distorting.

Then there was Bella's voice again, barely more than a gurgle, pleading for help.

Did Sam beg for his life? she wondered.

Did he gasp for breath?

Huh.

She sat very still as she watched Nurse Rossi slip right beneath the surface.

Eleanor closed her eyes. As the boat rocked gently, her thoughts felt muffled by alcohol.

Strangely, she heard Sam's voice. It was so warm and familiar, as if he were in the rowing boat, talking to her. She remained still, wanting to catch every word. She waited to hear his casual tone – as if life were only a ride, a bit of a pleasing joke and he was in on it, and if she stuck with him, she would be, too.

'Help,' he said.

Eleanor was thinking, *Yes, I'll help you. I will do whatever you want . . .*

'Help!'

Her eyes snapped open because it wasn't Sam but Bella.

Her fingers were raking at the sea as she slipped under, disappearing.

Like Sam had disappeared.

No, it was wrong. All wrong!

Eleanor yanked an oar from its rowlock and thrust it towards her. 'Grab on!'

Bella lunged for it, gasping, thrashing. Her fingers reached it – and Eleanor braced herself against Bella's weight as she pulled her towards the boat.

When she was near enough, she reached down, grabbing Bella by the shoulders and dragging her upwards. The boat rocked wildly, Bella's breath hot in her face, wet fingers grasping at Eleanor's clothes. She felt herself unbalancing, leaning too close to the water. She couldn't go over! Couldn't swim!

Eleanor ripped Bella's hands away – slamming back to the far side of the boat, hearing the splash as Bella plunged back into the sea. She cried out, her voice desperate, fingers clawing against the hull.

Eleanor knew she should help her.

She really should.

Eleanor had spent a long time hating this woman. She'd wanted her to suffer, just like Sam had, yet now – in this moment, when she had the choice of whether Bella lived or not – she knew she couldn't let Bella Rossi die.

She crossed the boat, keeping her knees bent and her body braced against the rocking. Then she reached down, grabbing Bella firmly by the shoulders. With a fierce surge of exertion, she hauled her over the side.

They both collapsed into the boat, a tangle of limbs, Bella soaked and gasping, a sodden red wrap knotted at her neck.

Eleanor peeled it free, then gathered the dry blanket from the boat floor and draped it around Bella's shoulders.

Bella was shaking hard, sobbing, unable to catch her breath. Her face was wretched in the moonlight, hair pasted across her forehead, lips peeled back, breathing hard. 'I could've drowned.'

Eleanor stared at her. 'Yes,' she said. 'You almost did.'

73

Bella

Bella hugged the blanket tight around herself. Her entire body trembled. She kept replaying the moment she'd gone over the cliff edge: the dry-mouthed plummet towards the sea, then the punch of water slamming into her body – like something solid, not liquid. She must have blacked out for a few moments, as all she remembered after that was floating on the surface, winded, alone, certain she was going to die . . .

But Eleanor saved her.

She took a breath. Air, beautiful air in her lungs! She pressed her feet into the solid wood of the boat. Drew another breath. The sea rocked them steadily, like a mother's touch against a cradle.

'Thank you,' Bella said after a time, looking at Eleanor. 'You saved my life.'

'And you,' Eleanor said, her voice low, thoughtful, 'ended another.'

Bella blinked, uncomprehending.

'Sam Maine,' Eleanor said.

Just two words. A name that echoed in the darkest corner of Bella's mind. She waited, unsure whether this was real . . . whether Eleanor had said that name . . . whether it was the shock of falling . . . She shook her head. Tried to speak, but no words came out.

Eleanor said, 'Sam Maine was my fiancé. You're the nurse who killed him.'

Her eyes widened. 'You . . . you were his fiancée?'

She nodded.

'My God . . . I . . . I had no idea . . .' A hand lifted to her throat. 'How long have you known who I am?'

'Since you sent the email about the hen weekend. I recognised your name. It was in the disciplinary report.'

Her head spun. 'That's why you came on the hen weekend?'

'Yes. I needed to see you. Look you in the eye. Know who you were.'

Bella felt her wet hair soaking into the blanket. 'Eleanor . . . I . . . I don't know what to say . . .'

Eleanor's hands gripped the edges of the wooden bench. 'I want you to tell me what happened.'

Bella wiped a hand across her mouth. Tried to focus. She was still shivering hard and pulled the blanket tighter. 'I was on nights at the hospital,' she began, her voice hoarse. She swallowed. Tried again. 'I'd been out the evening before with Lexi. I should've gone to bed the next day, slept, but the sun was out and I spent the afternoon in a beer garden. I didn't drink,' she added, looking square at Eleanor. 'I never, ever, drank before a shift.'

Bella remembered going into work with the feel of the sun still on her shoulders, the bustle and hum of the pub on her skin. She told Eleanor, 'I met Sam when I came onto shift. I liked him, straightaway. He made me laugh. Told me he'd come to Bournemouth for his stag do. He said his fiancée had just been in – delivered him a Walnut Whip and a Marvel comic. I told him, "1985 is on the phone. They want their lifestyle back." He laughed at that, said, "That's nothing. You should see our VHS collection."'

There was the briefest softening of Eleanor's features.

'It was about two a.m. when I started to flag.' It was almost like motion sickness, as if her blood were too hot for her body, eyes dry and stinging. 'I was in the treatment room preparing his next dose of antibiotics. I remember setting out the tray and reconstituting the vial of co-trimoxazole. That's what I thought I'd picked up. That's what I could've sworn I'd picked up. I knew Sam was allergic to penicillin – it was on his chart and on the red band he wore on his wrist. I knew. But right next to it, there was co-amoxiclav – and that's the one I picked up.' Tears stung her eyes. 'I reached for the wrong one. I didn't double-check.'

In her hand, she had been holding the drug that would kill him. That would act like a poison to his body, that would cause his blood vessels to leak, his blood pressure to drop and send his body into shock.

'Even when I got to his bedside, asked him his name, date of birth, whether he had any allergies, I still didn't realise I was about to give him the wrong antibiotic. So I attached it to his drip. Signed his chart. Told him to behave, and continued with my round.'

Eleanor was completely still, knuckles white where she gripped the seat. 'Go on.'

'Ten minutes later, the ward alarm rang.' She remembered the squeak of plimsolls sprinting down the corridor, the metal clang of the crash trolley as it was pushed into his bay. 'The crash team were there in moments – getting out defibrillator pads, administering adrenalin, putting in a bigger line for liquids. A doctor asked what drugs he'd been given and I answered, "Co-trimoxazole." As soon as I said it – I knew I must've got it wrong.

'I ran to the treatment room. The tray was still there, the vial out. I saw my mistake. And fuck, oh fuck . . .' Her voice splintered. Tears streamed down her face. 'Everything was spinning – the walls, the shelves. I couldn't breathe. I sprinted back to Sam, yelling at the doctors that I'd given him the wrong drug. That it had penicillin in! I wanted to do something, help, but he was already being rushed to intensive care.'

She'd just stood there in his empty bay, her body numb, her mind strangely blank. 'I told the charge nurse it was my fault, and she said she'd need to write this up. Let the family know. Then she told me to go home. That's what I did. I left.'

The streets were empty, the night warm; a few revellers were on their way home. Her thoughts were looped and fierce: the whites of Sam's eyes, his legs bare beneath the sheet, an awful wheeze sounding from his throat.

Twenty-four hours later, the team on intensive care made the decision, alongside his family, to withdraw support. And that was it. Sam Maine, comic-book lover, Walnut Whip-eater, VHS-owner, was dead.

And it was her fault.

'I was suspended from work,' she told Eleanor. 'There was a disciplinary hearing later. You'll have seen the report. I made no excuse. NMC ruled that I could return to my job in a more junior role. But I could never go back to nursing.

How could I? All it took was one momentary lapse in concentration, and someone – your Sam – died.'

Bella pushed a hand across her wet face. 'I didn't tell anyone outside of work what'd happened. I couldn't. Not even Lexi. Not my family. I found a job in a jeweller's and packaged it as a lifestyle change. Some days it felt almost possible that I could live with it, that this was a choice. But it's always there, in me. Knowing what I did. That I killed Sam.' She looked up at Eleanor. 'And now, here you are.'

The sea licked at the boat.

Her heart rate flaring, Bella fought to steady her voice: 'I think about you: Sam Maine's fiancée. I think about you every single day. Try to imagine who you are. How your life has changed. I think about the wedding day that you never got to have. I think about your wedding dress – and wonder whether you'd already chosen it, whether you kept it, whether you get it out of your wardrobe some days and try it on.'

'It's in the spare room. I kept it. Will always keep it. But I've never put it on.'

Bella nodded slowly. 'You know what Sam told me when I was teasing him about the comic you'd brought in? He told me, "I'm the luckiest man in the world." That's what he said.'

Eleanor tipped back her head. Looked up to the stars as if she could see something there that Bella could not.

Bella locked her arms tighter around herself, nails digging into her flesh, waiting. Whatever was coming, she knew she deserved it.

Out of all the words she could have responded with, Eleanor chose only two: 'Thank you.'

74

Lexi

Lexi hurried up the stone steps towards the villa. Her breath was high in her chest. Her thoughts felt hot, scattered. She didn't want it to be true: Ed was Luca's father.

He'd been lying to her.

Ana had been lying.

Bella had known.

Behind her, lost high in the distant cliffs, she thought she heard a shout. She paused, listening.

Beyond the chorus of cicadas she could hear nothing but her racing pulse.

She hurried towards the darkened villa. There was no breeze away from the sea and she felt sweat prickling against her skin. A wash of nausea rose from her stomach. She took a deep breath – concentrating on setting each foot firmly in front of the other – and gradually the sensation subsided.

When she reached the terrace, she hesitated. The villa lights were off to keep the mosquitoes from flooding in, and now the building looked eerie – as ancient and unyielding as the cliff from which it was hewn.

In the distance, a vehicle light trailed over the mountains like a search beam. She moved towards the front of the villa, thinking how strange it was to see headlights carving through the night when the road ended here, at the villa.

She listened as the low roar of an engine grew louder. Then suddenly a car crested the top of the hill, full beam startling her as it swung into the drive. Instinctively, she raised her hands, shading the blinding light from her eyes.

A taxi.

The passenger door opened, and a figure stepped out.

Dazed, she squinted into the glare.

A man crossed the driveway, coming straight towards her. She stepped back.

His shape, the breadth of his shoulders, the length of his stride – were familiar. 'Ed?'

Then he was standing in front of her. Right there, in Greece, saying her name.

She stared back at him, lost. Here, out of context, he seemed unrecognisable to her. A stranger.

The taxi pulled away in a spray of gravel, casting Ed in the eerie red glow of the taillights. Rising dust from the drive made him seem faint, unknown, his smile wavering.

He swallowed. 'Hello, Lexi.'

She and Ed faced one another in the dark. The lingering smell of petrol and dust hovered in the still air.

'What are you doing here?' Lexi asked, her voice sounding strange, narrow.

Ed didn't step closer. He was wearing a white shirt, unbuttoned at the neck, which looked ghostly in the moonlight. 'We need to talk.'

She stared at him: her fiancé; Luca's father; Ana's lover, once.

'Shall we go inside?'

She glanced towards the villa, with its cave-thick walls. For some reason she didn't want him in there, as if that space were for other things, not him. 'We'll go onto the terrace.'

She turned; he followed.

Neither of them noticed the shape of someone standing in the shadow of the lemon tree, back pressed to the trunk, watching.

75

Robyn

Robyn was breathing hard, calf muscles burning as she ran. Tiny pebbles stabbed against her bare feet as she made for the shoreline, where the rowing boat was drawing in. It had come into view only minutes ago and now she was squinting through the darkness, able to make out the shape of one . . . two people on board.

She lurched into the shallows and, as the boat came towards her, she could see Eleanor rotating the oars. At the back, Bella was huddled beneath a blanket, wet hair pasted to her scalp.

'Bella! Oh Bella!' Robyn cried, water splashing up her legs as she grabbed the nose of the boat. 'You're alive! My God! You're safe!'

Hunched within a blanket, Bella glanced up, face pale in the moonlight.

'Are you hurt?'

'No,' Bella claimed, although Robyn caught the way she winced as she shifted in the boat.

'When you went over the edge . . . I . . . thought we'd lost you.' Robyn's voice was broken with emotion. 'I'm sorry . . . It was all my fault . . . I'm so sorry, Bella! For all of it!'

Eleanor cut across her, saying, 'Let's get her back on land. Warm her up, shall we?'

Robyn nodded quickly. 'Sorry. Yes. Here.' She guided the boat towards the beach, the hull grinding along the pebbled seabed.

Robyn bore most of Bella's weight, helping her climb from the boat. She was shivering violently as she limped through the shallows. Reaching the shoreline, Bella stumbled to her knees, digging her fingers into the pebble beach. Her head hung down, the curve of her spine prominent through the wet fabric of her dress.

After a few moments, Bella took a deep breath, then rose, releasing the pebbles. She turned. Faced Eleanor.

The two women looked at one another for a long moment, something passing between them. 'I won't forget,' Bella said, a fierceness in her tone that caused goosebumps to rise across Robyn's neck.

Eleanor nodded once. After a beat, she turned to Robyn, instructing, 'Help me with the boat.'

Together they heaved it from the water, dragging it onto the shoreline. Eleanor retrieved the sodden red wrap Bella had been wearing. She wrung the water from it, then draped it over her arm, linking the other through Bella's. 'Come,' she said. 'Let's get you warm.'

Robyn's gaze swung to the cliff line. Fen was still out there, searching. They shouldn't have separated. Fen shouldn't be alone in the darkness. She'd help Bella back to the villa, fetch a torch, then go after her.

A drift of wood smoke curled from the fire as the three of them crossed the beach in silence. Eleanor's step faltered. Robyn glanced at her and saw her gaze was lifted towards the villa. 'What?'

The three of them were silent, listening.

'Voices,' Eleanor said.

Robyn heard them, too. First, a woman's voice – sharpened and rising – then cut across by the strong blow of a man's shout.

76

Lexi

On the terrace a few lanterns were still lit. The scent of chlorine rose from the swimming pool, chemical and sharp.

Lexi stopped beneath the pergola, placing her fingertips on the table where empty glasses and a bottle of wine waited to be cleared. The bronze statue stood at its centre and she found herself reaching for it, feeling something grounding in the cool weight of the bronze, the rasp of metal against her skin.

Ed's gaze followed hers. 'Is this you?'

She nodded, turning the bronzed body towards the light of the candle, the flame catching her curves, her expression of rapture.

A dancer, once.

And now? Who was she now?

Carefully, she set down the sculpture, suddenly feeling overwhelmingly tired. She didn't have the energy to deal with this. She wanted to unknow everything she'd heard about Ana, about Luca.

She wanted Ed to still be the man she thought he was, not this new, shadowed version of himself.

Ed pulled out a chair for her, and she lowered herself down.

A petal, loosened from her floral crown, fluttered into her lap. She stared at it for a moment, then lifted it lightly between her fingertips. Slowly, she pressed her fingernail into its delicate velvet texture, until she felt it tear. Then she pushed a hand into her hairline and tugged out the remaining flowers, letting them scatter to the floor.

'Lex,' he said, sitting close, elbows on his knees. His shirt sleeves were rolled up, exposing his tanned, strong forearms. 'I needed to see you. I was hoping to be the one to tell you. But you already know, don't you?'

She held his eye. 'You have a son.'

He hung his head. 'Yes.'

Lexi felt the blow of his admission.

'I'm so, so sorry,' he said, and she could hear the emotion thickening his voice. When he lifted his gaze, she was surprised to see his eyes shining with tears. 'I should've been the one to tell you. I'm devastated that you've found out like this – out here. Lex, I should have told you months ago, I know that.'

'Why didn't you?'

He swallowed. 'I was ashamed. Not that I have a son – but that I have no contact with him. I've heard the way you talk about your dad. You can't forgive him for abandoning his other daughter. You've barely got a relationship with him because of it.'

That was true.

'I wanted to be honest – tell you about Luca – I really did, but it felt impossible. I didn't want to risk losing you. I love you, Lexi Lowe.'

She could smell his aftershave warmed on his skin. She felt a softening. This was Ed. Her Ed. Who brought her breakfast in bed; who loved to wash her hair in the bath; who called during his lunch break because he missed her. When she was with him, she felt valued. Treasured. She wanted to lean into him and feel his arms wrapped around her.

'I'm pregnant.' The words slipped out so unexpectedly, so quietly, that her surprise almost matched his.

'What?' His eyes widened.

'I found out just before the hen. You were in Ireland. I wanted to tell you in person. I'm eleven weeks.'

Ed ran a hand across his jawline. 'Jesus Christ. Pregnant. You're pregnant.' His gaze travelled over her face, sliding down to her stomach. 'A baby,' he said, his voice low. 'How do you feel?'

If she thought only of the baby – of the bundle of cells multiplying inside her, making a home deep in her body, sharing her oxygen, her blood, her nutrients, her energy – she felt full, happy. 'I want this baby. I'm happy about it.'

His mouth broadened into a wide, spontaneous smile. 'This is . . . this is wonderful!'

'We said we never wanted children.'

'I said that because I thought it was what *you* wanted.' He stood, taking her fingers in his, drawing her to her feet, circling his arms around her. His body was warm, firm. He pressed his lips against the top of her head. 'God, I love you. And I'm going to love our baby.'

It was the right thing to say. The right thing to do. She

waited to feel a stirring of comfort, or desire, or happiness – but none of those feelings emerged. He was holding her too tightly, pinning her body to his. Her stomach felt compressed, restricted. She could feel the soft crush of petals beneath her bare feet.

She edged out of his grip.

Ed looked at her, head angled. 'What is it?'

'Luca.' Just saying his name aloud made the whispering in Lexi's chest grow louder. 'Your son, Luca. Why don't you see him?'

'Christ, I was so young. Juliana – Ana – and I weren't even in a relationship. It was, well, you can imagine – a . . . one-off.'

'A one-night stand.' It felt important that he name this, be clear.

He nodded. 'Weeks later, she turned up telling me she's pregnant. I was honest with her right away. Said I didn't want to be a dad. I was too young. Still a kid. I'd not long graduated. I had this whole big plan of how life was going to roll out – and then there was this girl I'd met once telling me she was having my baby. I was terrified.'

'What about her?'

He blinked. 'Sorry?'

'Ana. How do you think she felt? Don't you think she was terrified, too?'

His tone changed, sharpened. 'She didn't have to keep the baby. At least she got a choice.'

A moth flew towards the candle on the terrace, dancing erratically above the flame, before its wing tip caught alight. Lexi smelt burning as it spiralled down, falling to the table. It dragged its body in a pitiful circle. Ed picked up the sculpture, crushing the moth beneath the bronze base.

A kindness, she knew – and yet she found herself looking into his eyes, searching for a suggestion of something else. Something hinted at in the way Eleanor spoke of her brother. Something that explained Bella's wariness of Ed. Something to make sense of the anxiety Lexi had felt building all weekend. She tried to read his expression, to feel the truth of who he was.

It had been so easy for Ed to walk away from Luca. The same way her father had walked away from Sadie. Both men had the frightening ability to detach, compartmentalise.

In the bay below, she could see the faint glow of the beach fire. She pressed her fingertips into her hairline. 'Why hasn't Ana spoken to you in all these years? Why befriend me?'

'She's obviously got issues – tracking me down, pretending to be your friend, coming out here on your hen do, for God's sake! I'm only sorry that you've been dragged into this. I hate that she's duped us all.'

Is that it? Lexi's thoughts felt muddied, as if she couldn't tally the two versions of Ana: the friend she'd grown close to over recent months, admiring her strength and spirit – and then this newly glimpsed Ana who'd been concealing secrets, lying.

'I plan to seek legal advice. It may be that we need to consider a restraining order.'

'Really?'

'For all we know, she could be dangerous.'

There was movement across the terrace, footsteps so light and soft that Lexi didn't hear someone stealing towards them until they'd reached Ed's shoulder.

'Dangerous,' Ana said, coming to a halt. Her face was in shadow, but Lexi could determine the hard cast of her gaze, eyes fixed on Ed. Her red dress cloaked her like a warning. 'There's an interesting word.'

77

Ana

Here he was. Standing in front of her. Edward Tollock. In his white shirt, sleeves casually rolled.

Luca's father.

It had been almost sixteen years since she'd been this close to him – but her body remembered: a shiver travelling down her spine; a tightening across the back of her neck, like invisible hackles rising; a retraction in the soft flesh at her middle, drawing herself in, away.

'What are you doing here? You need to leave,' he instructed in a low voice intended to command authority.

'I'm not going anywhere,' she said, blood roaring in her ears. 'There are things Lexi needs to hear.'

'Neither of us are interested in anything you have to say,' Ed said, matter-of-factly.

Footsteps sounded behind them, causing Ana to turn. Eleanor and Robyn were guiding a shivering Bella onto the terrace. Her dress was soaked and make-up streaked her face.

'My God, what's happened?' Lexi asked.

'It's okay, I'm fine,' Bella said, her voice shaken. She looked at Ed. 'What's he doing here?'

Eleanor was staring at him, too, her expression creased with confusion.

'I came to talk to Lexi.'

Ana noted the way Lexi's spine stiffened as he placed his hand against the small of her back.

Lexi turned from him, facing Ana. 'What is it I need to hear?'

Can I go through with this? Right here, in front of them all? She glanced at Ed, a look of impatience pricking his features. Her heart was pounding, but she steadied herself by drawing air deep into her lungs. 'A year ago, Luca asked to meet his father,' she told Lexi. 'It shouldn't have come as a surprise – I knew one day he'd ask that question. I said that he needed to wait until he was sixteen. If he still wanted to find his father then, I'd help him.'

'I made it clear I didn't want to be involved,' Ed said, his voice studiously level.

To him, Ana said, 'Luca is a strong-minded, intelligent boy. Even if I'd told him that I wouldn't help, he'd have gone looking for you himself. If he tracked you down, I needed to know who he'd find. So I looked you up. Found out where you were working. Went to your office. I waited outside to talk to you. But when I saw you . . . I just . . . I couldn't do it . . .' She'd started to tremble, her whole body overtaken by a cold fear. Her throat constricted, shallowing her breath until she could barely snatch a breath.

'Why couldn't you talk to Ed?' Lexi asked, hands balled into fists at her sides.

Ana's gaze fixed on Ed, who was standing with his feet

planted wide, a stance associated with control, authority. Yet she also noticed the knot of tension in his jaw, the narrowed eyes, the tell of a hand moving fleetingly to the back of his neck.

'Do you want to tell Lexi about the night I got pregnant?'

He baulked. 'You expect me to talk my fiancée through a quick shag, sixteen years ago, that I can barely remember?'

'I remember,' Ana said, drawing herself up from her core. 'You'd just graduated and you threw a house party to celebrate. My roommate knew one of your friends, so we came along. It was my birthday.' Ana didn't usually drink heavily – couldn't afford to – but it was her nineteenth birthday and her friends had taken her for happy-hour cocktails. She'd arrived at the party feeling giddy, light-headed, lit with a bloom of false confidence. She remembered dancing in the lounge, enjoying the way this handsome graduate stood in the doorway, watching.

'You approached me, asked if I'd like a drink somewhere quieter. You were holding a bottle of vodka. I followed you upstairs.' She remembered being flattered that this well-spoken man in his smart leather shoes was so taken with her. 'When we walked into your bedroom, you locked the door.' She swallowed, recalling the first breath of unease. 'You uncapped the vodka and passed me the bottle. Didn't offer me a glass.' There'd been something in his expression, a hint of amusement, as if he were setting her a test. She drank straight from the bottle, the alcohol scorching her throat. 'Then you took down your trousers and said, *Put your mouth there.*'

'Christ's sake!' Ed burst out. 'I'm not listening to this!'

Ana's heart was beating fiercely. Shame burned hot in her cheeks, travelling all the way to her scalp. She wanted to run, leave, get away from Ed. She wanted to be at home with Luca, watching a film and eating popcorn. She ground her teeth together. Forced herself to continue.

'Everything felt wrong. The locked door. The way you spoke to me, like I wasn't your equal. I said, "No, thank you." You laughed. Imitated my voice. *No, thank you,* as if refusing were a joke to you. Then you grinned at me. Said, "We both know what happens in this room." You pulled me onto the bed. Climbed on top of me. Pushed your hands beneath my clothes.' She stated each fact slowly, voice as level as she could manage, like she was reading aloud from a document.

She could feel the collective gaze of Lexi and the hens. Listening.

Hearing her.

'You had sex with me. I didn't say, *No,* because I was scared. I was terrified of what would happen if I said that one word. What it'd mean if you didn't listen.' Because once she'd voiced it, once she said that word in a loud, clear voice like she'd been taught by all the women before her, then he had a choice to respect her – or not. 'So I lay still on your bed, and you did what you did.'

She felt the heat of her emotions simmering. She'd always kept them in check, containing them, pushing them down, keeping her cool – but now they were bubbling dangerously to the surface. 'Do you remember,' she went on, voice rising, 'what you said while you fucked me?'

In the brief widening of Ed's eyes, she could see that he did. He knew exactly what he'd said, his mouth pressed to her ear, his hot whisper cutting deep.

'You called me a *dirty bitch. A filthy whore.*'

She heard the intake of breath from the others.

Ana's temples throbbed; the muscles in her neck spasmed. Those words were worse than what he was doing to her body. They left scars. They made her see those things when she looked at herself in the mirror.

'When you'd finished, you climbed off me. Pulled up your trousers, then left. You didn't say a single word. Just rejoined the party like I was nothing.' She snatched a breath. 'I never said the word *no*. I never told you to *stop*. I was terrified – so I lay still and quiet. I was a Black girl at a white boy's party. But you knew I didn't want it. You knew what you were doing was wrong, but you did it anyway.'

There was silence.

Ed, clench-jawed, said, 'We had a one-night stand. I won't let you insinuate it was something darker than that. When you turned up a couple of months later, pregnant, you conveniently didn't mention any of this. You seemed quite happy to take my regular pay cheques.'

'Happy?' Hot fingers of tension jabbed at her brow. 'You've no idea, have you? I was a nineteen-year-old student from Brixton. Families like mine – they don't have a kid at university. It was *everything* that I got a place. I didn't want to drop out. I didn't want to see my parents' heartbreak that I'd thrown it all away. That I was another statistic. But I also knew I couldn't go through with an abortion – no matter what financial incentive you and your father dangled.' She shook her head, disgusted. 'You even insisted on a DNA test to check Luca was yours!'

'How did I know who you'd been sleeping with?'

'You.' Her voice was deathly quiet. 'You were the only person.'

Her statement hung there on the dark terrace, weighted and taut.

'Oh God,' Lexi whispered into her fingers.

'You paid me off. Made me sign a contract that agreed to a higher rate of maintenance, as long as I'd never let my child know your identity. And I agreed.'

She accepted it all. She had no money, rent to pay, parents who couldn't look her in the eye, and a baby growing in her belly.

When that first amount landed in her bank account, all she had thought was: *He was right. Now I am a whore.*

78

Lexi

Lexi knew Ana was an accomplished liar – after all, she'd been lying to Lexi ever since she'd turned up at her first yoga class – so could she trust what she was saying now?

Her gaze moved to Ed. A knot of tension pulsed in his jawline as he ground his teeth. But he'd been lying to her too, omitting Luca from his history.

Eleanor, Bella and Robyn were grouped close, a jury gathering information, waiting to pass judgement.

Into the silence, Ed began to laugh. 'This is ridiculous!' He turned to Lexi. 'We slept together once, and now she's trying to paint me as some monster and destroy my relationship with you! Sure, I was probably a twenty-one-year-old arsehole experimenting with talking dirty – I can barely remember, it was all so long ago – but what I do know is that it was consensual.'

Lexi thought of the way Ed was when they were alone:

tender, considerate, loving. He looked at her with adoration, told her she was beautiful, brilliant, kind. Could he be the same person who'd once hissed, *Dirty bitch* and *Filthy whore*?

'Lexi,' he said, coming towards her. 'You know me. You know this is all nonsense, don't you? If Ana is such a great friend, as she claims to be – and if this, this story of hers is true, that I am a monster – then why didn't she warn you about me? Why did she come out to Greece to celebrate your hen weekend and say nothing?'

It was a good question. An important one.

Lexi looked to Ana. 'Yes, why?'

79

Ana

Ana had let Lexi down, she knew that.

'I didn't know how to deal with what happened to me. It was easier to kid myself that it was only a one-night stand. It was better if I believed that for the baby's sake.'

Every time Ana felt a rising of emotion that suggested otherwise – the tightening in her chest if she was alone with a man, the flickering of fear if a door was locked behind her, the smell of vodka on someone's breath – she told herself to toughen up.

'When I saw Ed again all those years later, as a grown woman, I felt it in my body. I knew. I understood that what happened between us wasn't right. I hadn't misremembered anything. I had shut it out.' She kept her gaze on Lexi. 'The strength of that remembering, that feeling, was terrifying. I was standing outside his office, shaking. And then . . . then you came towards him. You looked so lovely, so happy, so pleased to see him. You beamed at Ed. Kissed him.' Ana shook her head. 'I was so confused. I thought: Ed can't be this person, not the one I'm remembering, if he's with someone like you.'

Lexi listened intently.

'You were carrying a yoga tote with the name of a studio on. It was close to where I lived, so the next day, I went there. It wasn't some big plan. I . . . I just wanted to see who you were. To understand why you were with Ed. Work out who he was, what had happened to me. I didn't expect us to become friends.' Ana had never had a group of close girlfriends. She had colleagues, she had her sister, she knew mothers from school, but she'd never had someone like Lexi in her life – and her friendship felt like a gift.

'I should have walked away. I know that. But I liked spending time together. You know what I hoped? That you'd break up with Ed, and that when it ended, you and I could keep on being friends.'

'I'm sure you would've loved that,' Ed said thinly.

'I shouldn't have said *yes* to the hen weekend. I know that. But you were so excited about it, so insistent that I be here – and I wanted to be. Part of me still hoped that I was wrong about Ed. How could he be the same person who did what he did to me – yet be someone entirely different with you? But then, out here, I started hearing things. There were red flags in the way Eleanor spoke about Ed, plus I overheard a conversation between Bella and Robyn about a lap dancer who knew Ed – and I knew this wasn't all in my mind. Ed is just extremely clever at hiding that side of himself.'

'Your claims are growing absurd,' Ed declared, with a careful note of pity in his voice. He turned towards his sister. 'You know me better than anyone. You know I would never have done this awful thing Ana is claiming.'

Eleanor's gaze travelled across her brother's face.

Ana could see the similarities now in the structure of their noses, the squareness of their jawlines, the broadness of their shoulders.

Everyone stared expectantly.

Ed bobbed his head at Eleanor, gesturing for her to speak.

The quiet grew, gathering close, all of them waiting for Eleanor's answer.

80

Eleanor

The night thrummed with heat and the low drone of insects. Eleanor could feel the pinch of salt streaking her bare legs, the fading warmth of the stone terrace beneath her soles.

She stared at her brother. Strange, Ed, right here, in this setting. He didn't seem to fit, like he was in the wrong place with his shiny leather shoes and pressed shirt, when they were all barefoot, shoulders tanned. It was the first time Eleanor had felt, *I belong; it's you who doesn't.*

'Tell them, Eleanor. You know me.'

You know me.

Oh yes, she knew Ed.

She knew that on her first day at senior school, she'd waved to Ed in the corridor and he'd blanked her. 'Who was that?' a red-haired boy had asked, and Ed had shrugged and said, 'Just some retard.'

She knew at fifteen, when Ed had been upset about a

disagreement with their parents and she'd made him a hot chocolate – just the way he liked it, with freshly whipped cream and chocolate grated over the top. She'd carried it into his bedroom and he'd slung a cushion at her, sloshing scalding milk down her front. 'I'm not a child! A hot chocolate won't fix shit!'

But she also knew that when she had her first series of sculptures accepted into a gallery, he'd been the one to congratulate her, arriving on her doorstep with a bottle of champagne. 'Proud of you, little sis.'

She knew that when she'd lost Sam, he'd cleared his diary and hadn't left her side for forty-eight hours.

She knew that, four months later, he'd looked at her, sitting in her pyjamas at midday, and his lips had curled as he said, 'Frankly, this is just indulgent now.'

She knew that Ed could be charming, loving, and generous – but he could also be cruel, hot-tempered, jealous.

He was deeply flawed.

But he was her brother.

He stared at her, eyes shining. 'Come on, Eleanor.'

It was a trial and she'd been brought forward as a character witness. The night held them close. She could feel the damp fabric of Lexi's red wrap still draped over her forearm. Could feel the others close to her, watching, waiting.

Ed said, 'I would never have done that to Ana.'

Eleanor wanted, more than anything, for her brother's claim to be true.

81

Bella

Bella watched Eleanor's gaze fall to the ground, the smallest downturn of her shoulders. *Cowed.* That was the word. Before her brother, straight-talking, spiky Eleanor Tollock looked cowed.

Ana's lips were pressed together, her expression mask-still. That account of hers – Ed's house party, the locked door, the description of his cold, brutal behaviour – there was an echo to it. She knew where she'd heard a whisper of it before: from Cynthia, who'd recognised him from the lap-dancing club.

Ed was wearing a controlled expression, but there was a hint of smugness in the upturn of his lips. He thought he was going to get away with it. Bella stepped forward. 'Ana's telling the truth.'

Ed looked her up and down. 'It would suit you to believe the worst, wouldn't it?'

'What suits me is seeing my friends happy. But look at Lexi – she doesn't look very happy right now, does she? And Ana – she's trembling like a leaf. And what about Eleanor? My guess is she's afraid of you.'

He laughed. 'Have you met my sister? She's scared of no one.' He stepped towards Bella, voice lowered so the others couldn't hear. 'You'd do well to mind your own business, Nurse Rossi.'

'There's no need to whisper,' she said, 'because Eleanor knows I was the nurse who gave Sam the wrong medication. I made a mistake. A mistake with terrible, terrible consequences. I've got to work out a way to live with that mistake without letting it eat me alive. And I've not got that figured out just yet. But you do not get to hold that mistake over me like a threat. Not anymore'.

There was silence on the terrace.

Bella could feel every pair of eyes trained on her. Her chest heaved with the suffocating weight of her guilt and grief. But beneath that, there was another sensation, just the lightest hint of relief that she was finally being honest.

'Wait—' Eleanor said, brow dipping. She looked at Ed. Her voice was a whisper. 'You knew Bella was the nurse?'

His expression faltered. 'Well, I did all the paperwork, dealt with the hospital for you. So yes, I recognised her name.'

'You encouraged me to go on the hen weekend, telling me it would do me good, when you knew all along I would be out here with her?'

'I thought you needed a holiday.' His tone was calm and level – the tone of an older brother who knows best. 'You needed a break after losing Sam. I was trying to look out for you. You know how much I care about you.'

Bella arched her brow. 'If it hadn't been for you and your

fucking antics on the stag do – Sam would never even have been in hospital.'

Eleanor went very still. 'What?'

'If Sam hadn't hurt his shoulder on the stag that night, he wouldn't have been admitted,' Bella said.

Eleanor was staring at her blankly. 'Sam hurt his shoulder *after* the stag. He fell down the hotel stairs the morning after.'

She really doesn't know?

Bella glanced at Ed. She could see it in his expression, a narrowing of his eyes. A tightening of his lips.

He'd not told her.

82

Lexi

Lexi stood with her arms hugged to her middle. Unseen in the dark, a chorus of cicadas trilled. Thousands of them calling together, a crashing sound that left no space in her head.

She wanted to leave. Exit stage left – like it was only a performance, and she could return to the dressing room and it'd be over. None of it mattering.

Except everything, right now, mattered.

Eleanor looked at Ed. 'Sam told me that after the stag, he'd checked out and was leaving the hotel. He was hungover and tripped over his luggage. Fell down the concrete entrance steps, landed on his shoulder. That's what happened, isn't it?'

Ed picked up the bronze sculpture, his grip loose, as if at any moment it could slip through his fingers, dashed onto the terrace flagstones. Lexi watched the quick dart of his

eyes, thinking: he's stalling, working out what to say. He
voice cut through his silence. 'Answer your sister.'

Ed's eyes widened at Lexi's tone. 'Look, Sam did trip,' h
explained, 'but it happened a few hours earlier, okay? That
all. We were on our way back from a club. We didn't know
Bournemouth well. Could barely remember where the hote
was. Sam was steaming drunk. He tripped, fell. It was an
accident. Sam decided to tell you that it happened *after* th
stag – I suppose he was embarrassed that he'd let himsel
get in such a state – so what could I do? I had to follow hi
lead.'

The way he said it, Lexi thought, it almost sounded mag
nanimous.

Almost.

Eleanor's lips barely moved as she asked, 'How did h
fall?'

Ed pushed his free hand into his pocket, then took it ou
again, opening his palm. 'It was the normal boys-on-a-stag
routine – all of us drinking too much, you know? His othe
mates had bailed early, so we were walking back. There wa
an underpass, which we thought would lead us back to the
hotel. Sam came at it wrong. Tripped. I feel bad because
should've booked us a cab. Made sure he got back safely.
He lifted his hands in surrender, Lexi's sculpture raised to
the night. 'I take full responsibility.'

'You blindfolded him,' Bella said, her voice deadly cool
'You made him walk home blindfolded – and he was suppose
to trust you to steer him right.'

Eleanor blinked.

'You called it Blind Person's Trust, but instead of looking
out for him, you steered him towards an underpass, didn't
you? You didn't warn him that he was nearing a set of

concrete steps. You led him there – and waited for him to fall.'

A cold wave of horror washed over Lexi.

'No!' Ed said.

'Sam told me about it when I came on duty. How his brother-in-law had plied him with drinks. That his other friends left early because of his domineering attitude. That there was a dangerous edge to his brother-in-law that he didn't like. I remember asking, "You sure you want to marry into a family like that?" And Sam smiled and said, "Ah, but his sister. She's worth it."'

Eleanor was staring at Ed, fingers curled at her sides, her face white.

'It was an accident,' Ed said, stepping towards her. 'Sure, Sam was blindfolded – and I should've been more careful with where I led him – but I was about to tell him there were steps coming up when he stumbled. I didn't mean for Sam to get hurt! He was my brother-in-law. I liked him. We were mates.'

Slowly, Eleanor's head shook from side to side. 'No, you weren't *mates*.' Her voice grew in volume as she went on, 'Sam never said a bad word about anyone. But you – oh, he didn't like you. I never told him what it was like growing up – how you used to throw things at me from the back of the school bus, encouraging your friends to do the same, or how you'd stand behind me in the school canteen, whispering, *Freak. Move. You're putting me off my food*! But Sam sensed you were a bully.'

Lexi felt the blood draining from her face as she remembered a passing comment Eleanor had made about being bullied at school. She'd assumed Eleanor had been talking about her classmates – but it had been Ed. Instinctively, she took a step towards Eleanor.

'Sam said you talked down to me. Dismissed me. And he was right. He saw you. Really saw you. I've been the blind one, trusting you.' She looked sadly at the sculpture that was still in Ed's hand. 'We've all made a mistake, trusting you. Lexi is far too good for you. We all are.'

Lexi watched it happening, the change in Ed's face – a tightening of his features, the way his eyes narrowed, pure fury glittering there. It was like a mask slipping off, revealing a wholly new Ed.

'You!' he spat at Eleanor, the word thin and damning. She'd belittled him, humiliated him in front of Lexi and her friends. Ed pointed the statue at her face. 'How fucking dare you!' The calm, controlled tone had disappeared, replaced by a rage-filled boom.

Lexi watched as something instinctive and fearful rose in Eleanor's expression. She recoiled towards the stone wall.

'No . . .' Lexi whispered, aware of the lethal drop behind Eleanor.

Ed's knuckles turned white where he gripped the raised statue, Eleanor cowering before him. In that moment, Lexi could imagine the dynamics of their childhood, Ed's charm masking the darker shades of himself in front of their parents, teachers, friends, leaving Eleanor to bear his cruelty in silence.

Ed drew back his arm.

Eleanor's hands lifted to protect her face.

Lexi went to say something – *Stop! Don't! Please!* – but already his arm was crashing forward.

It was too late.

83

Fen

By the time Fen returned to the bay, it was deserted. The fading embers of their beach fire glowed weakly, a thin drift of smoke hanging in the still air. A low beat from the speaker strummed eerily into the empty night.

She planted her hands on her hips, catching her breath as she turned on the spot. The rowing boat had been abandoned on the shoreline, oars jutting like elbows from its sides. *They made it back,* she thought, relieved.

After Bella's terrible fall into the sea, Fen had sprinted along the clifftop, breath ragged, adrenaline spiking in her veins. She'd scrambled down the steep path to reach the hidden cove where she and Robyn had once swum. At the water's edge she'd yanked off her clothes, wading into the inky black water, calling Bella's name.

As she swam out, sticking close to the cliff line, she'd spotted the shadow of a rowing boat. Through the darkness, she was able to make out Eleanor's frame as she reached down, hauling Bella from the water. Flooded with relief, Fen had called to them – but was too far away to be heard.

Where is everyone? Fen thought now. She lifted her gaze towards the villa, which stood castle-like on the cliff edge. In the high moonlight, she searched for Bella among the moving silhouettes. As she watched, two people stepped close to the terrace edge.

Too close.

She narrowed her eyes, trying to discern who they were.

She knew that terrace; knew the danger of the sheer drop onto a fatal bed of rock, the low structure of the wall. 'Careful . . .' she whispered.

There was a sudden movement, an arm raised with force. Hairs rose on the back of her neck.

In a beat, the arm had shot forward, launching something from the terrace.

She watched as an object twisted through the night.

What the . . . ?

There was the crash of something heavy landing against rock.

Fen started to run.

84

Eleanor

The launched sculpture missed Eleanor's head by inches. She turned, watching it twist magnificently, moonlight hitting the curve of bronze.

She thought of the hours and hours she'd dedicated to creating the sculpture, trailing the shape of Lexi's figure, wanting it to be perfect.

It landed with a distant clunk, like the dense thud of bone against rock.

'I can't believe you did that!' Robyn said, voice high with outrage.

Eleanor could.

She knew how Ed, enraged, was dangerous. She had the scars to prove it: butterfly stitches beneath her chin when he pushed her into a wall after she beat him in a running race; a scar below her knee when she was knocked from their treehouse; another scar on her shoulder after he'd tipped over her kitchen stool and she'd landed on a broken plate

What saddened her was that she'd allowed herself to hop that meeting Lexi had changed Ed. Yet now she realised he' been putting his best foot forward because he saw Lexi his equal; her beauty and success matched his. He'd hidde the darker shades of himself with such conviction that he' fooled them all.

Slowly, Eleanor lowered her hands, which had been guard ing her face. She became aware of the others drawing clos to her shoulder. She knew Ana's pain as she'd described wha Ed had done behind a locked door. She shared Bella's disgu that Ed had blindfolded Sam, and Robyn's disbelief that h had destroyed the sculpture. She understood Lexi's shock seeing the real Ed.

The women were standing near, almost a circle. She dre strength from their closeness, pulling back her shoulders an raising her chin. Despite the roar of blood in her ears, sh would not be afraid anymore. 'That sculpture wasn't your to destroy.'

Ed was glaring at her, eyes bright with rage. 'Lexi hardl wanted it! It's odd, Eleanor. A sculpture of her! These aren your friends. You've never had any friends. You're a joke!

The words shouldn't have stung – after all, she'd heard s many variations of them over the years – yet there was sti a part of her that flinched. That couldn't help thinking: *Mayb he is right*.

The women drew tighter. A pack.

But maybe he isn't, she thought.

'You and Sam suited one another,' Ed went on. He ha always hated it when he failed to get a rise. Had to push further. An older brother knowing the exact tender place t pinch. 'You suited one another because he was laughable, too!

390

Sam. My Sam. The most glorious person she'd ever known. The man who she'd loved with her whole being. Who was kind and easy and never judged others. Who Ed had blind-folded and steered to the top of a flight of concrete steps.

'What a pathetic pair you made!'

Ana stepped forward, a fierce vision, her red dress swishing once, then settling around her knees. 'Watch your fucking mouth!'

It happened so quickly that Eleanor didn't even have time to warn her. Ed lifted his left hand – his dominant hand – and swung the palm of it, swiftly, violently, across Ana's cheek.

Her head snapped back.

Lexi's mouth opened in a perfect O of shock.

Bella gasped.

They were all there. All watching. All saw the way Ana staggered back towards the wall.

Fell.

85

Fen

Fen flew up the stone steps, elbows pumping. A male voice, loud and scornful, cut across the others. Then she heard Ana shouting, 'Watch your fucking mouth!'

Fen ground to a halt, head craned towards the villa.

It all happened so fast. Everyone too near the terrace edge. That low, low wall. She knew the fear of being pinned there by Nico, the terror of understanding there was nothing but night at her back.

From this angle, she couldn't see who it was, not clearly. She only saw a figure stumbling, as if they were about to rest on the wall, but instead of sitting, they leaned back – too far back – arms widening into wings, legs lifting off the ground, rising.

In silent horror, she watched as the figure tipped over the edge of the terrace wall, falling through the night.

Arms windmilling.

A guttural, raw cry.
Dropping like a stone.
Red material swirling.
Down.
Down.
Down.
Then the dull, hard blow of a body against rock.
Silence.
Nothing more.
The sea stilled.
The sky blinking stars.
Fen was rooted to the spot, blood hot in her throat.
Then, from the terrace, she heard someone scream.

86

Lexi

The cry was piercing and wild, cutting high into the night. It echoed off the stone villa and the lonely, sheer cliff.

Lexi dug her fingernails into her throat, clawing her scream into silence.

No . . . no . . . no . . .

Robyn rushed forwards, gripping the wall as she peered down towards the rocks. 'Oh my God . . .' she gasped, shoulders beginning to shake.

No one moved. No one did anything.

'Call an ambulance,' Lexi whispered, her voice strange, hoarse.

But she knew.

They all knew.

It was a sheer drop of over a hundred feet onto jagged rock.

No one survives a fall like that.

87

Ana

Ana remained motionless. She felt as if all the blood had been drained from her body, a cool, hollow feeling suffusing her.

She blinked.

Stared at the empty space in front of the wall.

One moment she'd been standing on the terrace, listening as Ed said those awful things about Sam. She could not be witness to that, watching as Ed's words destroyed someone else. So she'd stepped forward, told him, *Watch your fucking mouth!*

Without warning, his hand had cut through the air, connecting with her cheek. The slap had been bone-shakingly hard and she'd slammed into the wall, fallen to the ground. Her cheek had flamed with an instant, bright pain. She'd put her fingertips to her skin, amazed to find there was no blood.

When she'd dragged her gaze to Ed, he'd no longer been

looking at her. He was staring at Eleanor, chin jutting forward, eyes narrowed. Ana realised it was not the first time Ed had hit a woman. It was all right there, pulsing in the space between brother and sister.

In the moonlight, Eleanor's skin looked white, her gaze burning. Her whole body trembled, alight with rage.

'You!' she'd snarled.

One word. Filled with fire and spit and hate.

And that's when it'd happened. When Eleanor's lips had peeled back from her teeth, and she'd charged.

88

Eleanor

He shouldn't have said it, that thing about Sam.

That he was laughable.

Eleanor had once believed that she was the only person Ed treated with easy cruelty – and that, somehow, she deserved it for being odd, for not acting like other people, for showing him up. She'd internalised that belief because it was less painful to imagine herself as strange than admit that her big brother – who was meant to love and protect her – was callous.

Watch your fucking mouth! Ana had warned.

Ed had barely glanced at her as he'd swung his palm hard at her cheek, like she was nothing.

'You!' Eleanor heard herself growl, an electric tingle spreading down to her fingertips, a rush of blood pounding in her ears.

Ed raised an eyebrow in contempt. It was the dismissiveness

of the gesture. That none of it – none of what he had done to her, to Sam, to Ana – mattered, because he saw himself as better. White noise filled her head and something that had been smouldering inside her for too long finally ignited.

She felt herself moving, storming forward, head down, charging. It was motion fuelled by instinct and anger and a lifetime of cruelties and hurts. Love flying so very close to hate.

She heard the grunt of air being expelled from Ed's lungs as her shoulder connected with his chest. He staggered towards the low wall but, rather than catching him – breaking his fall like it had done for Ana – the wall took his legs out from beneath him.

Eleanor was aware of his body tipping away from her, from the terrace, from safety. His expression shifted from surprise to fear as he reached out, grabbing for her.

Everything slowed: she could feel the damp press of the red wrap, still draped over her arm, beneath his grip; she could feel her bare feet sliding across the flagstone, desperate for purchase; she could feel her body, destabilising, lurching forwards with his.

Then suddenly there were other hands – small, warm, strong hands – grabbing for her, holding tight, pinning her to the terrace, and to them.

Ed's fingers slipped as the red wrap loosened, pulling free.

She watched his arms begin to windmill, the wrap swirling above him like a blood-red ribbon display.

Her brother, not flying – but falling.

She saw the whites of his eyes as his gaze swivelled, taking them all in – the circle of women holding tight to his sister – imploring them to help.

But they could do nothing.

If Eleanor could've reached out, caught him, she would have.

One of them would have.

Wouldn't they?

89

Lexi

Lexi's hands were clamped over her mouth. She could feel the heat of her breath against her palms. Her thoughts were fragmented, like jagged shards of broken glass reflecting distorted images.

Ana was still slumped on the ground, fingertips pressed to her swelling cheek. Nearby, Eleanor was rocking on her heels, arms hugged tight to her body.

Fen rushed onto the terrace. 'Was that Ed?'

Robyn nodded urgently, her feet making tiny frantic steps as she stared over the edge.

Lexi raked her fingers through the roots of her hair, nails digging into her scalp. Just seconds ago, Ed had been standing right there.

She'd been talking to him.

He was there.

And now . . .

He wasn't.

She was aware of her feet moving, carrying her across the terrace, stopping in front of the stone wall. The scent of oregano lifted from a nearby terracotta pot, strange and earthy. She placed her fingertips to the chalky surface of the wall, leaned forward. A dizzying rush of blood to her head made her lurch.

There was a hand on her shoulder, steadying her.

Someone was saying her name.

She looked.

'I can't see him.' Was she speaking? Or someone else?

She blinked. The oceanic roar of blood in her ears.

She angled her head. A vertiginous wave of nausea gripped her, knees buckling, saliva slickening her throat.

'Breathe,' someone said, the pressure on her shoulder increasing.

She drew air into her lungs.

Continued to stare down, down.

There. The pale shadow of his white shirt. A darkening on the rocks. Moonlight catching against something silver. A watch?

Ed.

Unmoving.

She knew it. Felt it in her body.

Dead.

90

Bella

Bella held Lexi firmly by the shoulders. She seemed like a spectre, as if she might drift over the edge, dissolve into the night.

'Come away,' Bella instructed.

Lexi allowed herself to be guided across the terrace, her body boneless and yielding as she was ushered towards a chair. She collapsed into it, spine rounding. Her expression was vacant, unreachable.

Bella crouched at Lexi's feet, her wet dress clinging to her spine. She placed her hands on the cool skin of her knees. 'I'm right here.'

Lexi's eyes were wide, unseeing.

'It's okay, Lex,' she said. 'I'm here. I've got you.'

'Is this real?'

'Ed went over the terrace wall. No one could have survived that fall. He's dead, Lexi. I'm sorry, but he's dead.'

Lexi's head shook from side to side, refusing the information. She blinked rapidly, her breath fast and shallow.

Bella gathered Lexi's trembling hands. She squeezed, pressing them to her lips. She felt the cold edges of the diamond engagement ring. There was nothing Bella could do to make this better, other than hold Lexi.

Behind them, Robyn spoke in a rushed, frayed tone. 'We need to call the police! An ambulance!'

Ana was beside Eleanor now, a gentle hand on her back, rubbing in slow smooth circles, like a mother soothing a child. She spoke in a calming voice, whispering words to try to reach her, but Eleanor made only a low, keening wail.

Earlier, in the rowing boat, when Eleanor had chosen to save Bella, hauling her out of the dark sea, she'd witnessed her capacity for love, for forgiveness.

I won't forget, Bella had promised her.

'We need to call the police!' Robyn repeated, her tone growing shrill, hands rising around her face.

'Yes,' Bella agreed. Her voice was steady as she said, 'They need to know there's been a terrible *accident.*'

91

Robyn

Robyn stared at Bella.

No, she can't mean what that statement implies.

Could she?

Bella was crouched beside Lexi, her wet dress ruched. He
expression was calm, focused as she returned Robyn's que
tioning gaze. 'He is dead,' Bella said slowly. 'How he fe
changes nothing.'

Silence.

Even the cicadas had stopped their symphony. All Roby
could hear was the thunder of her own heartbeat.

'I agree,' Ana said clearly, locking eyes with Bella. 'We te
the police there was an accident. If we say Eleanor charge
into him . . . if they think she did it on purpose . . .' Sh
didn't need to finish the sentence. They all understoo
Eleanor would go to prison.

Robyn was shaking her head. 'We've got to tell the truth

Tell the police what happened!' She always told the truth. That was how she'd been brought up. She looked to Fen, who was staring over the wall, her expression unreadable in the darkness. But then Robyn had also been brought up to believe many things that needed questioning. Her thoughts whirled. 'There'll be a police investigation. Interviews!'

'Yes,' Bella said.

'How can you be so calm? Ed is fucking dead! Right now! Down there! He's dead, Bella! And we all saw what happened!' Eleanor had charged at him. Sent him crashing towards the wall. She'd have gone over too if they hadn't grabbed her.

Robyn couldn't lie.

This is madness.

'I'm getting my phone,' Robyn said, breaking free of Bella's gaze and hurrying into the villa.

It was a relief to step away from the others. She flicked on the light and stood in the centre of the kitchen, heart pounding, blinking into the glare.

She found her phone on the kitchen side, the screen coming to life at her touch.

Glancing towards the terrace, she saw her friends still framed in the flickering lantern light. Eleanor had been guided to the cushioned area and now sat hunched forward, fists gripping her top as if she needed something to hang onto.

When she'd charged at Ed, had she intended to send him over the wall?

Robyn didn't think so, but how could she know for certain?

All she knew was that Ed was lying at the bottom of a cliff, dead.

Those were the facts.

She needed to stick to them.

Tell the truth.

Fingers trembling, she dialled.

92

Lexi

Lexi tried to swallow, but her mouth was too dry. There was an intense throbbing pressure in her temples. She pulled her hands free of Bella's and squeezed them against the sides of her head.

Ed. He was dead. Her fiancé was dead.

She kept repeating these facts – yet she felt detached from them, like she couldn't *feel* them.

She looked up to see Robyn exiting the villa, phone in hand. 'I'm calling the police. I need to do it on the cliff.'

No one spoke.

No one told Robyn, *Don't*.

No one told her, *Do*.

Robyn's gaze found Lexi. Was there a beat of hesitation, a question in the rise of her brow? Was she silently asking, *What do you want?*

Soon the terrace, the villa, the rocks below, would be

overtaken by search beams, flashing blue lights, uniformed
police officers. For now – for a few more minutes – it was
only them.

What do I want?

She got to her feet, passing Robyn, crossing the terrace
towards the stone wall. Heart pounding, she planted her
palms and looked down.

What she wanted was for Ed to get up! She wanted him
to dust himself off, climb the villa steps, look her in the eye,
and start talking! She wanted him to hold her, tell her he
loved her, loved their baby – and that everything else she'd
heard was a mistake!

She gripped the wall, thinking about the way Ed had once
held her hands, saying, *One day soon I'm going to ask you
to marry me.* She'd felt like there was a light shining in the
centre of her chest. They'd been happy. She had felt happy,
hadn't she?

Yet right here, she'd seen the coldness in his expression as
he'd slapped Ana. He'd changed in front of her eyes, like
there had been another Ed lurking beneath his persona of
charm the whole time. Maybe she'd glimpsed it before. Just
flickers – like a static energy that suddenly, fleetingly, sparks.

Lexi was overtaken by a violent trembling, like she was
cold on the inside.

Slowly, she turned. Bella was watching her, eyes large with
concern. Robyn was standing at Fen's shoulder, phone in
hand, the emergency number dialled. Beyond them, Ana was
kneeling beside Eleanor, who sat with her knees hugged to
her chest.

She thought of Eleanor growing up with Ed as an older
brother. The relentless, inescapable bullying that followed her
from home to school and back again. Then Eleanor had met

Sam, someone kind and genuine, who she'd loved with her whole being, who she was going to marry, spend a lifetime with. But Ed had blindfolded Sam. Instructed him: *Trust me*.

Lexi pictured Eleanor in a courtroom, sitting before a faceless jury who didn't know her. Who hadn't been standing on this terrace watching how years of insidious bullying had led to one burning flash of fury.

But Lexi had.

They all had.

She looked again to Eleanor, whose face was shock-white. She was rocking on her haunches, silent, tears running down her cheeks. 'This is what happens next,' Lexi said authoritatively, knowing what she wanted.

Her friends were all looking right at her. The night felt stilled, a dark heat pressing close to her skin. Beyond them she caught the drift of smoke rising from the embers of the fire.

'I am going to ring the police. I am going to say . . .' Her gaze travelled deliberately over each of the women in turn: Fen, then Ana, then Bella, then Eleanor – finally resting on Robyn.

The two women held one another's eye for a long moment, years of history, of friendship, of understanding, weighed in that steady gaze.

'We are *all* going to say that there was an accident. No one touched Ed. He fell.'

~

The hen weekend was never meant to end that way: Ed's body broken on the rocks. Us pacing the terrace, stricken, waiting for the police to arrive. Each of us silently replaying the moment we chose to reach for Eleanor, not Ed.

We all had our part to play.

One of us asked, 'But, what do we say? How do we explain?'

– We say Ed travelled out here to surprise Lexi.

– We were all in on the surprise. Were happy to see him.

– Definitely happy.

– He was sitting on the terrace wall, chatting to us.

– That's right. We were just chatting.

– Those gifts – the ones we gave out on the first night – we were talking about them. Showing Ed.

– Yes! The sculpture. He'd been admiring his sister's sculpture.

– He'd set it down on the wall, carried on talking, but then he caught it by accident with his elbow.

– Turned to grab it . . .

– Tried to reach for it . . .

– But . . . but the movement unbalanced him.
– He went to right himself . . .
– But couldn't.
– It all happened so quickly.
– It did. So quickly.
– He fell.
– Yes.
– Ed fell.
– That's what I saw.
– Me too.
– Me too.
– Me too.
– Me too.
– Me too.

When we looked up, blue flashing lights were already travelling across the dark mountainside. The police were almost upon us. We watched in silence as they grew nearer, closing in.

No one said it. We didn't need to because we all remembered. We were standing right there on the terrace when we'd agreed it. The third rule. The final rule. The promise we'd made to each other at the very beginning.

'What happens on the hen weekend, stays on the hen weekend.'

THE WEDDING

(Sixteen months later)

93

Lexi

Lexi was sitting nearest the aisle, ankles crossed. The late-September sun cast golden light across the field, the swaying grass glowing amber. Beyond the scent of wheat, she caught the salted hint of the sea. In the fields, cattle grazed beneath billowing white clouds. Later she'd need the jacket that was draped over the back of her chair, but for now she was just right.

It was a beautiful location for a wedding: a rolling hillside in West Dorset that sloped lazily towards the sea, thirty wooden chairs set on either side of a mown grass aisle. An archway of flowers in place of an altar. There was no church or priest in robes; there were no dust-lined hymn books.

If Lexi had planned her perfect wedding this, she decided, would be it. Small, intimate, among close friends and family. Nothing like the wedding she and Ed had organised.

Had life worked out differently – had the hen weekend

ended a day sooner – she would be married now, and Ed would be sitting beside her, a wedding band worn on the tanned hand that he'd once placed tenderly around hers as he told her he loved her. The same hand that had sliced through the herb-scented night, slapping Ana. The same hand that had knocked Eleanor backwards off a kitchen stool. The same hand that had steered Sam towards a flight of concrete steps, blindfolded.

She wondered when she'd have first noticed the cracks – because she would have. She'd already sensed a low, beating feeling inside her that said, *Wait! I'm not sure*, but instead of listening to that rising instinct, she'd thought the problem was with *her*. Strange the way women so often do that – look for the fault within themselves.

The months following Ed's death had dragged Lexi to a dark, breathless place. The changing terrain of her grief was tangled so tightly with guilt and fear that for a time there was no light, only doubt: *Could I have reached for Ed? Would it have made a difference? Should we have told the truth?*

Struggling to cope alone in the city, Lexi had returned to Bournemouth to be closer to Bella, to Robyn – and surprisingly, to her mother. On the hardest days, the beach offered her solace, when all she felt able to do was walk its wintery shores. But gradually, gradually, as her stomach swelled, the first glimmers of light returned.

Even though she couldn't be certain whether she was mourning Ed or an image of him that had never existed, she finally allowed herself to remember the happy moments, too. Ed was still the man she'd danced with to Prince, both of them in their pyjamas; still the man who'd brought her breakfast in bed; still the man who'd given her the most exquisite and startling gift of her life . . .

She looked at their baby, Wren. She was ten months old now. Her little fists gripped at the neckline of Lexi's top as she pulled herself up to standing, tiny feet pressing into Lexi's thighs. Lexi dipped her head, placing a kiss on the tip of her pink nose. Wren giggled, delighted.

Lexi searched, as she often did, for traces of Ed in her daughter's face, finding them in the almond-shaped eyes, the strong brow. Wren reached for Lexi's necklace, drawing it towards her gummy mouth.

Watching Wren, Lexi knew that she had a choice. She could mourn the past, the things that could have happened differently, the misjudgements she'd made about Ed – or she could choose to live in the moment.

And this moment – her daughter safe and thriving – was enough.

94

Ana

Ana stole a glance at her son. Seventeen and already two inches taller than her. He looked so handsome in an open-necked shirt, his curious dark gaze turned to the sky, where a buzzard circled.

Now that he'd started college, the crowd Luca used to mix with were already beginning to slip away. There was a girl on the scene, too. Zelda. Ana hadn't been afforded the privilege of meeting her yet, but from the way Luca laughed more often and easily, her presence was welcome.

The past year had been hard on them both. She'd decided to tell Luca about his father, providing the broadest of outlines about his death. There was no mention of the hen weekend. No mention of a locked student bedroom years earlier.

Luca was furious that he would never have the chance to meet Ed. He blamed Ana. His anger and hurt and resentment were a vast ocean, and she had to simply wait out the storm.

– hold steadfast as rock – while those waves of emotion crashed against her. But, like any storm, it eventually subsided, and she was grateful that Luca could hold onto an impression of Ed that wouldn't be challenged by meeting him. It felt important for a son growing up to have that, at least.

In the row in front, Lexi was holding Wren, murmuring to her softly as Wren began to fret.

Luca leaned forward, resting his hand on the back of Lexi's chair. 'I'll take her for a walk.'

Lexi turned, cheekbones shimmering. 'Really? You sure?'

'Better than watching a wedding.' He grinned.

Motherhood was a series of questions and doubts, Ana decided. She wrestled with whether she'd given Luca enough love – or indulged him. Whether she should be working harder – or be at home more. Whether she should have introduced him to Ed when she'd had the chance – or done the right thing by not. The worries and second-guessing were endless but, as she looked at Luca taking Wren carefully in his arms, light falling softly across the back of his neck as he talked quietly to her, Wren's legs pumping as she awarded him an open-mouthed smile, she thought, *I've done okay*.

Returning her gaze to the front, she saw Lexi was watching them, too.

Ana's friendship with Lexi was something tentative, fragile – the foundations of it having been built on a lie. It would have been easier to simply let each other go, but there were Luca and Wren. Half-siblings. The sweet relationship they'd watched growing over the past few months was something they both wanted to nurture.

Lexi caught her eye. They looked at one another. Mother to mother. Friend to friend. Woman to woman.

Smiled.

95

Eleanor

Eleanor wasn't one for weddings. Sitting pin-straight on the wooden chair, hands clamped together, she thought, *Too much can go wrong*.

Look at her and Sam.

Look at Lexi and Ed.

Still, this one would be different.

The morning had gone well, so far. She'd booked her usual blow-dry, but when she'd arrived at the salon, Reece had steered her towards the mirror. He stood at her shoulder, smoothing her hair back from her face, as he said, 'I'd like to try something different. What about we go a bit shorter today? Like this. Frame your face here and here? Bring out these cheekbones?'

She'd looked at herself in the mirror. Right in the eye. 'Yes. Let's.'

Two hours later, she'd returned to the flat, ducking as she

crossed the lounge. 'Don't look!' she whispered to Sam's ashes before closing the bedroom door. She'd unhooked the dress that Ana had helped her choose – a maxi-dress in midnight blue that Ana claimed brought out her eyes – and she'd tugged it over her vacuum-packing underwear.

She inspected herself in her bedroom mirror (you could never tell if you really liked a new haircut until you'd checked it in your *own* mirror). *There,* she thought. *Ready.*

She swished into the lounge, shoulders back, making a slow twirl before the urn. 'So, what d'you think?'

She could feel Sam's smile warming her from the inside. Could hear his low whistle. *Smokin'!*

Eleanor grinned.

She'd have given anything for Sam to be sitting next to her at this wedding. To feel the heat of his hand around hers. To have him take her home at midnight so they could eat Frazzles standing in their kitchen, chatting about the day they'd shared.

But Eleanor knew that focusing on all that you don't have was a path of suffering. It was one of the things her weekly sessions with a therapist had taught her. So instead, she thought about what she was grateful for. She looked around and saw Luca walking at the edge of the field carrying Wren. Her niece and nephew. Thriving.

She had that.

Then she touched the back of her head. *And the good hair, of course.*

After the hen weekend, Eleanor and Lexi hadn't spoken for months. Eleanor had tried – she'd called, left messages, written long emails – but her efforts were met with silence. She understood: Lexi was torn apart by grief and anger and didn't have the capacity to assuage Eleanor's guilt and sadness.

When baby Wren was born, Eleanor had sent a card, along with a small music box which had once belonged to Ed. When the lid was opened, a tiny bird turned and turned on its perch, singing its brightening tune. Lexi, after seven months of silence, called the morning she received it, asking, 'Would you like to meet your niece?'

Eleanor, voice solemn, hands trembling as she gripped the phone, said, 'Yes. Yes, I'd like that very much.'

Eleanor didn't know what to do with babies, but she knew how to do food, and it turns out that in the early months, that's about the biggest gift you can deliver to a new mother: parcels of delicious, home-cooked meals with a simple note: *Heat for twenty minutes and enjoy. Best served with WINE.*

That's what she did for Lexi. She drove from London to Bournemouth, twice a month, to visit her niece and deliver food. That was her way of saying all the things they couldn't speak of. Lexi had her grief – and Eleanor hers. They didn't need to talk about it. So instead they focused on other things, like the way Wren could now build a tower out of colourful blocks, or how she liked to bob up and down when music was playing.

Eleanor had made sure Lexi and the baby were cared for financially from Ed's estate, splitting everything he had evenly between Wren and Luca. It was the least she could do: those two children would never know their father because of her.

Did she regret charging at Ed?

Absolutely.

He was her brother and, despite everything, she had loved him.

If the wall had been higher, he'd still be here. If Eleanor hadn't been ablaze with anger, he'd still be here. If the others had chosen to reach for him, not her, he'd still be here. In the same way that if Bella had picked up a different vial, Sam would still be here. Life was fragile and fleeting and mostly out of your control, and all you could do was surround yourself with good people, do your best.

The music began to play. The guests rose to their feet. Eleanor turned to look at the bride.

96

Robyn

Robyn waited at the entrance of the aisle, palms sweating.

Her heart was racing with excitement, with nerves, with the giddiness that this – *this* was happening.

The sun had come out now, a warm burst of it, a relic of the summer that was ending. She thought, as she often did of the tiny island of Aegos where this all began. It would forever be a place of two halves. An island where there was death and deceit and the cold sweat of lying in a police interview – but also the beauty of a kiss on a clifftop with a woman she'd fallen in love with.

That small, beautiful seed that had been planted on the hen weekend was too fragile to survive the trampling of police enquiries and Ed's death. Robyn and Fen agreed not to see one another after they left Greece.

Instead, they wrote. Pen to paper, truths inked within envelopes and sealed with their tongues. By hand, Robyn found her voice. She shared news of how she'd finally moved out of her parents' home and was renting a two-bedroom cottage in the New Forest. She described how, on Saturdays, her parents looked after Jack and she went hiking. She took those walks alone, pounding the wind-blown clifftops in the Purbecks, the slicing January cold stealing into her bones.

After six months of writing to one another, they met.

It was like nothing she'd ever experienced. Like magnets finding their opposing force. It was love in all the ways she had never known.

There was everything to learn about each other.

Everything to unlearn about herself.

Now, she took in the small group of guests gathered in the sunlight, searching out her parents. They were sitting in the front row, a little stiffly perhaps, yet as her mother turned to speak to her father, she could see she was smiling.

Earlier this morning, as her mother had placed the orchid in Robyn's hair, she'd squeezed her shoulder, saying, 'We just want you to be happy.'

Robyn could finally answer: 'I am.'

Now, at her side, she felt a light prod against her hip.

'Mummy,' Jack whispered, face serious. 'Time to do the walk.'

She held out her hand, and he put his soft, tiny fingers in hers. Then the two of them began to move down the aisle, to where Fen was waiting beneath an archway of flowers.

97

Fen

Fen could hear the music begin to play.

She smoothed down her white shirt. The cotton was crisp, freshly ironed, buttoned to the top. Her tailored trousers ended in a pair of tan leather Converse she'd deliberated over, deciding their informality balanced the suit.

In her peripheral vision, she could see her aunt seated at the front. She was dressed in a cobalt blue kaftan, an absence of jewellery setting off its clean lines. Over dinner last night, her aunt had told Fen and Robyn that the sale of the Greek villa had finally gone through after months of delays. As she'd been clearing out her belongings, she'd come across a photo of Fen tucked at the back of a cupboard. 'I wondered if you wanted this,' she'd said, taking it from her purse.

Fen had held the picture of her younger self, looking at the brilliance of her smile, the openness of her expression. She'd once hidden the photo away because, when she'd looked at herself, it was Nico's voice she'd heard: *No one will want you*. But when she'd studied the photo again last night, on the eve of her wedding, with Robyn sitting beside her, she'd heard her own voice clearly. It told her that she was a woman who was both strong and vulnerable, who was brave and sometimes scared, who was loved and who loves. 'Thank you,' she'd told her aunt. 'I'd love to keep the photo.'

Now, behind her, Fen caught the delighted murmurings of the guests as they rose to their feet. She couldn't wait a moment longer.

She turned.

Robyn moved easily down the grass aisle, her hand in Jack's, the two of them grinning wildly. She was wearing a simple cream dress, with flat shoes, her hair swept back into a low bun, a single orchid weaved within it. She was luminous.

There she is, Fen thought, eyes warming with tears.

Robyn moved to Fen's side. Jack slipped his hand free of his mummy's, lifting it towards Fen for a high five. She laughed as their palms connected, then watched him bound towards his grandparents, plonking himself on the seat between them, legs swinging.

Then it was just her and Robyn, hands joining, looking one another full in the eye.

She kissed the bride.

98

Bella

Did they have to kiss for quite that long? Bella thought.

In fairness, it did look like a sensational kiss. Being the only person in the audience who'd kissed them both, she'd know! See – she was making jokes! Smiling! She almost felt a genuine flush of happiness for Robyn and Fen.

There were many things that were taking time and adjustment. After the hen weekend, she'd handed in her notice at the jeweller's, which had felt like a good step. Still haunted by Sam's death, she knew she'd never return to nursing, but she'd found a new role working in a residential home for the elderly. Old people loved her – and she loved them. Eleanor came in twice a month, after visiting Wren, to run the table-tennis club, and Bella would slip off-duty for a few minutes to give her a game. She rarely got a point off Eleanor, who had a particularly deadly backhand, but it didn't stop Bella baiting her.

Strange that she and Eleanor had become friends of sorts. Life. What a big fucking mystery! Other people, smarter than her, could try and figure it out.

Lexi, standing next to her, slipped her hand into Bella's. Squeezed.

She squeezed back.

She adored this woman with her whole being. Always would. Lexi's ride into motherhood hadn't been easy. A difficult labour followed by complications from an emergency C-section, followed by two spells of mastitis, meant those early months as a single parent were particularly tough. Bella tried to stay over a couple of nights each week, bringing takeout, cabbage leaves, and pretty outfits for Wren, as what girl wanted to be dressed in neutral-toned organic vests Monday to Sunday?

The biggest surprise of Bella's life was how hard she'd fallen for that little milky splodge of a baby. It was ironic to think she'd campaigned so hard to keep party-girl-Lexi aflame – when it was motherhood that deepened their friendship in new ways.

When Wren was three days old, Bella had carried her reverently from the maternity ward, clicking her baby seat into the back of her freshly valeted car, double-checking the Isofix. Then she'd helped Lexi shuffle into the front, reaching across to buckle her in, mindful of her C-section wound. Lexi had caught Bella's arm. 'I'd like you to be Wren's godmother.'

Bella had turned to look at Wren, a tiny, perfect being, swamped within a car seat, eyes closed, lips pursed. So innocent and unmarked.

Bella had shaken her head. 'I'm sorry. I can't. I'm not a good role model.'

Lexi had looked Bella straight in the eye. Her skin was pale and wan, mauve shadows ringing her eyes – but her voice was fierce as she said, 'You might have made mistakes, Bella, but you got back up again. That makes you an excellent role model for my daughter.'

Tears spilled onto Bella's cheeks.

'Anyway,' Lexi added, 'who else is going to teach her how to walk in four-inch stilettos?'

So, godmother she was.

Robyn visited Lexi often – and sometimes those visits coincided with Bella's. At first their encounters were painfully raw, but over time, they gradually began adjusting to a new dynamic. It wasn't easy, and there were often heated arguments – usually when wine was involved – but there was a fresh honesty between them, and that was something.

There'd been one evening, a few months ago now, when Robyn had seemed edgy, unable to sit still. She kept getting up to fetch more wine, open bags of crisps, check her phone. 'D'you want to tell us what's going on?' Bella had asked impatiently.

Robyn had cleared her throat, pressed her hands at her sides as if she were about to deliver a school presentation. 'Fen and I are engaged.'

Bella had waited a beat, employing the technique her counsellor recommended of simply taking a breath or two before speaking. Eventually she'd smiled. 'I'm really happy for you.' She said those words and, as she did, she realised she meant them. She *was* happy.

As they'd raised their glasses to toast the wedding to come, Bella had to say it, didn't she?

'Shall I organise the hen weekend?'

Author's Note

Over the past few years, I've been lucky enough to visit several Greek islands, which have shaped and influenced this novel. However, I chose to set *One of the Girls* on the fictional island of Aegos, because I wanted the hens to have full artistic licence to explore a setting that arises from imagination.

Acknowledgements

Firstly, thank you to Charlotte Brabbin and Kim Young, who are everything I could want in an editor and publisher. I am so grateful for your creativity and thoughtfulness, your passionate vision for my books, and your smart editorial input. I am incredibly lucky to work with a team of talented people at HarperCollins, including Jaime Frost and Alice Hill in Publicity; Hannah O'Brien, Maddy Marshall, Katy Blott, and Jeannelle Brew in Marketing; Sarah Munro and Izzy Coburn in UK Sales; Alice Gomer in International Sales; and Claire Ward in Cover Design. I'm so thankful for everything you do for me and my books.

Thank you to my beloved agent, Judith Murray at Greene & Heaton, who heard the idea for *One of the Girls* when it was no more than a one-line pitch and said, 'Yes! That one! It's given me goosebumps!' Your instincts are as sound as the great care you take of each of your authors. Thank you also to the brilliant Kate Rizzo for handling my international rights, and to Sally Oliver for her continued support.

Thank you to my US agent, Grainne Fox at Fletcher & Co, who has found me my dream publishing home in the

US at Putnam Books. Danielle Dietrich and Sally Kim, your vision for *One of the Girls* has blown me away and I'm so excited to see where this journey leads.

Thank you to Hannah Turner for the laughter-filled video call about your role as a BSL interpreter; thank you to Alex Hixson for the saves on the professional dancing front; thank you to Sandra Gamper for her medical expertise discussed while sitting two-metres apart on a sunny spring morning.

Thank you to all the people who have read early drafts of this novel, including Faye Buchan, Laura Crossley, Becki Hunter, Heidi Perks, Emma Stonex and of course, my first reader: my mum!

Thank you to the booksellers, librarians, bloggers, and readers who champion my novels, cheer me along via social media, and press my books into the hands of people they hope will enjoy them, too. It means so much and is at the heart of why I keep writing.

Thank you to Mimi Hall. This book is dedicated to you because you've lived every step of this novel alongside me. Your daily voice notes (limos!) bring so much joy and richness to my writing life. I love journeying across the page together.

Thank you to my parents, brother, in-laws, and friends for your ongoing support in all the forms it takes, whether that's reading manuscripts, helping with the children, rearranging the shelves in every bookstore you visit(!), or riding the highs and the lows alongside me.

Thank you, finally, to James, Tommy and Darcy for making this life bright and beautiful and wild.